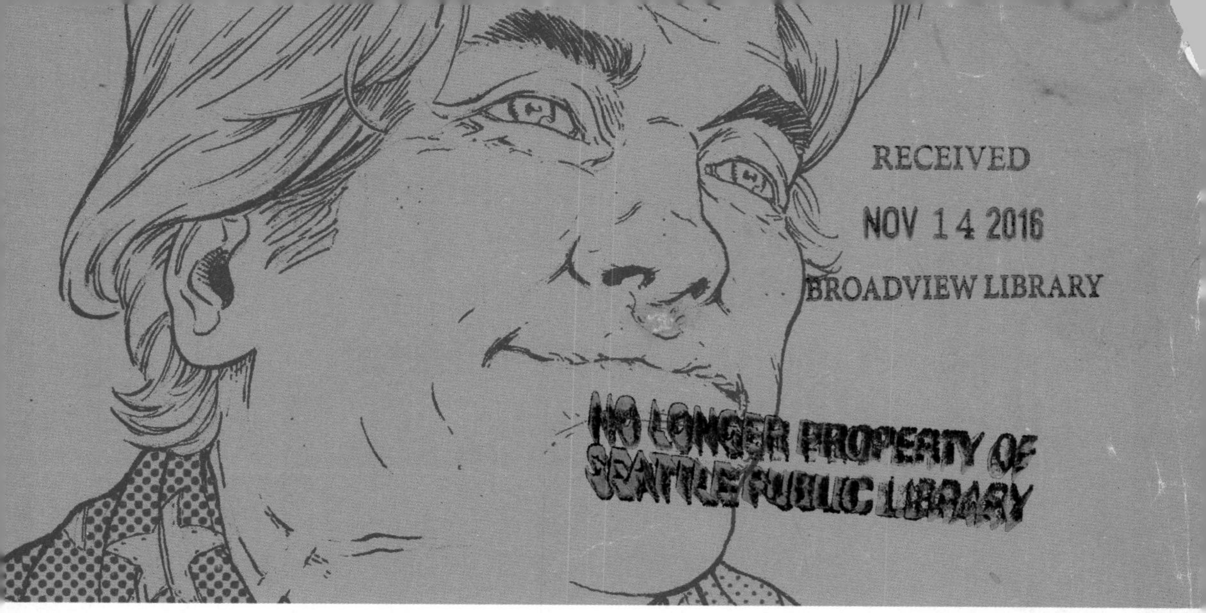

CITIZEN JACK™

VOLUME ONE

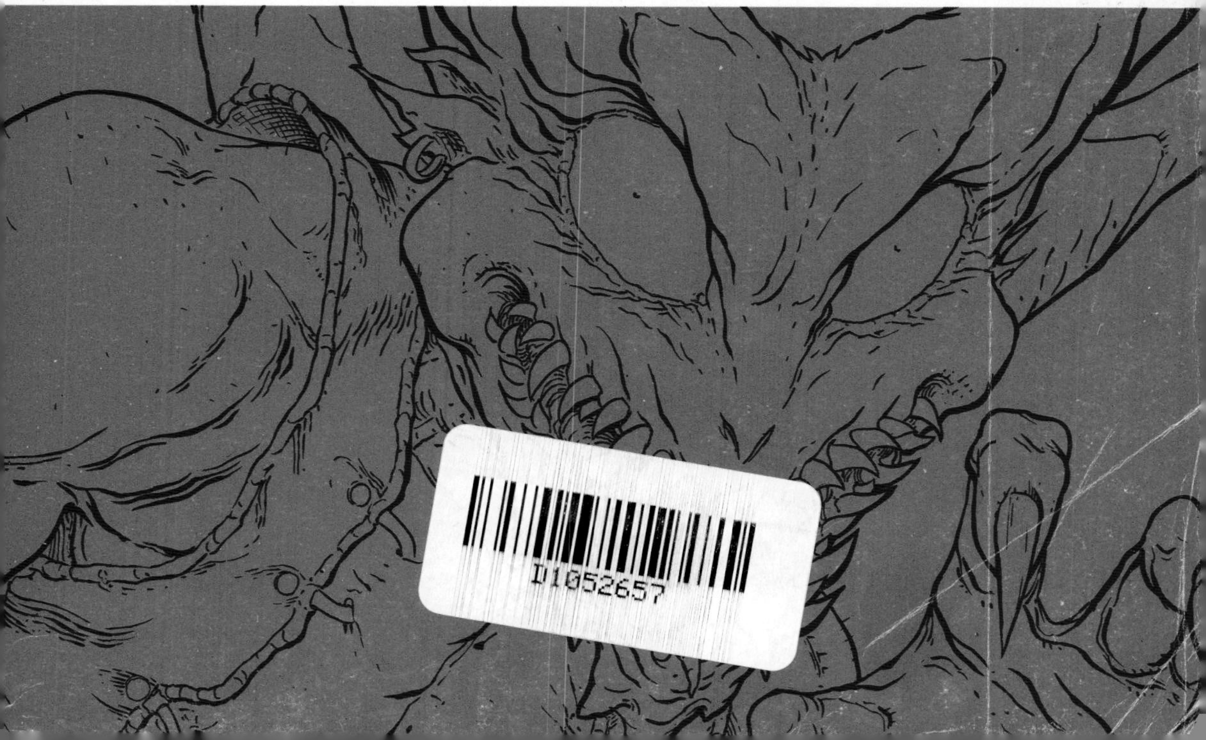

WRITER **SAM HUMPHRIES**

ARTIST **TOMMY PATTERSON**

COLORIST **JON ALDERINK**

LETTERER **RACHEL DEERING**

DESIGNER **DYLAN TODD/BIG RED ROBOT**

EDITOR **JEANINE SCHAEFER**

COVERS **TOMMY PATTERSON & DYLAN TODD,**

CHIP ZDARSKY, MING DOYLE,

PHIL JIMENEZ & ROMULO FAJARDO,

JEFF LEMIRE, RILEY ROSSMO,

RYAN STEGMAN & JON ALDERINK

COLOR FLATTERS **JOEL BARTLETT, JAY STINSON, CARLOS LIMA**

PUBLICITY **JEREMY ATKINS**
LEGAL **BRENDAN MCFEELY FOR KANE KESSLER, P.C.**
MANAGEMENT **DAVID ENGEL FOR CIRCLE OF CONFUSION**

CREATED BY **SAM HUMPHRIES**
AND **TOMMY PATTERSON**

CITIZEN JACK, VOLUME 01 | AUGUST 2016

COPYRIGHT © 2016 SAM HUMPHRIES & TOMMY PATTERSON. ALL RIGHTS RESERVED.

First printing. Published by Image Comics, Inc. Office of publication: 2001 Center Street, Sixth Floor, Berkeley, CA 94704. Originally published in single magazine form as CITIZEN JACK #1-6, by Image Comics. CITIZEN JACK, its logos, and all character likenesses herein are trademarks of Sam Humphries & Tommy Patterson unless expressly indicated. Image Comics® and its logos are registered trademarks and copyrights of Image Comics, Inc. All rights reserved. No part of this publication may be reproduced or transmitted, in any form or by any means (except for short excerpts for review purposes) without the express written permission of Sam Humphries & Tommy Patterson or Image Comics, Inc. All names, characters, events, and locales in this publication, except for satirical purposes, are entirely fictional, and any resemblance to actual persons (living or dead) or entities or events or places is coincidental. Printed in the USA. For information regarding the CPSIA on this printed material call: 203-595-3636 and provide reference # RICH-694659. For international rights, contact: foreignlicensing@imagecomics.com. ISBN: 978-1-63215-705-8

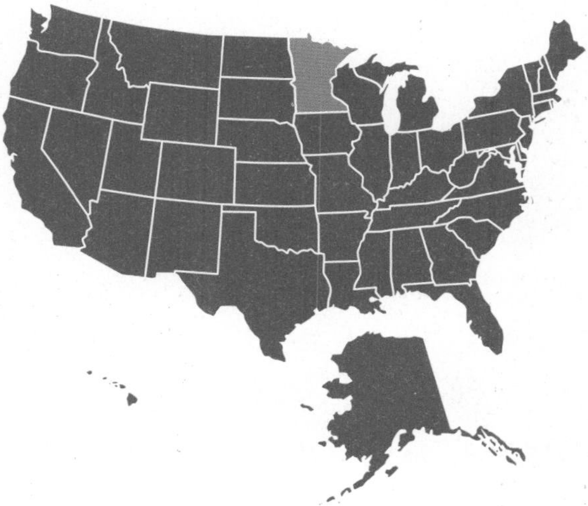

DEDICATED TO

VICE PRESIDENT WALTER F. MONDALE

WHO CAMPAIGNED BRAVELY IN 1984

AND LOST IN A LANDSLIDE DEFEAT,

CARRYING ONLY THE DISTRICT OF COLUMBIA

AND HIS HOME STATE,

MINNESOTA

CHAPTER 1

ONCE UPON A TIME IN MINNESOTA...

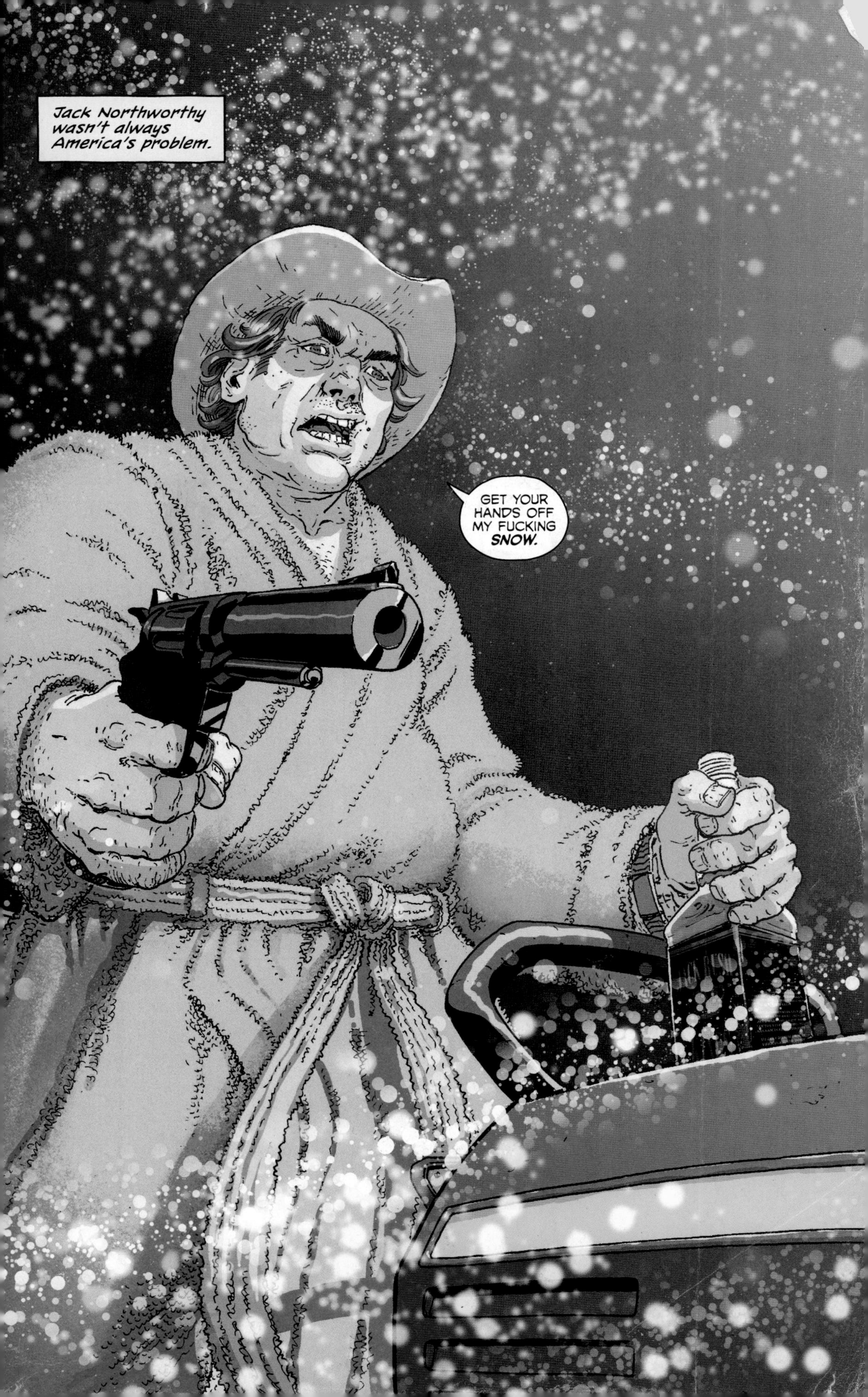
Jack Northworthy wasn't always America's problem.
GET YOUR HANDS OFF MY FUCKING SNOW.

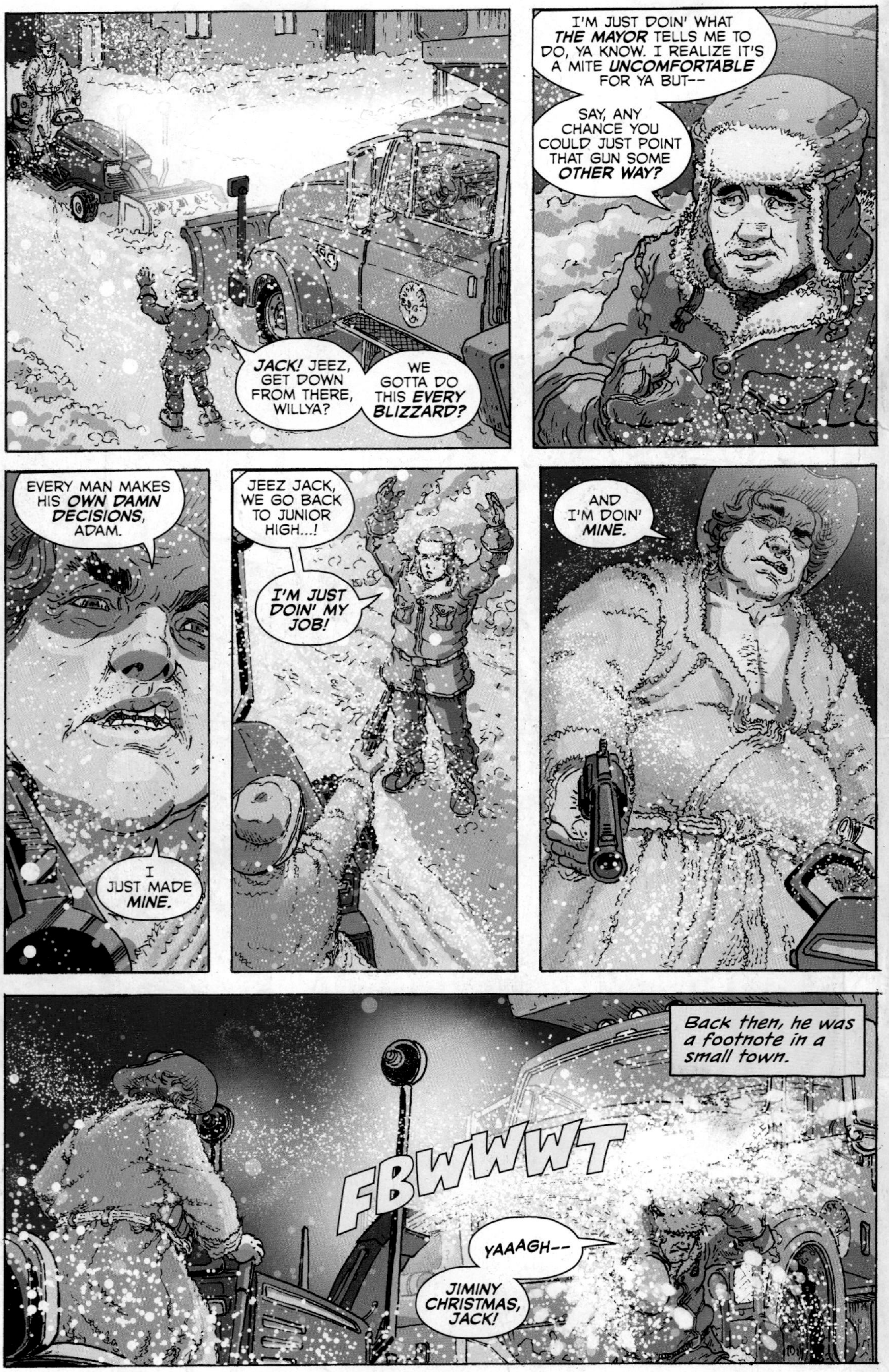
JACK! JEEZ, GET DOWN FROM THERE, WILLYA?
WE GOTTA DO THIS EVERY BLIZZARD?
I'M JUST DOIN' WHAT THE MAYOR TELLS ME TO DO, YA KNOW. I REALIZE IT'S A MITE UNCOMFORTABLE FOR YA BUT--
SAY, ANY CHANCE YOU COULD JUST POINT THAT GUN SOME OTHER WAY?
EVERY MAN MAKES HIS OWN DAMN DECISIONS, ADAM.
I JUST MADE MINE.
JEEZ JACK, WE GO BACK TO JUNIOR HIGH...!
I'M JUST DOIN' MY JOB!
AND I'M DOIN' MINE.
Back then, he was a footnote in a small town.
FBWWWT
YAAAGH--
JIMINY CHRISTMAS, JACK!

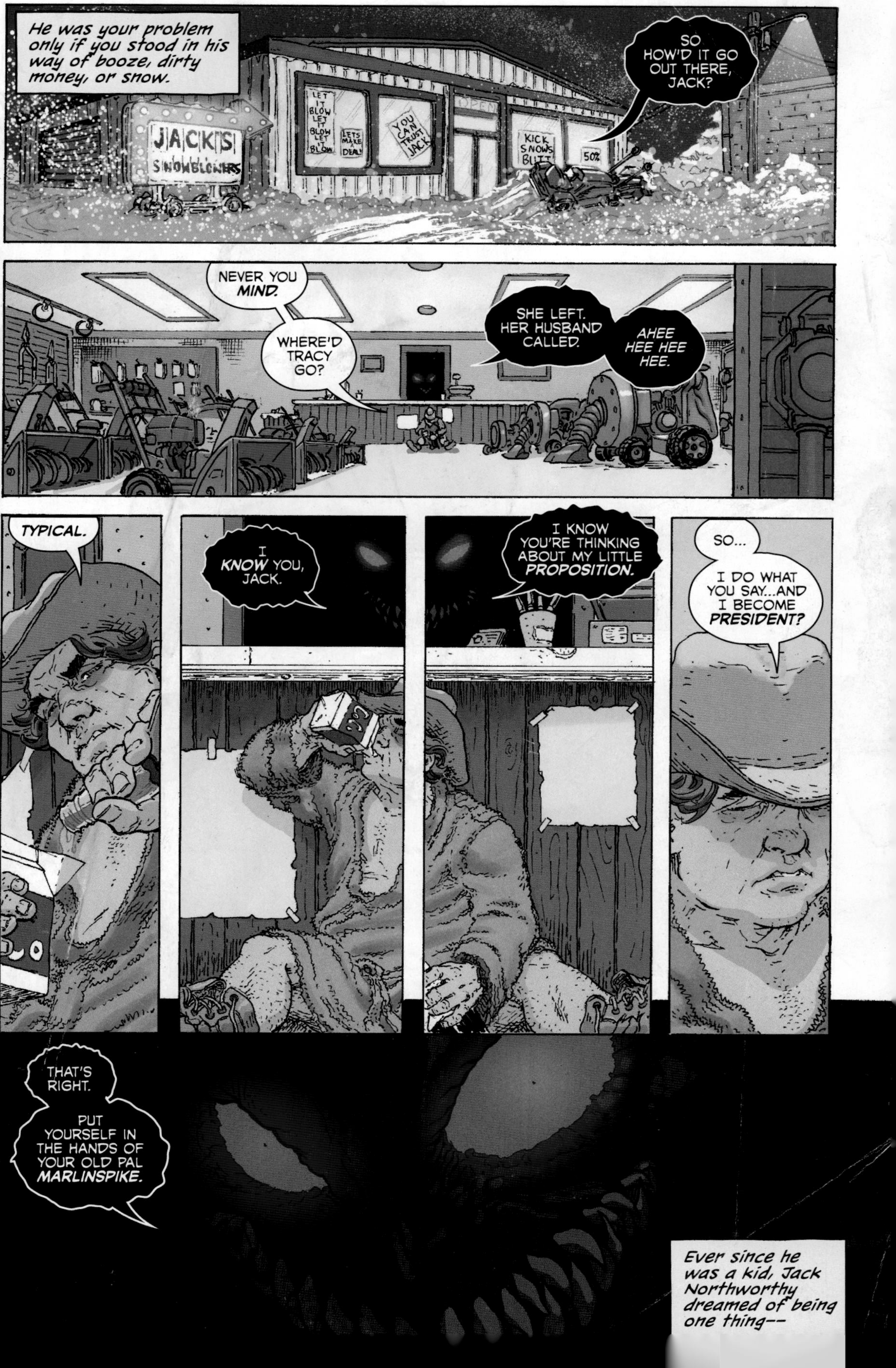
He was your problem only if you stood in his way of booze, dirty money, or snow.
JACK'S SNOWBLOWERS
LET IT BLOW LET IT BLOW LET IT BLOW
LETS MAKE A DEAL!
YOU CAN TRUST JACK
OPEN
KICK SNOWS BUTT
50%
SO HOW'D IT GO OUT THERE, JACK?
NEVER YOU MIND.
WHERE'D TRACY GO?
SHE LEFT. HER HUSBAND CALLED.
AHEE HEE HEE HEE.
TYPICAL.
I KNOW YOU, JACK.
I KNOW YOU'RE THINKING ABOUT MY LITTLE PROPOSITION.
SO...
I DO WHAT YOU SAY...AND I BECOME PRESIDENT?
THAT'S RIGHT.
PUT YOURSELF IN THE HANDS OF YOUR OLD PAL MARLINSPIKE.
Ever since he was a kid, Jack Northworthy dreamed of being one thing--

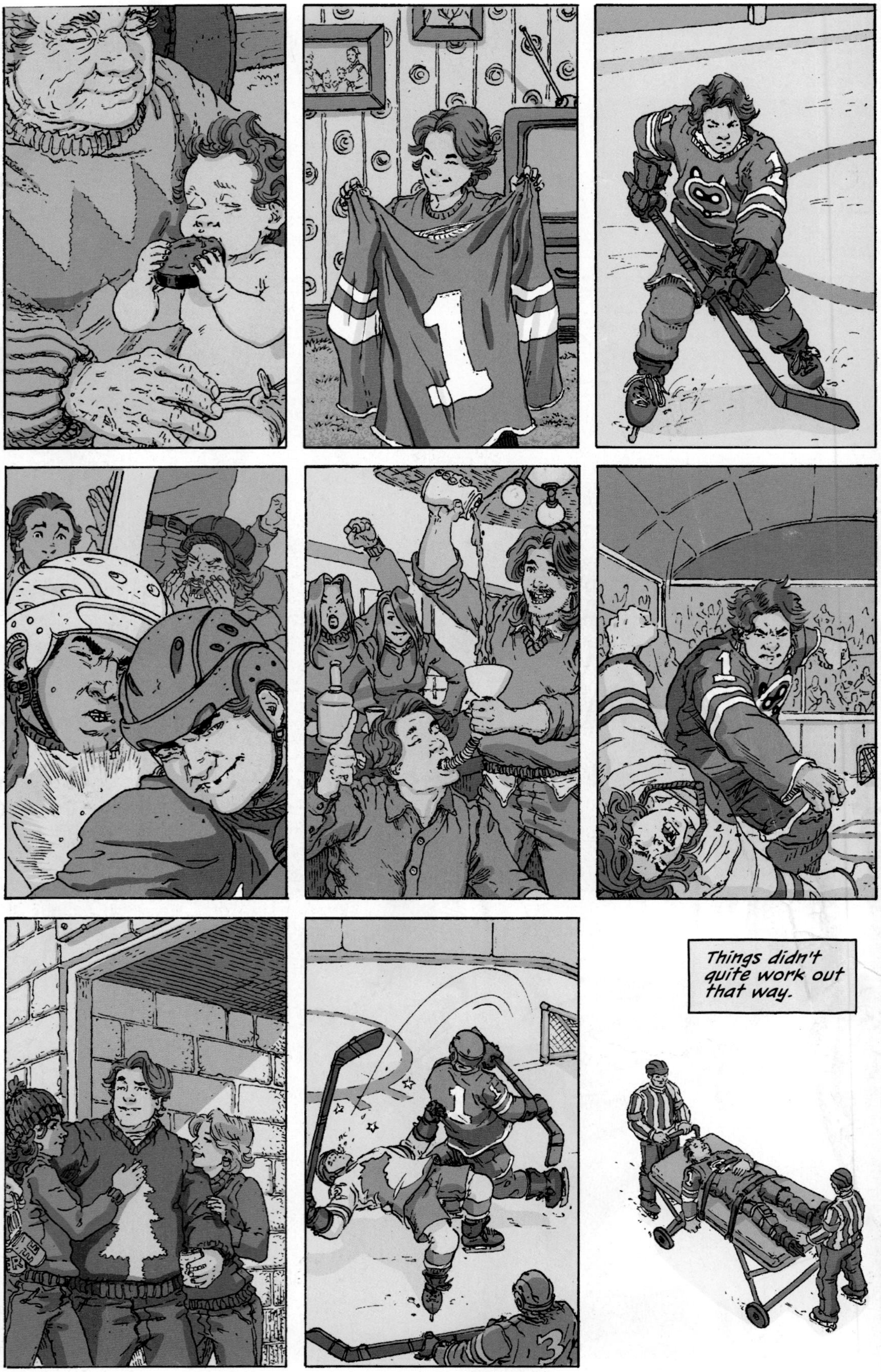
Things didn't quite work out that way.

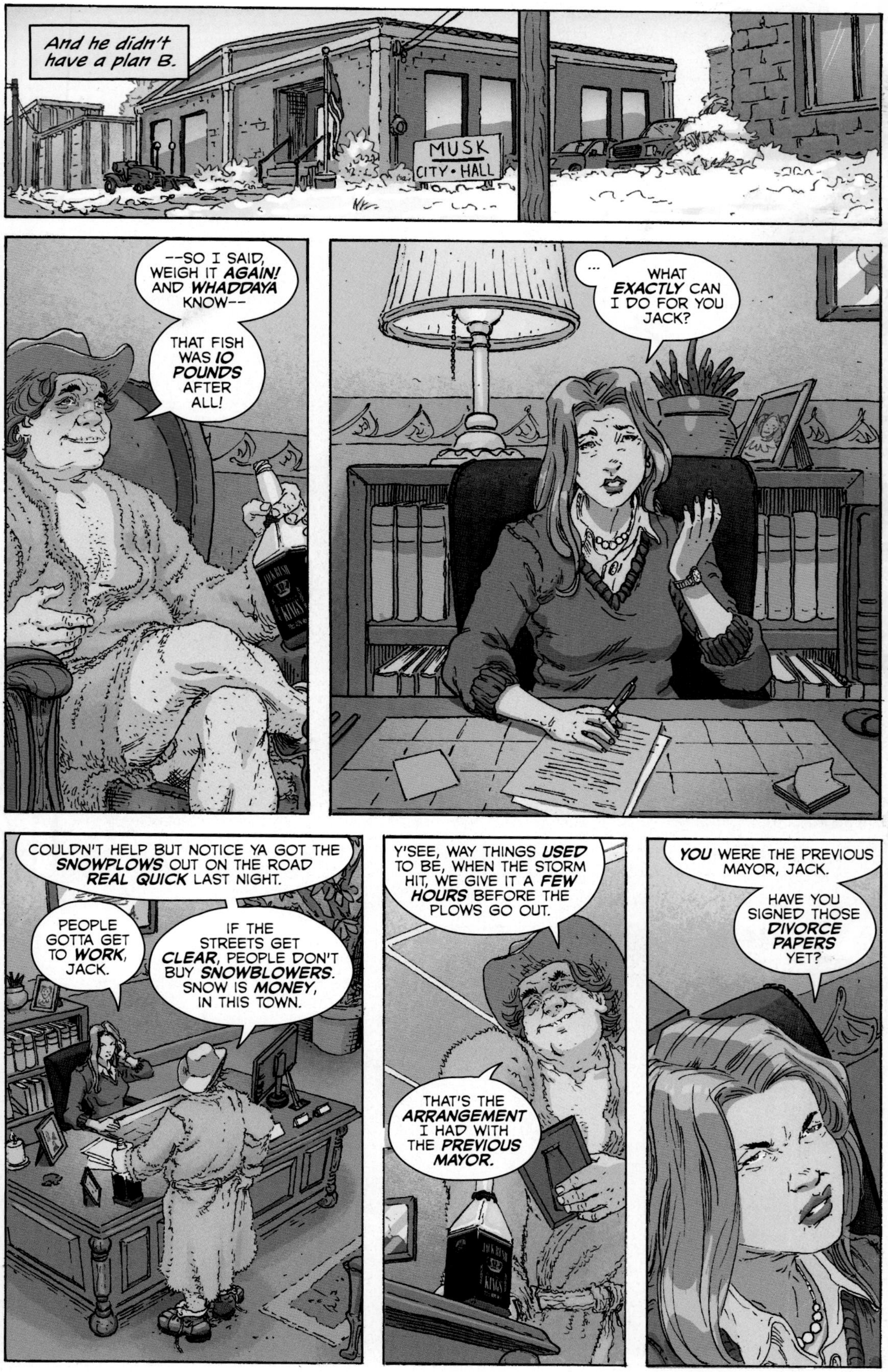
And he didn't have a plan B.
MUSK CITY • HALL
--SO I SAID, WEIGH IT AGAIN! AND WHADDAYA KNOW--
THAT FISH WAS 10 POUNDS AFTER ALL!
... WHAT EXACTLY CAN I DO FOR YOU JACK?
COULDN'T HELP BUT NOTICE YA GOT THE SNOWPLOWS OUT ON THE ROAD REAL QUICK LAST NIGHT.
PEOPLE GOTTA GET TO WORK, JACK.
IF THE STREETS GET CLEAR, PEOPLE DON'T BUY SNOWBLOWERS. SNOW IS MONEY, IN THIS TOWN.
Y'SEE, WAY THINGS USED TO BE, WHEN THE STORM HIT, WE GIVE IT A FEW HOURS BEFORE THE PLOWS GO OUT.
THAT'S THE ARRANGEMENT I HAD WITH THE PREVIOUS MAYOR.
YOU WERE THE PREVIOUS MAYOR, JACK.
HAVE YOU SIGNED THOSE DIVORCE PAPERS YET?

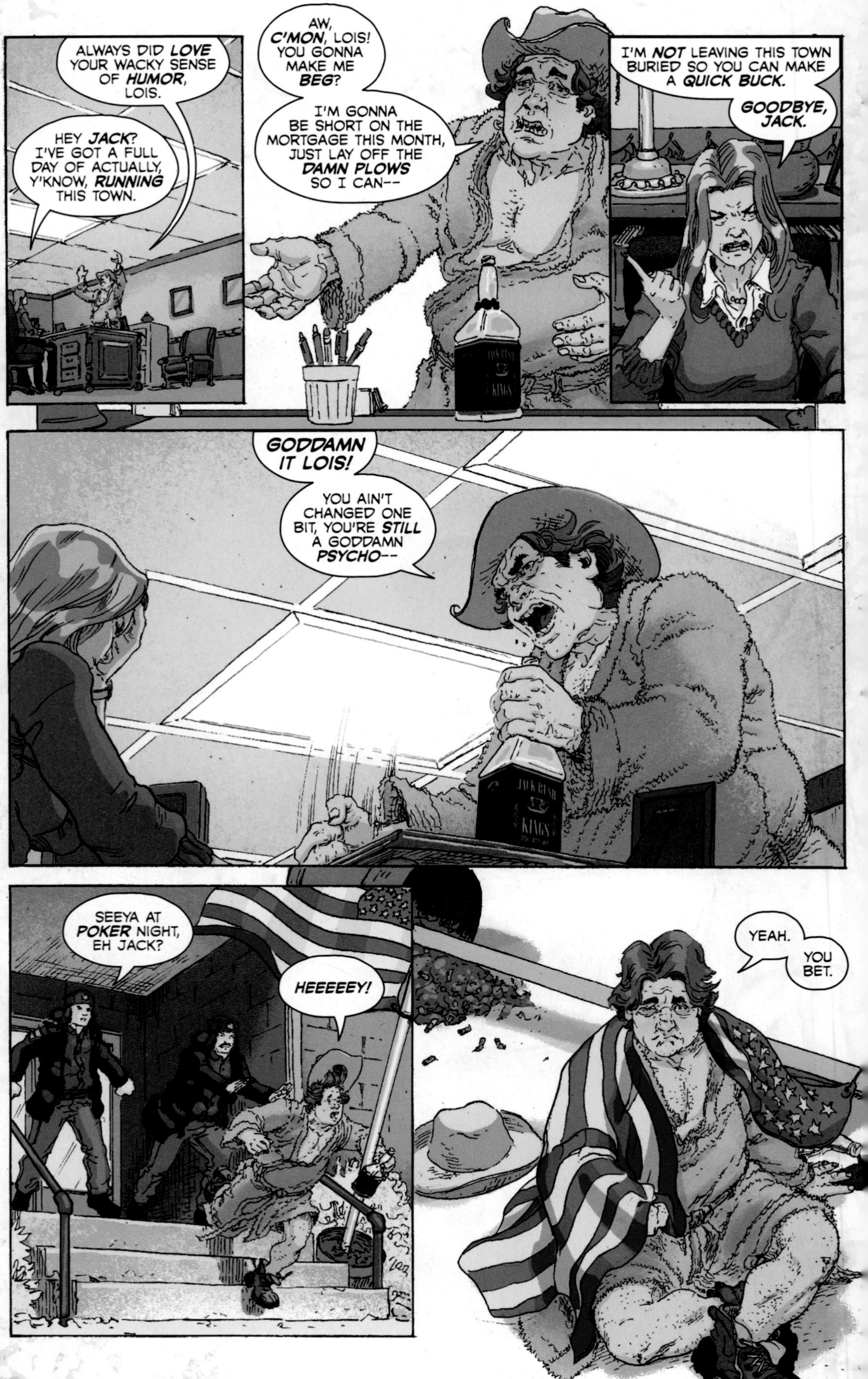
ALWAYS DID LOVE YOUR WACKY SENSE OF HUMOR, LOIS.
HEY JACK? I'VE GOT A FULL DAY OF ACTUALLY, Y'KNOW, RUNNING THIS TOWN.
AW, C'MON, LOIS! YOU GONNA MAKE ME BEG?
I'M GONNA BE SHORT ON THE MORTGAGE THIS MONTH, JUST LAY OFF THE DAMN PLOWS SO I CAN--
I'M NOT LEAVING THIS TOWN BURIED SO YOU CAN MAKE A QUICK BUCK.
GOODBYE, JACK.
GODDAMN IT LOIS!
YOU AIN'T CHANGED ONE BIT, YOU'RE STILL A GODDAMN PSYCHO--
SEEYA AT POKER NIGHT, EH JACK?
HEEEEEY!
YEAH.
YOU BET.

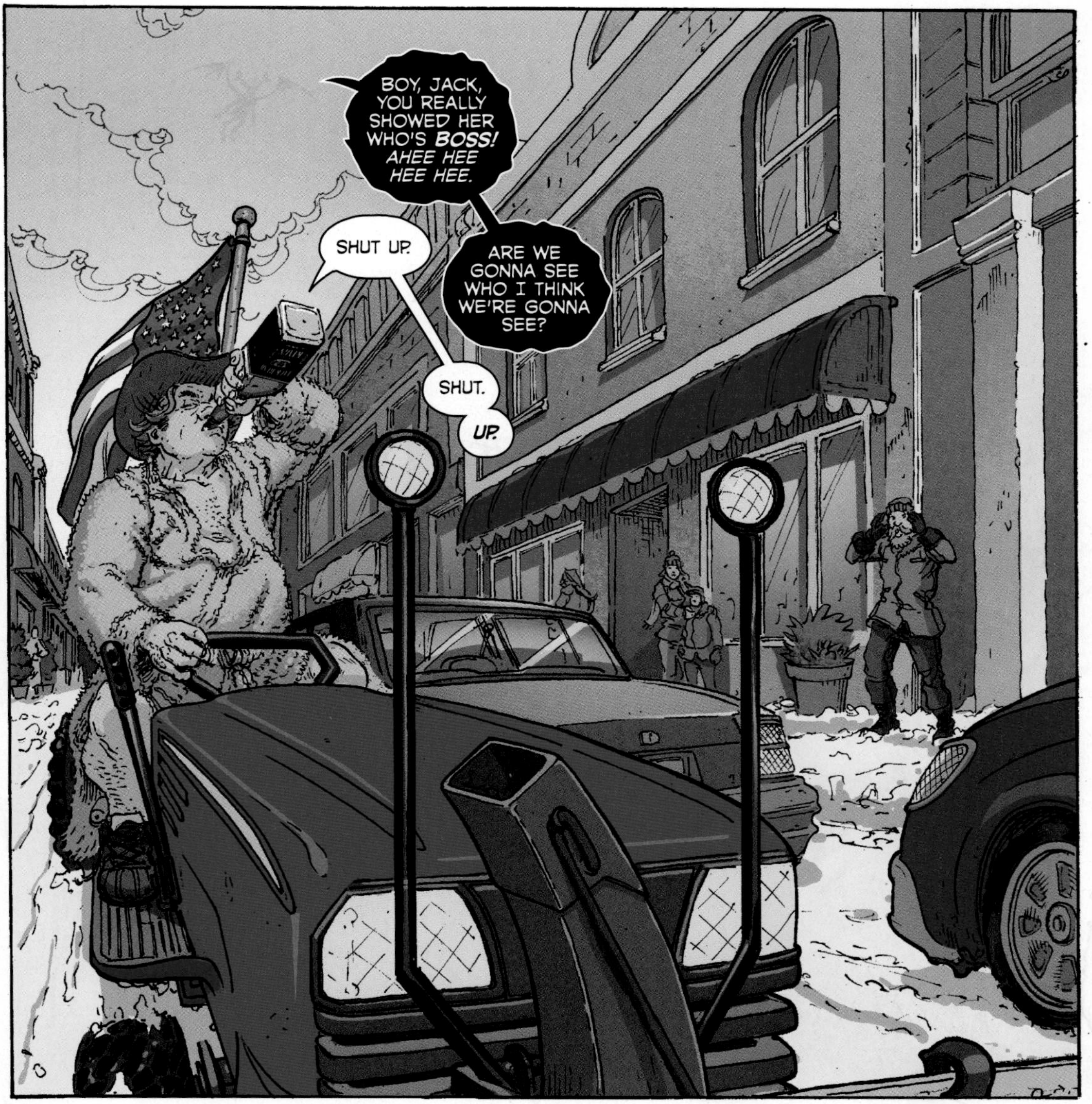
BOY, JACK, YOU REALLY SHOWED HER WHO'S *BOSS!* *AHEE HEE HEE HEE.*
SHUT UP.
ARE WE GONNA SEE WHO I THINK WE'RE GONNA SEE?
SHUT.
UP.

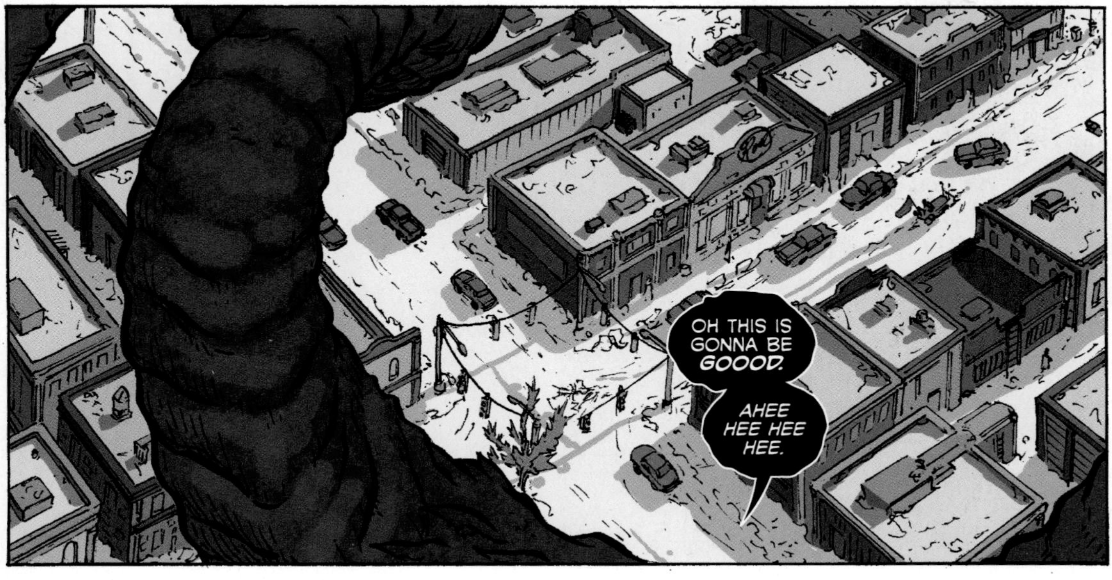
OH THIS IS GONNA BE *GOOOD.*
AHEE HEE HEE HEE.

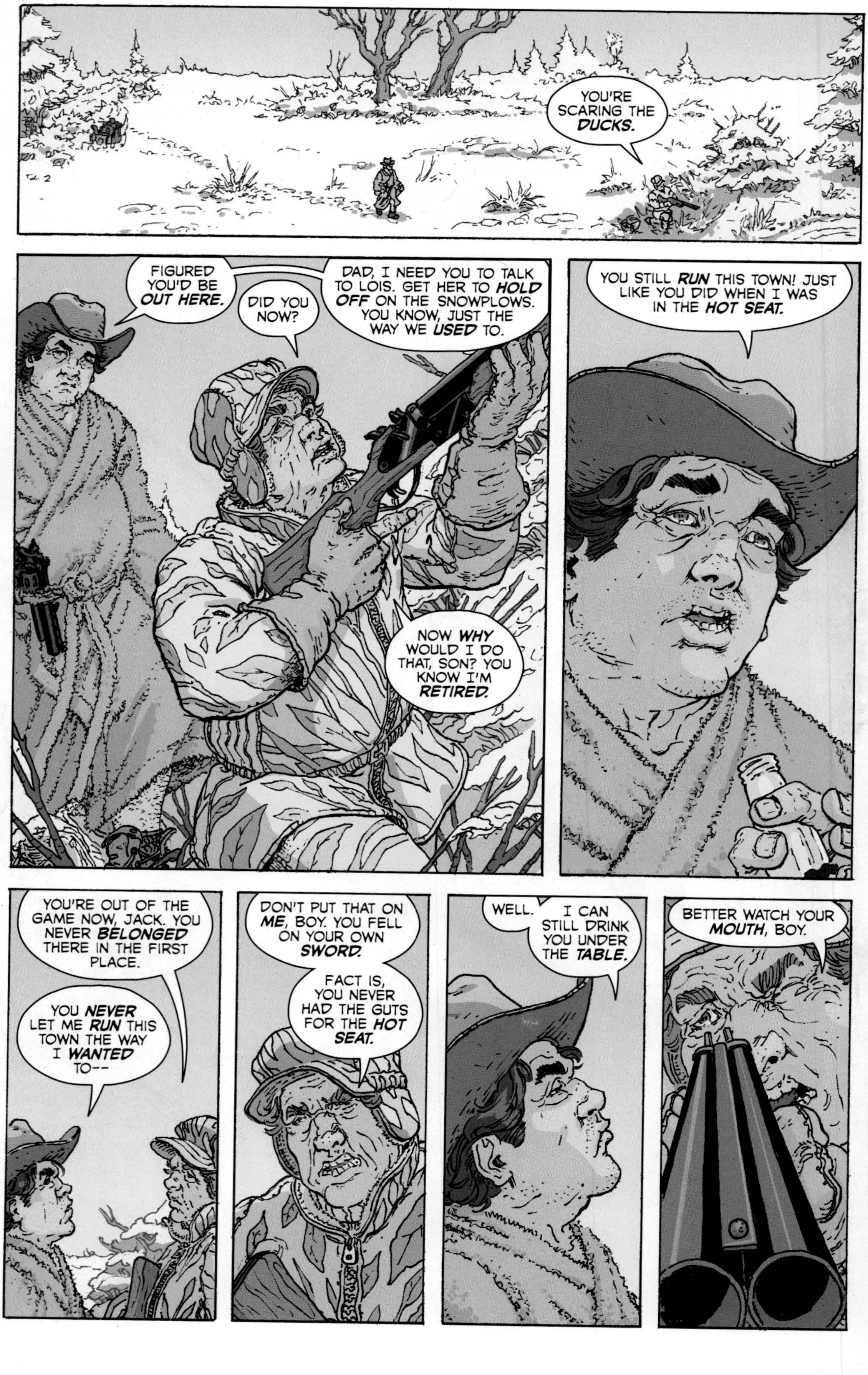
YOU'RE SCARING THE DUCKS.
FIGURED YOU'D BE OUT HERE.
DID YOU NOW?
DAD, I NEED YOU TO TALK TO LOIS. GET HER TO HOLD OFF ON THE SNOWPLOWS. YOU KNOW, JUST THE WAY WE USED TO.
NOW WHY WOULD I DO THAT, SON? YOU KNOW I'M RETIRED.
YOU STILL RUN THIS TOWN! JUST LIKE YOU DID WHEN I WAS IN THE HOT SEAT.
YOU'RE OUT OF THE GAME NOW, JACK. YOU NEVER BELONGED THERE IN THE FIRST PLACE.
YOU NEVER LET ME RUN THIS TOWN THE WAY I WANTED TO--
DON'T PUT THAT ON ME, BOY. YOU FELL ON YOUR OWN SWORD.
FACT IS, YOU NEVER HAD THE GUTS FOR THE HOT SEAT.
WELL.
I CAN STILL DRINK YOU UNDER THE TABLE.
BETTER WATCH YOUR MOUTH, BOY.

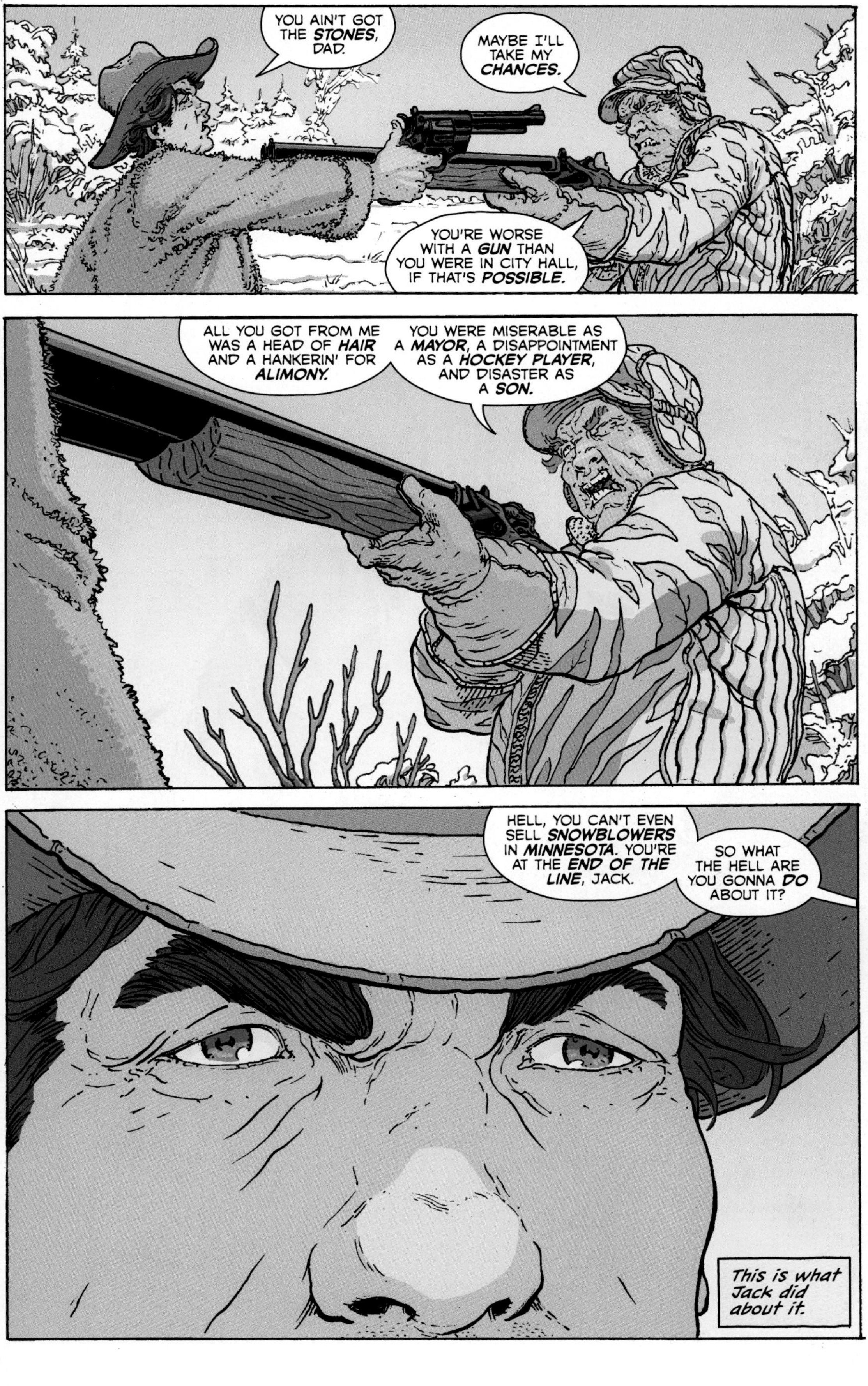
YOU AIN'T GOT THE STONES, DAD.
MAYBE I'LL TAKE MY CHANCES.
YOU'RE WORSE WITH A GUN THAN YOU WERE IN CITY HALL, IF THAT'S POSSIBLE.
ALL YOU GOT FROM ME WAS A HEAD OF HAIR AND A HANKERIN' FOR ALIMONY.
YOU WERE MISERABLE AS A MAYOR, A DISAPPOINTMENT AS A HOCKEY PLAYER, AND DISASTER AS A SON.
HELL, YOU CAN'T EVEN SELL SNOWBLOWERS IN MINNESOTA. YOU'RE AT THE END OF THE LINE, JACK.
SO WHAT THE HELL ARE YOU GONNA DO ABOUT IT?
This is what Jack did about it.

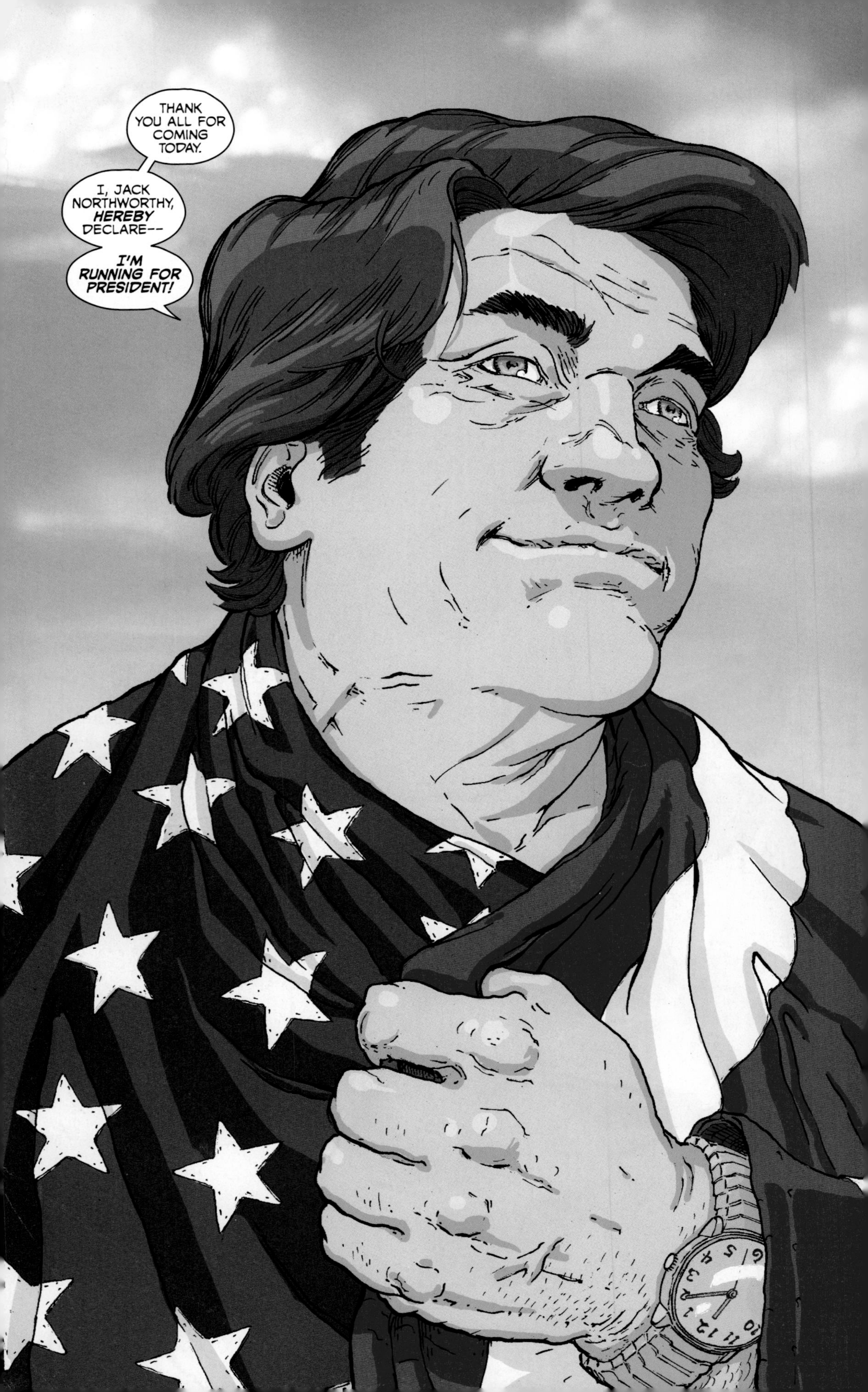
THANK YOU ALL FOR COMING TODAY.
I, JACK NORTHWORTHY, *HEREBY* DECLARE--
I'M RUNNING FOR PRESIDENT!

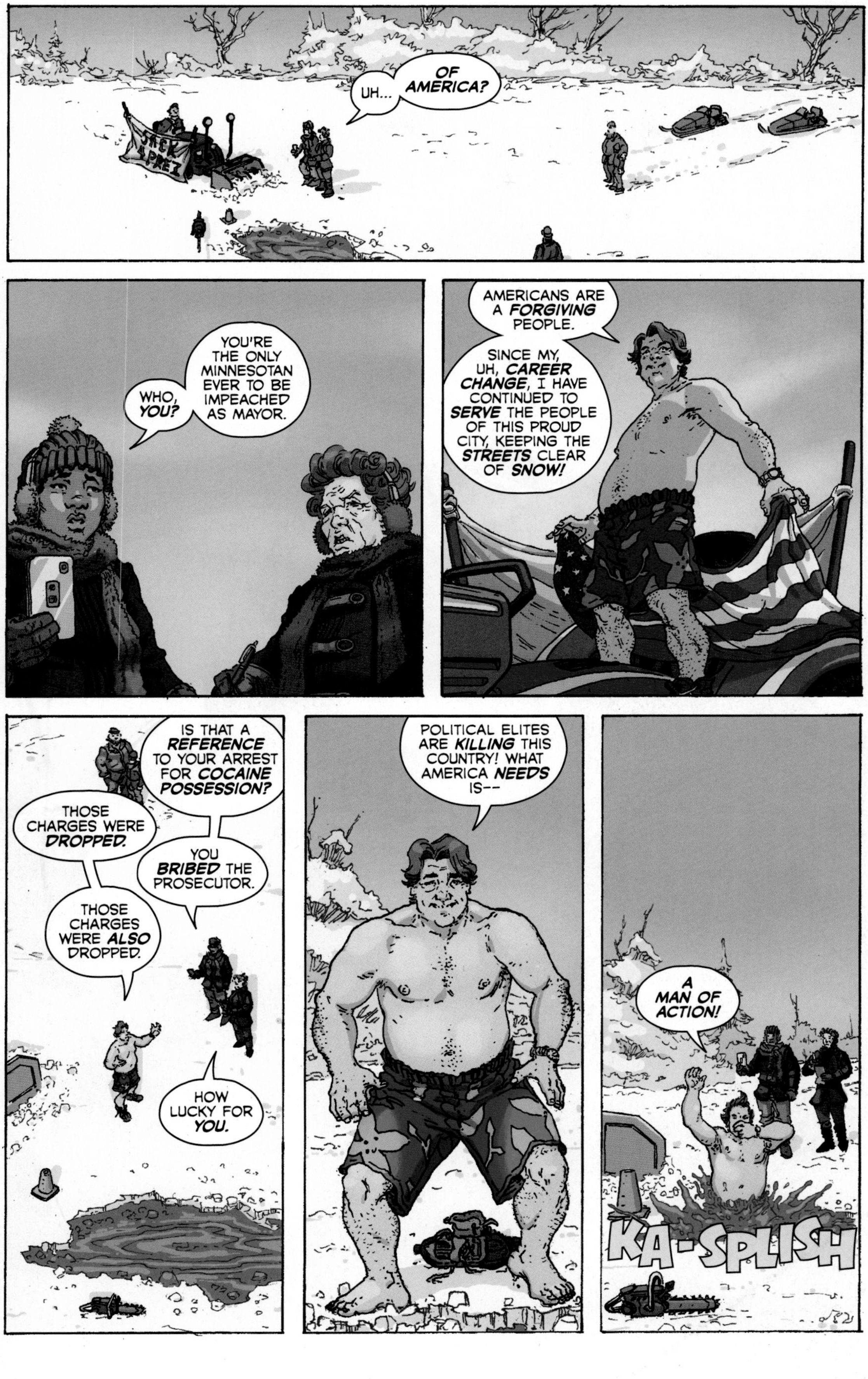
UH... OF AMERICA?
WHO, YOU?
YOU'RE THE ONLY MINNESOTAN EVER TO BE IMPEACHED AS MAYOR.
AMERICANS ARE A FORGIVING PEOPLE.
SINCE MY, UH, CAREER CHANGE, I HAVE CONTINUED TO SERVE THE PEOPLE OF THIS PROUD CITY, KEEPING THE STREETS CLEAR OF SNOW!
IS THAT A REFERENCE TO YOUR ARREST FOR COCAINE POSSESSION?
THOSE CHARGES WERE DROPPED.
YOU BRIBED THE PROSECUTOR.
THOSE CHARGES WERE ALSO DROPPED.
HOW LUCKY FOR YOU.
POLITICAL ELITES ARE KILLING THIS COUNTRY! WHAT AMERICA NEEDS IS--
A MAN OF ACTION!
KA-SPLISH

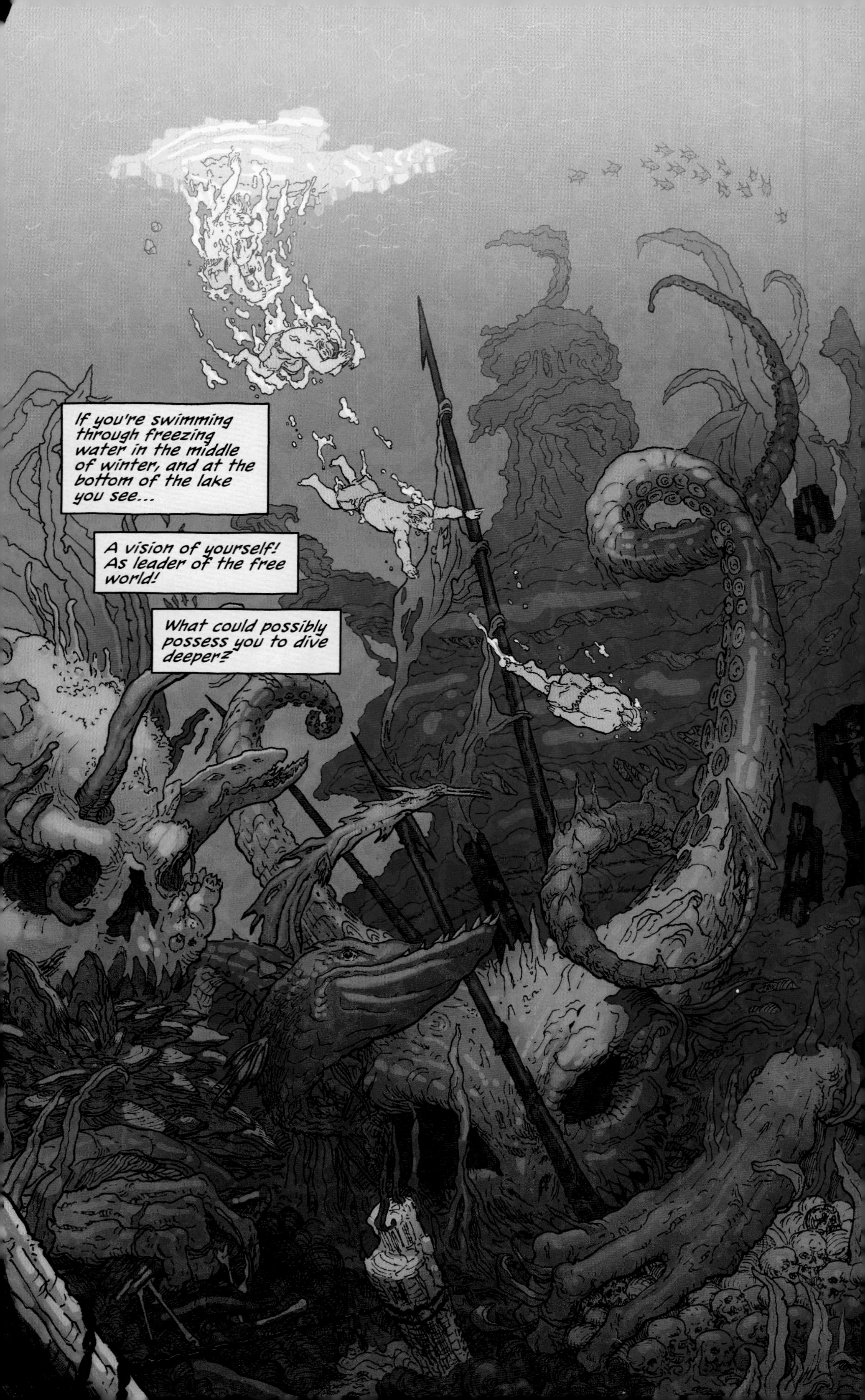
If you're swimming through freezing water in the middle of winter, and at the bottom of the lake you see...
A vision of yourself! As leader of the free world!
What could possibly possess you to dive deeper?

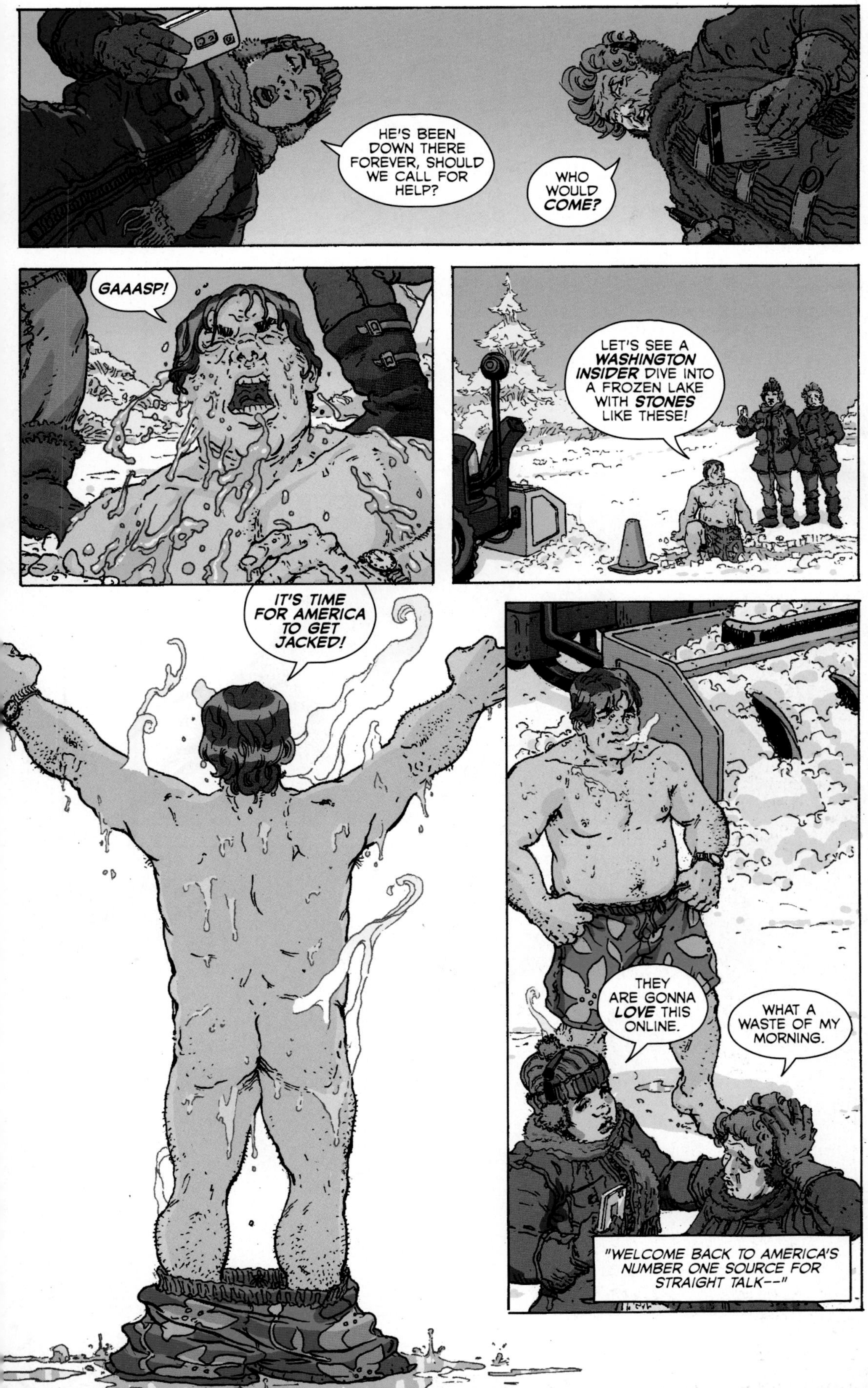
HE'S BEEN DOWN THERE FOREVER, SHOULD WE CALL FOR HELP?
WHO WOULD *COME?*
GAAASP!
LET'S SEE A ***WASHINGTON INSIDER*** DIVE INTO A FROZEN LAKE WITH ***STONES*** LIKE THESE!
IT'S TIME FOR AMERICA TO GET JACKED!
THEY ARE GONNA ***LOVE*** THIS ONLINE.
WHAT A WASTE OF MY MORNING.
"WELCOME BACK TO AMERICA'S NUMBER ONE SOURCE FOR STRAIGHT TALK--"

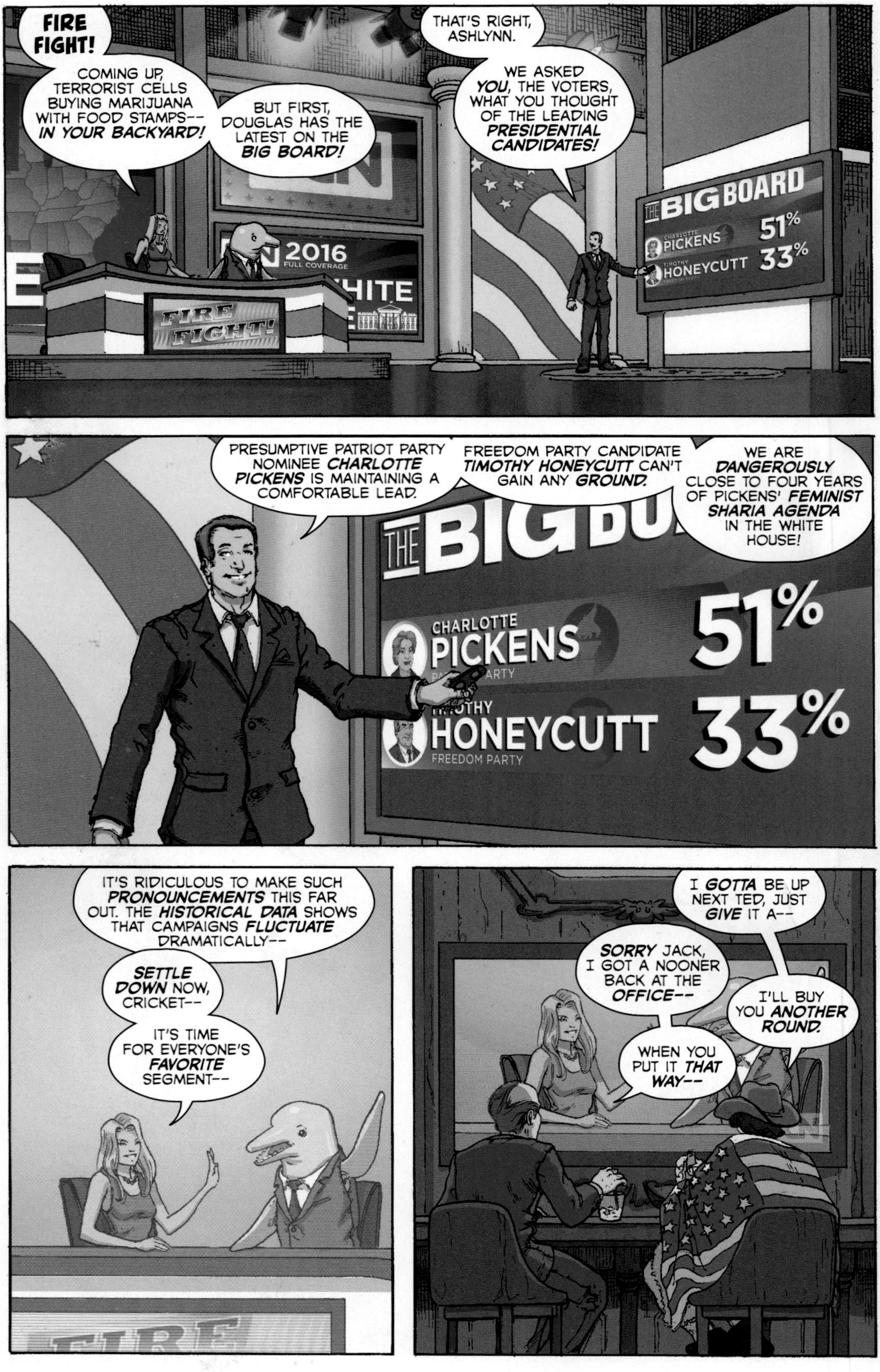
FIRE FIGHT!
COMING UP, TERRORIST CELLS BUYING MARIJUANA WITH FOOD STAMPS-- IN YOUR BACKYARD!
BUT FIRST, DOUGLAS HAS THE LATEST ON THE BIG BOARD!
THAT'S RIGHT, ASHLYNN.
WE ASKED YOU, THE VOTERS, WHAT YOU THOUGHT OF THE LEADING PRESIDENTIAL CANDIDATES!
2016 FULL COVERAGE
FIRE FIGHT!
THE BIG BOARD
PICKENS 51%
HONEYCUTT 33%
PRESUMPTIVE PATRIOT PARTY NOMINEE CHARLOTTE PICKENS IS MAINTAINING A COMFORTABLE LEAD.
FREEDOM PARTY CANDIDATE TIMOTHY HONEYCUTT CAN'T GAIN ANY GROUND.
WE ARE DANGEROUSLY CLOSE TO FOUR YEARS OF PICKENS' FEMINIST SHARIA AGENDA IN THE WHITE HOUSE!
CHARLOTTE PICKENS 51%
HONEYCUTT 33%
FREEDOM PARTY
IT'S RIDICULOUS TO MAKE SUCH PRONOUNCEMENTS THIS FAR OUT. THE HISTORICAL DATA SHOWS THAT CAMPAIGNS FLUCTUATE DRAMATICALLY--
SETTLE DOWN NOW, CRICKET--
IT'S TIME FOR EVERYONE'S FAVORITE SEGMENT--
FIRE
I GOTTA BE UP NEXT TED, JUST GIVE IT A--
SORRY JACK, I GOT A NOONER BACK AT THE OFFICE--
I'LL BUY YOU ANOTHER ROUND.
WHEN YOU PUT IT THAT WAY--

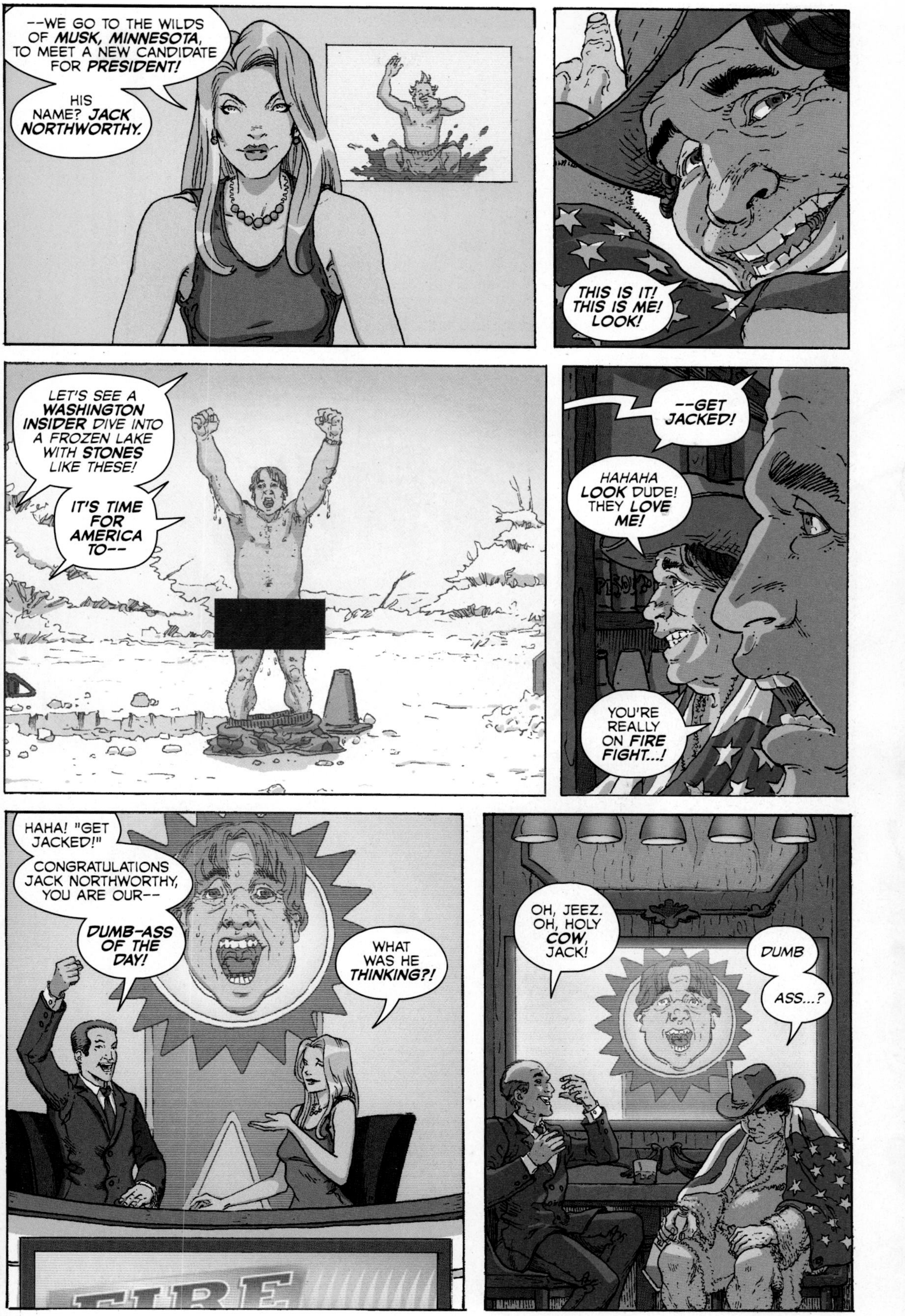
--WE GO TO THE WILDS OF MUSK, MINNESOTA, TO MEET A NEW CANDIDATE FOR PRESIDENT!
HIS NAME? JACK NORTHWORTHY.
THIS IS IT! THIS IS ME! LOOK!
LET'S SEE A WASHINGTON INSIDER DIVE INTO A FROZEN LAKE WITH STONES LIKE THESE!
IT'S TIME FOR AMERICA TO--
--GET JACKED!
HAHAHA LOOK DUDE! THEY LOVE ME!
YOU'RE REALLY ON FIRE FIGHT...!
HAHA! "GET JACKED!"
CONGRATULATIONS JACK NORTHWORTHY, YOU ARE OUR--
DUMB-ASS OF THE DAY!
WHAT WAS HE THINKING?!
FIRE
OH, JEEZ. OH, HOLY COW, JACK!
DUMB
ASS...?

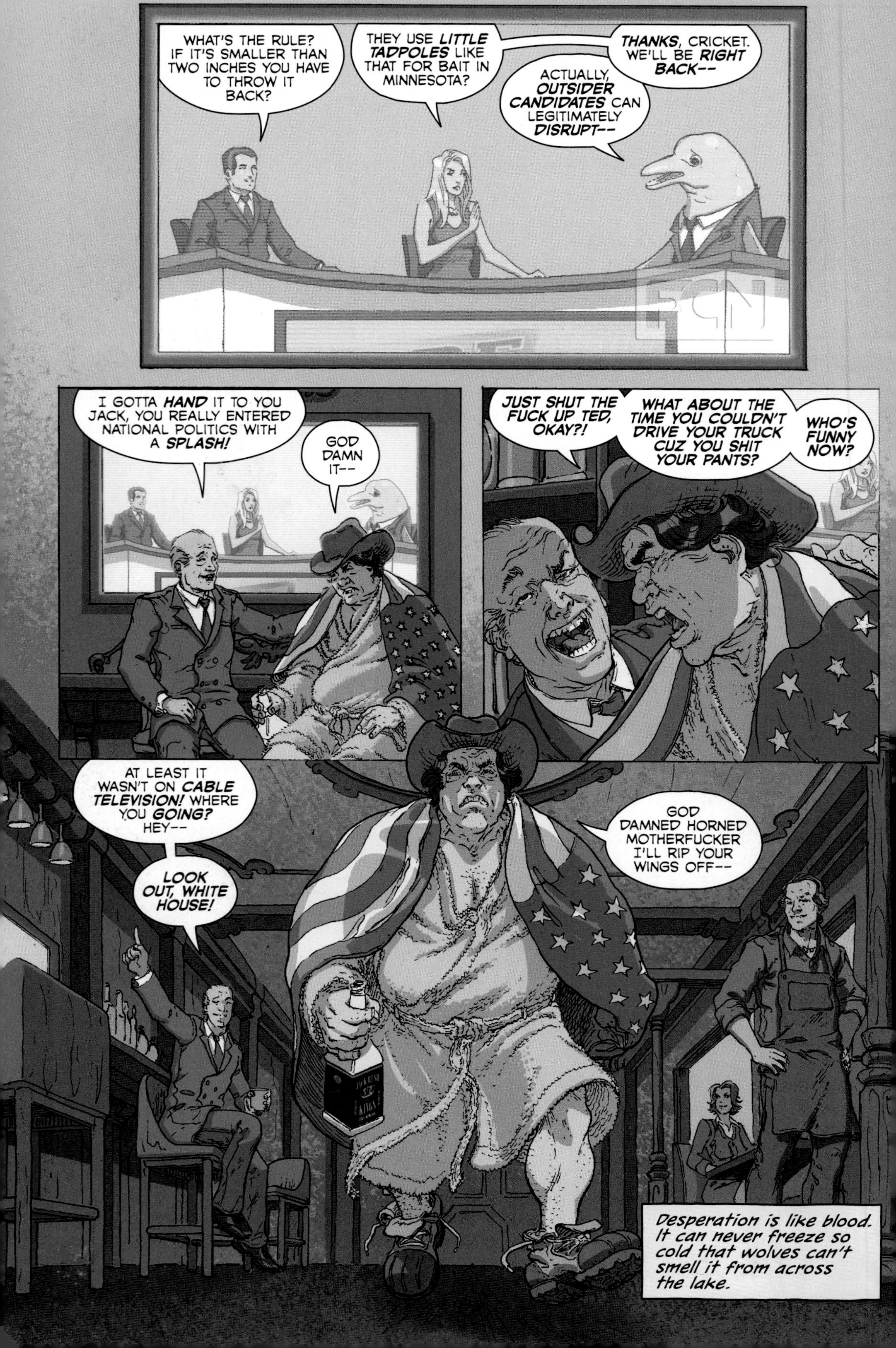
WHAT'S THE RULE? IF IT'S SMALLER THAN TWO INCHES YOU HAVE TO THROW IT BACK?
THEY USE LITTLE TADPOLES LIKE THAT FOR BAIT IN MINNESOTA?
ACTUALLY, OUTSIDER CANDIDATES CAN LEGITIMATELY DISRUPT--
THANKS, CRICKET. WE'LL BE RIGHT BACK--
I GOTTA HAND IT TO YOU JACK, YOU REALLY ENTERED NATIONAL POLITICS WITH A SPLASH!
GOD DAMN IT--
JUST SHUT THE FUCK UP TED, OKAY?!
WHAT ABOUT THE TIME YOU COULDN'T DRIVE YOUR TRUCK CUZ YOU SHIT YOUR PANTS?
WHO'S FUNNY NOW?
AT LEAST IT WASN'T ON CABLE TELEVISION! WHERE YOU GOING? HEY--
LOOK OUT, WHITE HOUSE!
GOD DAMNED HORNED MOTHERFUCKER I'LL RIP YOUR WINGS OFF--
Desperation is like blood. It can never freeze so cold that wolves can't smell it from across the lake.

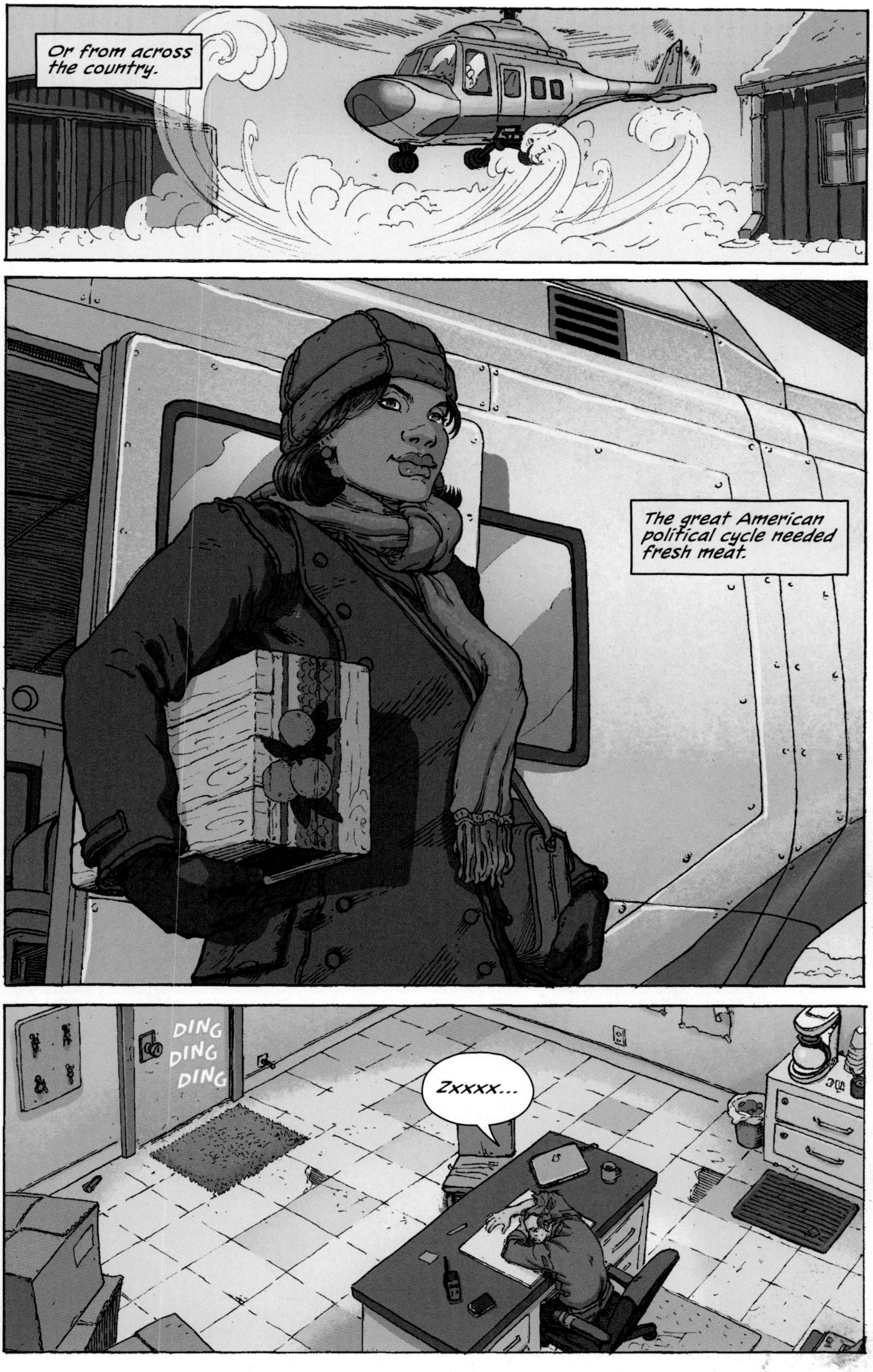
Or from across the country.
The great American political cycle needed fresh meat.
DING DING DING
Zxxxx...

HELLOOO-- GOOD AFTERNOON!

Zxxxx...

EXCUSE ME, COULD YOU PLEASE...?

Zxx!

Zxxxx...

Hmph.

AAAAH--!

SWACK

OKAY, I'M AWAKE, I'M AWAKE--

YOU MUST BE LOST OR SOMETHING. THE BIG CITY'S SOUTH OF--

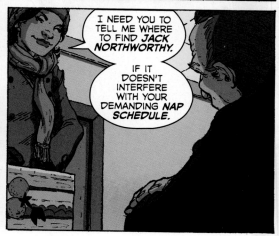

I NEED YOU TO TELL ME WHERE TO FIND JACK NORTHWORTHY.

IF IT DOESN'T INTERFERE WITH YOUR DEMANDING NAP SCHEDULE.

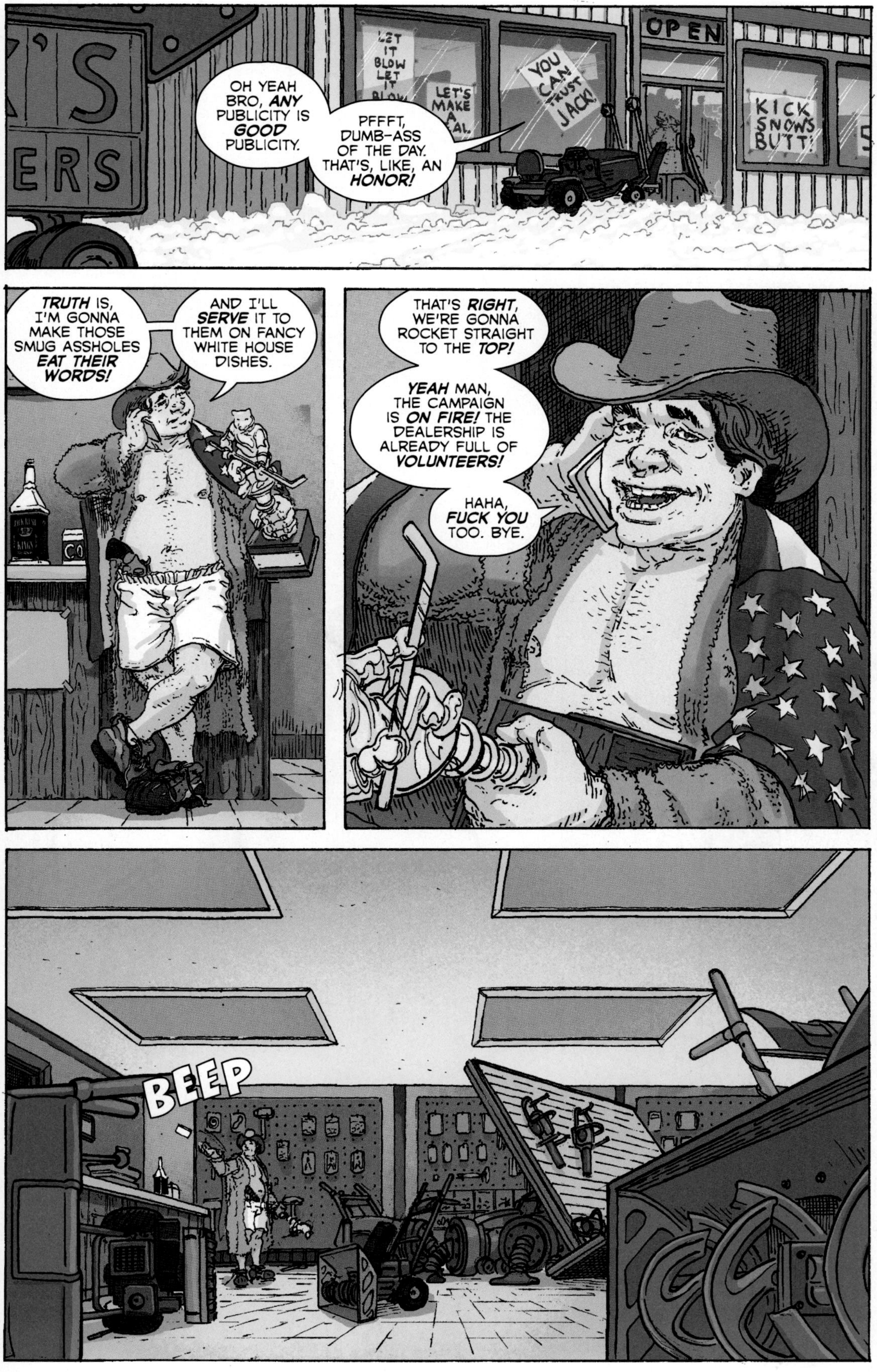
OPEN
LET IT BLOW LET IT BLOW
LET'S MAKE A DEAL
YOU CAN TRUST JACK!
KICK SNOWS BUTT!
OH YEAH BRO, ANY PUBLICITY IS GOOD PUBLICITY.
PFFFT, DUMB-ASS OF THE DAY. THAT'S, LIKE, AN HONOR!
TRUTH IS, I'M GONNA MAKE THOSE SMUG ASSHOLES EAT THEIR WORDS!
AND I'LL SERVE IT TO THEM ON FANCY WHITE HOUSE DISHES.
THAT'S RIGHT, WE'RE GONNA ROCKET STRAIGHT TO THE TOP!
YEAH MAN, THE CAMPAIGN IS ON FIRE! THE DEALERSHIP IS ALREADY FULL OF VOLUNTEERS!
HAHA, FUCK YOU TOO. BYE.
BEEP

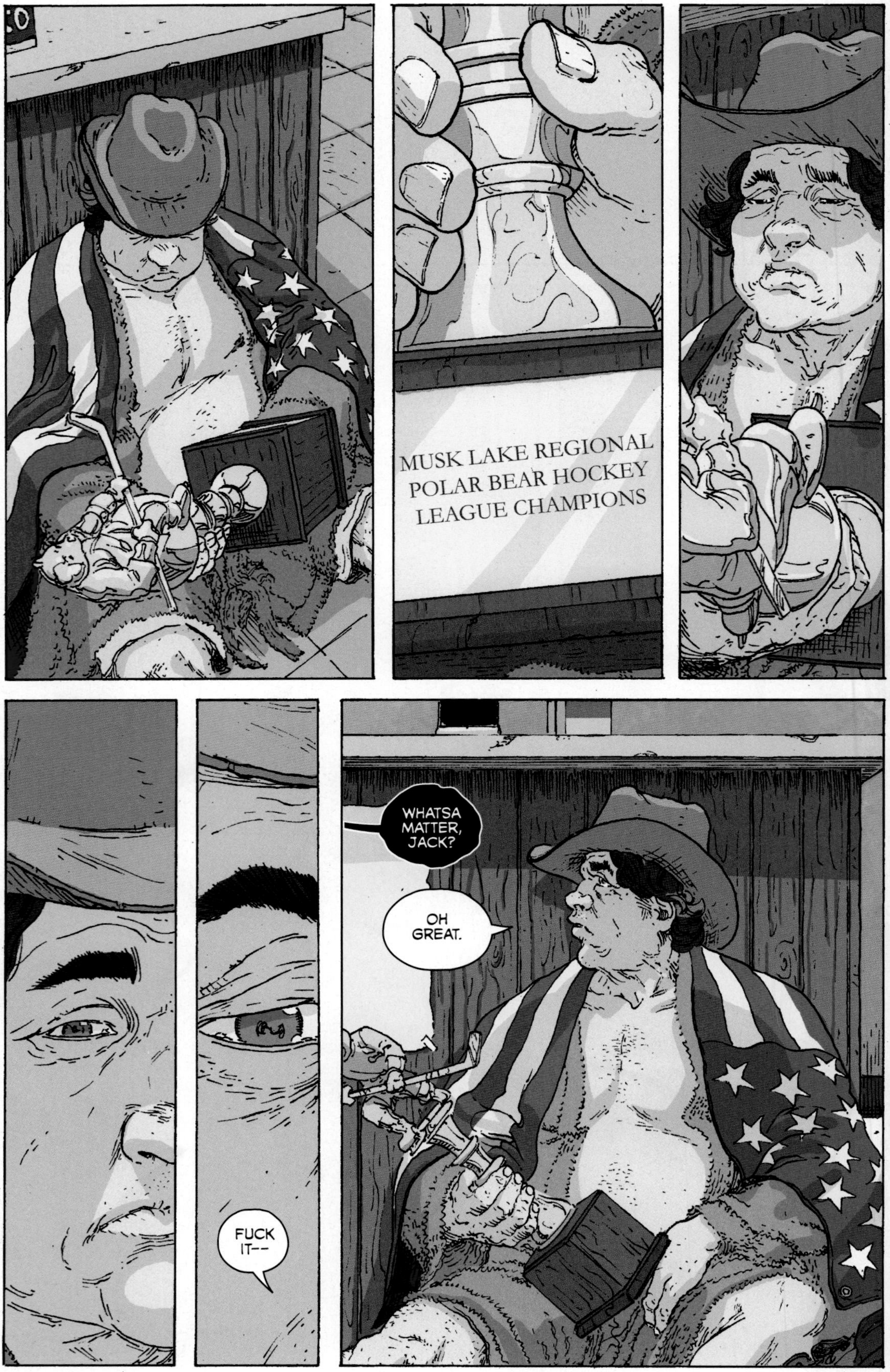
MUSK LAKE REGIONAL
POLAR BEAR HOCKEY
LEAGUE CHAMPIONS
FUCK IT--
WHATSA MATTER, JACK?
OH GREAT.

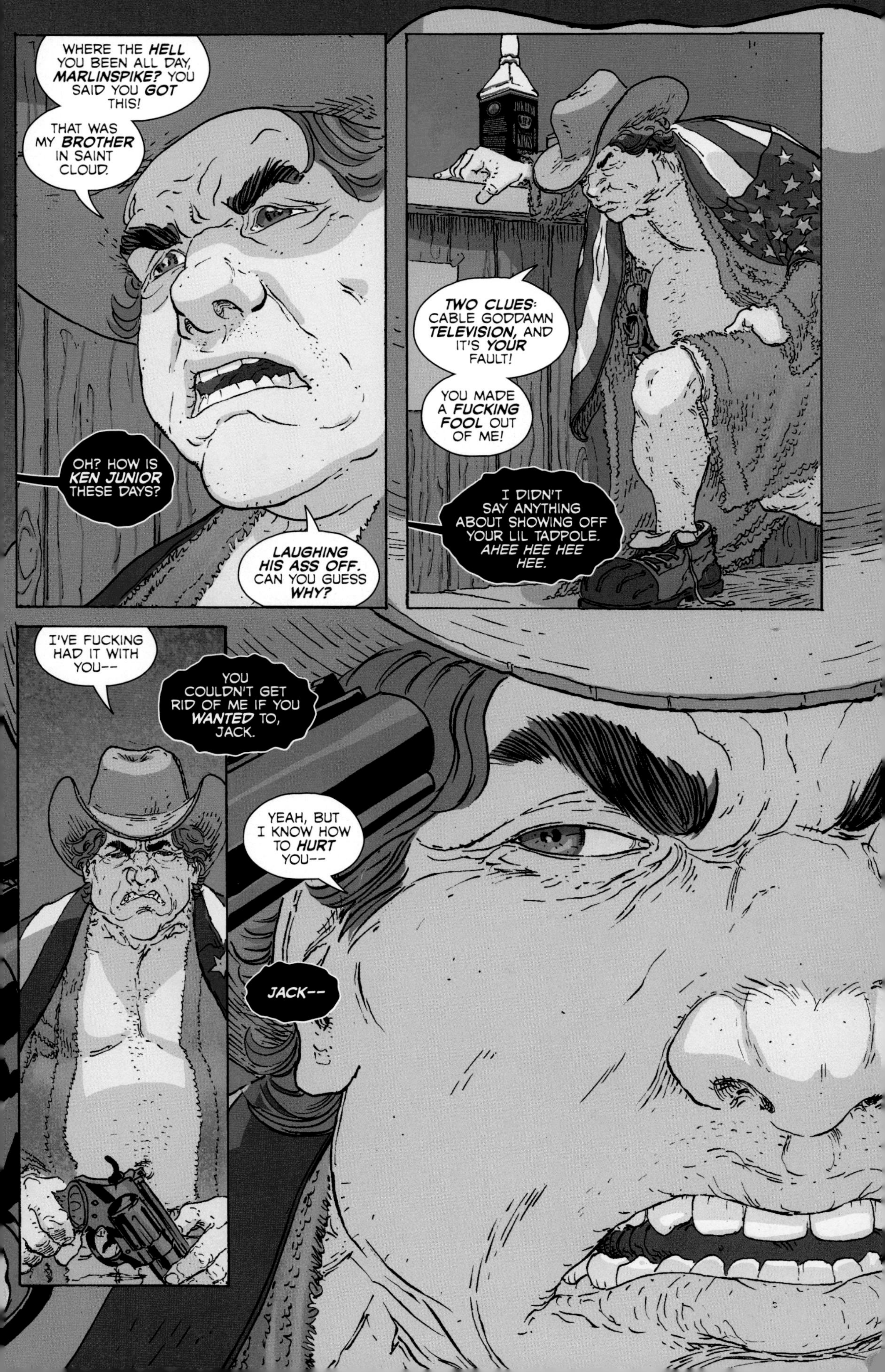

WHERE THE HELL YOU BEEN ALL DAY, MARLINSPIKE? YOU SAID YOU GOT THIS!
THAT WAS MY BROTHER IN SAINT CLOUD.
OH? HOW IS KEN JUNIOR THESE DAYS?
LAUGHING HIS ASS OFF. CAN YOU GUESS WHY?
TWO CLUES: CABLE GODDAMN TELEVISION, AND IT'S YOUR FAULT!
YOU MADE A FUCKING FOOL OUT OF ME!
I DIDN'T SAY ANYTHING ABOUT SHOWING OFF YOUR LIL TADPOLE. AHEE HEE HEE HEE.
I'VE FUCKING HAD IT WITH YOU--
YOU COULDN'T GET RID OF ME IF YOU WANTED TO, JACK.
YEAH, BUT I KNOW HOW TO HURT YOU--
JACK--

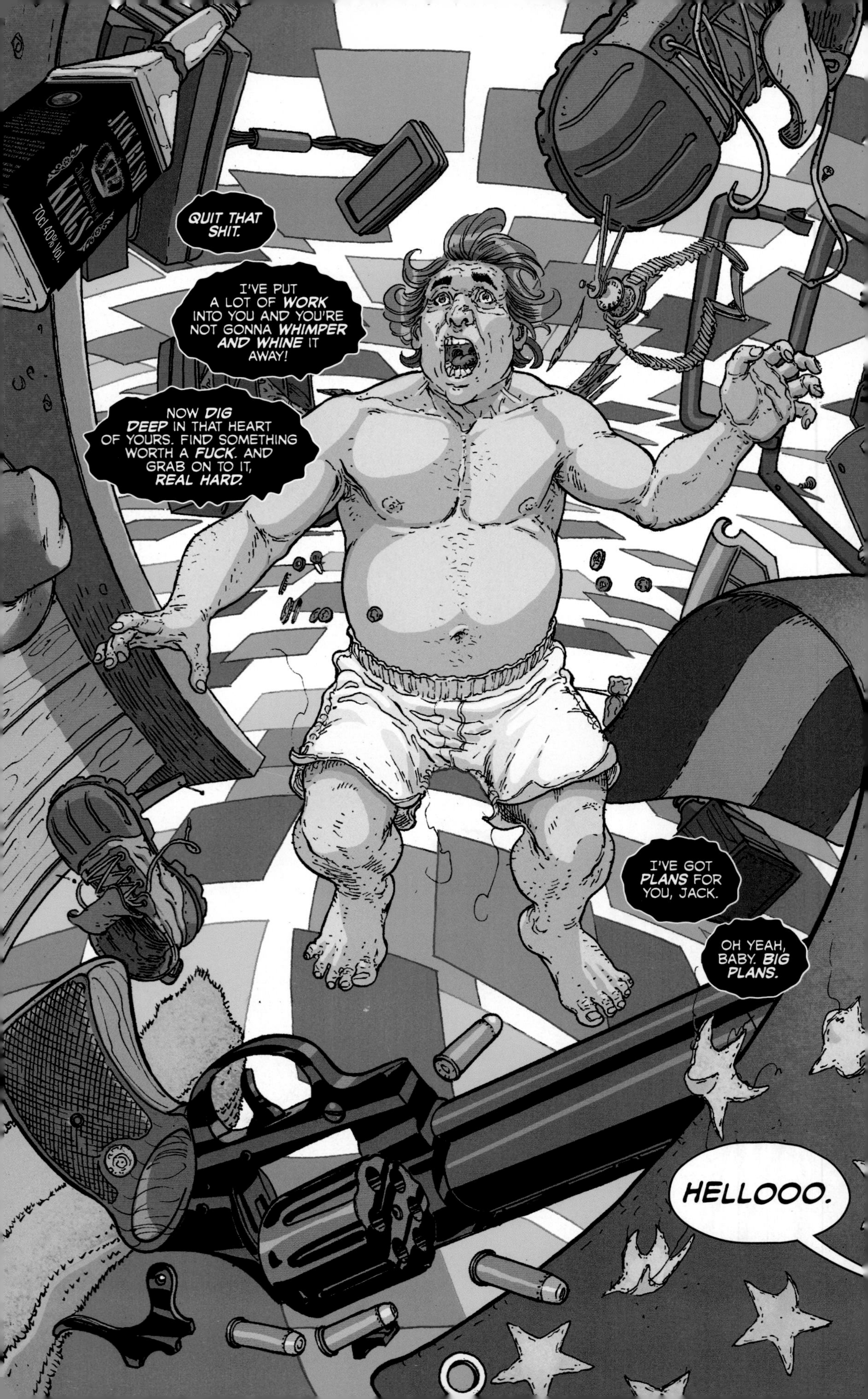
70cl 40% Vol.
QUIT THAT SHIT.
I'VE PUT A LOT OF WORK INTO YOU AND YOU'RE NOT GONNA WHIMPER AND WHINE IT AWAY!
NOW DIG DEEP IN THAT HEART OF YOURS. FIND SOMETHING WORTH A FUCK. AND GRAB ON TO IT, REAL HARD.
I'VE GOT PLANS FOR YOU, JACK.
OH YEAH, BABY. BIG PLANS.
HELLOOO.

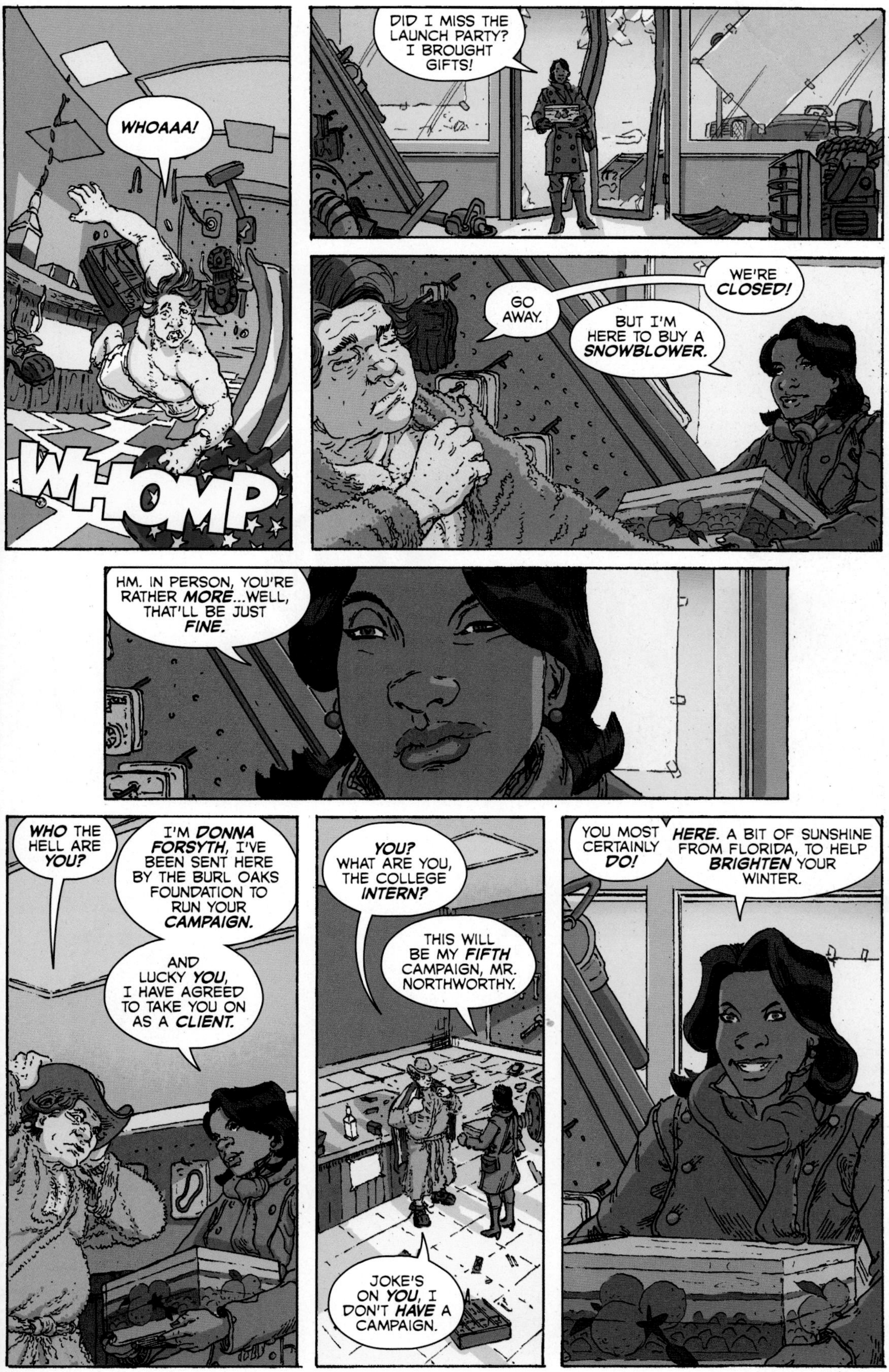
WHOAAA!
WHOMP
DID I MISS THE LAUNCH PARTY? I BROUGHT GIFTS!
WE'RE CLOSED!
GO AWAY.
BUT I'M HERE TO BUY A SNOWBLOWER.
HM. IN PERSON, YOU'RE RATHER MORE...WELL, THAT'LL BE JUST FINE.
WHO THE HELL ARE YOU?
I'M DONNA FORSYTH, I'VE BEEN SENT HERE BY THE BURL OAKS FOUNDATION TO RUN YOUR CAMPAIGN.
AND LUCKY YOU, I HAVE AGREED TO TAKE YOU ON AS A CLIENT.
YOU? WHAT ARE YOU, THE COLLEGE INTERN?
THIS WILL BE MY FIFTH CAMPAIGN, MR. NORTHWORTHY.
JOKE'S ON YOU, I DON'T HAVE A CAMPAIGN.
YOU MOST CERTAINLY DO!
HERE. A BIT OF SUNSHINE FROM FLORIDA, TO HELP BRIGHTEN YOUR WINTER.

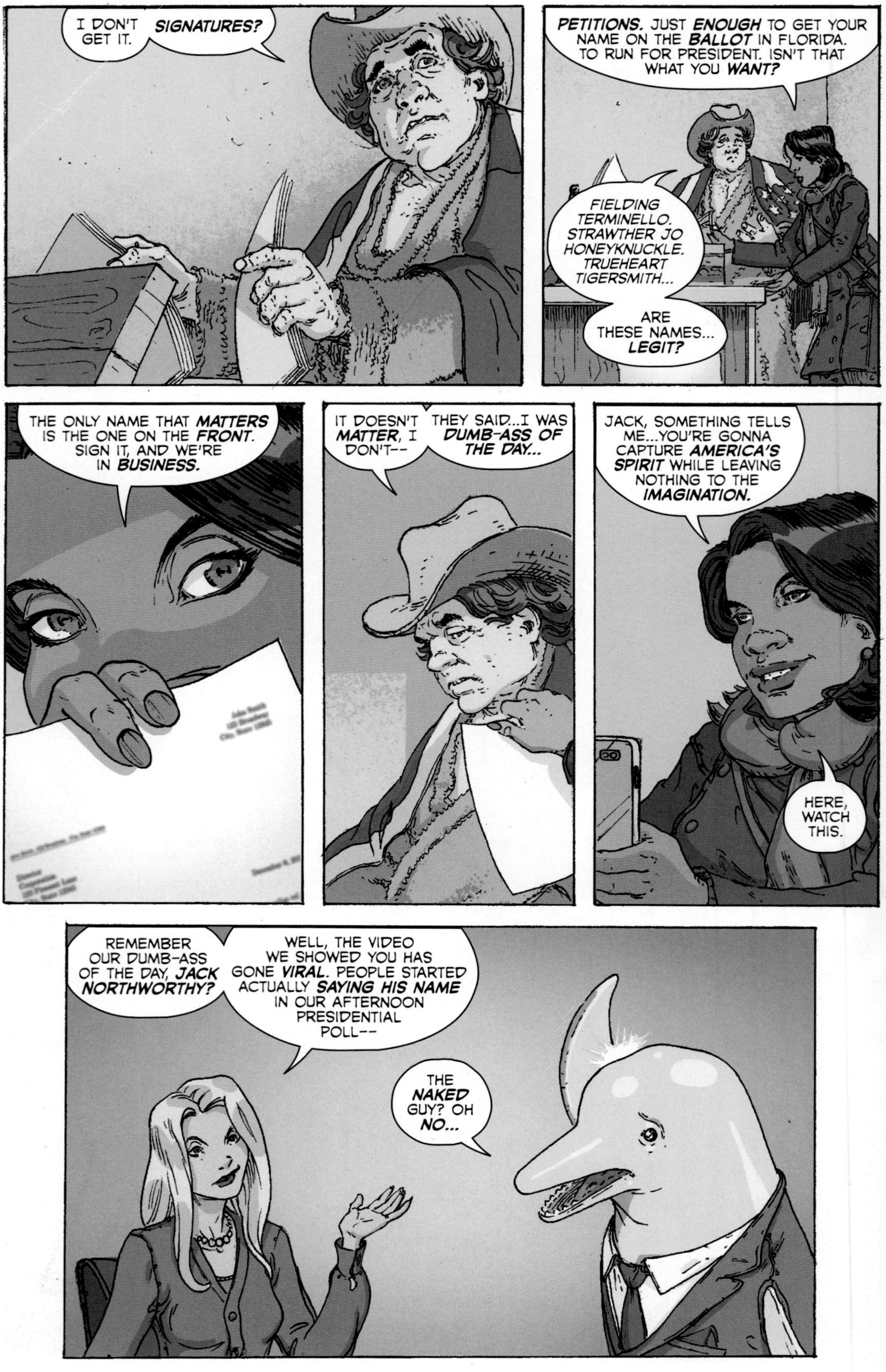
I DON'T GET IT.
SIGNATURES?
PETITIONS. JUST ENOUGH TO GET YOUR NAME ON THE BALLOT IN FLORIDA. TO RUN FOR PRESIDENT. ISN'T THAT WHAT YOU WANT?
FIELDING TERMINELLO. STRAWTHER JO HONEYKNUCKLE. TRUEHEART TIGERSMITH...
ARE THESE NAMES... LEGIT?
THE ONLY NAME THAT MATTERS IS THE ONE ON THE FRONT. SIGN IT, AND WE'RE IN BUSINESS.
IT DOESN'T MATTER, I DON'T--
THEY SAID...I WAS DUMB-ASS OF THE DAY...
JACK, SOMETHING TELLS ME...YOU'RE GONNA CAPTURE AMERICA'S SPIRIT WHILE LEAVING NOTHING TO THE IMAGINATION.
HERE, WATCH THIS.
REMEMBER OUR DUMB-ASS OF THE DAY, JACK NORTHWORTHY?
WELL, THE VIDEO WE SHOWED YOU HAS GONE VIRAL. PEOPLE STARTED ACTUALLY SAYING HIS NAME IN OUR AFTERNOON PRESIDENTIAL POLL--
THE NAKED GUY? OH NO...

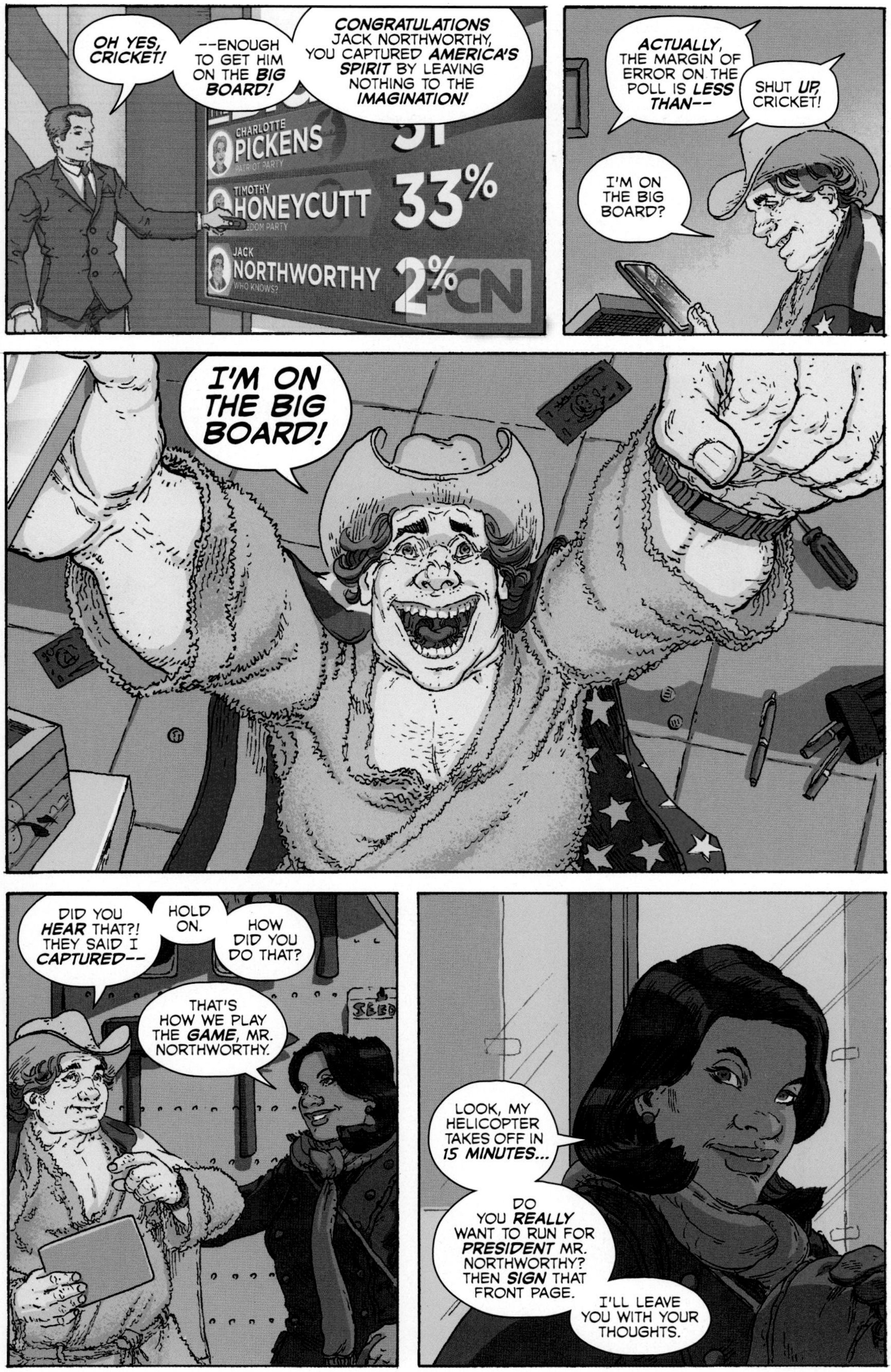
OH YES, CRICKET!
--ENOUGH TO GET HIM ON THE BIG BOARD!
CONGRATULATIONS JACK NORTHWORTHY, YOU CAPTURED AMERICA'S SPIRIT BY LEAVING NOTHING TO THE IMAGINATION!
CHARLOTTE PICKENS PATRIOT PARTY
TIMOTHY HONEYCUTT 33%
JACK NORTHWORTHY WHO KNOWS? 2%
FCN
ACTUALLY, THE MARGIN OF ERROR ON THE POLL IS LESS THAN--
SHUT UP, CRICKET!
I'M ON THE BIG BOARD?
I'M ON THE BIG BOARD!
DID YOU HEAR THAT?! THEY SAID I CAPTURED--
HOLD ON.
HOW DID YOU DO THAT?
THAT'S HOW WE PLAY THE GAME, MR. NORTHWORTHY.
LOOK, MY HELICOPTER TAKES OFF IN 15 MINUTES...
DO YOU REALLY WANT TO RUN FOR PRESIDENT MR. NORTHWORTHY? THEN SIGN THAT FRONT PAGE.
I'LL LEAVE YOU WITH YOUR THOUGHTS.

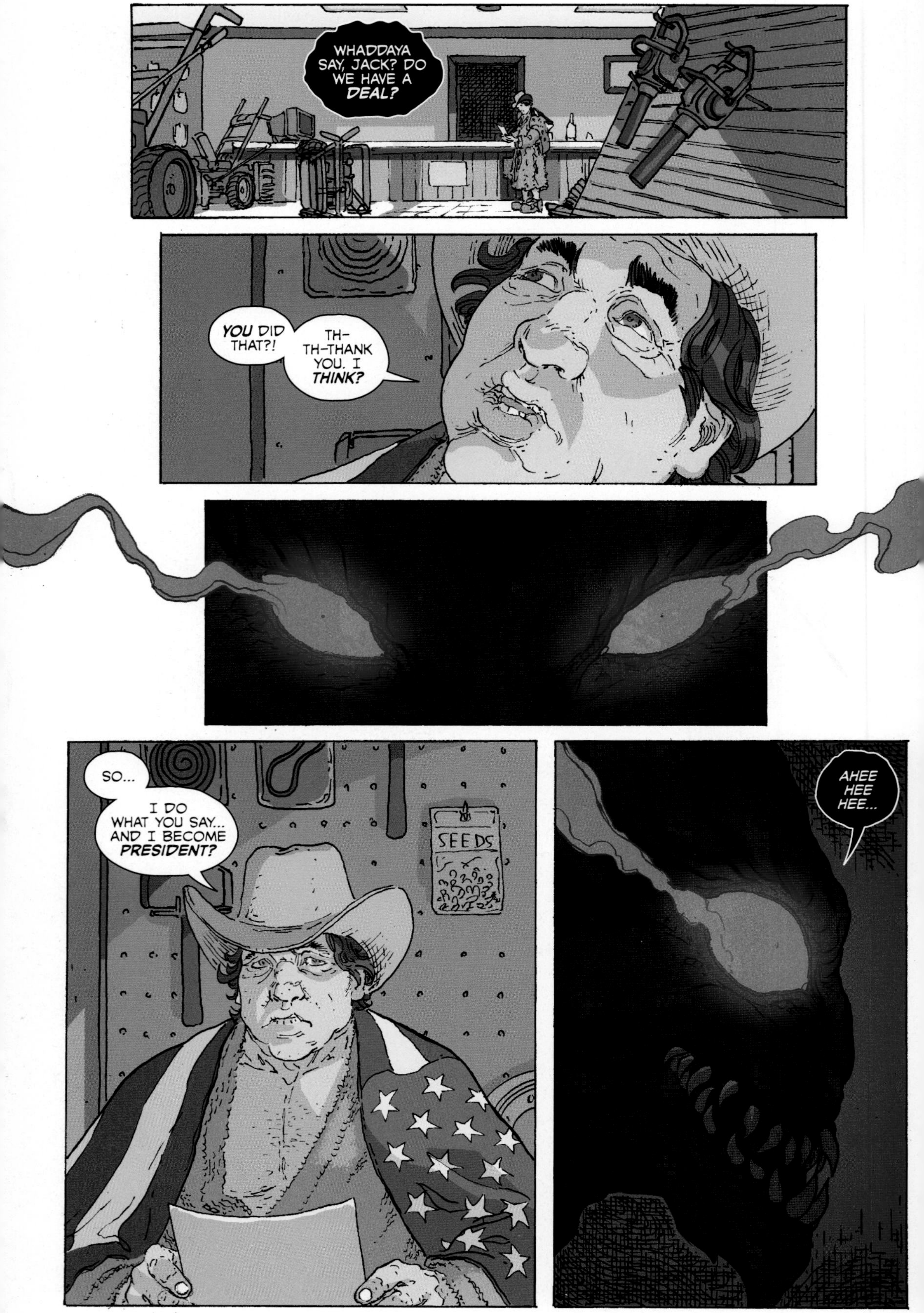
WHADDAYA SAY, JACK? DO WE HAVE A DEAL?
YOU DID THAT?!
TH- TH-THANK YOU. I THINK?
SO...
I DO WHAT YOU SAY... AND I BECOME PRESIDENT?
AHEE HEE HEE...

YOU KNOW WHAT? *FUCK IT.* SEEMS LIKE A FUN THING TO DO.

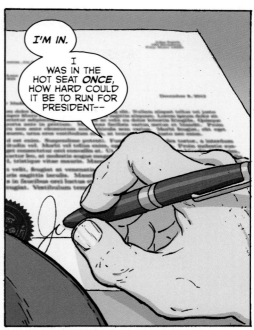

I'M IN.

I WAS IN THE HOT SEAT *ONCE,* HOW HARD COULD IT BE TO RUN FOR PRESIDENT--

THAT'S THE *SPIRIT,* JACK--

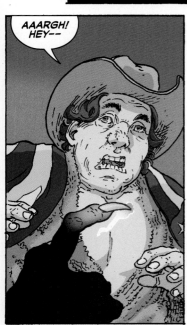

AAARGH! HEY--

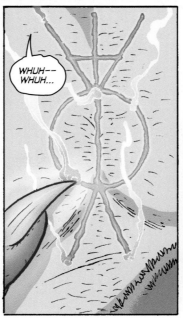

WHUH-- WHUH...

WHAT THE FUCK DID YOU DO THAT FOR?

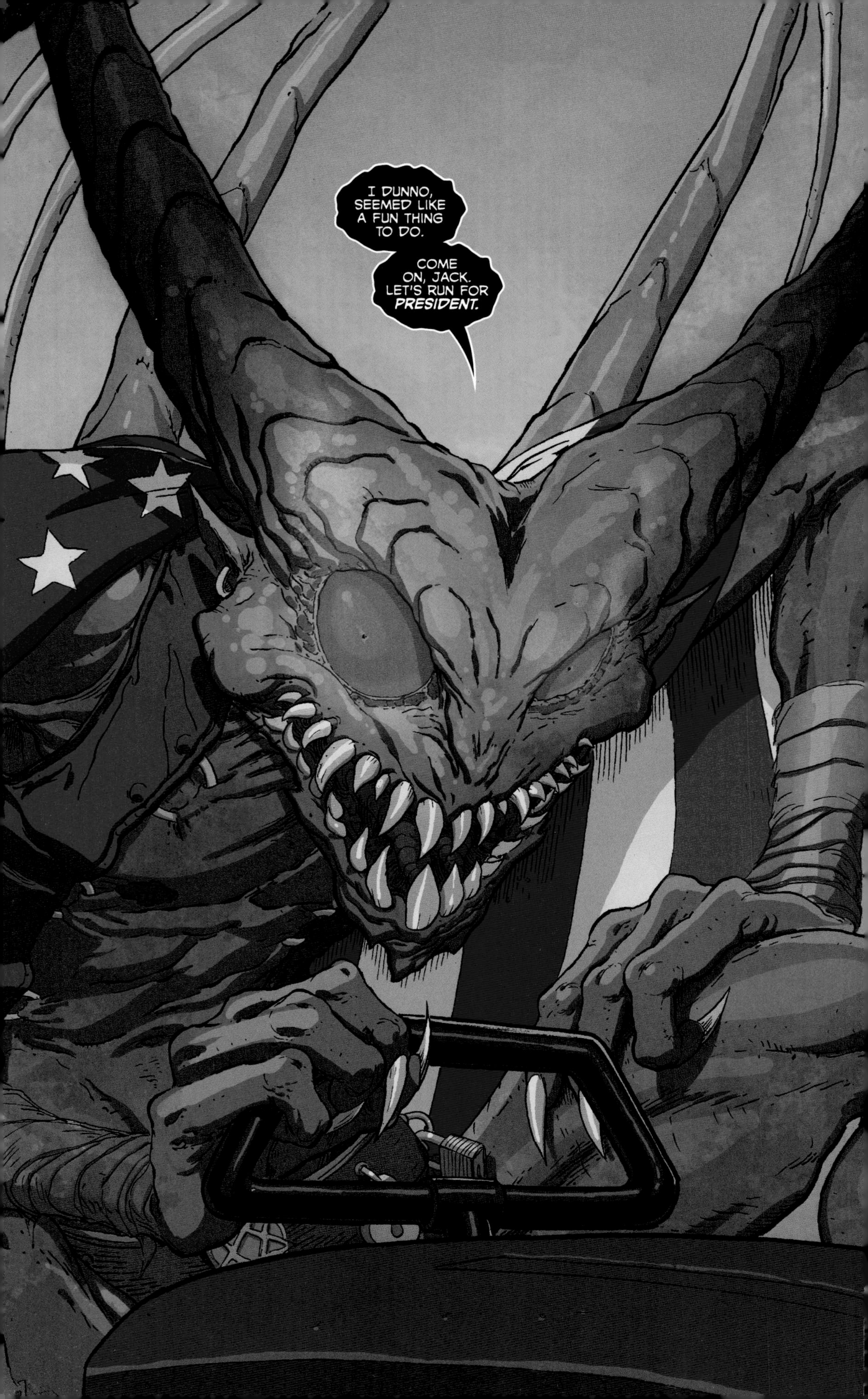
I DUNNO, SEEMED LIKE A FUN THING TO DO.
COME ON, JACK. LET'S RUN FOR ***PRESIDENT.***

CHAPTER 2
THE RETURN OF THE GOON

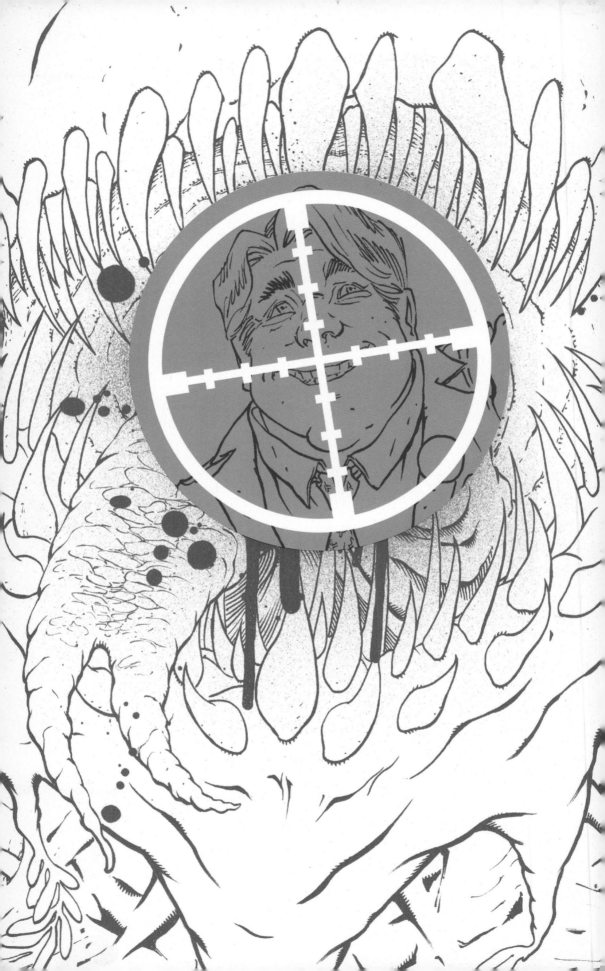

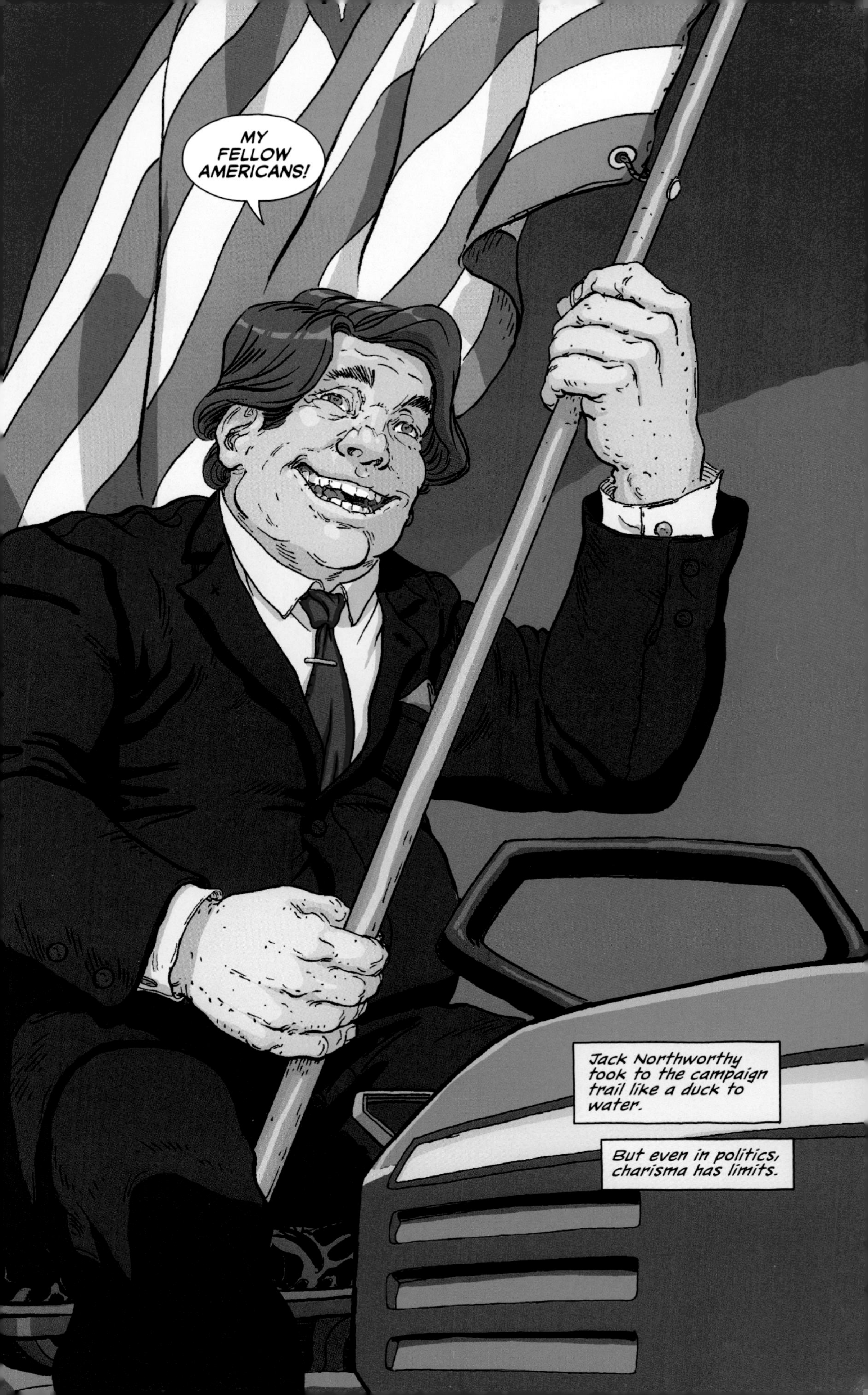

MY FELLOW AMERICANS!
Jack Northworthy took to the campaign trail like a duck to water.
But even in politics, charisma has limits.

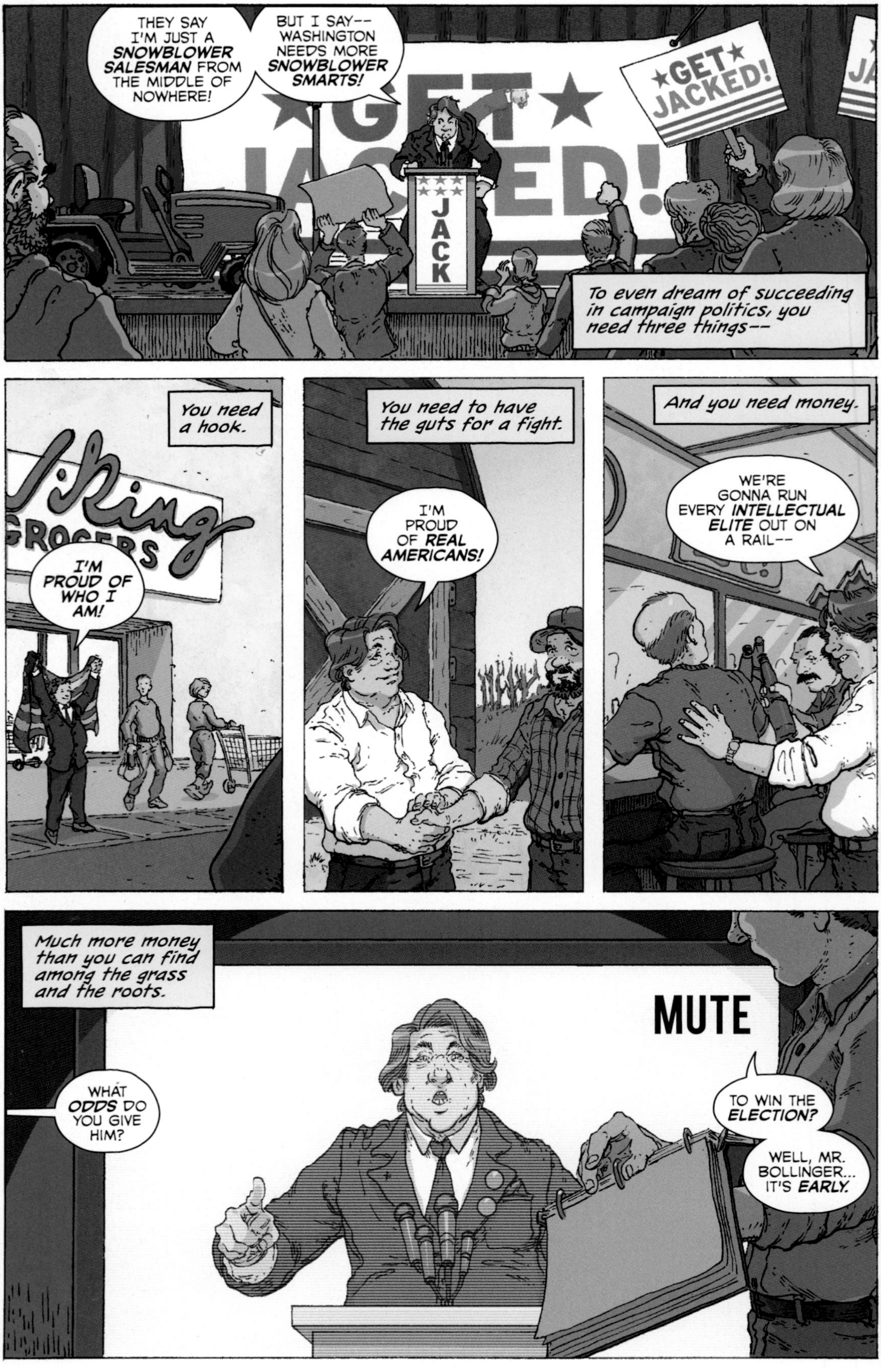
THEY SAY I'M JUST A SNOWBLOWER SALESMAN FROM THE MIDDLE OF NOWHERE!
BUT I SAY-- WASHINGTON NEEDS MORE SNOWBLOWER SMARTS!
★GET★ JACKED!
GET JACKED!
JACK
To even dream of succeeding in campaign politics, you need three things--
You need a hook.
I'M PROUD OF WHO I AM!
GROCERS
You need to have the guts for a fight.
I'M PROUD OF REAL AMERICANS!
And you need money.
WE'RE GONNA RUN EVERY INTELLECTUAL ELITE OUT ON A RAIL--
Much more money than you can find among the grass and the roots.
MUTE
WHAT ODDS DO YOU GIVE HIM?
TO WIN THE ELECTION?
WELL, MR. BOLLINGER... IT'S EARLY.

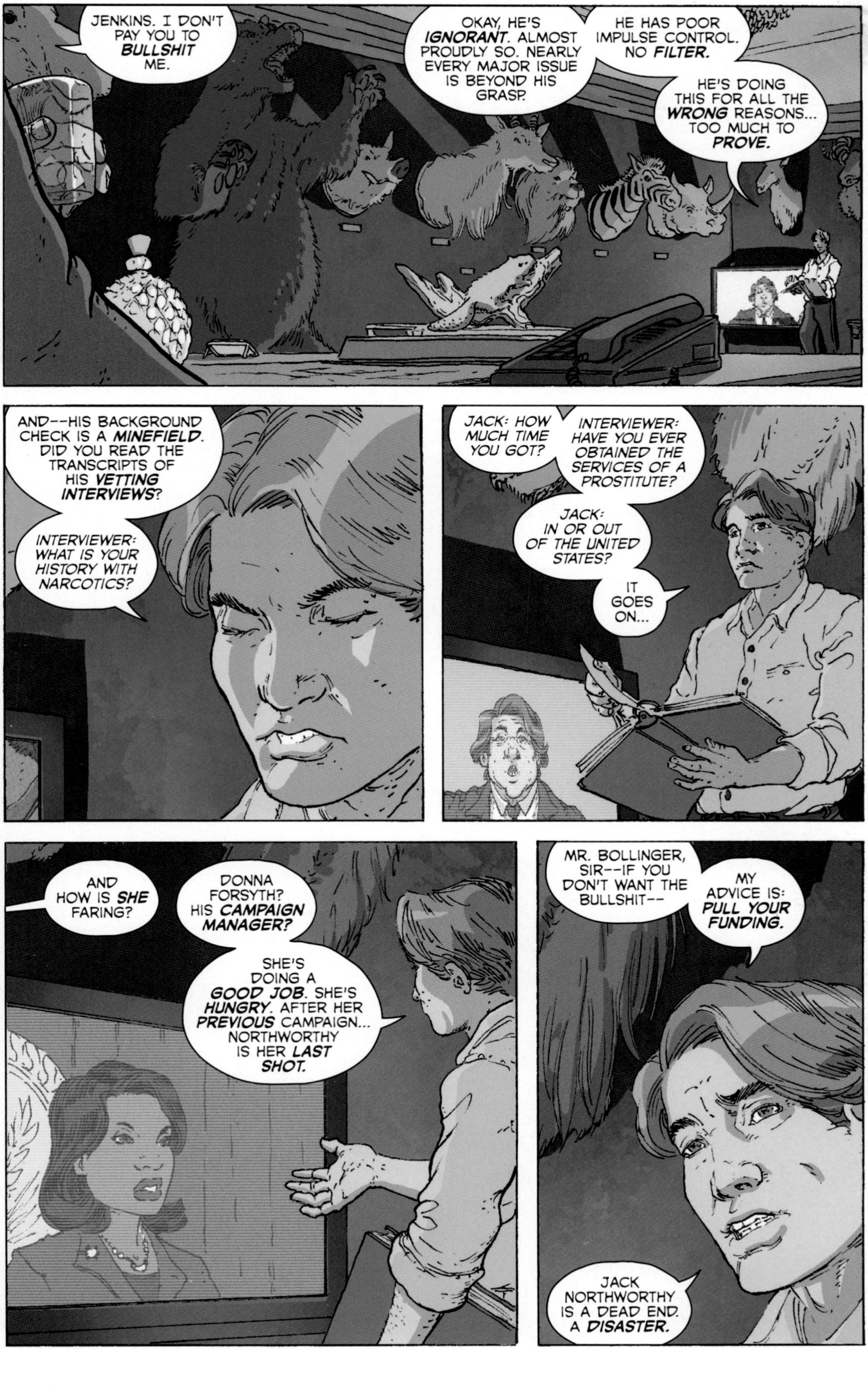
JENKINS. I DON'T PAY YOU TO BULLSHIT ME.
OKAY, HE'S IGNORANT. ALMOST PROUDLY SO. NEARLY EVERY MAJOR ISSUE IS BEYOND HIS GRASP.
HE HAS POOR IMPULSE CONTROL. NO FILTER.
HE'S DOING THIS FOR ALL THE WRONG REASONS... TOO MUCH TO PROVE.
AND--HIS BACKGROUND CHECK IS A MINEFIELD. DID YOU READ THE TRANSCRIPTS OF HIS VETTING INTERVIEWS?
INTERVIEWER: WHAT IS YOUR HISTORY WITH NARCOTICS?
JACK: HOW MUCH TIME YOU GOT?
INTERVIEWER: HAVE YOU EVER OBTAINED THE SERVICES OF A PROSTITUTE?
JACK: IN OR OUT OF THE UNITED STATES?
IT GOES ON...
AND HOW IS SHE FARING?
DONNA FORSYTH? HIS CAMPAIGN MANAGER?
SHE'S DOING A GOOD JOB. SHE'S HUNGRY. AFTER HER PREVIOUS CAMPAIGN... NORTHWORTHY IS HER LAST SHOT.
MR. BOLLINGER, SIR--IF YOU DON'T WANT THE BULLSHIT--
MY ADVICE IS: PULL YOUR FUNDING.
JACK NORTHWORTHY IS A DEAD END. A DISASTER.

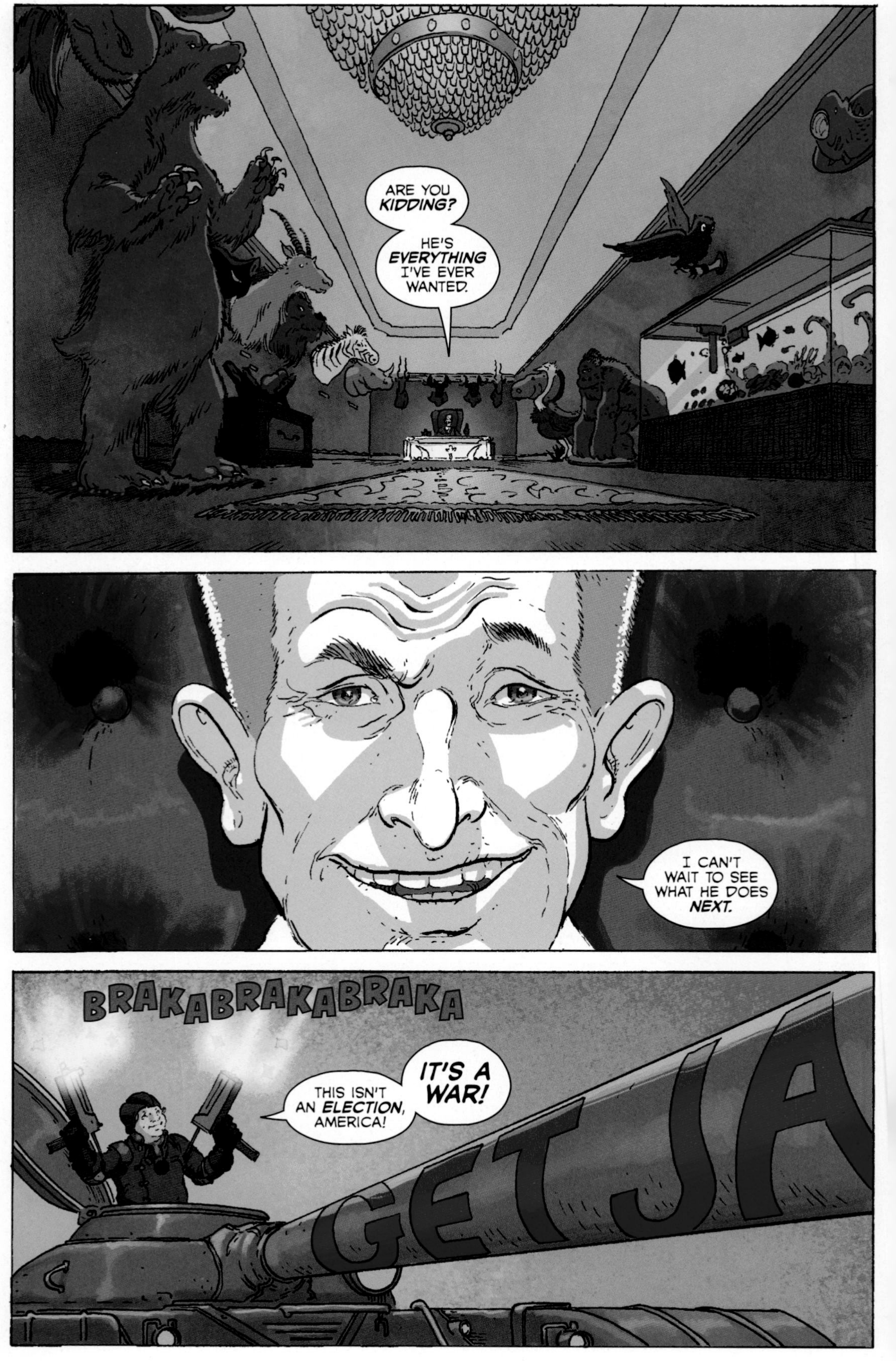
ARE YOU *KIDDING?*
HE'S *EVERYTHING* I'VE EVER WANTED.
I CAN'T WAIT TO SEE WHAT HE DOES *NEXT.*
BRAKABRAKABRAKA
THIS ISN'T AN *ELECTION*, AMERICA!
IT'S A WAR!
GET JA

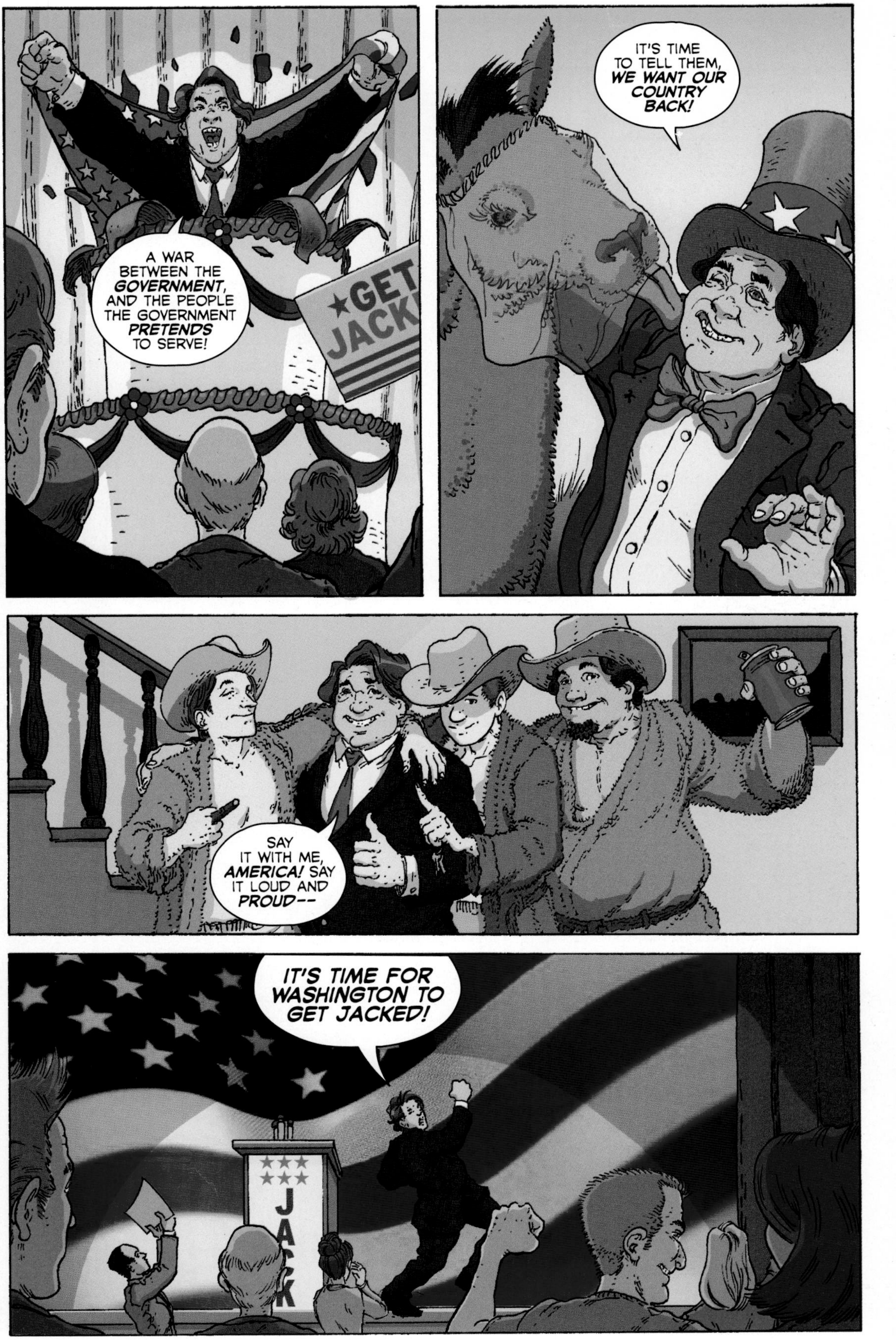
A WAR BETWEEN THE GOVERNMENT, AND THE PEOPLE THE GOVERNMENT PRETENDS TO SERVE!
★GET JACK!
IT'S TIME TO TELL THEM, WE WANT OUR COUNTRY BACK!
SAY IT WITH ME, AMERICA! SAY IT LOUD AND PROUD--
IT'S TIME FOR WASHINGTON TO GET JACKED!
JACK

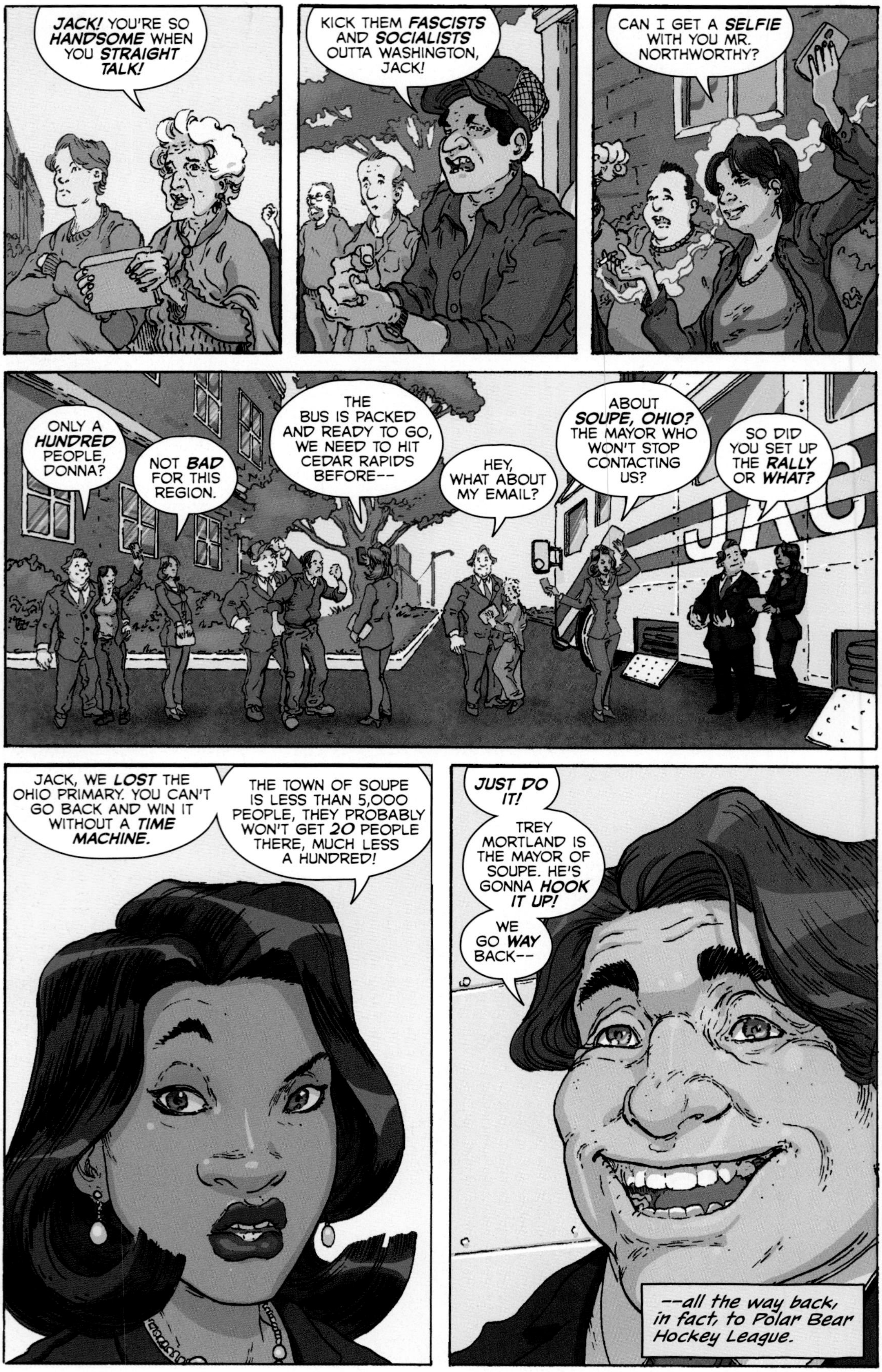
JACK! YOU'RE SO HANDSOME WHEN YOU STRAIGHT TALK!
KICK THEM FASCISTS AND SOCIALISTS OUTTA WASHINGTON, JACK!
CAN I GET A SELFIE WITH YOU MR. NORTHWORTHY?
ONLY A HUNDRED PEOPLE, DONNA?
NOT BAD FOR THIS REGION.
THE BUS IS PACKED AND READY TO GO, WE NEED TO HIT CEDAR RAPIDS BEFORE--
HEY, WHAT ABOUT MY EMAIL?
ABOUT SOUPE, OHIO? THE MAYOR WHO WON'T STOP CONTACTING US?
SO DID YOU SET UP THE RALLY OR WHAT?
JACK, WE LOST THE OHIO PRIMARY. YOU CAN'T GO BACK AND WIN IT WITHOUT A TIME MACHINE.
THE TOWN OF SOUPE IS LESS THAN 5,000 PEOPLE, THEY PROBABLY WON'T GET 20 PEOPLE THERE, MUCH LESS A HUNDRED!
JUST DO IT!
TREY MORTLAND IS THE MAYOR OF SOUPE. HE'S GONNA HOOK IT UP!
WE GO WAY BACK--
--all the way back, in fact, to Polar Bear Hockey League.

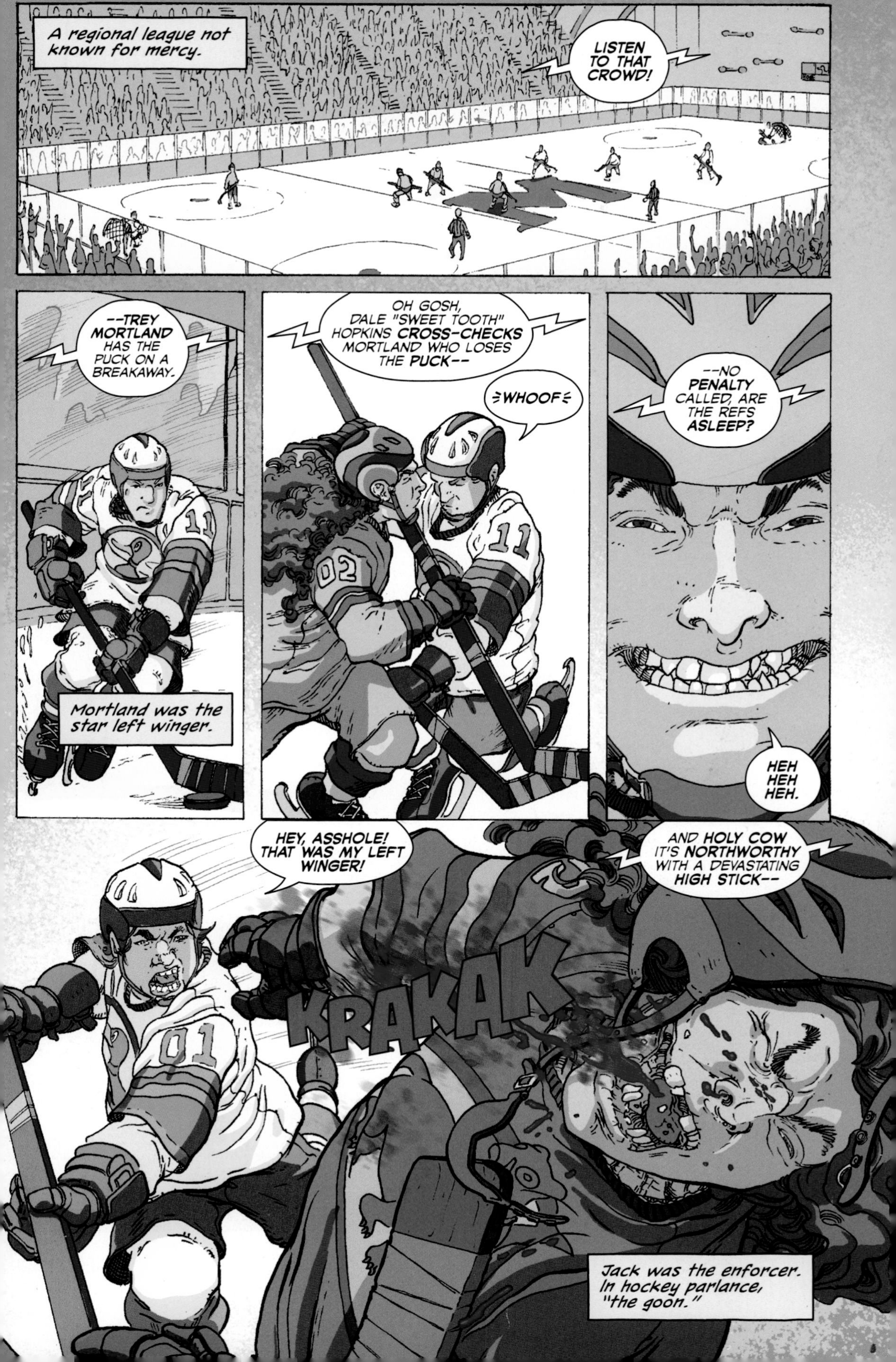

A regional league not known for mercy.
LISTEN TO THAT CROWD!
--TREY MORTLAND HAS THE PUCK ON A BREAKAWAY.
Mortland was the star left winger.
OH GOSH, DALE "SWEET TOOTH" HOPKINS CROSS-CHECKS MORTLAND WHO LOSES THE PUCK--
WHOOF
--NO PENALTY CALLED, ARE THE REFS ASLEEP?
HEH HEH HEH.
HEY, ASSHOLE! THAT WAS MY LEFT WINGER!
AND HOLY COW IT'S NORTHWORTHY WITH A DEVASTATING HIGH STICK--
KRAKAK
Jack was the enforcer. In hockey parlance, "the goon."

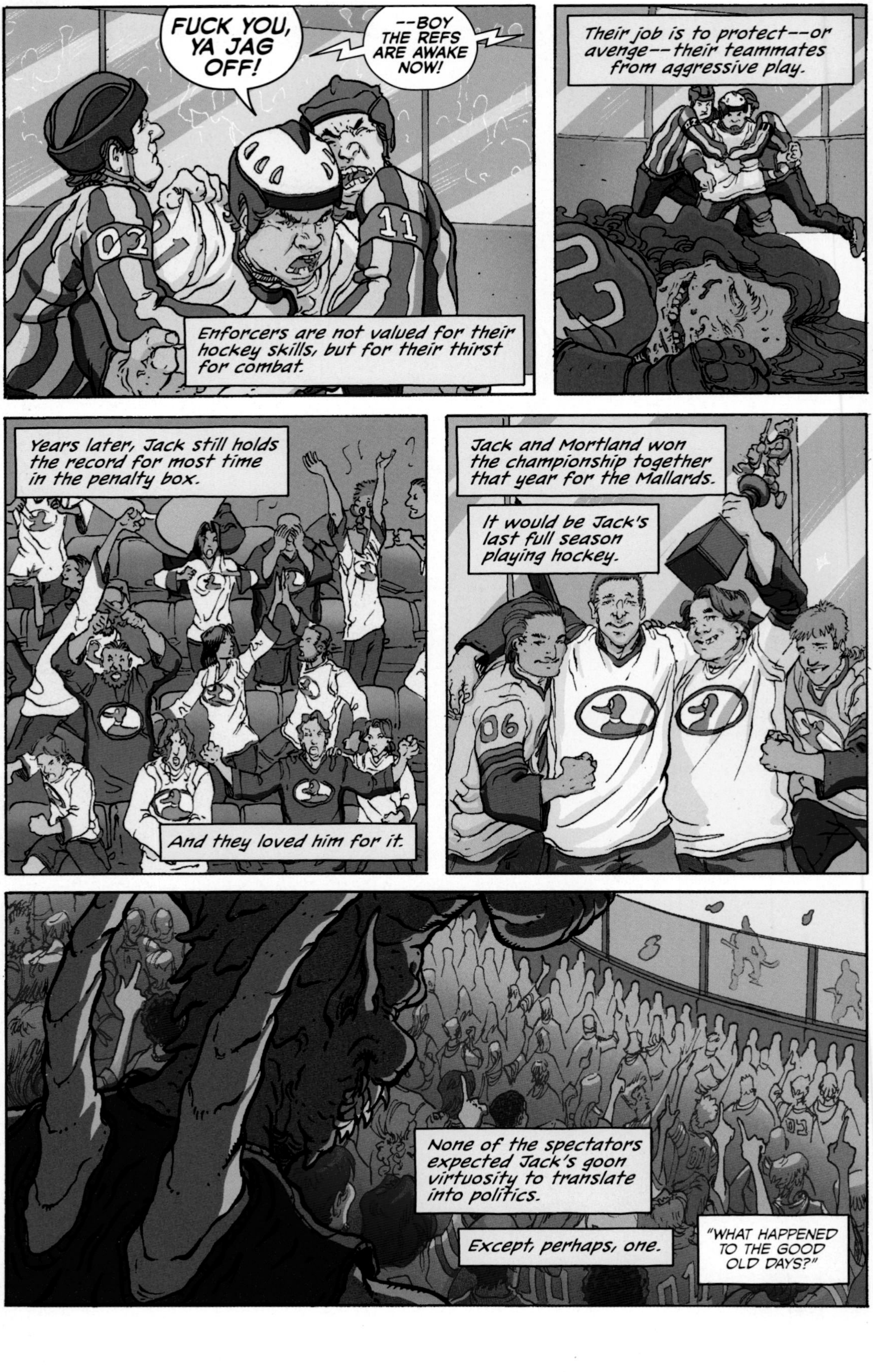
FUCK YOU, YA JAG OFF!
--BOY THE REFS ARE AWAKE NOW!
Enforcers are not valued for their hockey skills, but for their thirst for combat.
Their job is to protect--or avenge--their teammates from aggressive play.
Years later, Jack still holds the record for most time in the penalty box.
And they loved him for it.
Jack and Mortland won the championship together that year for the Mallards.
It would be Jack's last full season playing hockey.
None of the spectators expected Jack's goon virtuosity to translate into politics.
Except, perhaps, one.
"WHAT HAPPENED TO THE GOOD OLD DAYS?"

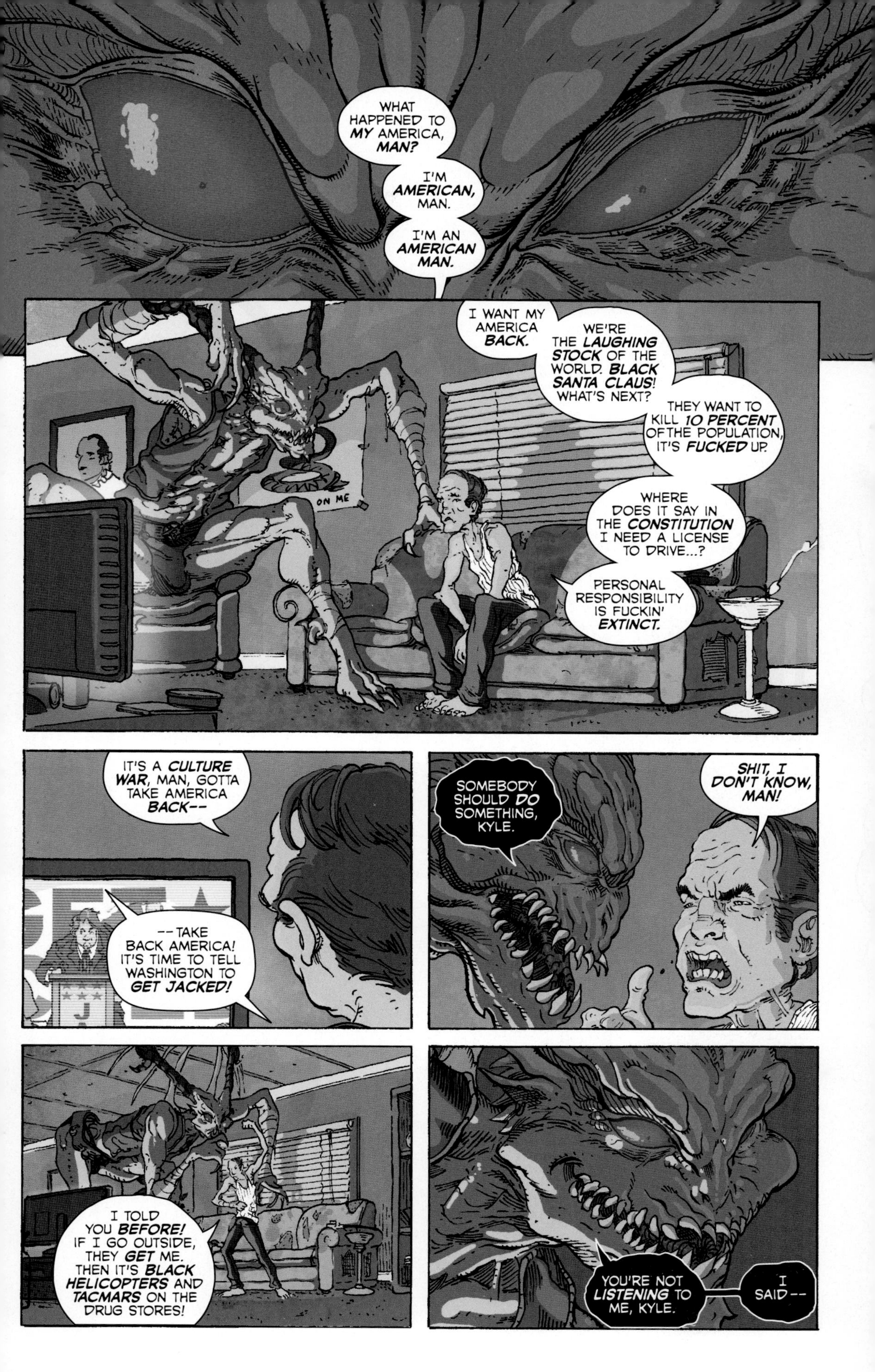

WHAT HAPPENED TO MY AMERICA, MAN?
I'M AMERICAN, MAN.
I'M AN AMERICAN MAN.
I WANT MY AMERICA BACK.
WE'RE THE LAUGHING STOCK OF THE WORLD. BLACK SANTA CLAUS! WHAT'S NEXT?
THEY WANT TO KILL 10 PERCENT OF THE POPULATION, IT'S FUCKED UP.
WHERE DOES IT SAY IN THE CONSTITUTION I NEED A LICENSE TO DRIVE...?
PERSONAL RESPONSIBILITY IS FUCKIN' EXTINCT.
ON ME
IT'S A CULTURE WAR, MAN, GOTTA TAKE AMERICA BACK--
--TAKE BACK AMERICA! IT'S TIME TO TELL WASHINGTON TO GET JACKED!
SOMEBODY SHOULD DO SOMETHING, KYLE.
SHIT, I DON'T KNOW, MAN!
I TOLD YOU BEFORE! IF I GO OUTSIDE, THEY GET ME. THEN IT'S BLACK HELICOPTERS AND TACMARS ON THE DRUG STORES!
YOU'RE NOT LISTENING TO ME, KYLE.
I SAID--

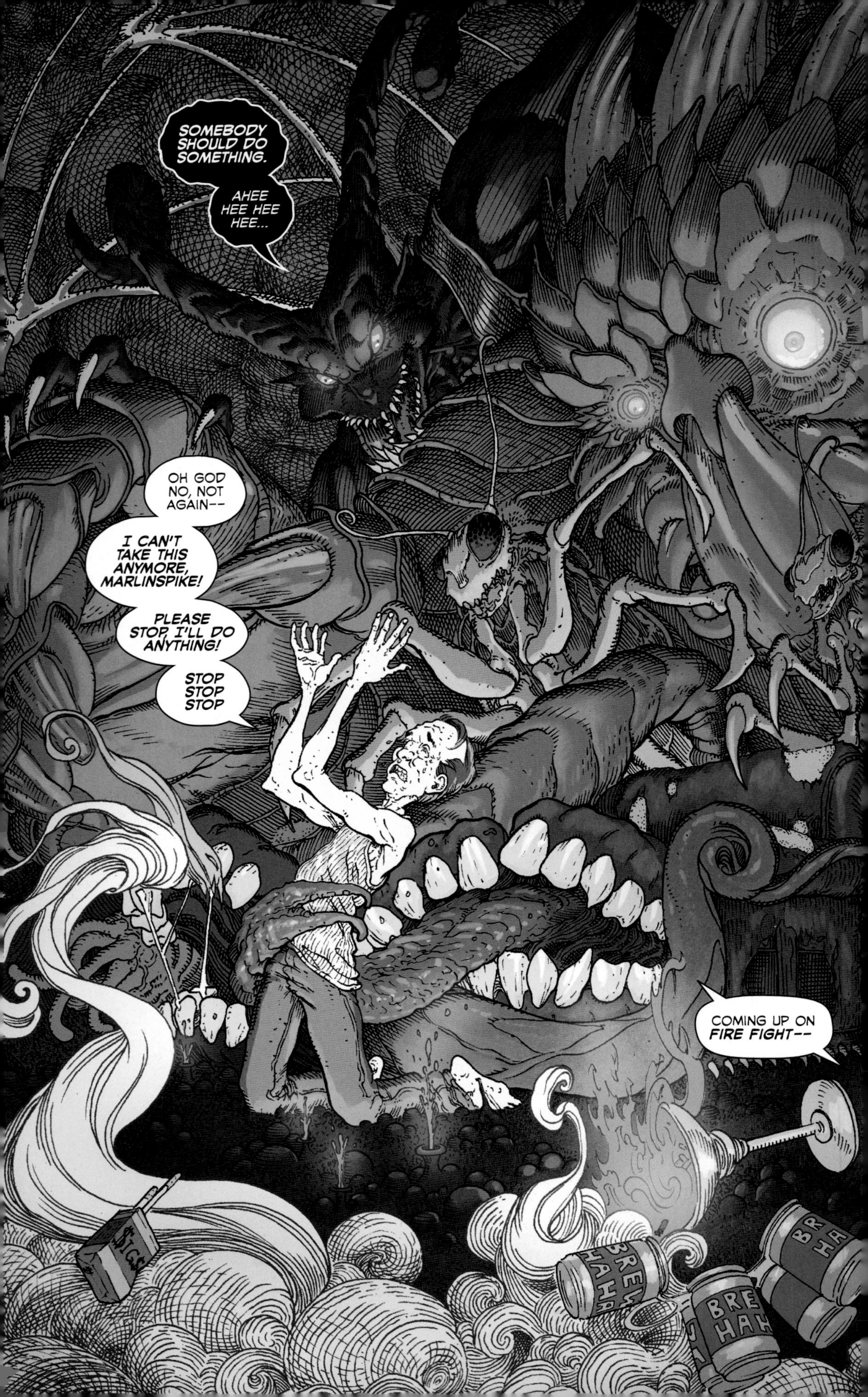
SOMEBODY SHOULD DO SOMETHING.
AHEE HEE HEE HEE...
OH GOD NO, NOT AGAIN--
I CAN'T TAKE THIS ANYMORE, MARLINSPIKE!
PLEASE STOP, I'LL DO ANYTHING!
STOP STOP STOP
COMING UP ON FIRE FIGHT--
BREW HAHA

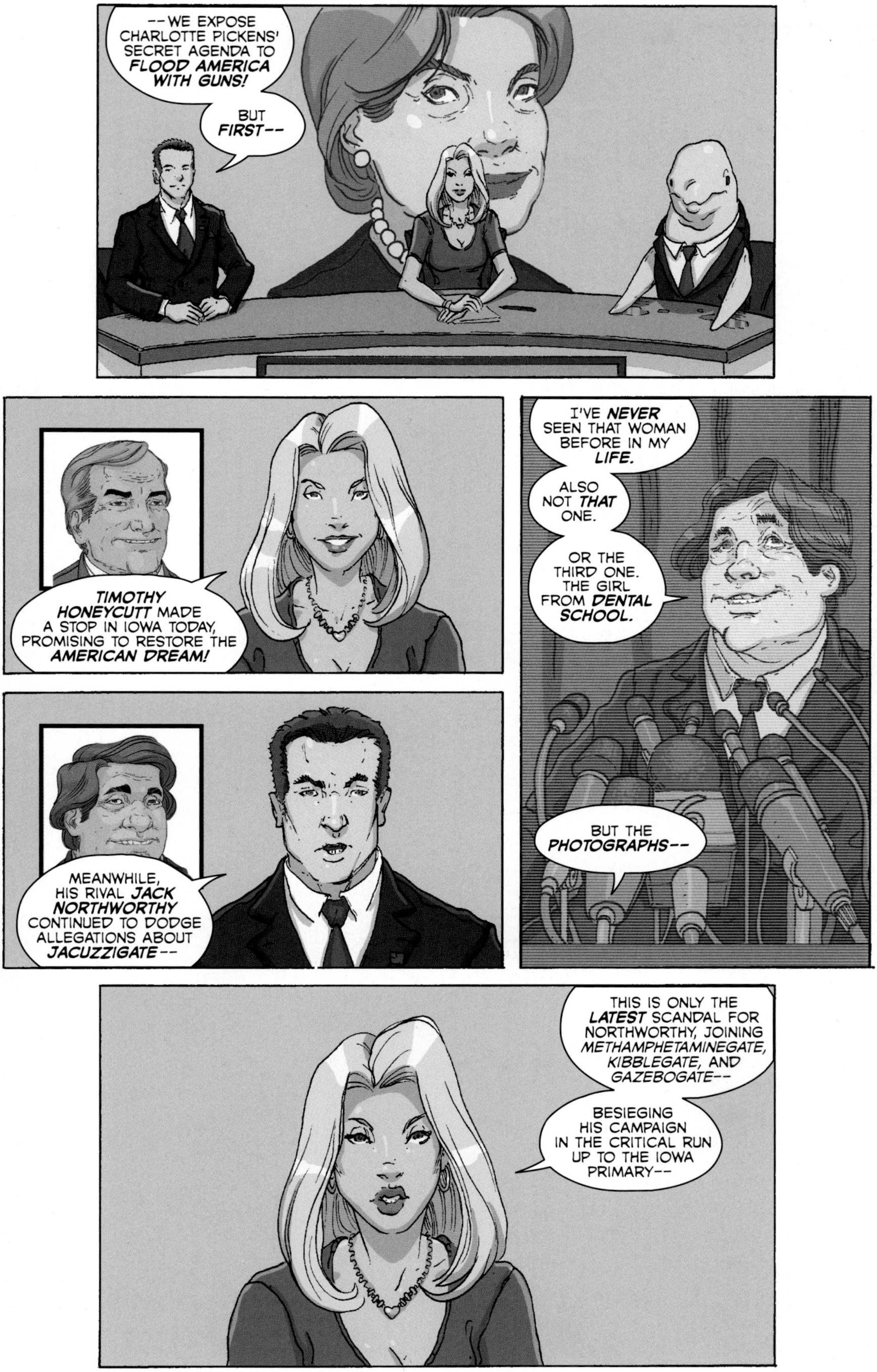
--WE EXPOSE CHARLOTTE PICKENS' SECRET AGENDA TO FLOOD AMERICA WITH GUNS!
BUT FIRST--
TIMOTHY HONEYCUTT MADE A STOP IN IOWA TODAY, PROMISING TO RESTORE THE AMERICAN DREAM!
MEANWHILE, HIS RIVAL JACK NORTHWORTHY CONTINUED TO DODGE ALLEGATIONS ABOUT JACUZZIGATE--
I'VE NEVER SEEN THAT WOMAN BEFORE IN MY LIFE.
ALSO NOT THAT ONE.
OR THE THIRD ONE. THE GIRL FROM DENTAL SCHOOL.
BUT THE PHOTOGRAPHS--
THIS IS ONLY THE LATEST SCANDAL FOR NORTHWORTHY, JOINING METHAMPHETAMINEGATE, KIBBLEGATE, AND GAZEBOGATE--
BESIEGING HIS CAMPAIGN IN THE CRITICAL RUN UP TO THE IOWA PRIMARY--

THE BIG BOARD
ELECTABILITY™©

TIMOTHY **HONEYCUTT** **85%**
FREEDOM PARTY

JACK **NORTHWORTHY** **11%**
FREEDOM PARTY

WHAT IS HURTING HIM IN THE FREEDOM PARTY PRIMARIES IS HIS *ELECTABILITY*™©.

TIMOTHY HONEYCUTT'S *ELECTABILITY*© IS *ROCK SOLID.* NORTHWORTHY IS POPULAR AMONG *FRINGE* AND *OUTSIDER* GROUPS--

BUT UNABLE TO *PERSUADE* THE CORE FREEDOM PARTY BASE THAT HE'S GOT WHAT IT TAKES TO WIN THE ELECTION AGAINST *CHARLOTTE PICKENS.*

AND YOU *NEED ELECTABILITY*™© IN ORDER TO WIN *ELECTIONS.*

UNLESS HE GETS SOME *ELECTABILITY*™©, JACK NORTHWORTHY IS DOOMED TO BE A *NOVELTY* CANDIDATE.

OH, COME ON--!

"ELECTABILITY" IS JUST SOME *BULLCRAP* WE INVENTED IN THE *WRITER'S ROOM.* IT HAS NO *BEARING* ON--

ENOUGH, CRICKET--

--THANKS FOR *NOTHING.*

UP *NEXT:* HOW CHARLOTTE PICKENS IS TRYING TO TAKE AMERICA'S GUNS *AWAY!*

YOU HEAR THAT?

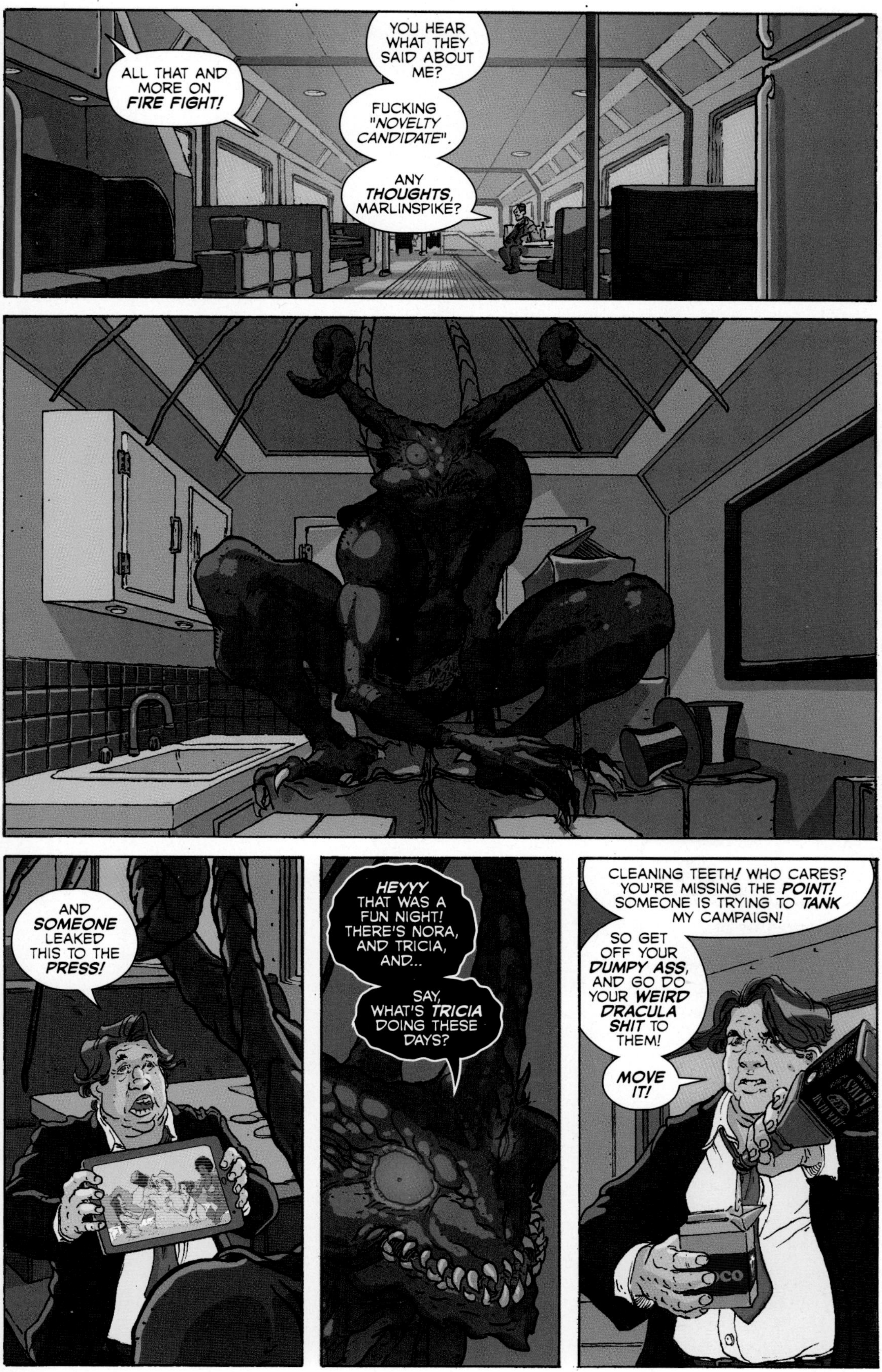
ALL THAT AND MORE ON FIRE FIGHT!
YOU HEAR WHAT THEY SAID ABOUT ME?
FUCKING "NOVELTY CANDIDATE".
ANY THOUGHTS, MARLINSPIKE?
AND SOMEONE LEAKED THIS TO THE PRESS!
HEYYY THAT WAS A FUN NIGHT! THERE'S NORA, AND TRICIA, AND...
SAY, WHAT'S TRICIA DOING THESE DAYS?
CLEANING TEETH! WHO CARES? YOU'RE MISSING THE POINT! SOMEONE IS TRYING TO TANK MY CAMPAIGN!
SO GET OFF YOUR DUMPY ASS, AND GO DO YOUR WEIRD DRACULA SHIT TO THEM!
MOVE IT!

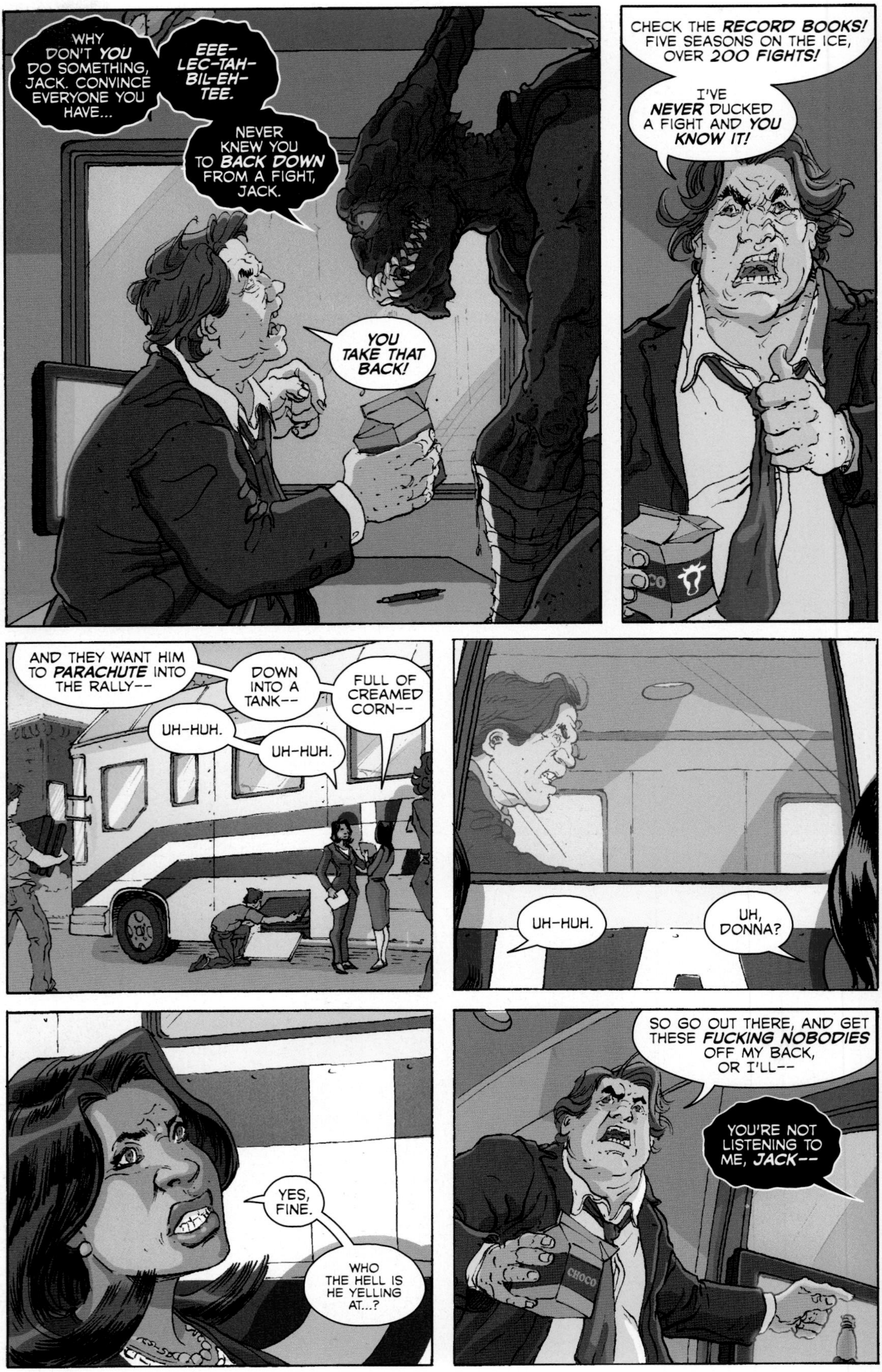

WHY DON'T YOU DO SOMETHING, JACK. CONVINCE EVERYONE YOU HAVE...
EEE-LEC-TAH-BIL-EH-TEE.
NEVER KNEW YOU TO BACK DOWN FROM A FIGHT, JACK.
YOU TAKE THAT BACK!
CHECK THE RECORD BOOKS! FIVE SEASONS ON THE ICE, OVER 200 FIGHTS!
I'VE NEVER DUCKED A FIGHT AND YOU KNOW IT!
CHOCO
AND THEY WANT HIM TO PARACHUTE INTO THE RALLY--
UH-HUH.
DOWN INTO A TANK--
UH-HUH.
FULL OF CREAMED CORN--
UH-HUH.
UH, DONNA?
YES, FINE.
WHO THE HELL IS HE YELLING AT...?
SO GO OUT THERE, AND GET THESE FUCKING NOBODIES OFF MY BACK, OR I'LL--
YOU'RE NOT LISTENING TO ME, JACK--
CHOCO

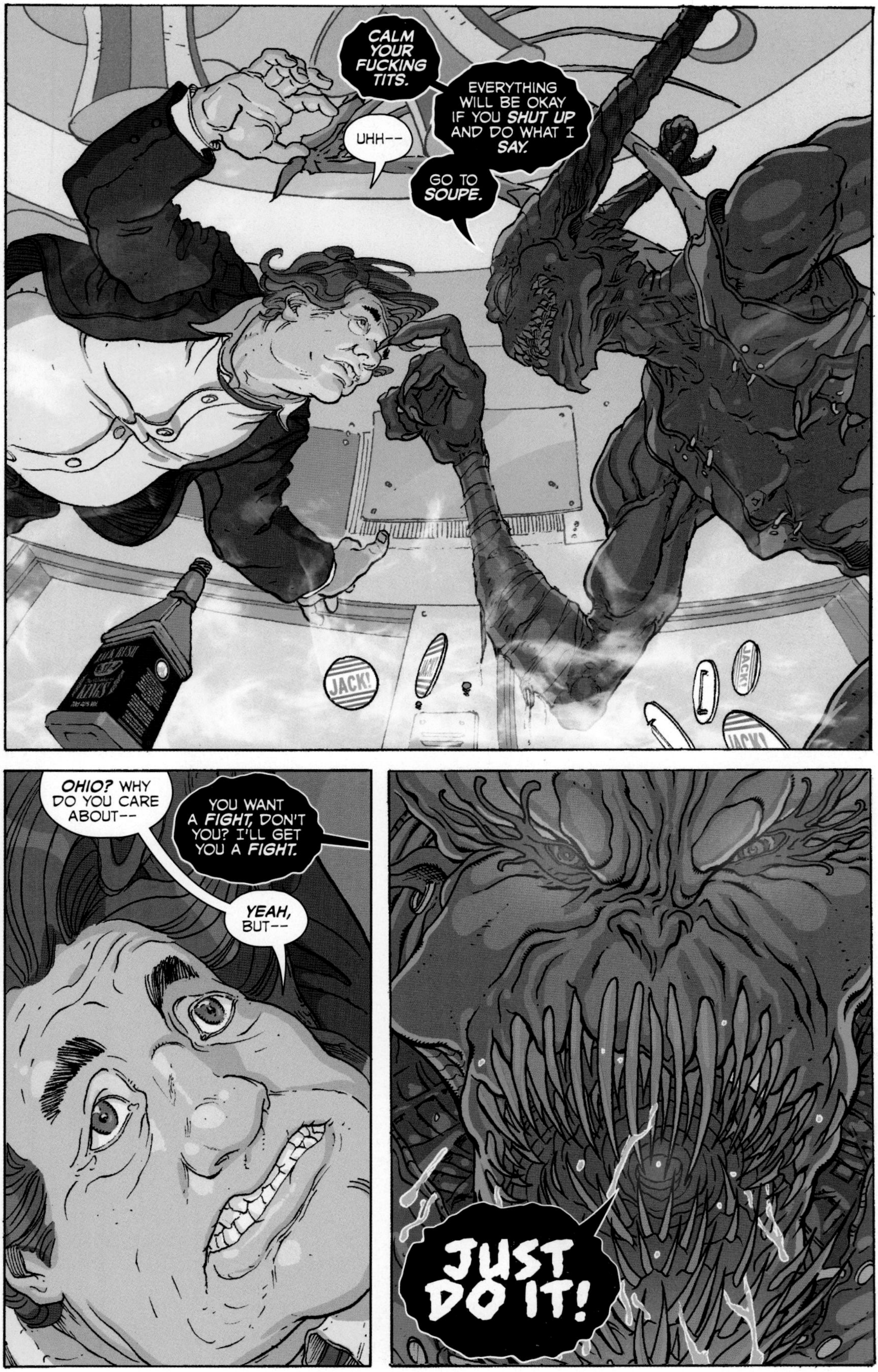
CALM YOUR FUCKING TITS.
UHH--
EVERYTHING WILL BE OKAY IF YOU SHUT UP AND DO WHAT I SAY.
GO TO SOUPE.
JACK!
OHIO? WHY DO YOU CARE ABOUT--
YOU WANT A FIGHT, DON'T YOU? I'LL GET YOU A FIGHT.
YEAH, BUT--
JUST DO IT!

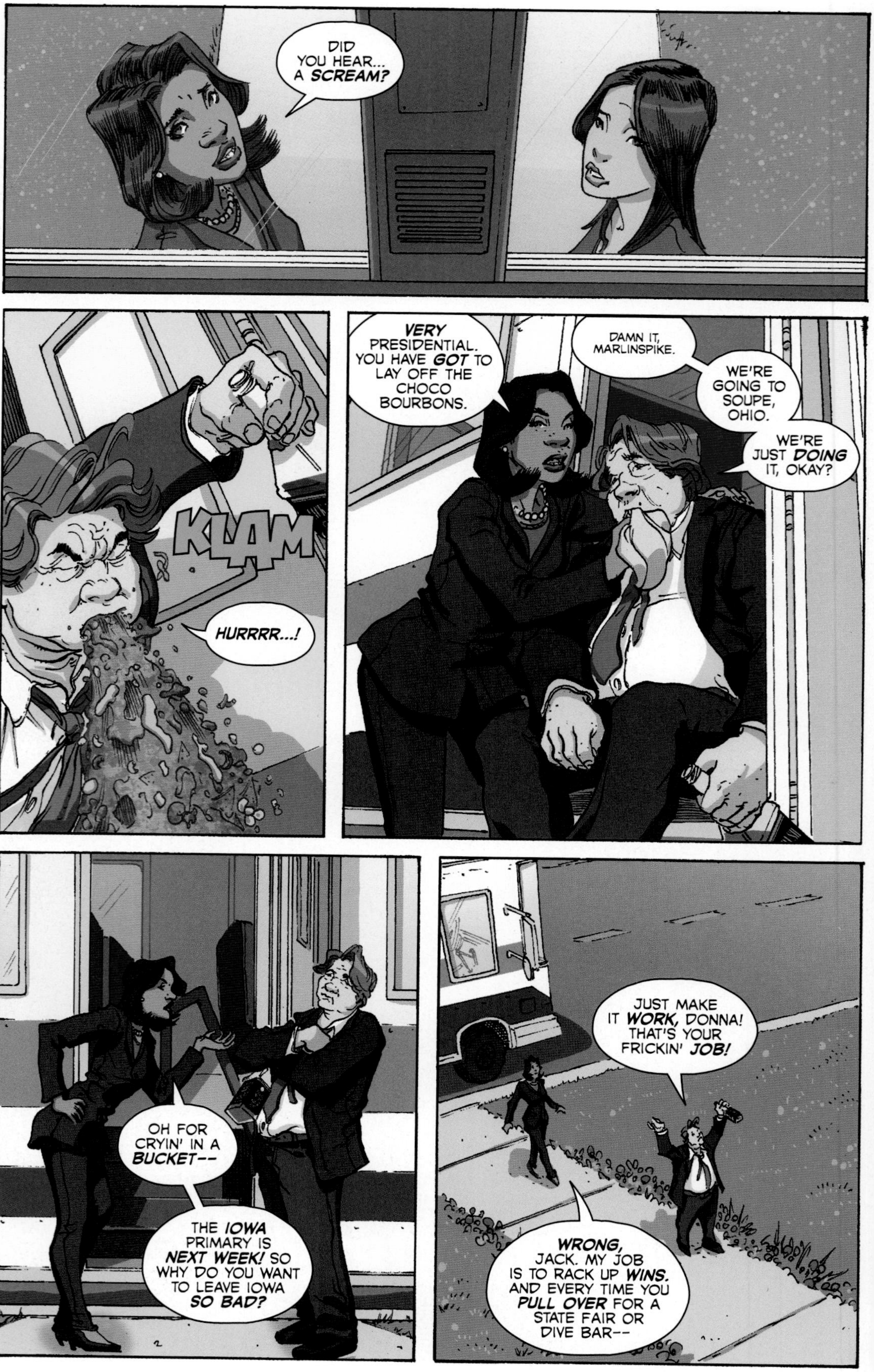

DID YOU HEAR... A SCREAM?
KLAM
HURRRR...!
VERY PRESIDENTIAL. YOU HAVE GOT TO LAY OFF THE CHOCO BOURBONS.
DAMN IT, MARLINSPIKE.
WE'RE GOING TO SOUPE, OHIO.
WE'RE JUST DOING IT, OKAY?
OH FOR CRYIN' IN A BUCKET--
THE IOWA PRIMARY IS NEXT WEEK! SO WHY DO YOU WANT TO LEAVE IOWA SO BAD?
JUST MAKE IT WORK, DONNA! THAT'S YOUR FRICKIN' JOB!
WRONG, JACK. MY JOB IS TO RACK UP WINS. AND EVERY TIME YOU PULL OVER FOR A STATE FAIR OR DIVE BAR--

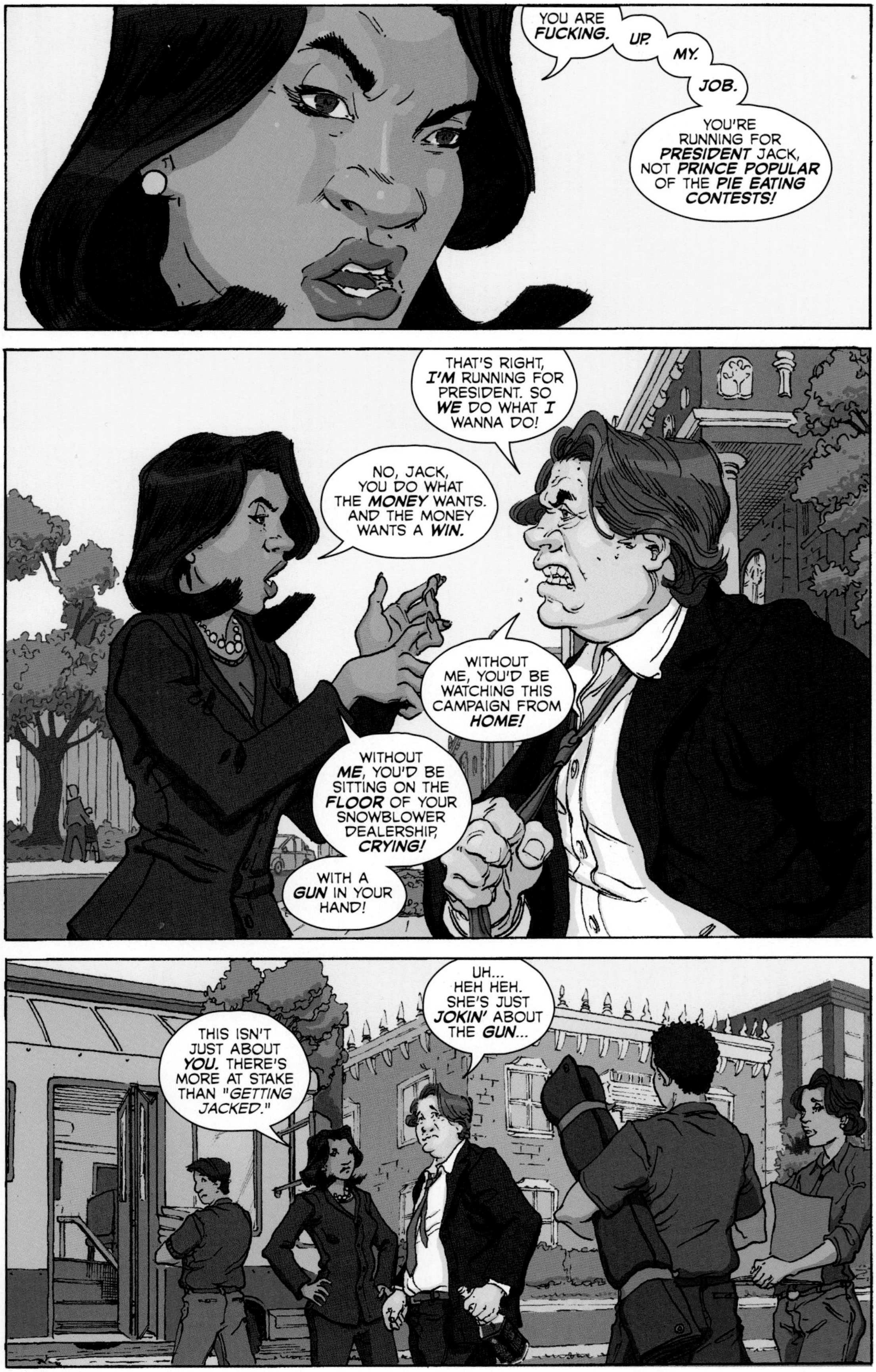
YOU ARE FUCKING.
UP.
MY.
JOB.
YOU'RE RUNNING FOR PRESIDENT JACK, NOT PRINCE POPULAR OF THE PIE EATING CONTESTS!
THAT'S RIGHT, I'M RUNNING FOR PRESIDENT. SO WE DO WHAT I WANNA DO!
NO, JACK, YOU DO WHAT THE MONEY WANTS. AND THE MONEY WANTS A WIN.
WITHOUT ME, YOU'D BE WATCHING THIS CAMPAIGN FROM HOME!
WITHOUT ME, YOU'D BE SITTING ON THE FLOOR OF YOUR SNOWBLOWER DEALERSHIP, CRYING!
WITH A GUN IN YOUR HAND!
UH... HEH HEH. SHE'S JUST JOKIN' ABOUT THE GUN...
THIS ISN'T JUST ABOUT YOU. THERE'S MORE AT STAKE THAN "GETTING JACKED."

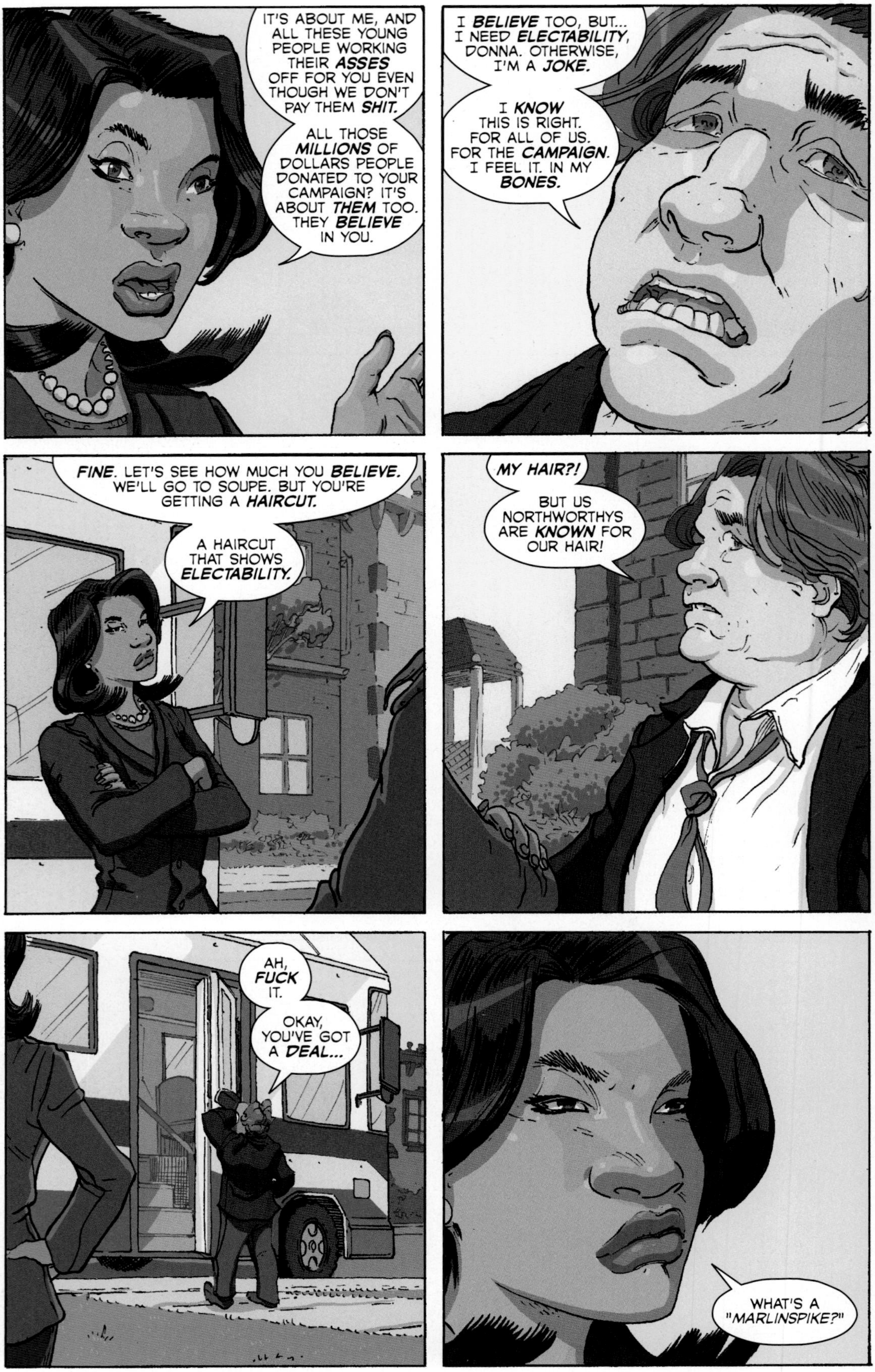
IT'S ABOUT ME, AND ALL THESE YOUNG PEOPLE WORKING THEIR ASSES OFF FOR YOU EVEN THOUGH WE DON'T PAY THEM SHIT.
ALL THOSE MILLIONS OF DOLLARS PEOPLE DONATED TO YOUR CAMPAIGN? IT'S ABOUT THEM TOO. THEY BELIEVE IN YOU.
I BELIEVE TOO, BUT... I NEED ELECTABILITY, DONNA. OTHERWISE, I'M A JOKE.
I KNOW THIS IS RIGHT. FOR ALL OF US. FOR THE CAMPAIGN. I FEEL IT. IN MY BONES.
FINE. LET'S SEE HOW MUCH YOU BELIEVE. WE'LL GO TO SOUPE. BUT YOU'RE GETTING A HAIRCUT.
A HAIRCUT THAT SHOWS ELECTABILITY.
MY HAIR?!
BUT US NORTHWORTHYS ARE KNOWN FOR OUR HAIR!
AH, FUCK IT.
OKAY, YOU'VE GOT A DEAL...
WHAT'S A "MARLINSPIKE?"

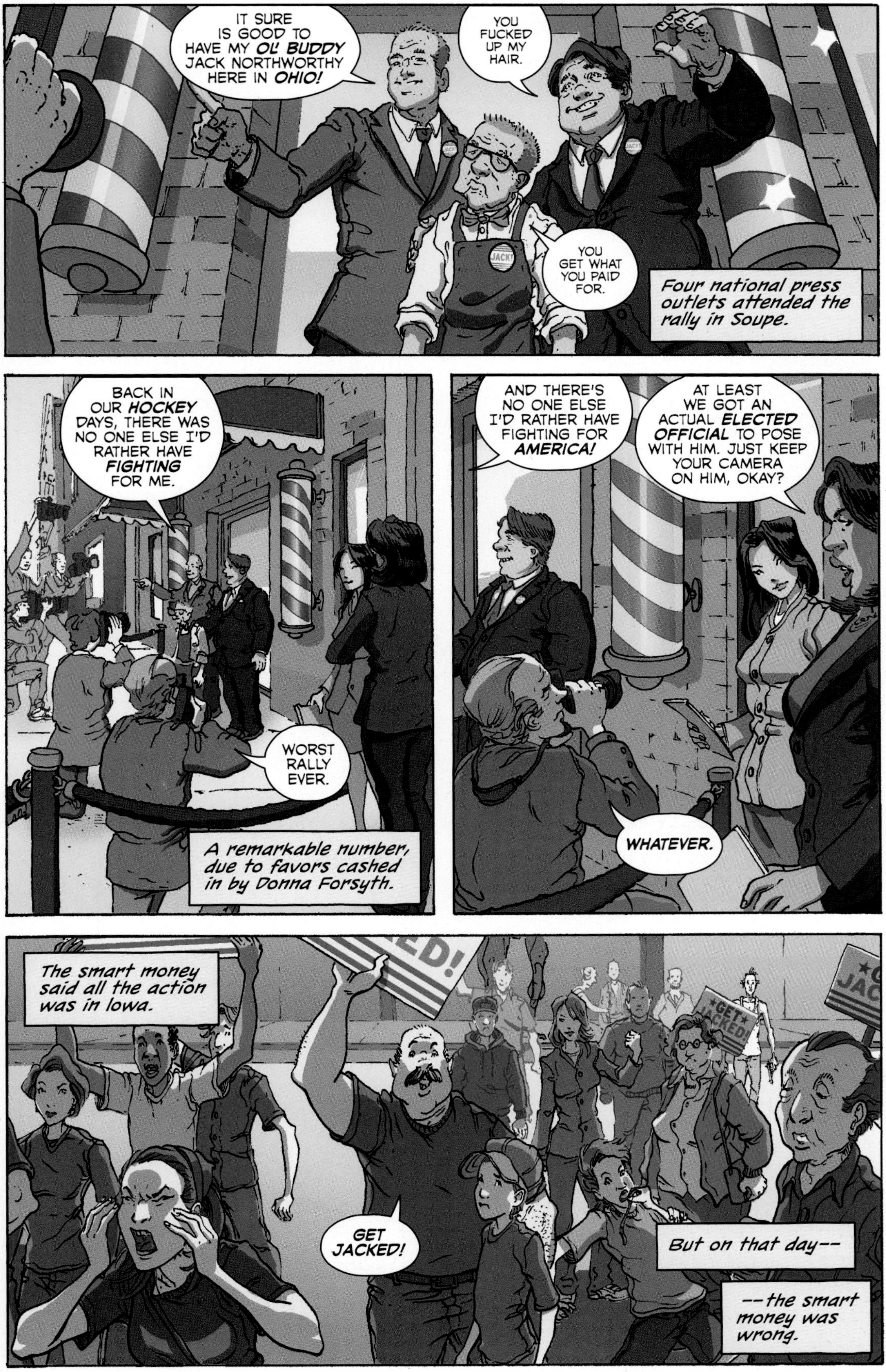
IT SURE IS GOOD TO HAVE MY OL' BUDDY JACK NORTHWORTHY HERE IN OHIO!
YOU FUCKED UP MY HAIR.
YOU GET WHAT YOU PAID FOR.
Four national press outlets attended the rally in Soupe.
BACK IN OUR HOCKEY DAYS, THERE WAS NO ONE ELSE I'D RATHER HAVE FIGHTING FOR ME.
WORST RALLY EVER.
A remarkable number, due to favors cashed in by Donna Forsyth.
AND THERE'S NO ONE ELSE I'D RATHER HAVE FIGHTING FOR AMERICA!
AT LEAST WE GOT AN ACTUAL ELECTED OFFICIAL TO POSE WITH HIM. JUST KEEP YOUR CAMERA ON HIM, OKAY?
WHATEVER.
The smart money said all the action was in Iowa.
GET JACKED!
But on that day--
--the smart money was wrong.

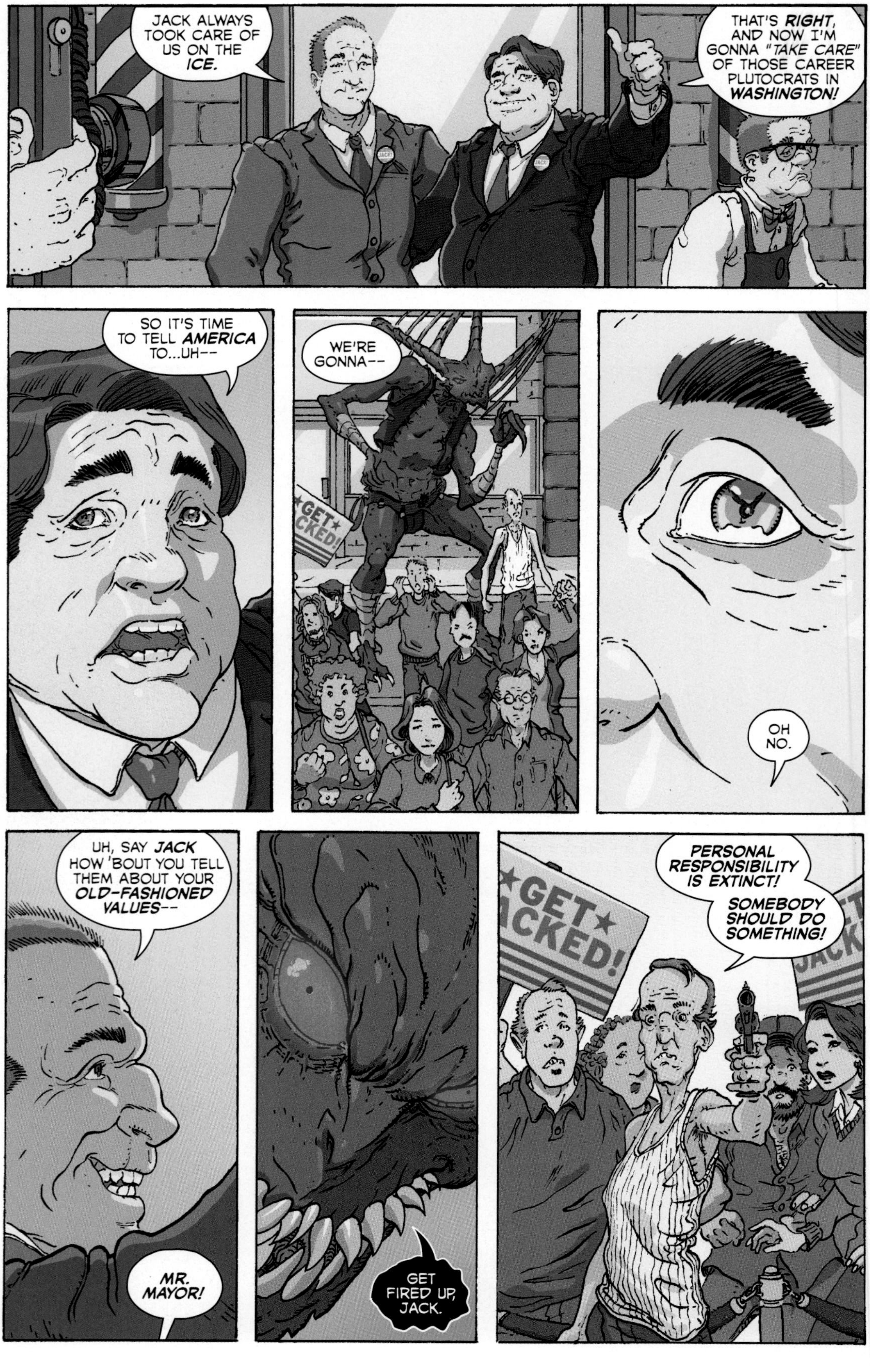
JACK ALWAYS TOOK CARE OF US ON THE ICE.
THAT'S RIGHT, AND NOW I'M GONNA "TAKE CARE" OF THOSE CAREER PLUTOCRATS IN WASHINGTON!
JACK!
SO IT'S TIME TO TELL AMERICA TO...UH--
WE'RE GONNA--
GET JACKED!
OH NO.
UH, SAY JACK HOW 'BOUT YOU TELL THEM ABOUT YOUR OLD-FASHIONED VALUES--
MR. MAYOR!
GET FIRED UP, JACK.
PERSONAL RESPONSIBILITY IS EXTINCT!
SOMEBODY SHOULD DO SOMETHING!
GET JACKED!

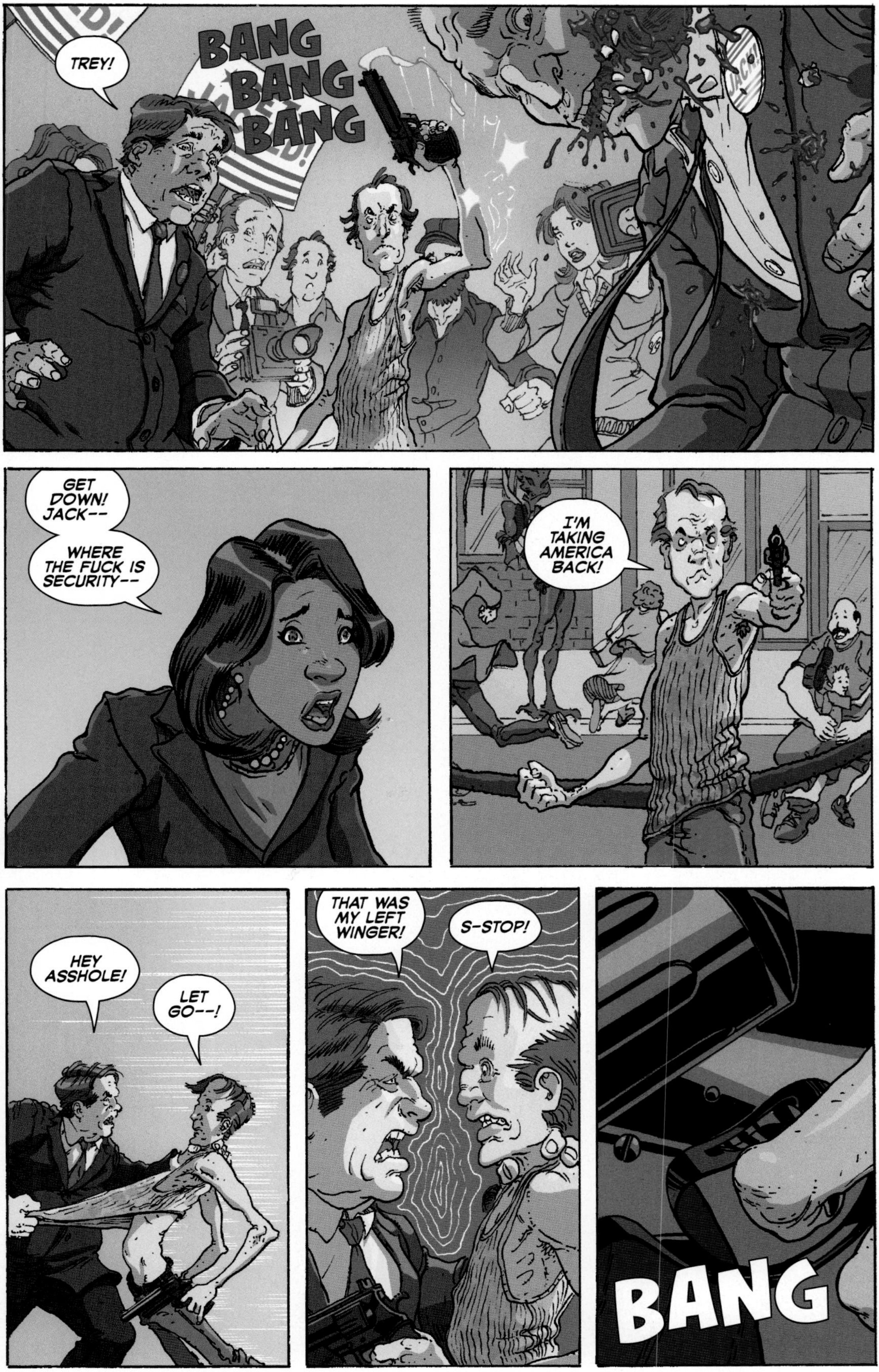
TREY!
BANG BANG BANG
GET DOWN! JACK--
WHERE THE FUCK IS SECURITY--
I'M TAKING AMERICA BACK!
HEY ASSHOLE!
LET GO--!
THAT WAS MY LEFT WINGER!
S-STOP!
BANG

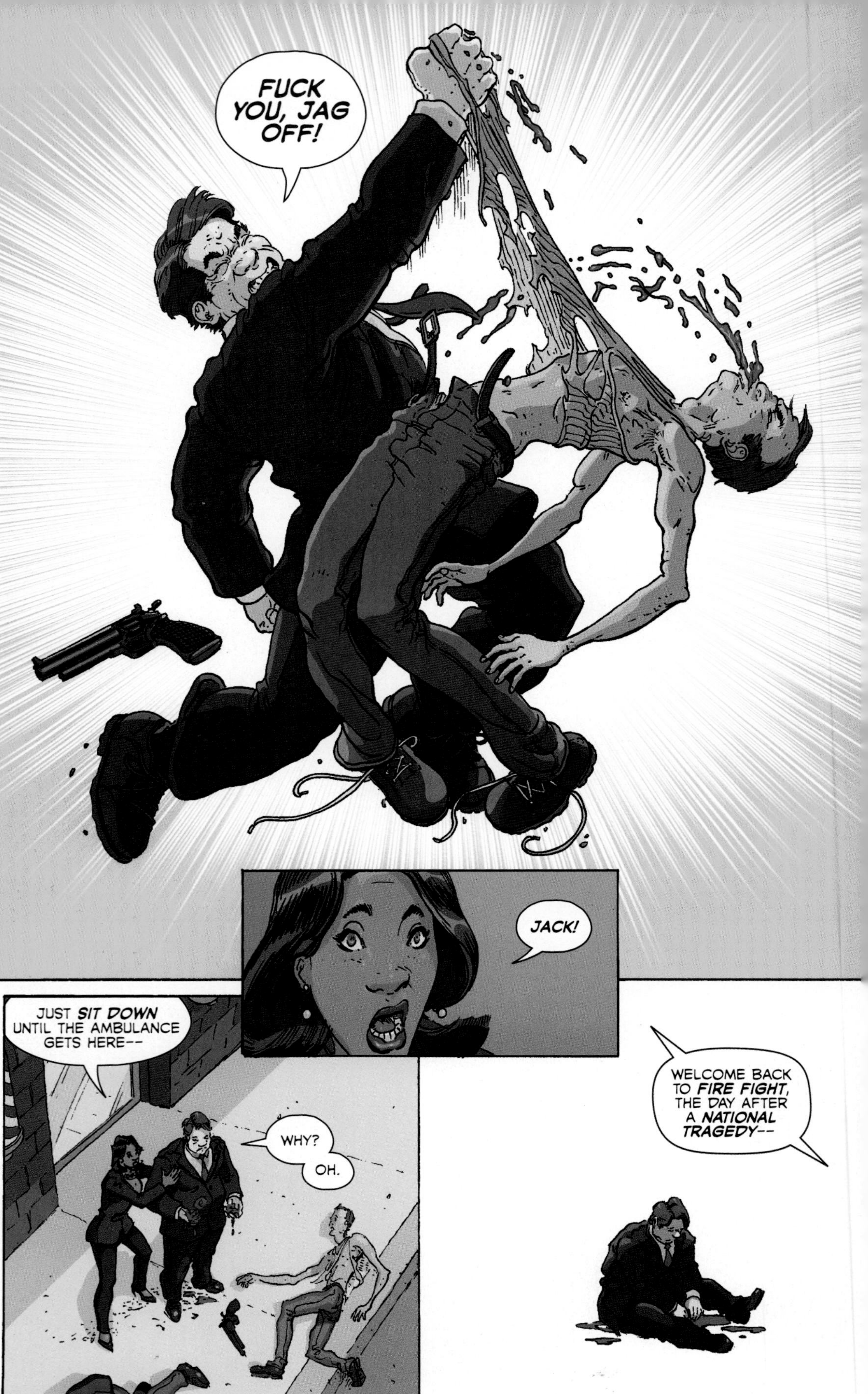
FUCK YOU, JAG OFF!
JACK!
JUST SIT DOWN UNTIL THE AMBULANCE GETS HERE--
WHY?
OH.
WELCOME BACK TO FIRE FIGHT, THE DAY AFTER A NATIONAL TRAGEDY--

America was transfixed by the assassination in Soupe.

Kyle Gratton died in police custody, under questionable circumstances.

But nobody questioned them.

Mayor Mortland's funeral services were broadcast live on the news networks.

And the attack transformed Jack's campaign overnight.

DID YOU SEE HIM *PUNCH* THAT DUDE WITH THE *GUN?!*

THAT GUY IS A *HERO!*

GET JACKED!

NORTHWORTHY'S ELECTABILITY™ © HAS SHOT THROUGH THE ROOF!

Jack took the Iowa primary out of Honeycutt's clutches just in time for the Freedom Party National Convention.

The shooting was a tragedy.

THE BIG ELECTABILITY™ ©

TIMOTHY **HONEYCUTT**
FREEDOM PARTY
46%

JACK N**ORTHWORTHY**
PARTY
45%

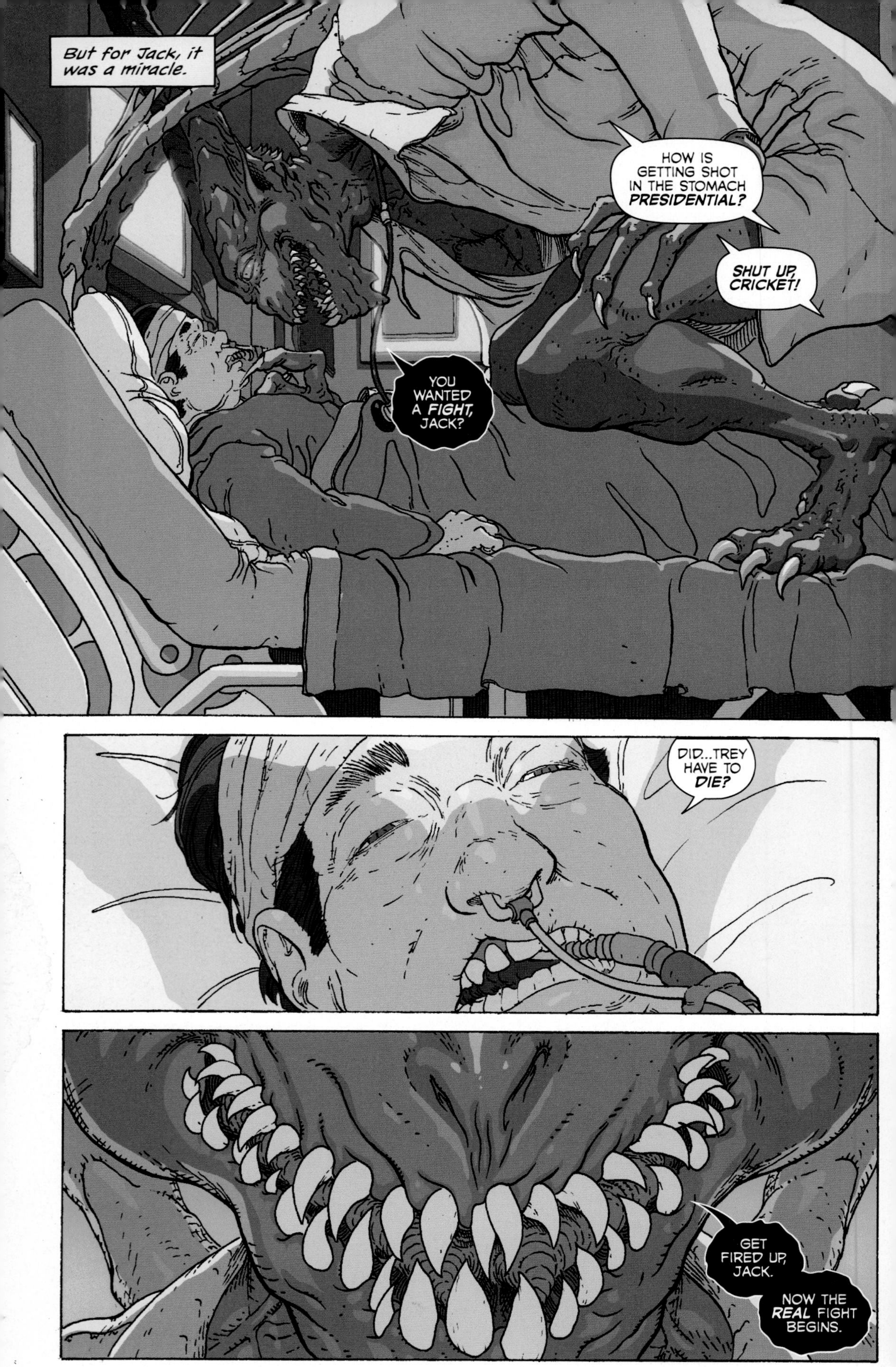
But for Jack, it was a miracle.
HOW IS GETTING SHOT IN THE STOMACH PRESIDENTIAL?
SHUT UP, CRICKET!
YOU WANTED A FIGHT, JACK?
DID...TREY HAVE TO DIE?
GET FIRED UP, JACK.
NOW THE REAL FIGHT BEGINS.

CHAPTER 3

THE CON

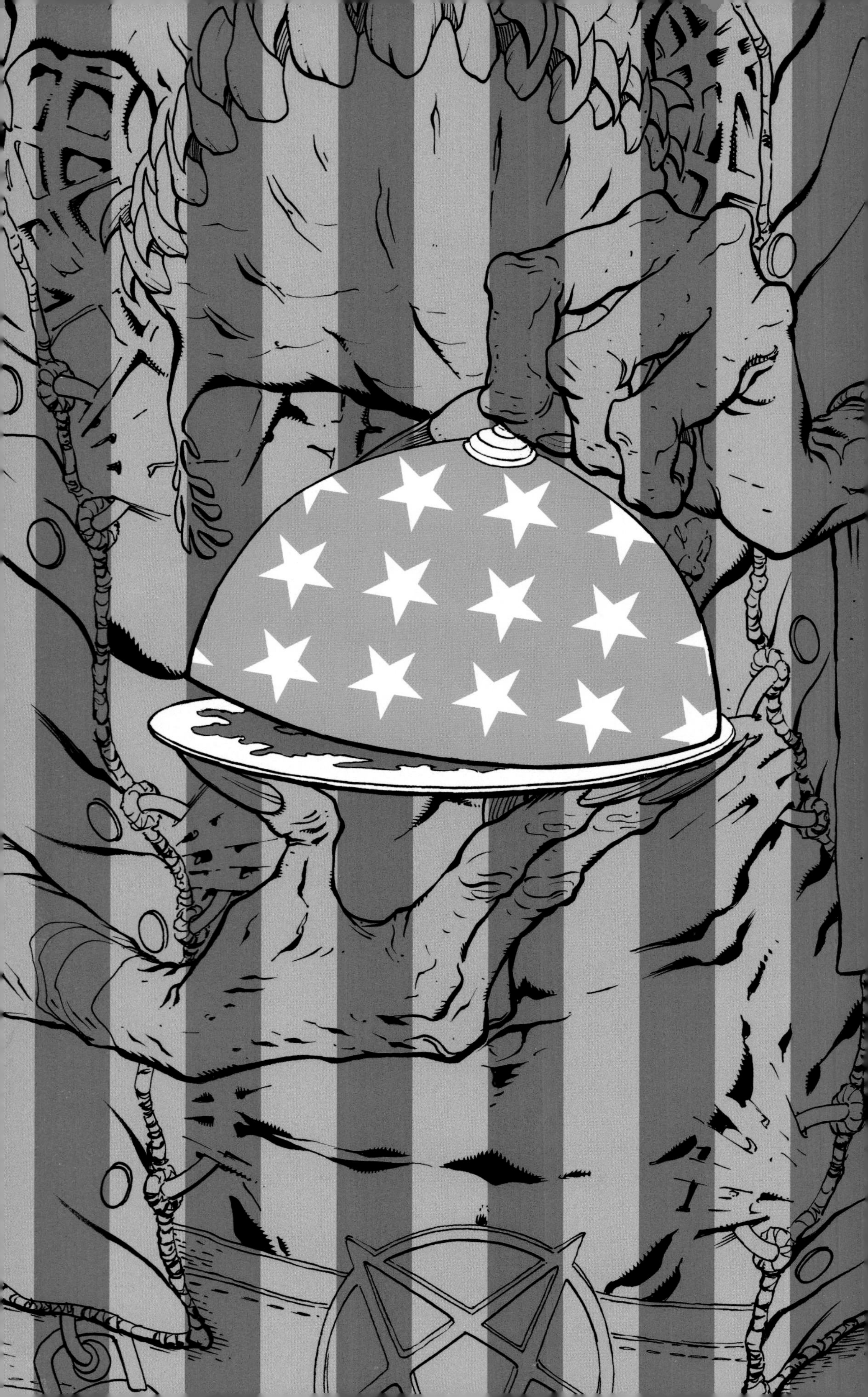

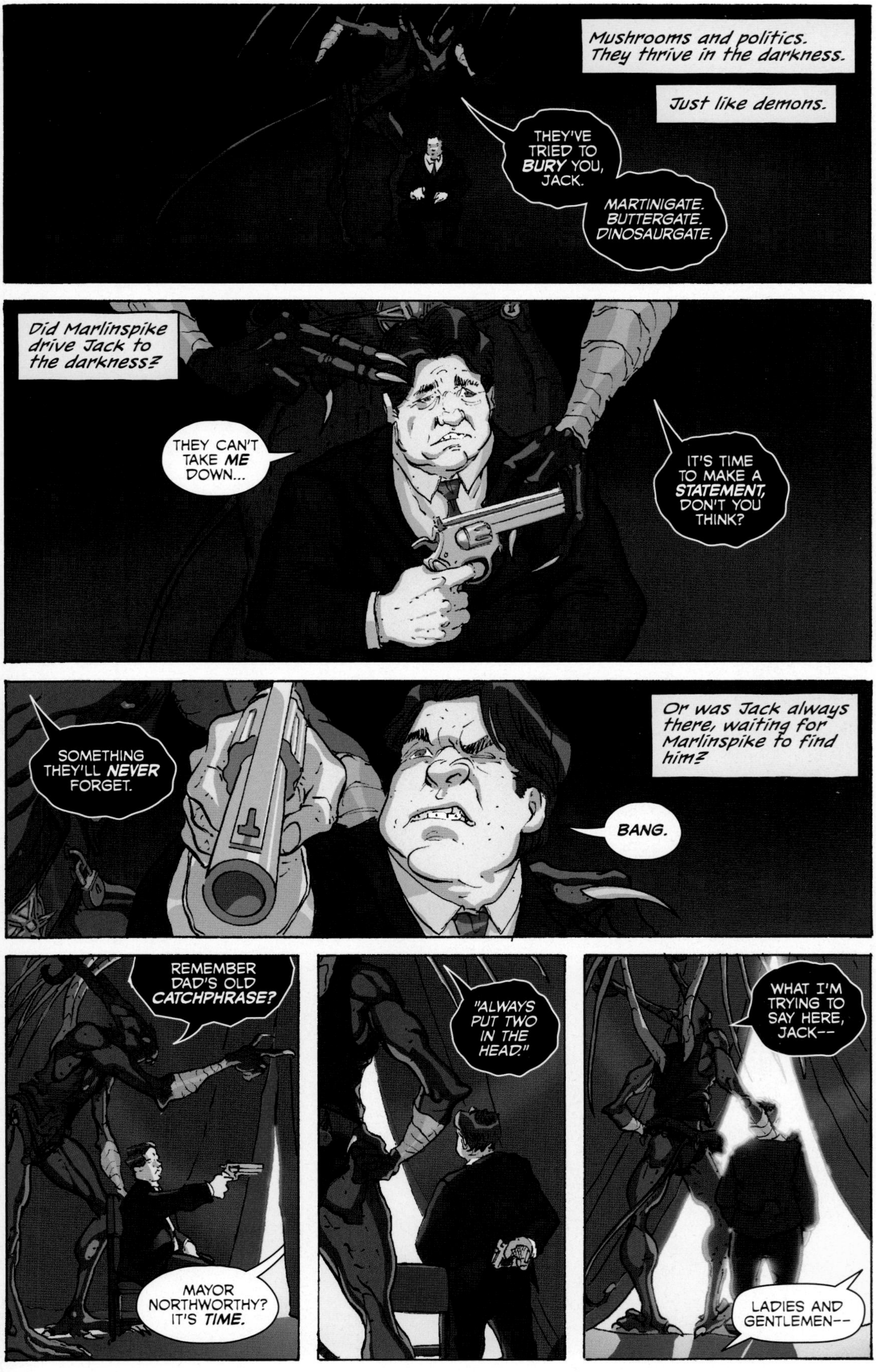
Mushrooms and politics. They thrive in the darkness.
Just like demons.
THEY'VE TRIED TO BURY YOU, JACK.
MARTINIGATE. BUTTERGATE. DINOSAURGATE.
Did Marlinspike drive Jack to the darkness?
THEY CAN'T TAKE ME DOWN...
IT'S TIME TO MAKE A STATEMENT, DON'T YOU THINK?
SOMETHING THEY'LL NEVER FORGET.
Or was Jack always there, waiting for Marlinspike to find him?
BANG.
REMEMBER DAD'S OLD CATCHPHRASE?
MAYOR NORTHWORTHY? IT'S TIME.
"ALWAYS PUT TWO IN THE HEAD."
WHAT I'M TRYING TO SAY HERE, JACK--
LADIES AND GENTLEMEN--

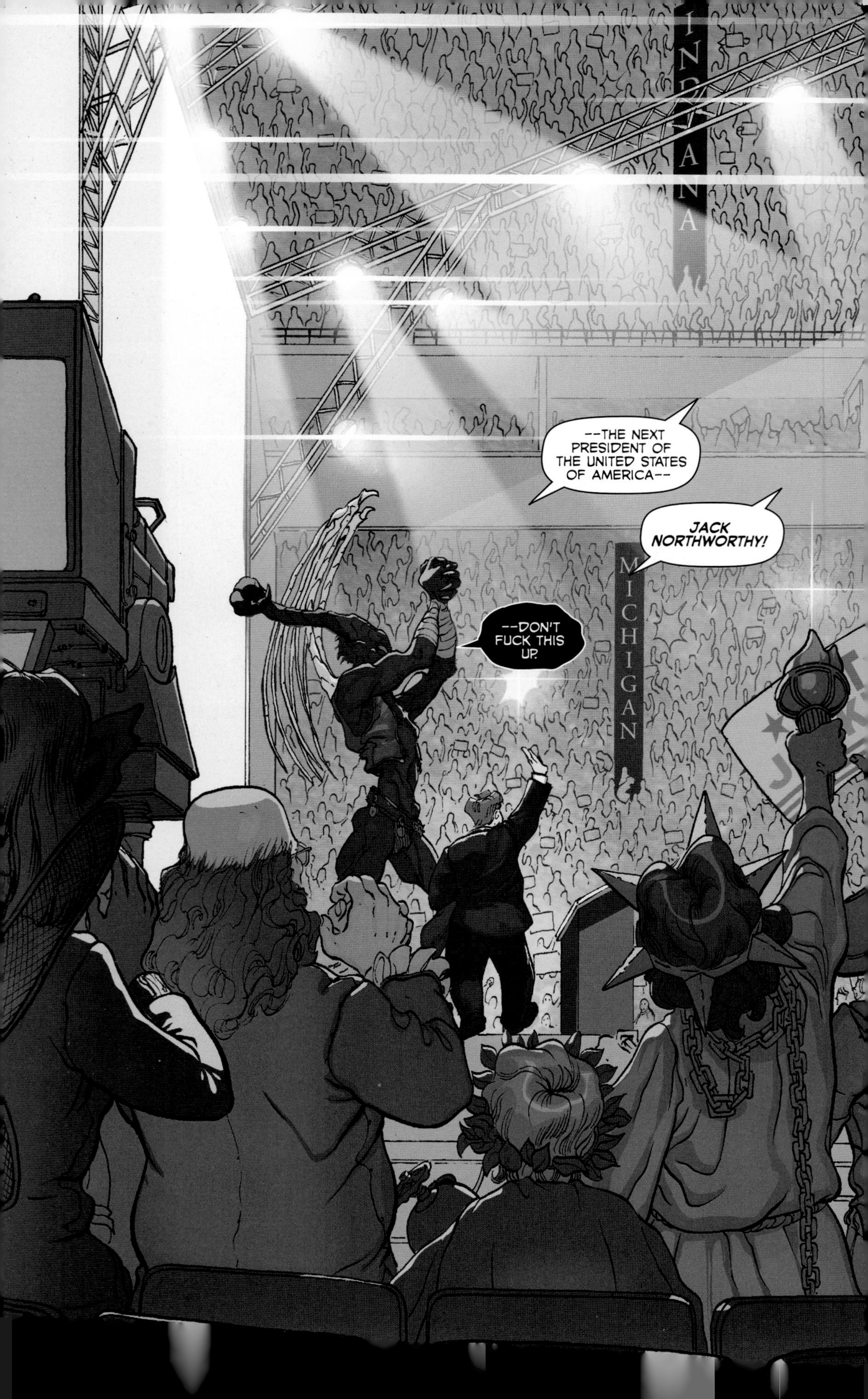
INDIANA
--THE NEXT PRESIDENT OF THE UNITED STATES OF AMERICA--
JACK NORTHWORTHY!
MICHIGAN
--DON'T FUCK THIS UP.

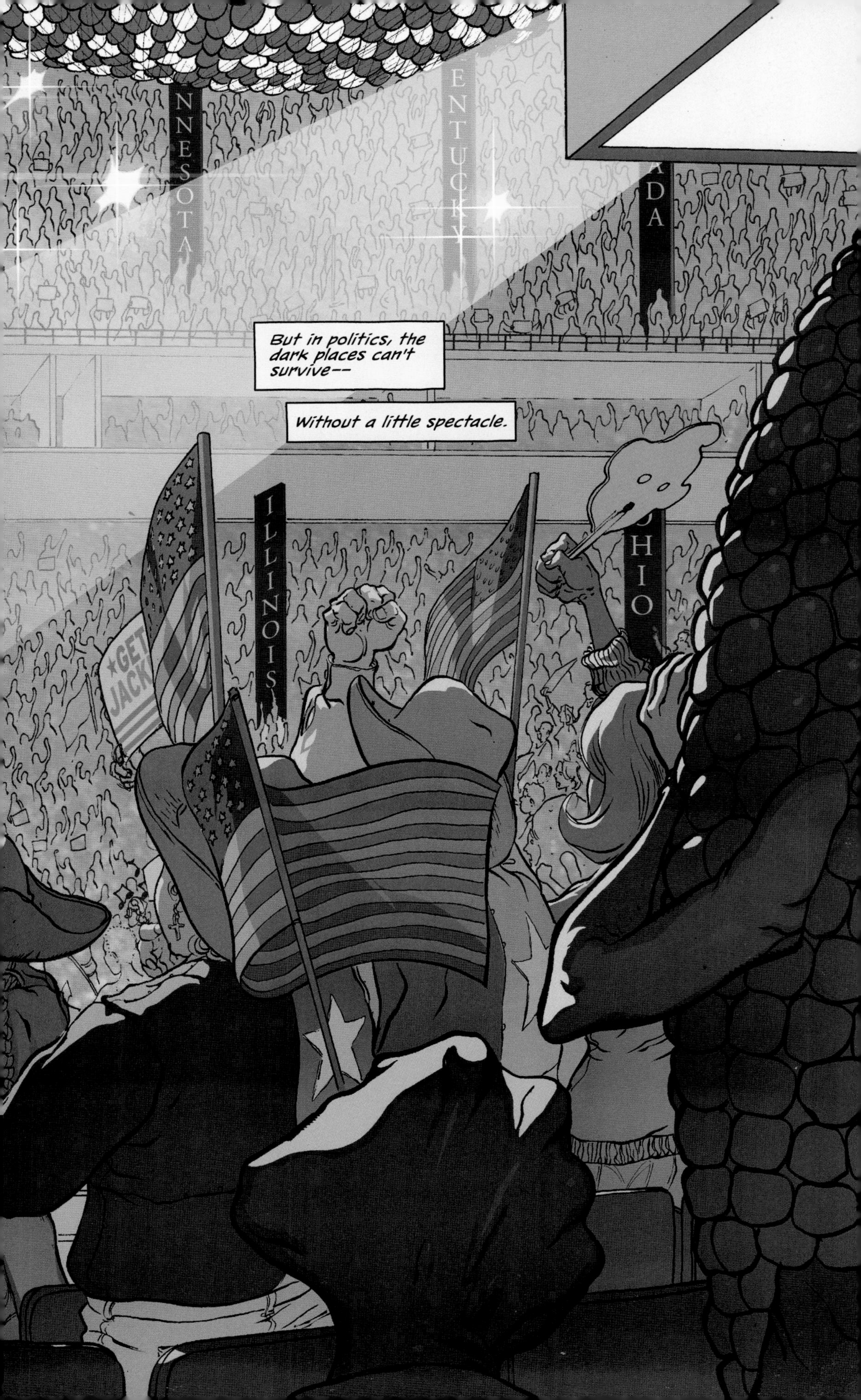
But in politics, the dark places can't survive--
Without a little spectacle.
ILLINOIS
OHIO

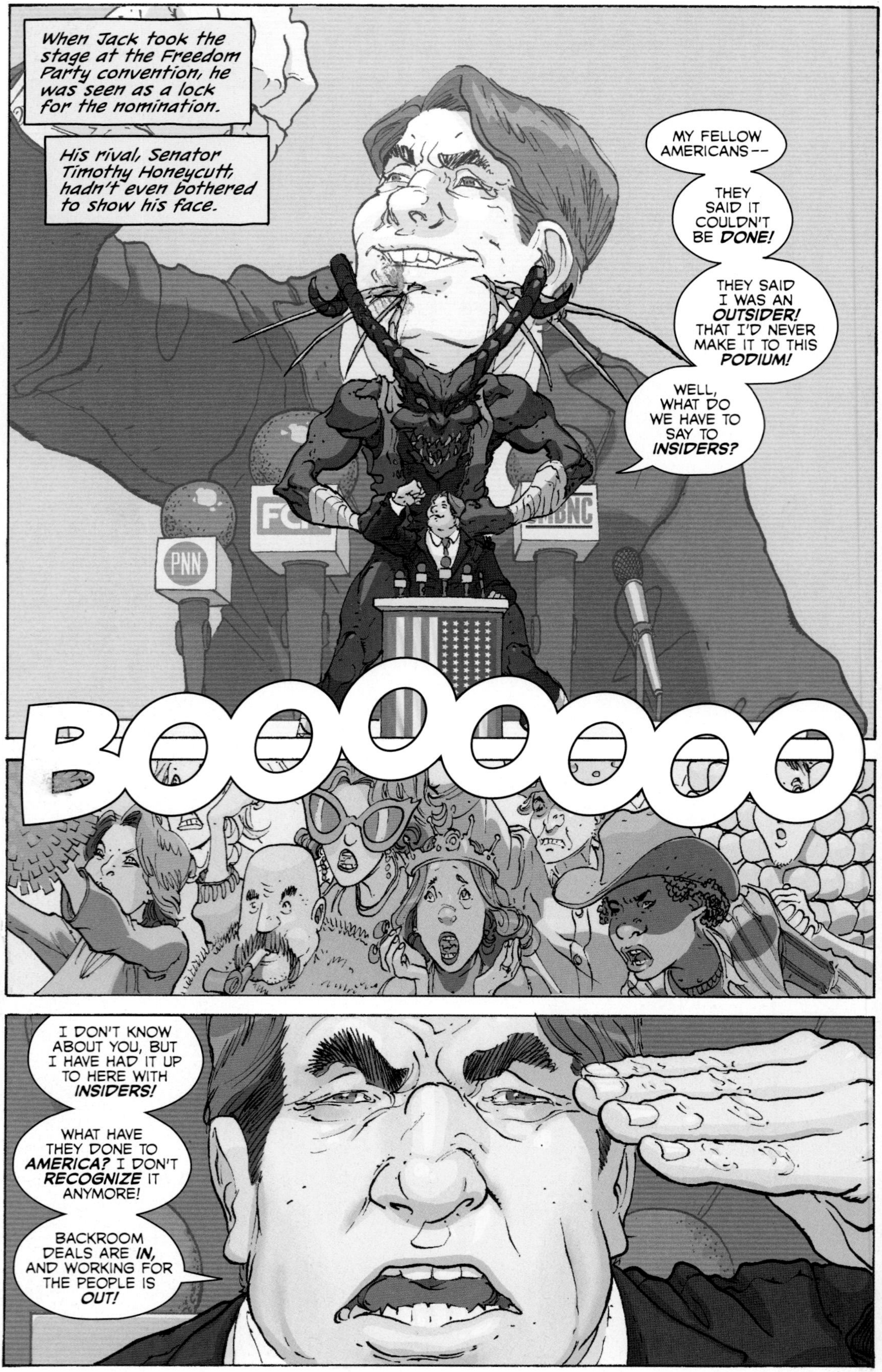
When Jack took the stage at the Freedom Party convention, he was seen as a lock for the nomination.
His rival, Senator Timothy Honeycutt, hadn't even bothered to show his face.
MY FELLOW AMERICANS--
THEY SAID IT COULDN'T BE DONE!
THEY SAID I WAS AN OUTSIDER! THAT I'D NEVER MAKE IT TO THIS PODIUM!
WELL, WHAT DO WE HAVE TO SAY TO INSIDERS?
PNN
FCN
MSNBC
BOOOOOOO
I DON'T KNOW ABOUT YOU, BUT I HAVE HAD IT UP TO HERE WITH INSIDERS!
WHAT HAVE THEY DONE TO AMERICA? I DON'T RECOGNIZE IT ANYMORE!
BACKROOM DEALS ARE IN, AND WORKING FOR THE PEOPLE IS OUT!

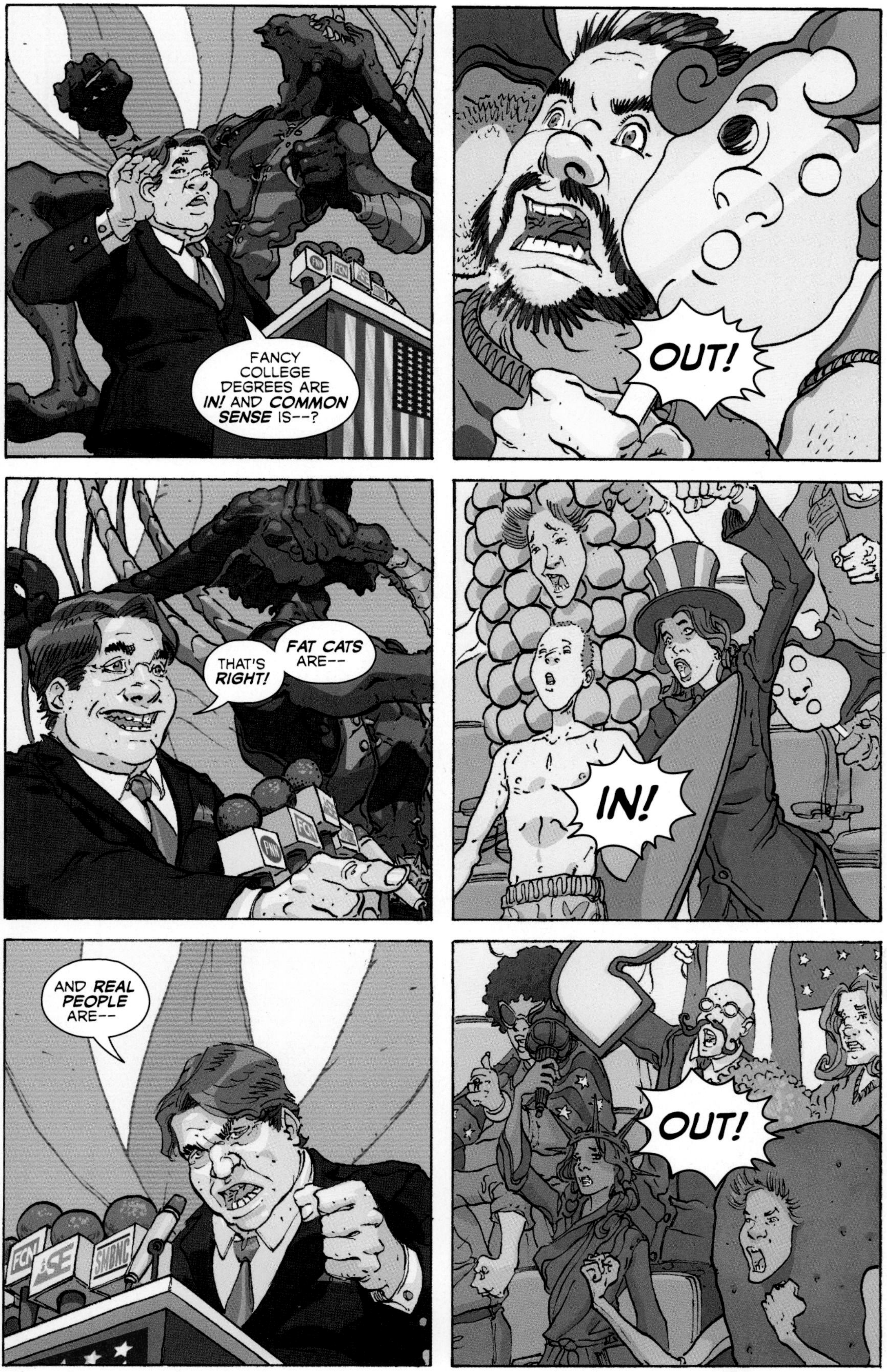
FANCY COLLEGE DEGREES ARE IN! AND COMMON SENSE IS--?
OUT!
THAT'S RIGHT!
FAT CATS ARE--
IN!
AND REAL PEOPLE ARE--
OUT!

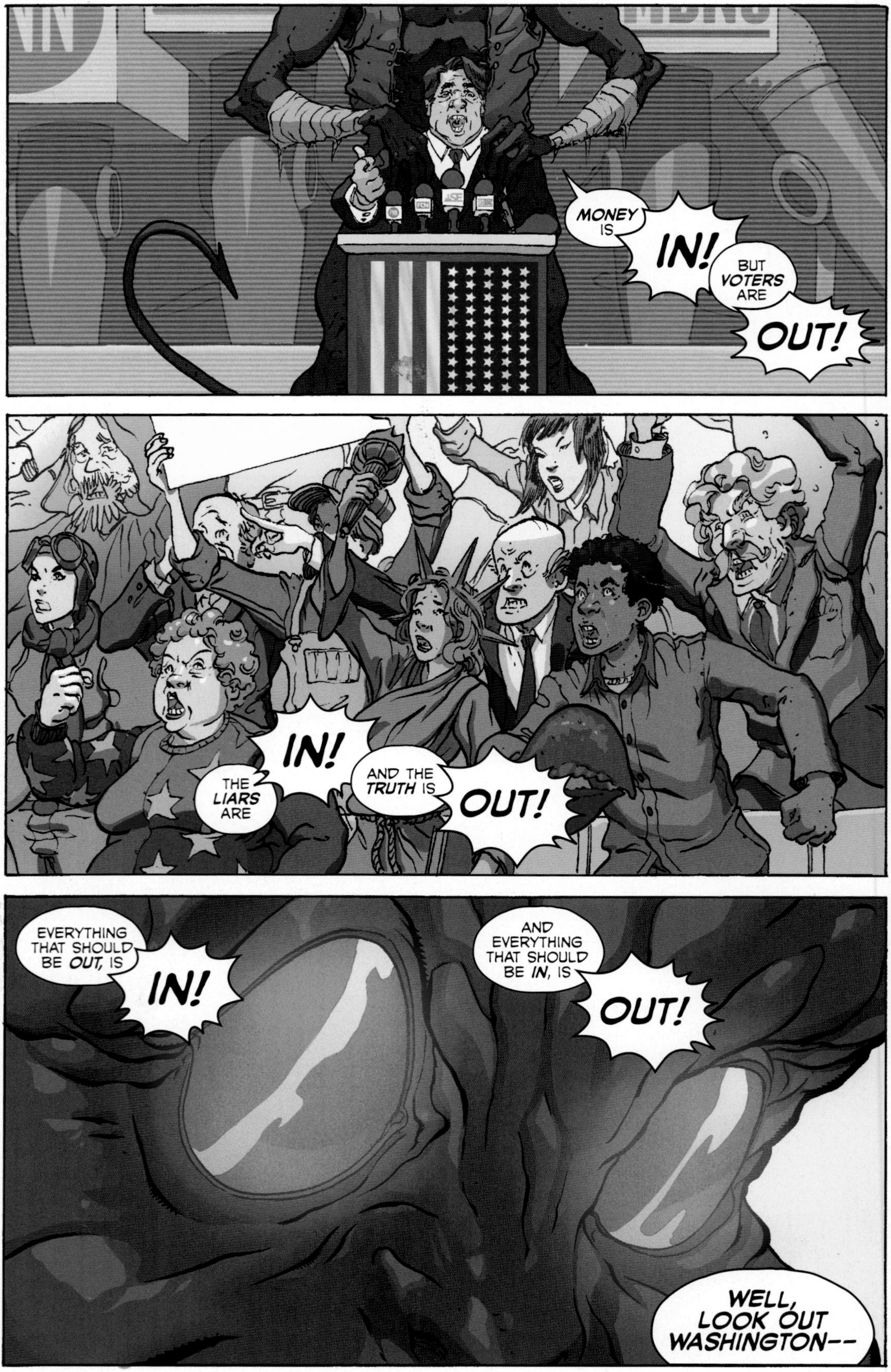

MONEY IS
IN!
BUT VOTERS ARE
OUT!
THE LIARS ARE
IN!
AND THE TRUTH IS
OUT!
EVERYTHING THAT SHOULD BE OUT, IS
IN!
AND EVERYTHING THAT SHOULD BE IN, IS
OUT!
WELL, LOOK OUT WASHINGTON--

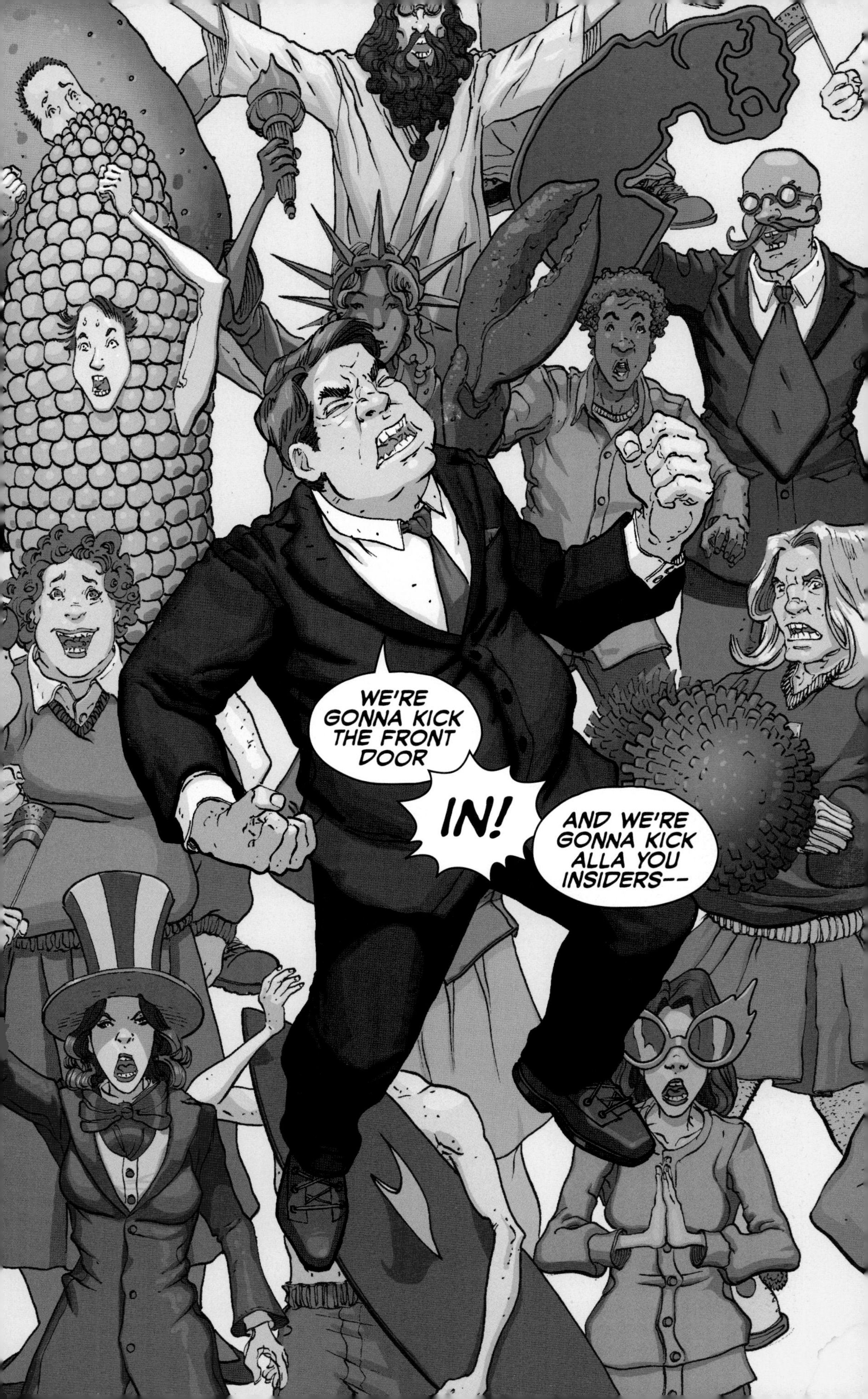
WE'RE GONNA KICK THE FRONT DOOR
IN!
AND WE'RE GONNA KICK ALLA YOU INSIDERS--

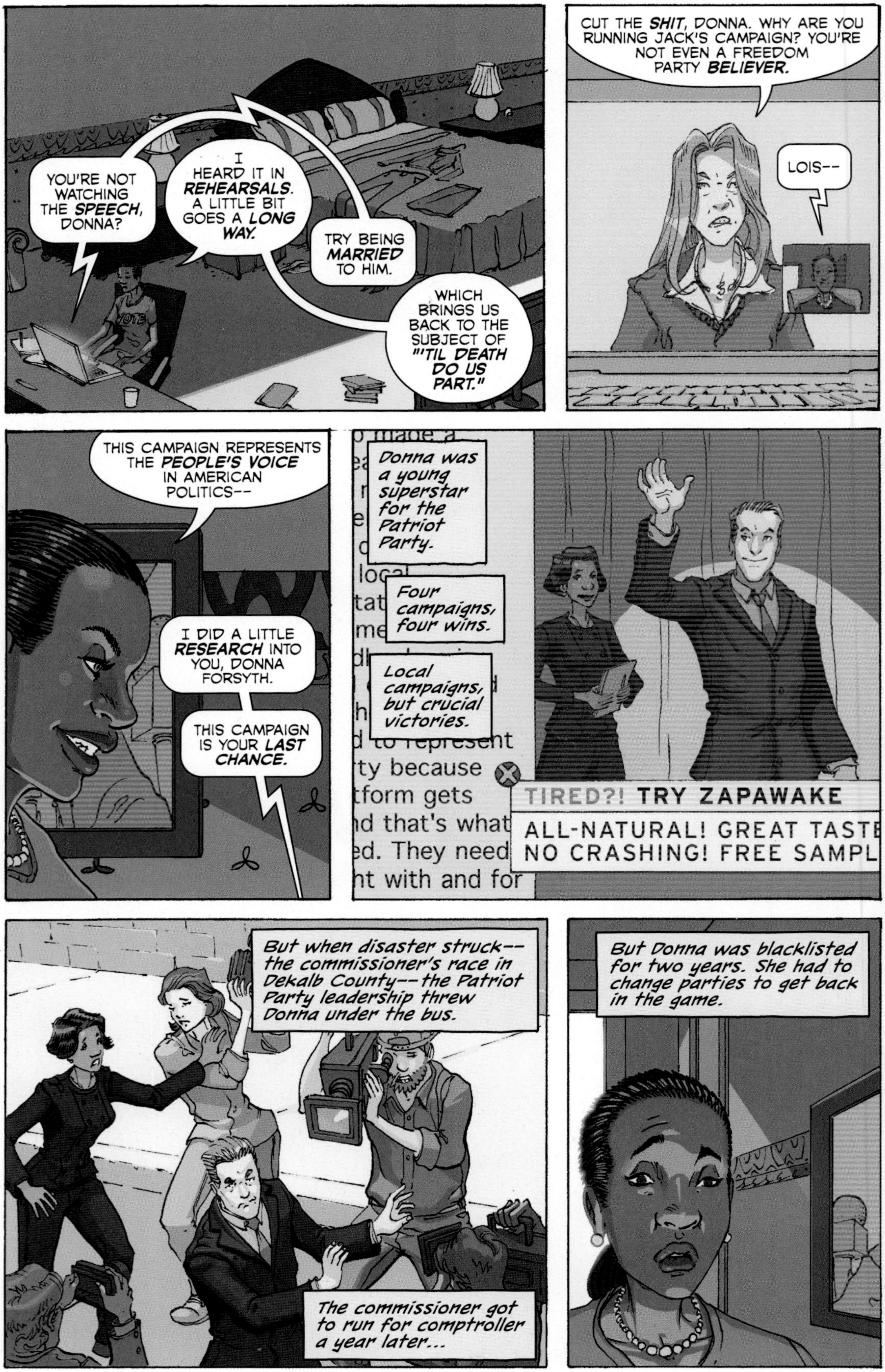
YOU'RE NOT WATCHING THE *SPEECH*, DONNA?
I HEARD IT IN *REHEARSALS*. A LITTLE BIT GOES A *LONG WAY.*
TRY BEING *MARRIED* TO HIM.
WHICH BRINGS US BACK TO THE SUBJECT OF *"'TIL DEATH DO US PART."*
VOTE
CUT THE *SHIT*, DONNA. WHY ARE YOU RUNNING JACK'S CAMPAIGN? YOU'RE NOT EVEN A FREEDOM PARTY *BELIEVER.*
LOIS--
THIS CAMPAIGN REPRESENTS THE *PEOPLE'S VOICE* IN AMERICAN POLITICS--
I DID A LITTLE *RESEARCH* INTO YOU, DONNA FORSYTH.
THIS CAMPAIGN IS YOUR *LAST CHANCE.*
Donna was a young superstar for the Patriot Party.
Four campaigns, four wins.
Local campaigns, but crucial victories.
TIRED?! TRY ZAPAWAKE
ALL-NATURAL! GREAT TAST
NO CRASHING! FREE SAMPL
But when disaster struck-- the commissioner's race in Dekalb County-- the Patriot Party leadership threw Donna under the bus.
The commissioner got to run for comptroller a year later...
But Donna was blacklisted for two years. She had to change parties to get back in the game.

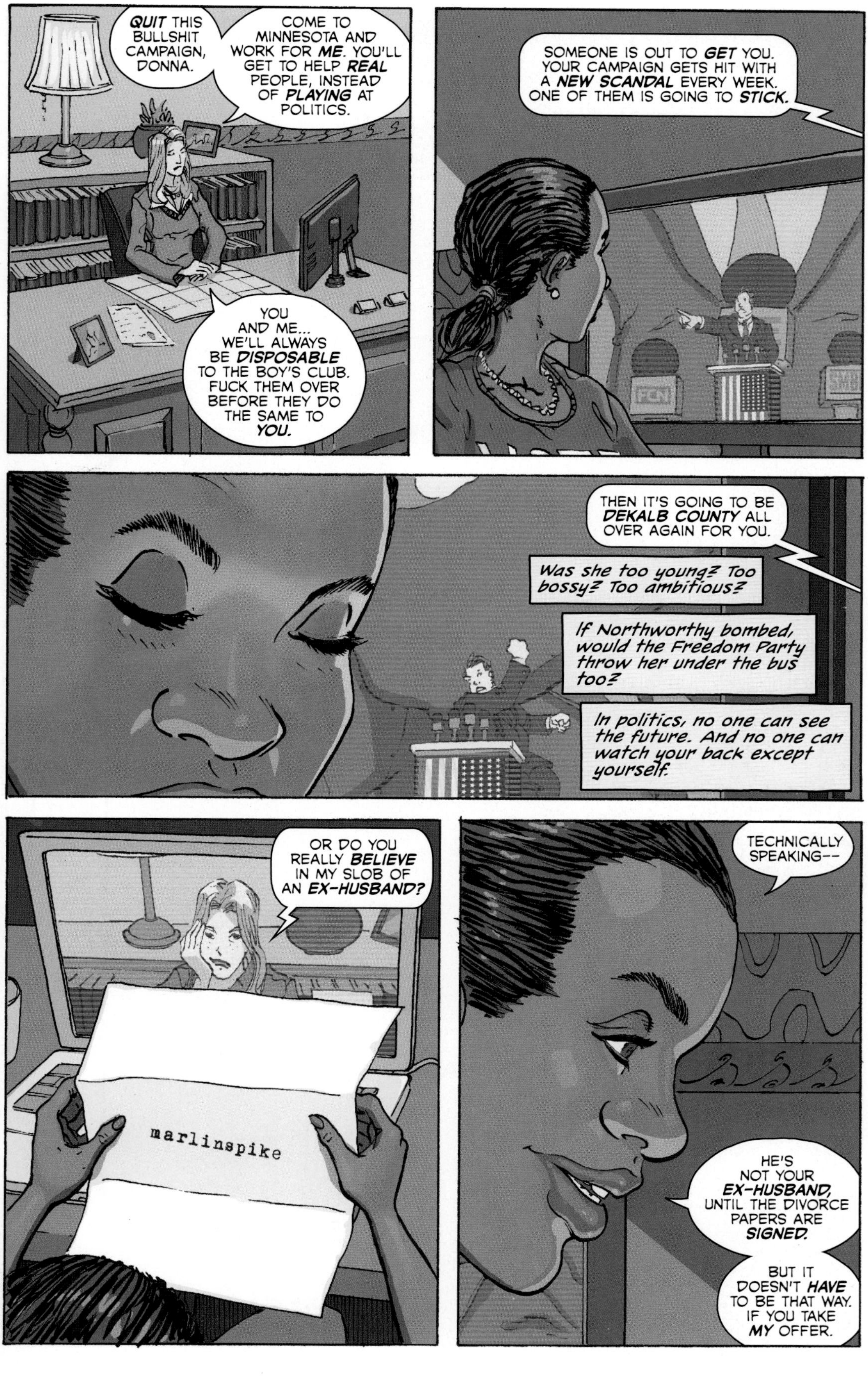
QUIT THIS BULLSHIT CAMPAIGN, DONNA.
COME TO MINNESOTA AND WORK FOR ME. YOU'LL GET TO HELP REAL PEOPLE, INSTEAD OF PLAYING AT POLITICS.
YOU AND ME... WE'LL ALWAYS BE DISPOSABLE TO THE BOY'S CLUB. FUCK THEM OVER BEFORE THEY DO THE SAME TO YOU.
SOMEONE IS OUT TO GET YOU. YOUR CAMPAIGN GETS HIT WITH A NEW SCANDAL EVERY WEEK. ONE OF THEM IS GOING TO STICK.
FCN
SMB
THEN IT'S GOING TO BE DEKALB COUNTY ALL OVER AGAIN FOR YOU.
Was she too young? Too bossy? Too ambitious?
If Northworthy bombed, would the Freedom Party throw her under the bus too?
In politics, no one can see the future. And no one can watch your back except yourself.
OR DO YOU REALLY BELIEVE IN MY SLOB OF AN EX-HUSBAND?
marlinspike
TECHNICALLY SPEAKING--
HE'S NOT YOUR EX-HUSBAND, UNTIL THE DIVORCE PAPERS ARE SIGNED.
BUT IT DOESN'T HAVE TO BE THAT WAY. IF YOU TAKE MY OFFER.

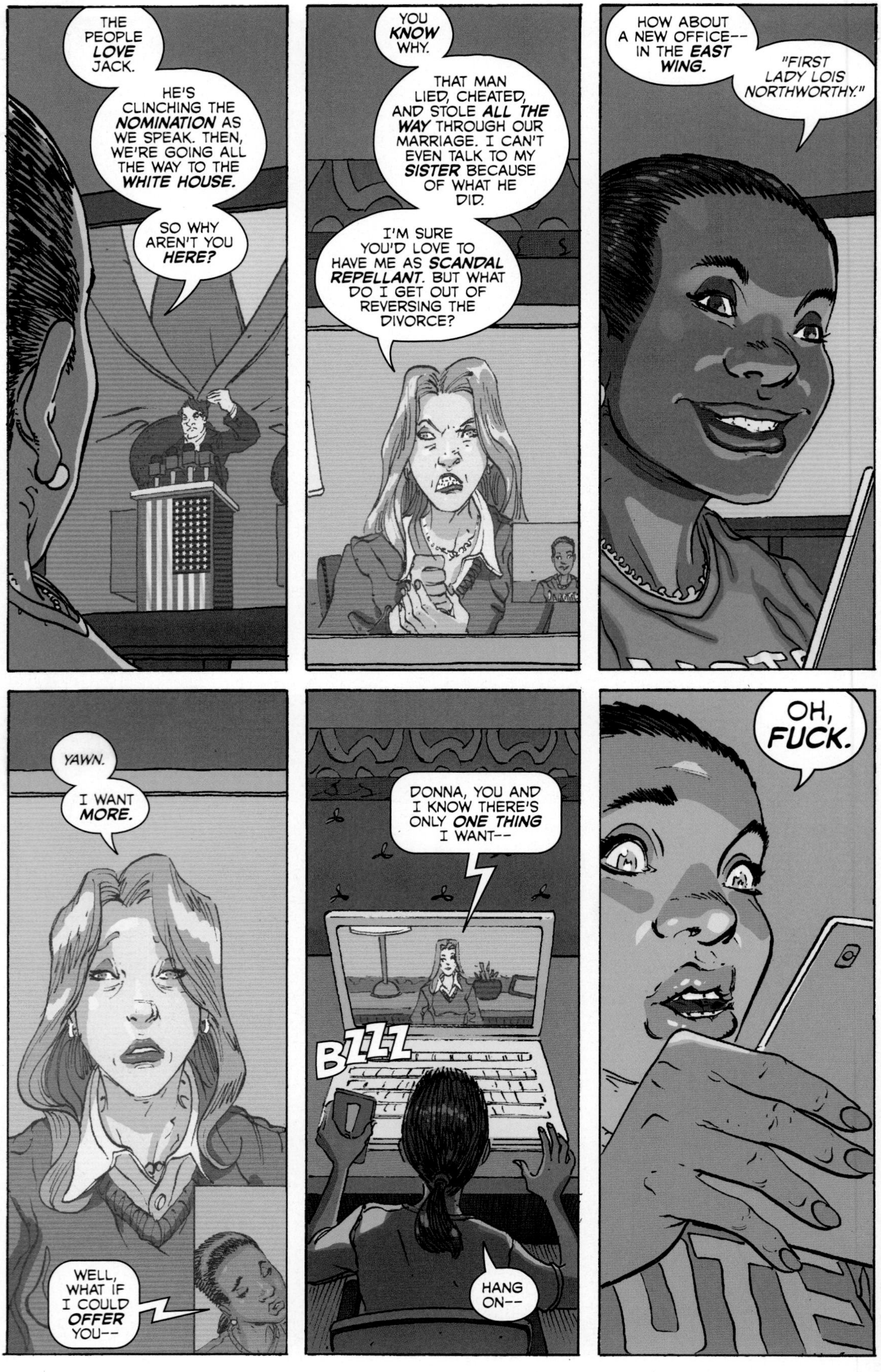
THE PEOPLE LOVE JACK.
HE'S CLINCHING THE NOMINATION AS WE SPEAK. THEN, WE'RE GOING ALL THE WAY TO THE WHITE HOUSE.
SO WHY AREN'T YOU HERE?
YOU KNOW WHY.
THAT MAN LIED, CHEATED, AND STOLE ALL THE WAY THROUGH OUR MARRIAGE. I CAN'T EVEN TALK TO MY SISTER BECAUSE OF WHAT HE DID.
I'M SURE YOU'D LOVE TO HAVE ME AS SCANDAL REPELLANT. BUT WHAT DO I GET OUT OF REVERSING THE DIVORCE?
HOW ABOUT A NEW OFFICE-- IN THE EAST WING.
"FIRST LADY LOIS NORTHWORTHY."
YAWN.
I WANT MORE.
WELL, WHAT IF I COULD OFFER YOU--
DONNA, YOU AND I KNOW THERE'S ONLY ONE THING I WANT--
BZZZ
HANG ON--
OH, FUCK.

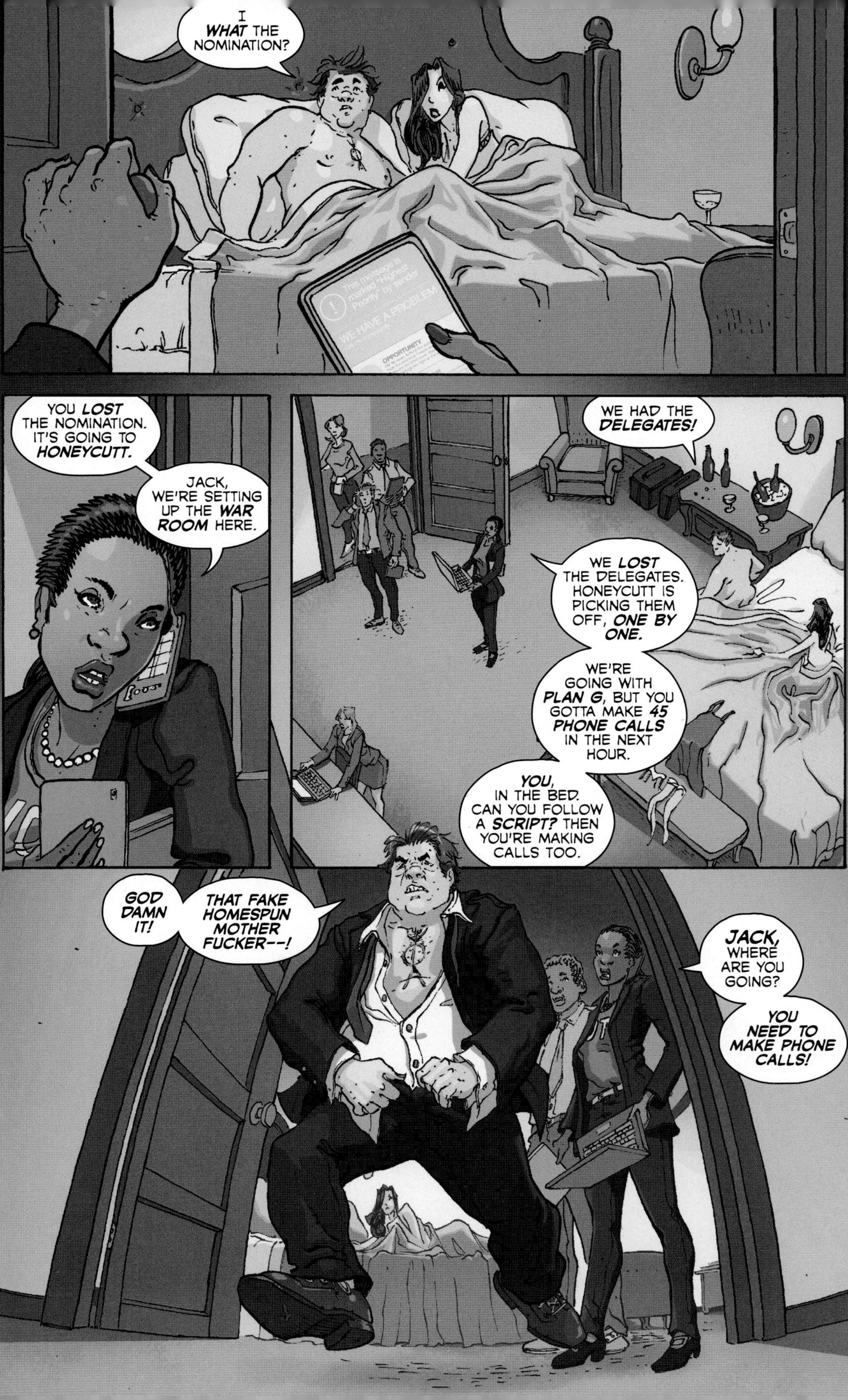
I WHAT THE NOMINATION?
This message is marked "Highest Priority" by sender
WE HAVE A PROBLEM
OPPORTUNITY
YOU LOST THE NOMINATION. IT'S GOING TO HONEYCUTT.
JACK, WE'RE SETTING UP THE WAR ROOM HERE.
WE HAD THE DELEGATES!
WE LOST THE DELEGATES. HONEYCUTT IS PICKING THEM OFF, ONE BY ONE.
WE'RE GOING WITH PLAN G, BUT YOU GOTTA MAKE 45 PHONE CALLS IN THE NEXT HOUR.
YOU, IN THE BED. CAN YOU FOLLOW A SCRIPT? THEN YOU'RE MAKING CALLS TOO.
GOD DAMN IT!
THAT FAKE HOMESPUN MOTHER FUCKER--!
JACK, WHERE ARE YOU GOING?
YOU NEED TO MAKE PHONE CALLS!

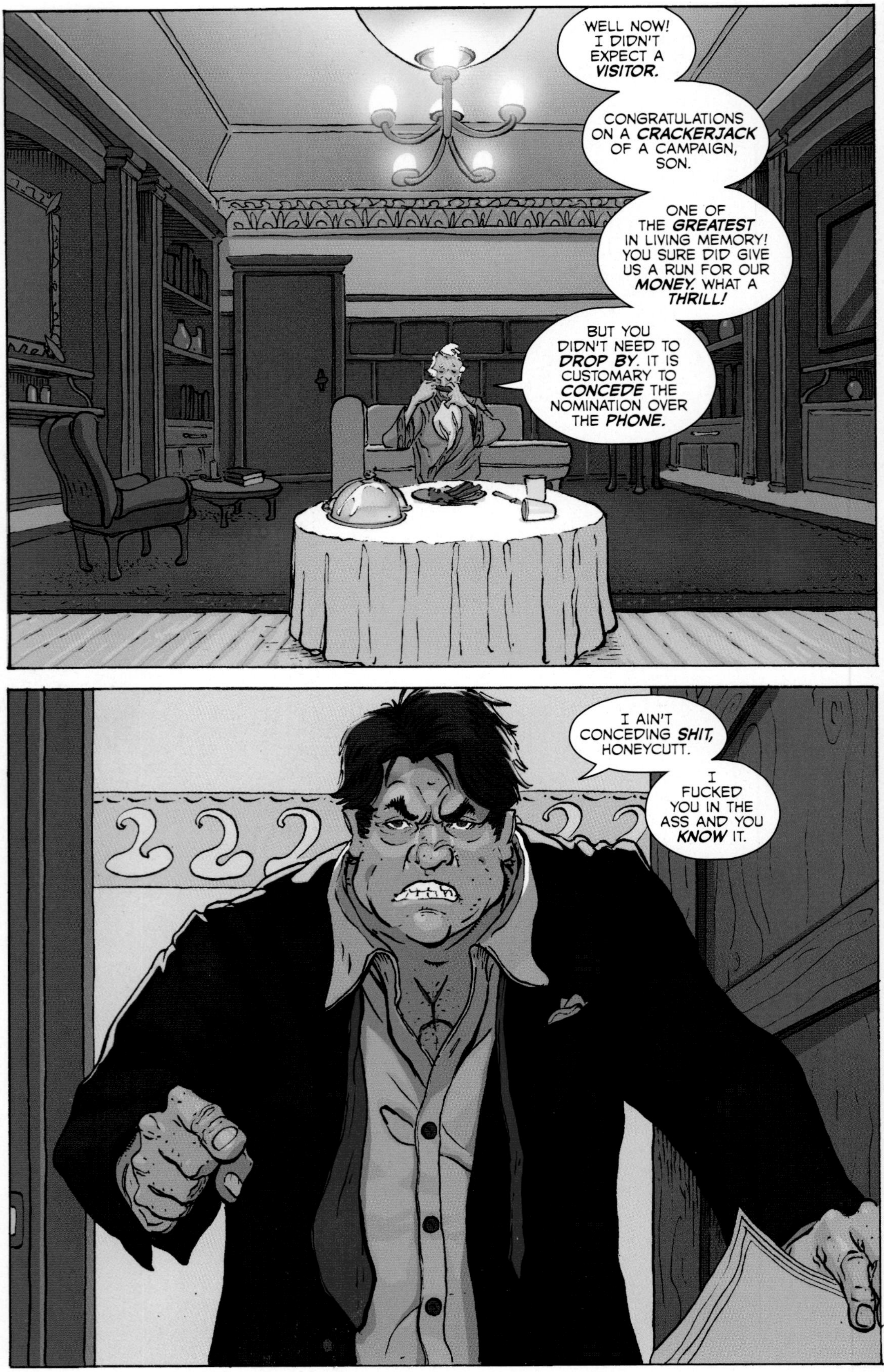
WELL NOW! I DIDN'T EXPECT A VISITOR.
CONGRATULATIONS ON A CRACKERJACK OF A CAMPAIGN, SON.
ONE OF THE GREATEST IN LIVING MEMORY! YOU SURE DID GIVE US A RUN FOR OUR MONEY. WHAT A THRILL!
BUT YOU DIDN'T NEED TO DROP BY. IT IS CUSTOMARY TO CONCEDE THE NOMINATION OVER THE PHONE.
I AIN'T CONCEDING SHIT, HONEYCUTT.
I FUCKED YOU IN THE ASS AND YOU KNOW IT.

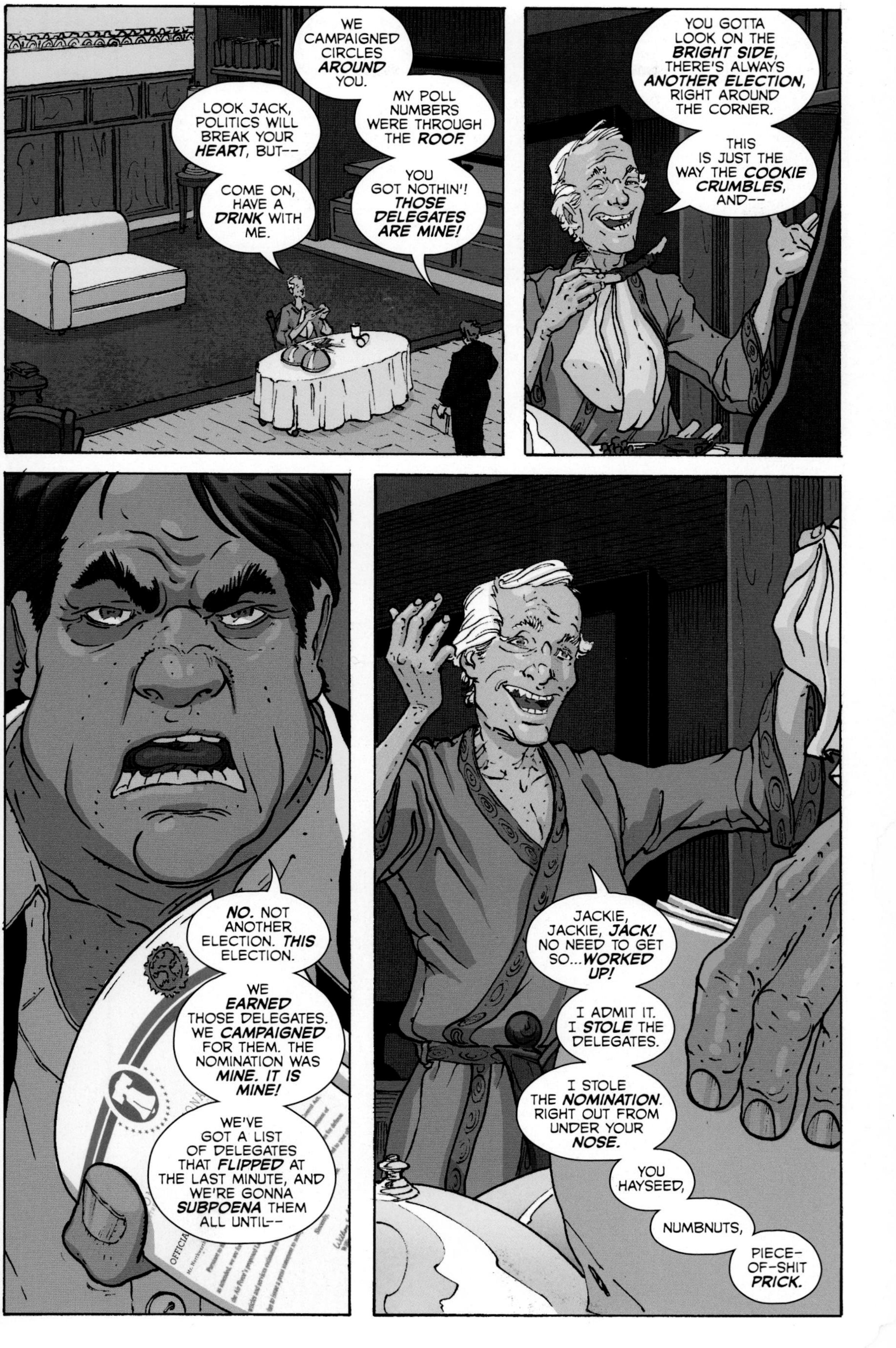
LOOK JACK, POLITICS WILL BREAK YOUR HEART, BUT--
COME ON, HAVE A DRINK WITH ME.
WE CAMPAIGNED CIRCLES AROUND YOU.
MY POLL NUMBERS WERE THROUGH THE ROOF.
YOU GOT NOTHIN'! THOSE DELEGATES ARE MINE!
YOU GOTTA LOOK ON THE BRIGHT SIDE, THERE'S ALWAYS ANOTHER ELECTION, RIGHT AROUND THE CORNER.
THIS IS JUST THE WAY THE COOKIE CRUMBLES, AND--
NO. NOT ANOTHER ELECTION. THIS ELECTION.
WE EARNED THOSE DELEGATES. WE CAMPAIGNED FOR THEM. THE NOMINATION WAS MINE. IT IS MINE!
WE'VE GOT A LIST OF DELEGATES THAT FLIPPED AT THE LAST MINUTE, AND WE'RE GONNA SUBPOENA THEM ALL UNTIL--
JACKIE, JACKIE, JACK! NO NEED TO GET SO...WORKED UP!
I ADMIT IT. I STOLE THE DELEGATES.
I STOLE THE NOMINATION. RIGHT OUT FROM UNDER YOUR NOSE.
YOU HAYSEED,
NUMBNUTS,
PIECE-OF-SHIT PRICK.

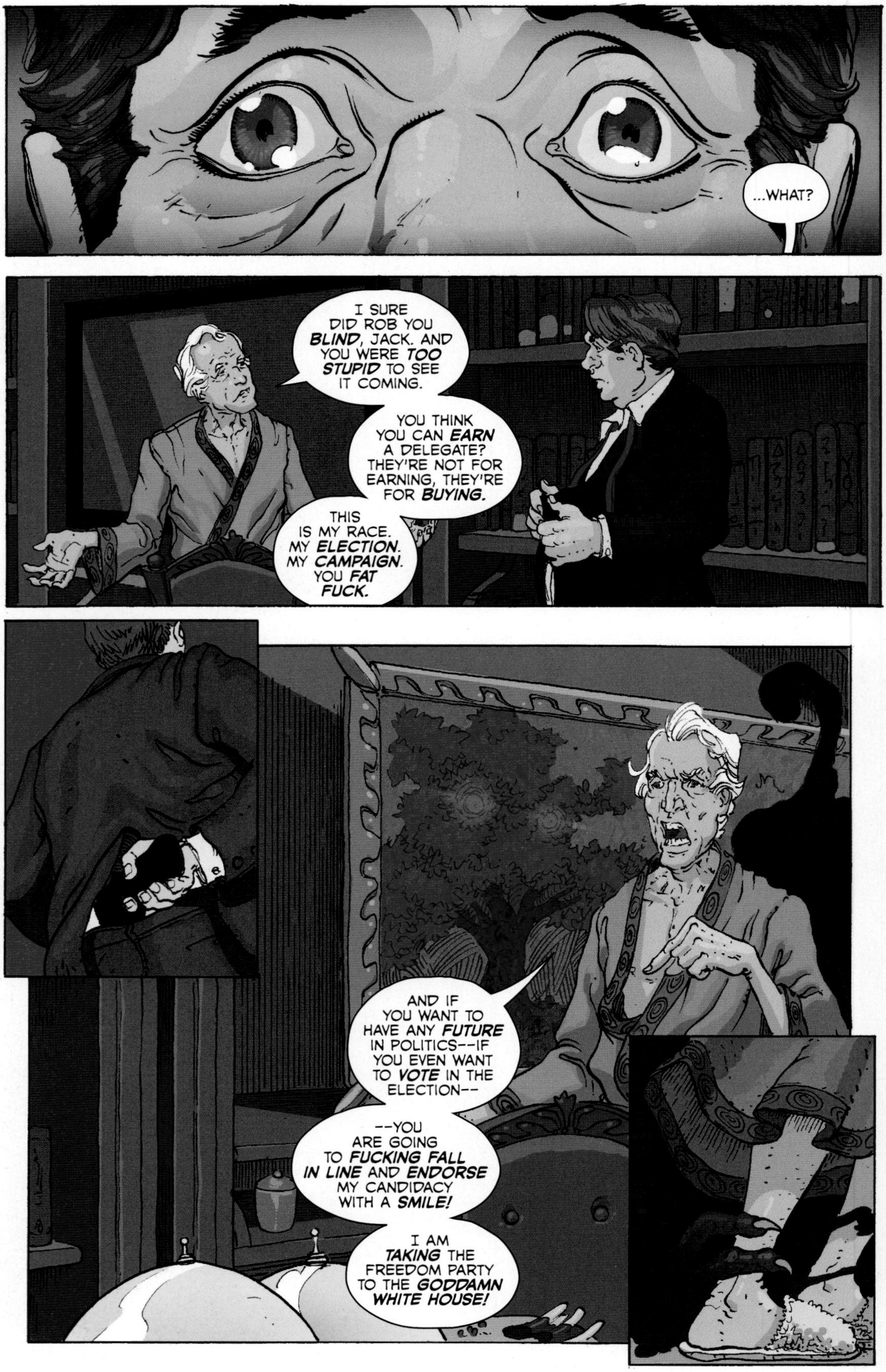
...WHAT?
I SURE DID ROB YOU BLIND, JACK. AND YOU WERE TOO STUPID TO SEE IT COMING.
YOU THINK YOU CAN EARN A DELEGATE? THEY'RE NOT FOR EARNING, THEY'RE FOR BUYING.
THIS IS MY RACE. MY ELECTION. MY CAMPAIGN. YOU FAT FUCK.
AND IF YOU WANT TO HAVE ANY FUTURE IN POLITICS--IF YOU EVEN WANT TO VOTE IN THE ELECTION--
--YOU ARE GOING TO FUCKING FALL IN LINE AND ENDORSE MY CANDIDACY WITH A SMILE!
I AM TAKING THE FREEDOM PARTY TO THE GODDAMN WHITE HOUSE!

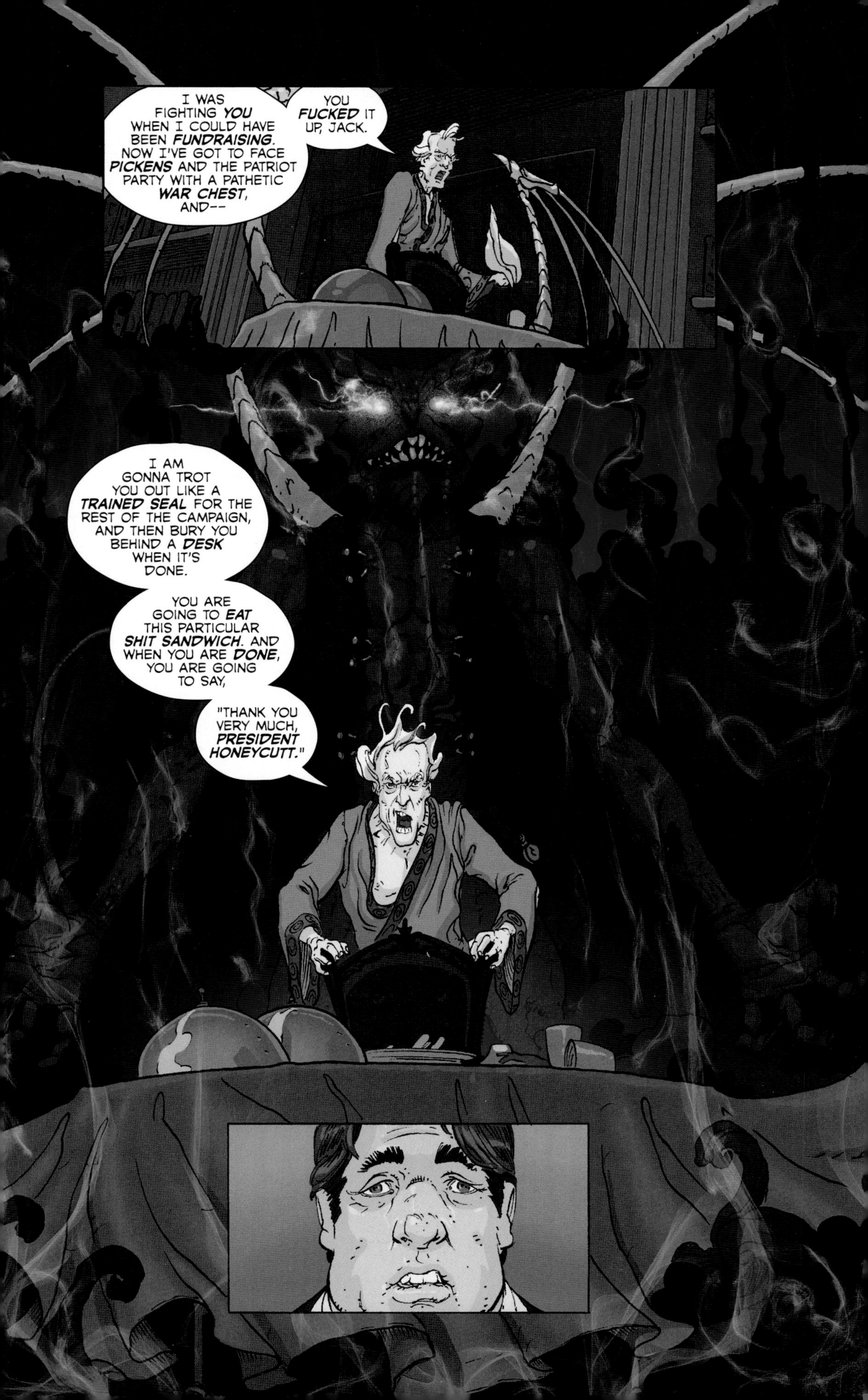
I WAS FIGHTING YOU WHEN I COULD HAVE BEEN FUNDRAISING. NOW I'VE GOT TO FACE PICKENS AND THE PATRIOT PARTY WITH A PATHETIC WAR CHEST, AND--
YOU FUCKED IT UP, JACK.
I AM GONNA TROT YOU OUT LIKE A TRAINED SEAL FOR THE REST OF THE CAMPAIGN, AND THEN BURY YOU BEHIND A DESK WHEN IT'S DONE.
YOU ARE GOING TO EAT THIS PARTICULAR SHIT SANDWICH. AND WHEN YOU ARE DONE, YOU ARE GOING TO SAY,
"THANK YOU VERY MUCH, PRESIDENT HONEYCUTT."

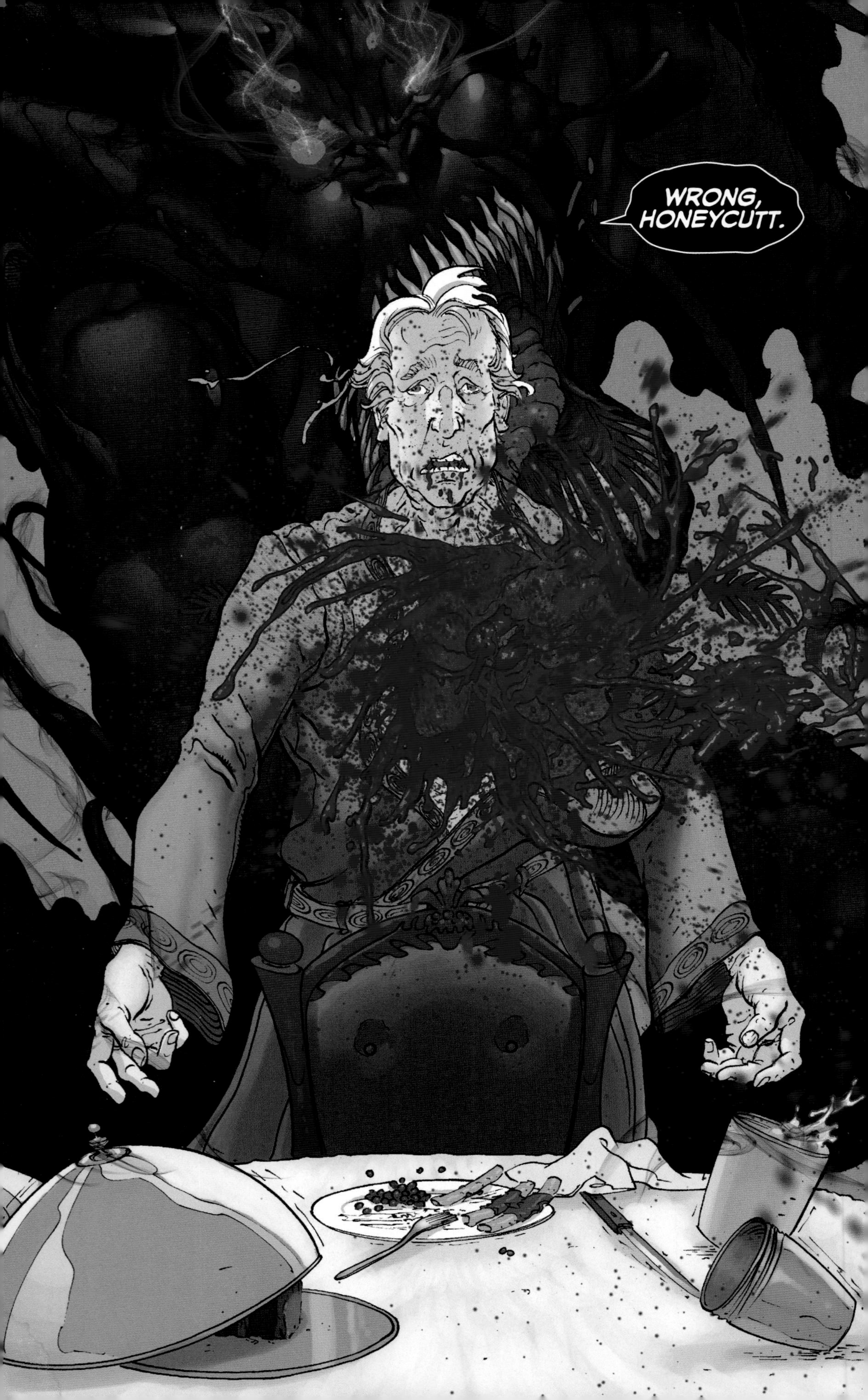
WRONG, HONEYCUTT.

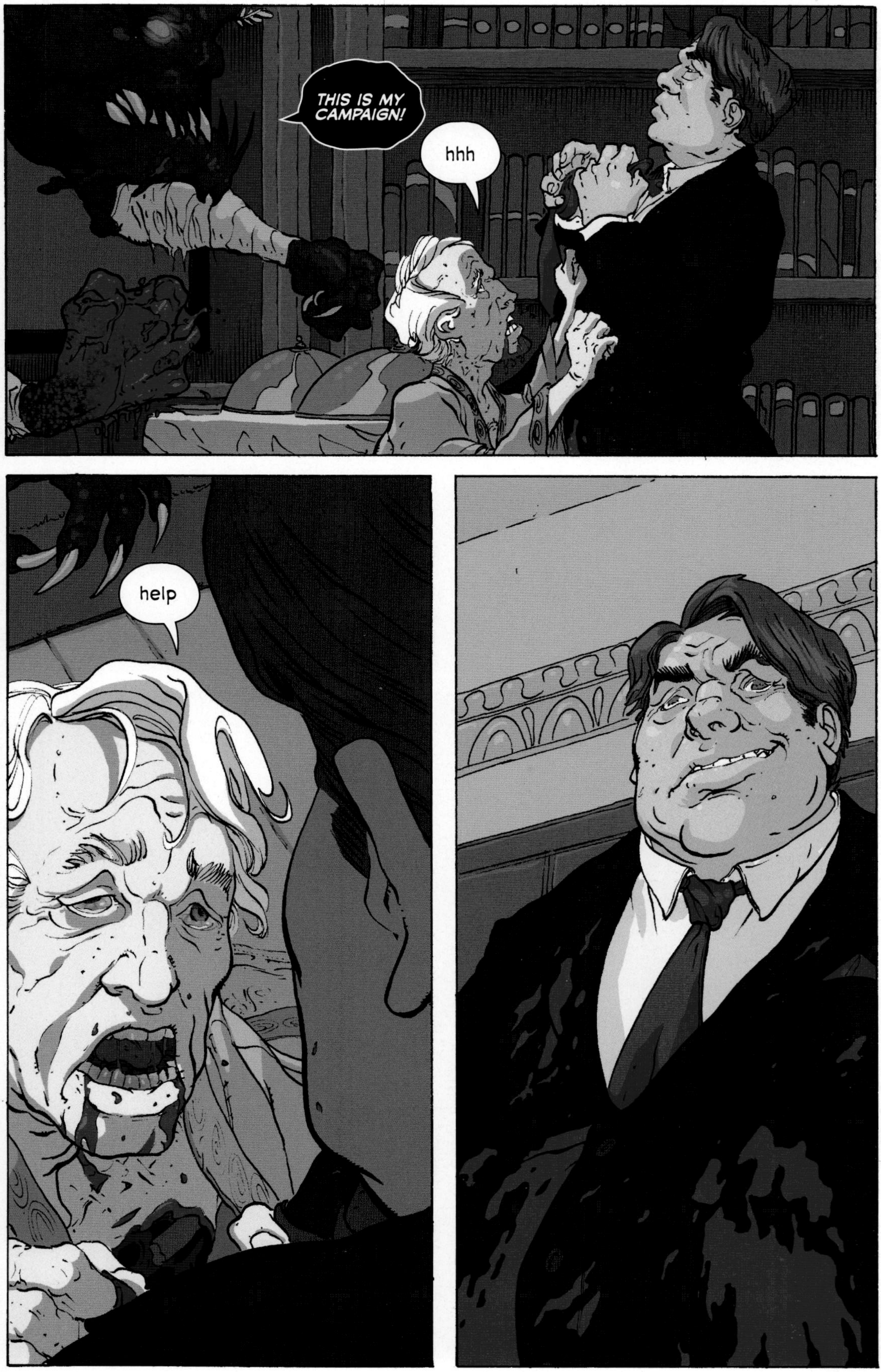
THIS IS MY CAMPAIGN!
hhh
help

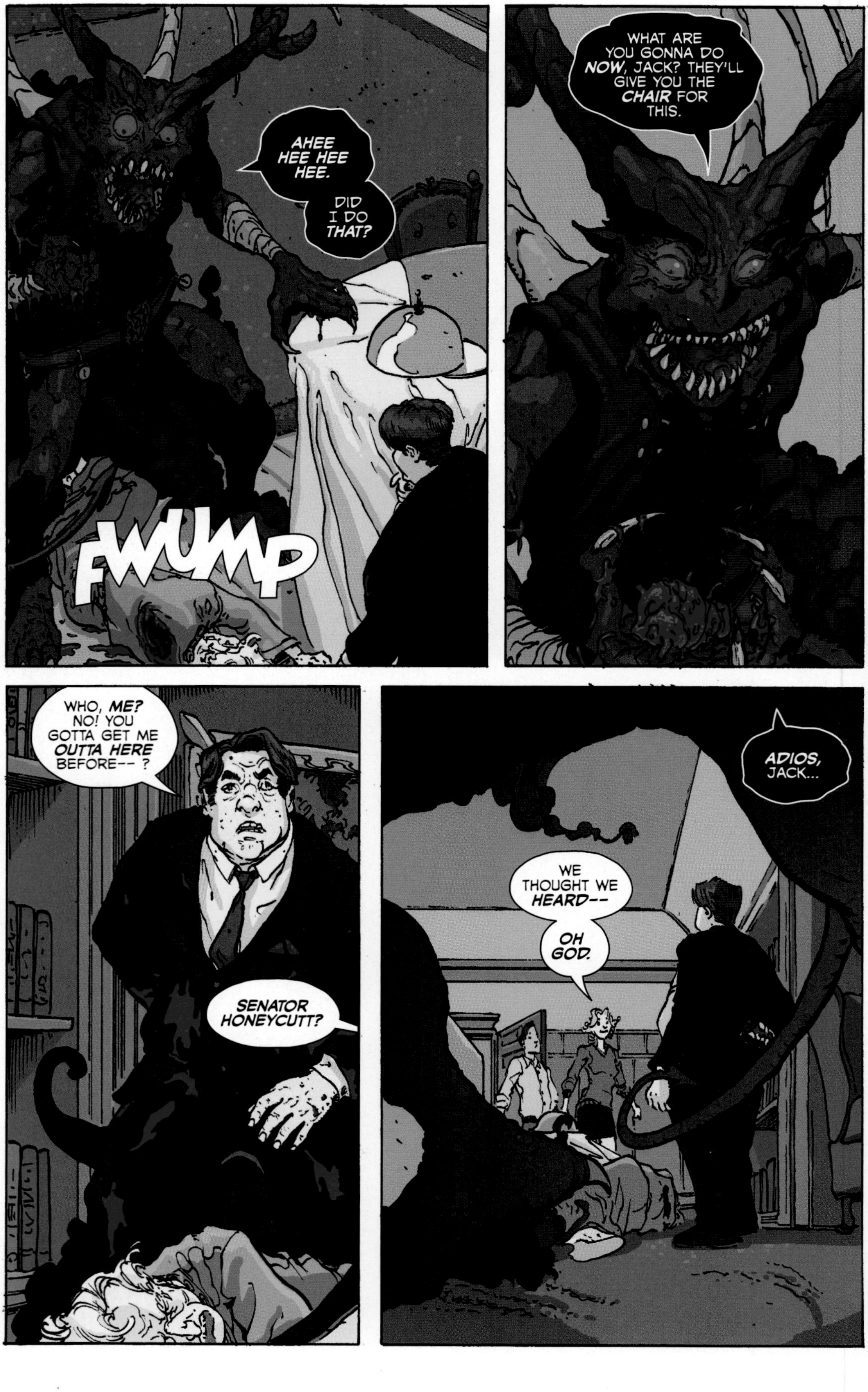
AHEE HEE HEE HEE.
DID I DO THAT?
FWUMP
WHAT ARE YOU GONNA DO NOW, JACK? THEY'LL GIVE YOU THE CHAIR FOR THIS.
WHO, ME? NO! YOU GOTTA GET ME OUTTA HERE BEFORE-- ?
SENATOR HONEYCUTT?
ADIOS, JACK...
WE THOUGHT WE HEARD--
OH GOD.

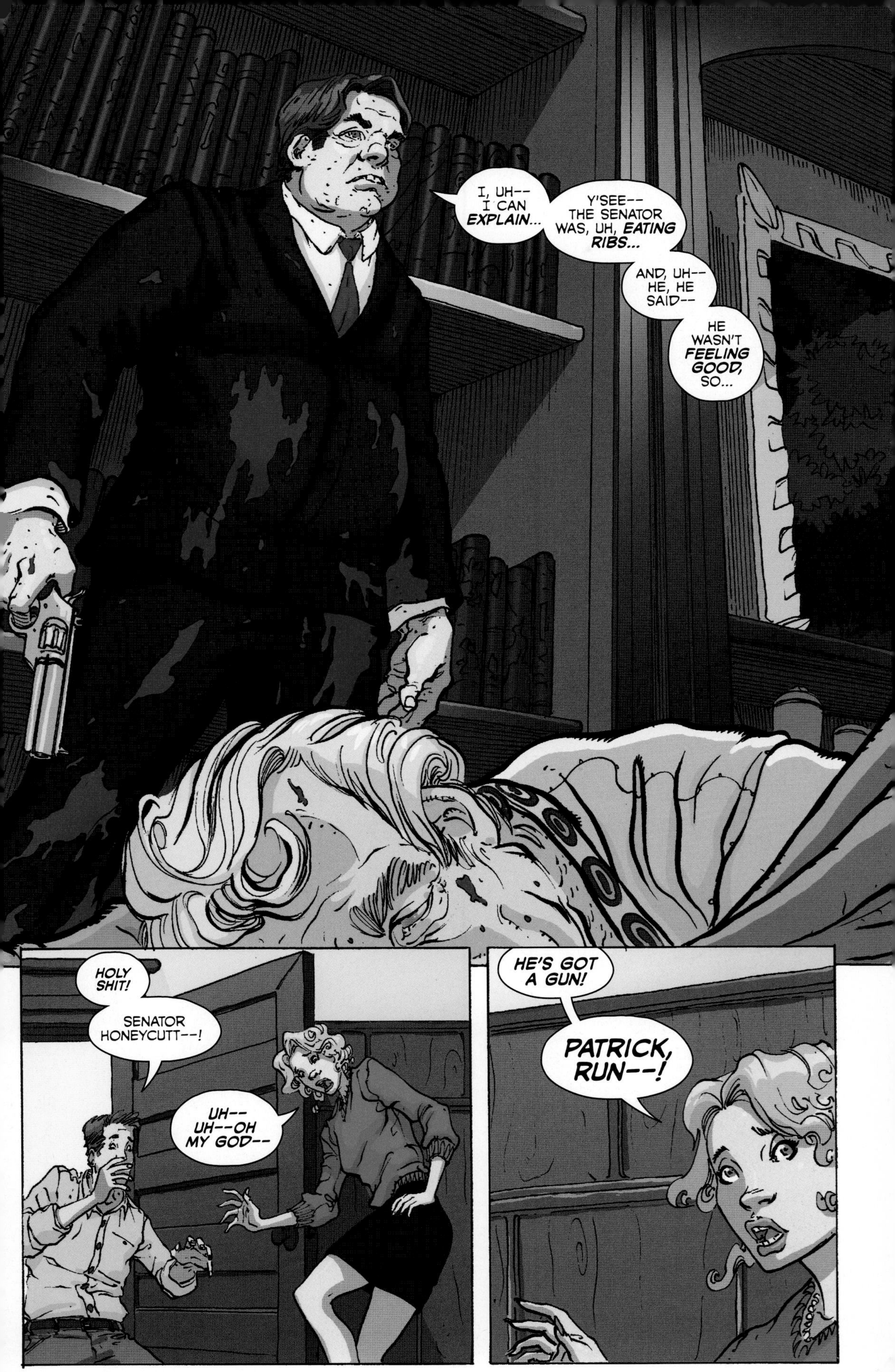
I, UH--
I CAN
EXPLAIN...
Y'SEE--
THE SENATOR
WAS, UH, EATING
RIBS...
AND, UH--
HE, HE
SAID--
HE
WASN'T
FEELING
GOOD,
SO...
HOLY
SHIT!
SENATOR
HONEYCUTT--!
UH--
UH--OH
MY GOD--
HE'S GOT
A GUN!
PATRICK,
RUN--!

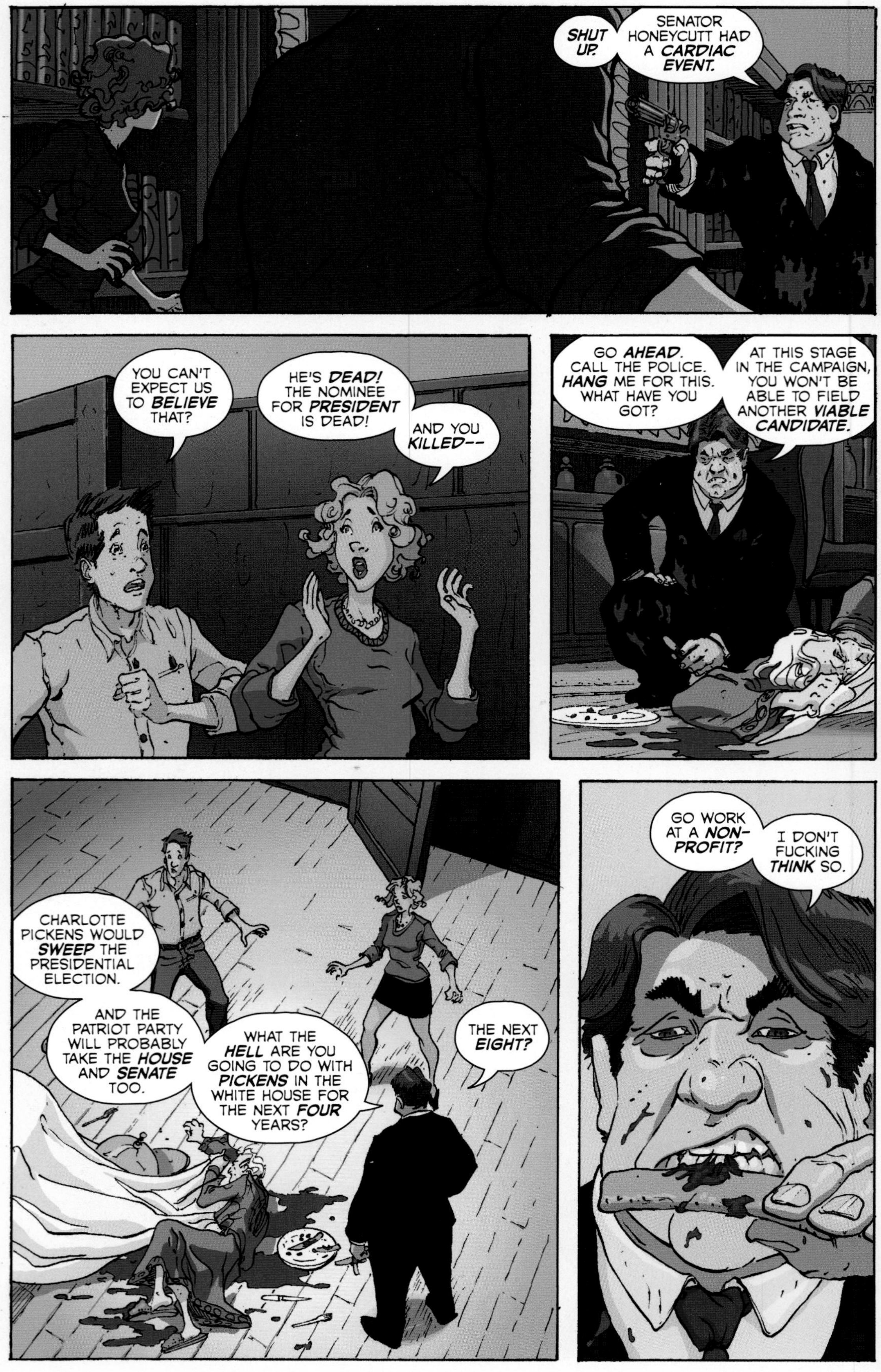
SHUT UP.
SENATOR HONEYCUTT HAD A CARDIAC EVENT.
YOU CAN'T EXPECT US TO BELIEVE THAT?
HE'S DEAD! THE NOMINEE FOR PRESIDENT IS DEAD!
AND YOU KILLED--
GO AHEAD. CALL THE POLICE. HANG ME FOR THIS. WHAT HAVE YOU GOT?
AT THIS STAGE IN THE CAMPAIGN, YOU WON'T BE ABLE TO FIELD ANOTHER VIABLE CANDIDATE.
CHARLOTTE PICKENS WOULD SWEEP THE PRESIDENTIAL ELECTION.
AND THE PATRIOT PARTY WILL PROBABLY TAKE THE HOUSE AND SENATE TOO.
WHAT THE HELL ARE YOU GOING TO DO WITH PICKENS IN THE WHITE HOUSE FOR THE NEXT FOUR YEARS?
THE NEXT EIGHT?
GO WORK AT A NON-PROFIT?
I DON'T FUCKING THINK SO.

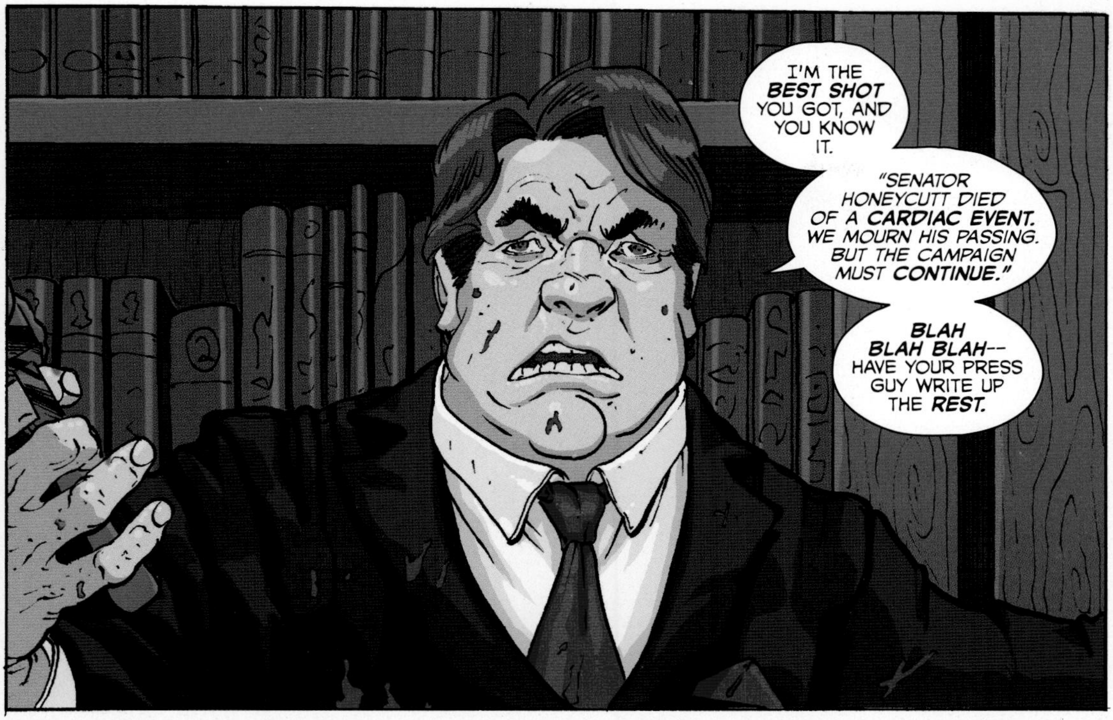
I'M THE BEST SHOT YOU GOT, AND YOU KNOW IT.
"SENATOR HONEYCUTT DIED OF A CARDIAC EVENT. WE MOURN HIS PASSING. BUT THE CAMPAIGN MUST CONTINUE."
BLAH BLAH BLAH-- HAVE YOUR PRESS GUY WRITE UP THE REST.

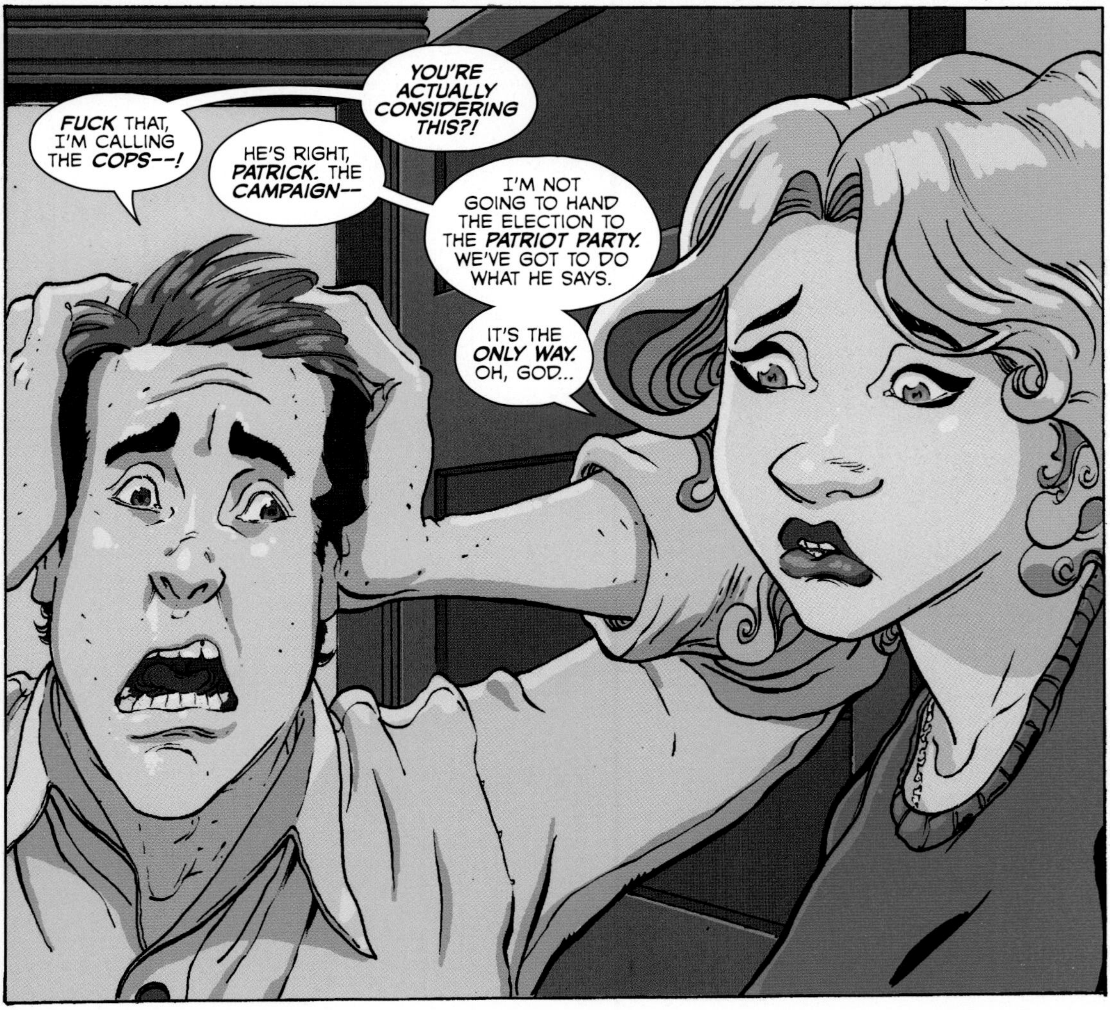
FUCK THAT, I'M CALLING THE COPS--!
YOU'RE ACTUALLY CONSIDERING THIS?!
HE'S RIGHT, PATRICK. THE CAMPAIGN--
I'M NOT GOING TO HAND THE ELECTION TO THE PATRIOT PARTY. WE'VE GOT TO DO WHAT HE SAYS.
IT'S THE ONLY WAY. OH, GOD...

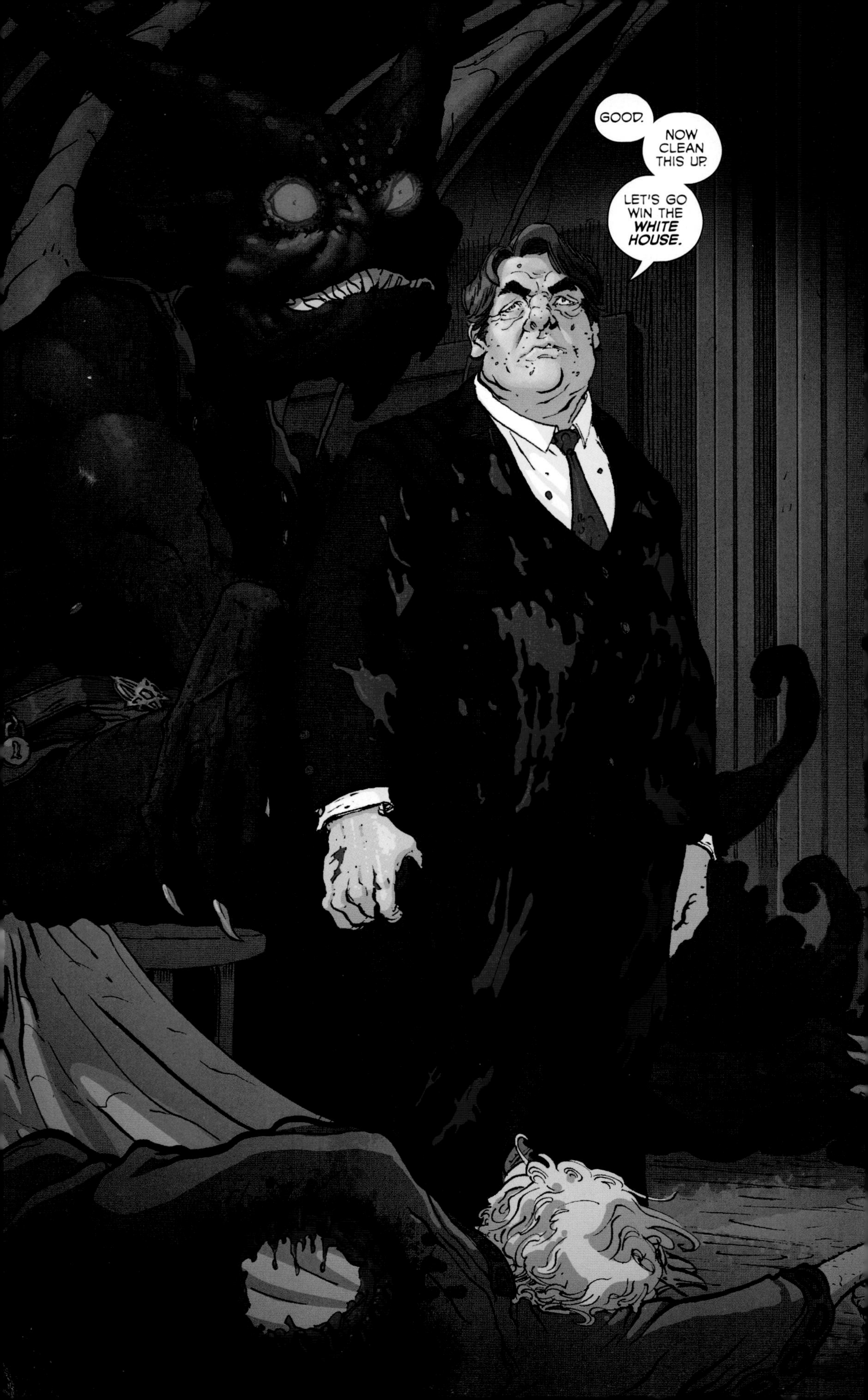
GOOD.
NOW CLEAN THIS UP.
LET'S GO WIN THE *WHITE HOUSE.*

CHAPTER 4
THE DEVIL INSIDE

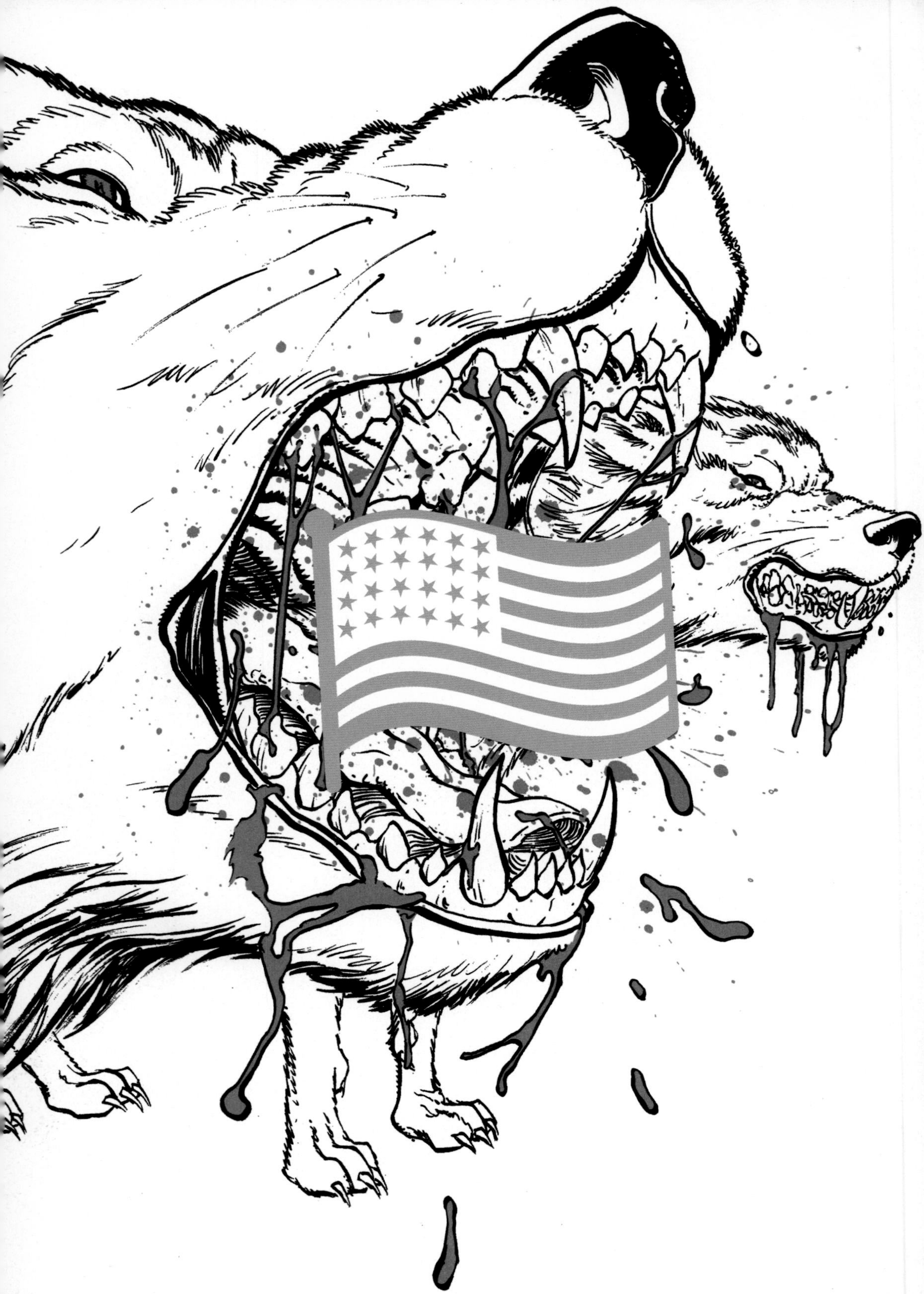

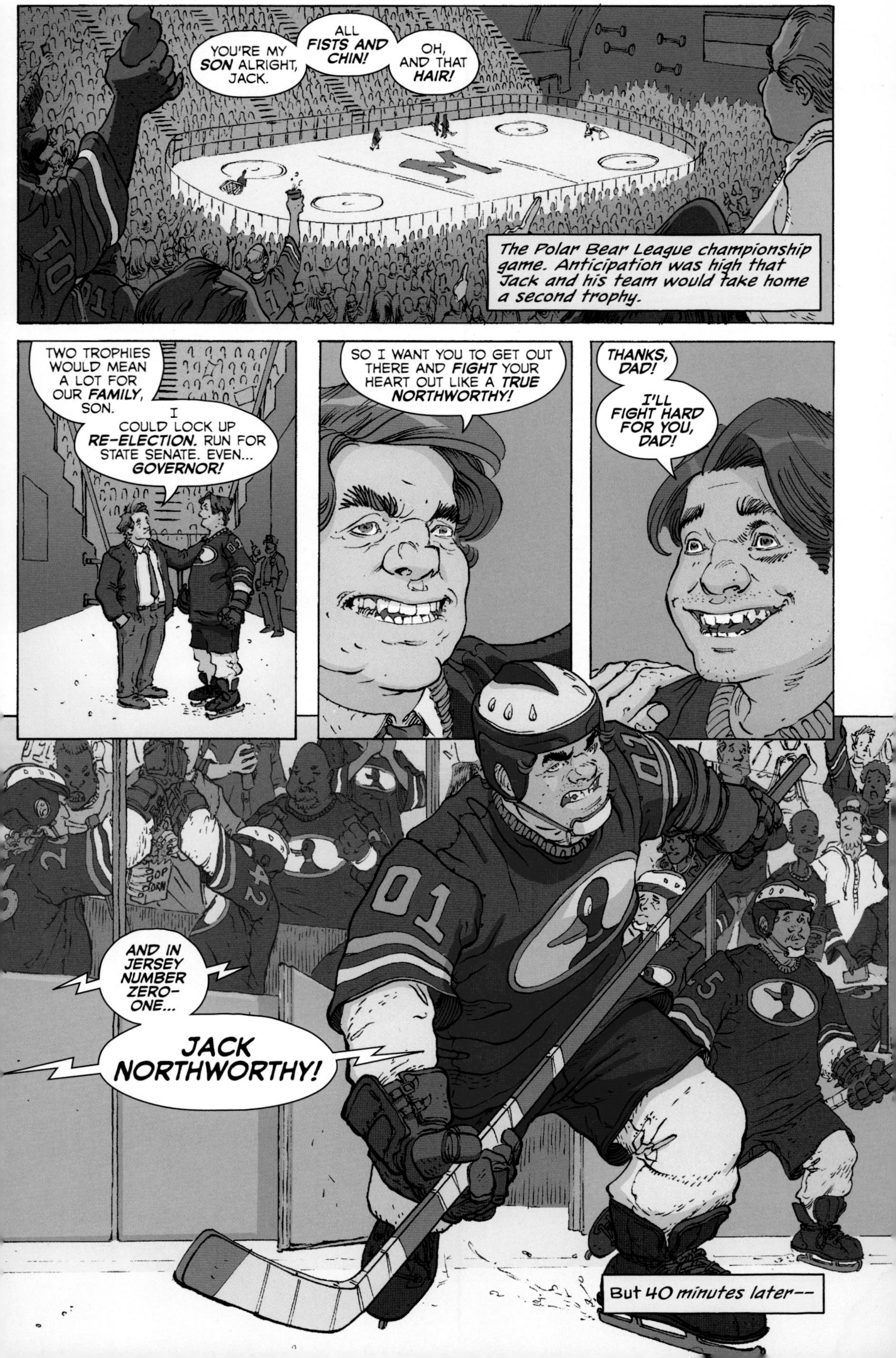

YOU'RE MY SON ALRIGHT, JACK.
ALL FISTS AND CHIN!
OH, AND THAT HAIR!
The Polar Bear League championship game. Anticipation was high that Jack and his team would take home a second trophy.
TWO TROPHIES WOULD MEAN A LOT FOR OUR FAMILY, SON.
I COULD LOCK UP RE-ELECTION. RUN FOR STATE SENATE. EVEN... GOVERNOR!
SO I WANT YOU TO GET OUT THERE AND FIGHT YOUR HEART OUT LIKE A TRUE NORTHWORTHY!
THANKS, DAD!
I'LL FIGHT HARD FOR YOU, DAD!
AND IN JERSEY NUMBER ZERO-ONE...
JACK NORTHWORTHY!
But 40 minutes later--

--an opposing player slammed Jack's head into the ice.

Four times.

WHERE'S... MY *DAD?*

DON'T TRY to *TALK,* JACK.

DID...DID HE SEE ME FIGHT *REAL HARD?*

DAD'S *GONE,* JACK. HE AND KEN JUNIOR *LEFT* AFTER THEY SCORED *FOUR POINTS* ON YOU.

AHEE HEE HEE HEE.

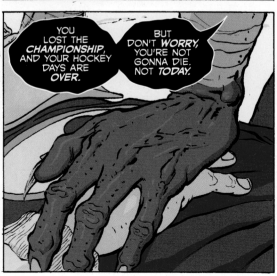

YOU LOST THE *CHAMPIONSHIP,* AND YOUR HOCKEY DAYS ARE *OVER.*

BUT DON'T *WORRY,* YOU'RE NOT GONNA DIE. NOT *TODAY.*

I'M NOT GONNA LET YOU *DOWN.*

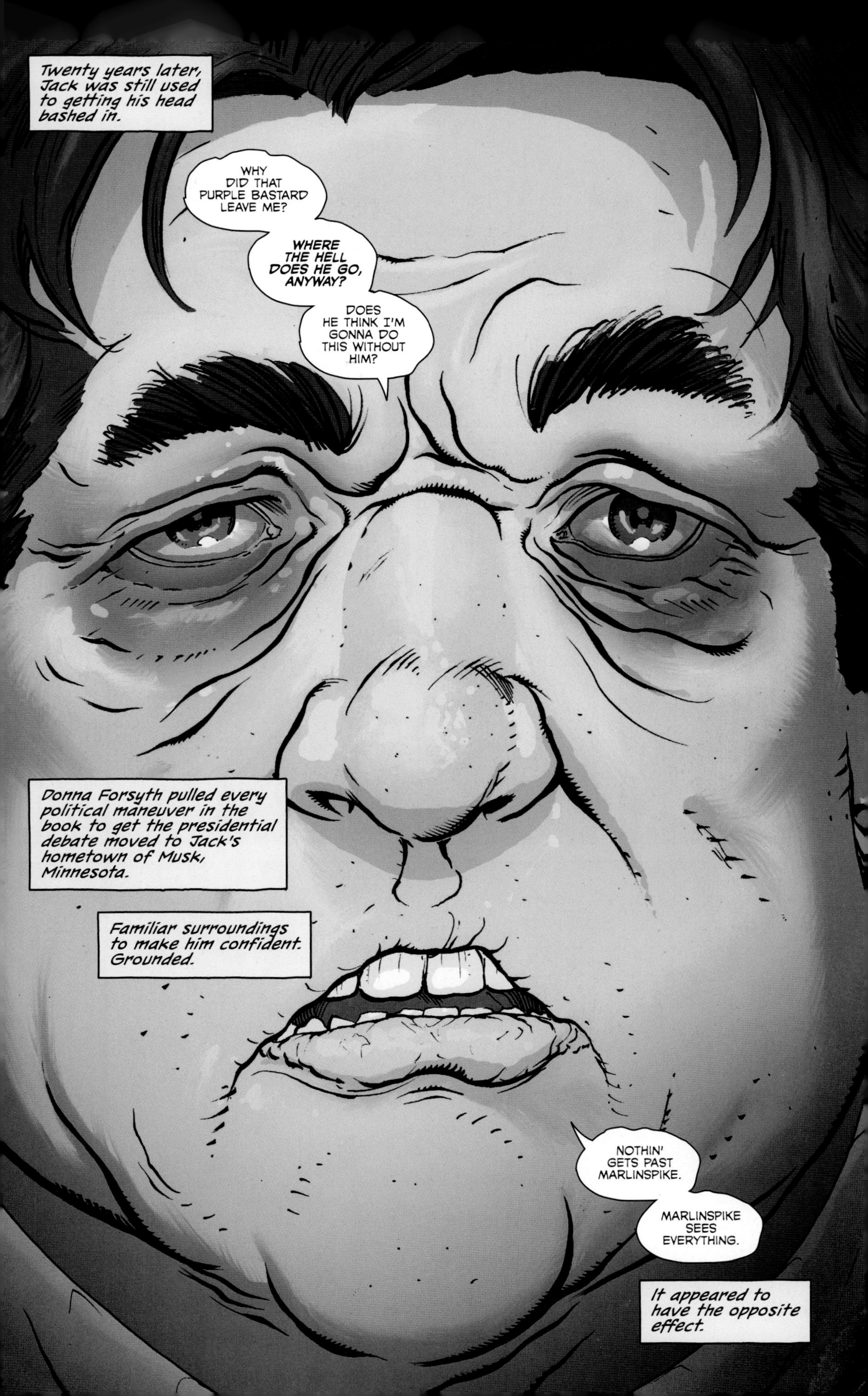
Twenty years later, Jack was still used to getting his head bashed in.
WHY DID THAT PURPLE BASTARD LEAVE ME?
WHERE THE HELL DOES HE GO, ANYWAY?
DOES HE THINK I'M GONNA DO THIS WITHOUT HIM?
Donna Forsyth pulled every political maneuver in the book to get the presidential debate moved to Jack's hometown of Musk, Minnesota.
Familiar surroundings to make him confident. Grounded.
NOTHIN' GETS PAST MARLINSPIKE.
MARLINSPIKE SEES EVERYTHING.
It appeared to have the opposite effect.

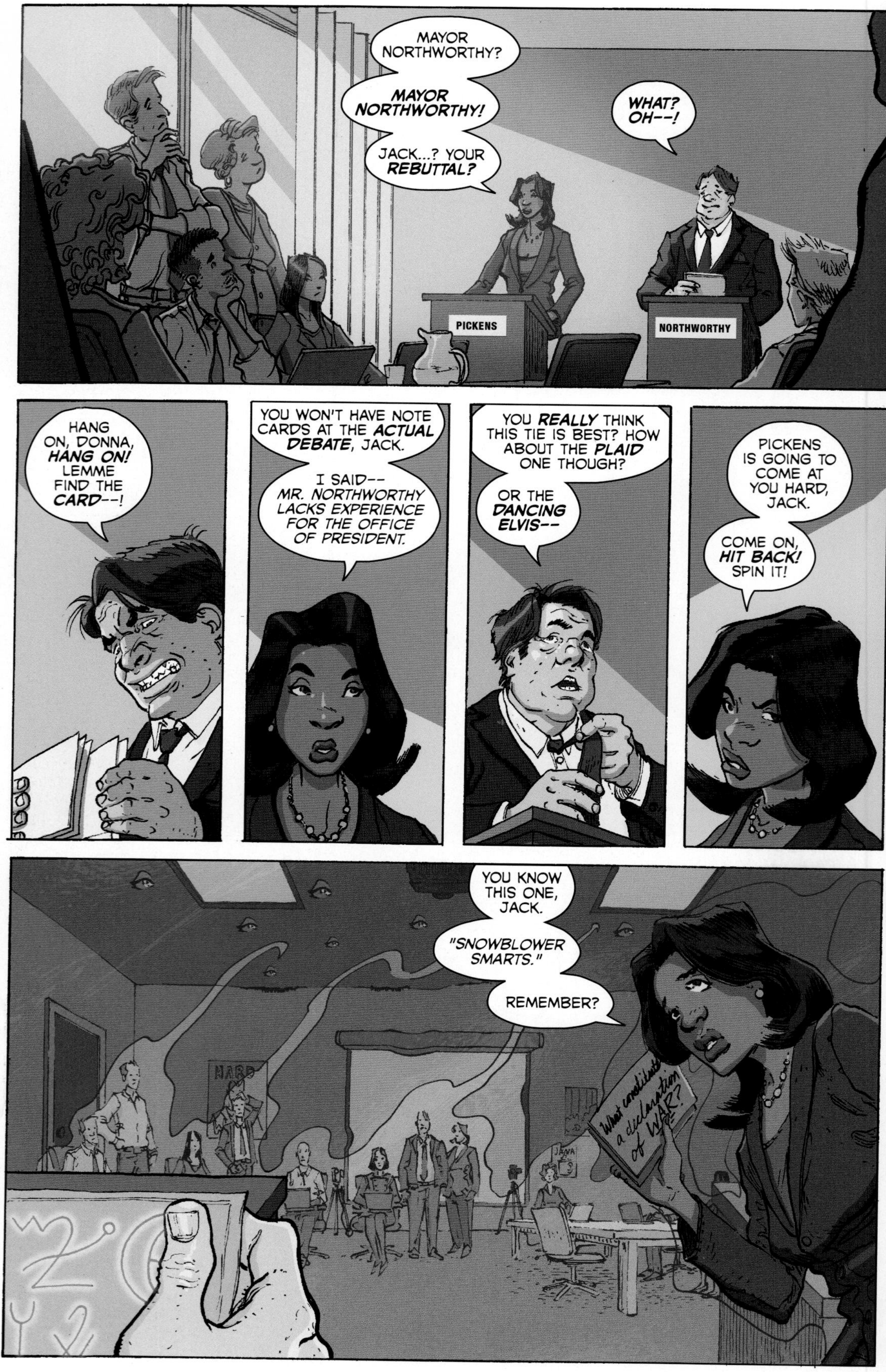
MAYOR NORTHWORTHY?
MAYOR NORTHWORTHY!
JACK...? YOUR REBUTTAL?
WHAT? OH--!
PICKENS
NORTHWORTHY
HANG ON, DONNA, HANG ON! LEMME FIND THE CARD--!
YOU WON'T HAVE NOTE CARDS AT THE ACTUAL DEBATE, JACK.
I SAID-- MR. NORTHWORTHY LACKS EXPERIENCE FOR THE OFFICE OF PRESIDENT.
YOU REALLY THINK THIS TIE IS BEST? HOW ABOUT THE PLAID ONE THOUGH?
OR THE DANCING ELVIS--
PICKENS IS GOING TO COME AT YOU HARD, JACK.
COME ON, HIT BACK! SPIN IT!
YOU KNOW THIS ONE, JACK.
"SNOWBLOWER SMARTS."
REMEMBER?
What constitutes a declaration of WAR?

WELL I DO HAVE **ONE** THING YOU'LL NEVER HAVE, **SENATOR PICKENS**, AND **THAT'S--**

CUT!

HALT!

FINITO!

TIME FOR **PRESIDENT NORTHWORTHY** TO HAVE A "HARD FIGHTIN'" **STEAK DINNER** WITH HIS **OLD MAN!**

THAT'S RIGHT! THAT OLD **DUSTBAG PICKENS** DOESN'T STAND A CHANCE, **RIGHT** JACK?

DAD...

MY SON'S GONNA BE THE **NEXT PRESIDENT!**

ALL YOU FOLKS CAN PICK UP **TOMORROW!**

BUT TOMORROW'S THE **DEBATE.**

≷SIGH≷ **EVERYONE--**

--WE'RE DONE HERE.

Hannah

5:41 PM

Contact

Today 8:32 AM

Marlinspike or Marlin Spike?

Could be either

Am I looking for a person, place, or thing?

I dunno. That's why I need you :)

I'm on the case

Thanks girl I owe you

Hey running out of time you got anything?

DONNA, WHAT ARE WE GOING TO DO ABOUT HIM? THE DEBATE IS **TOMORROW--**

GET THE **UNIFORM.** WHAT ELSE HAVE WE GOT?

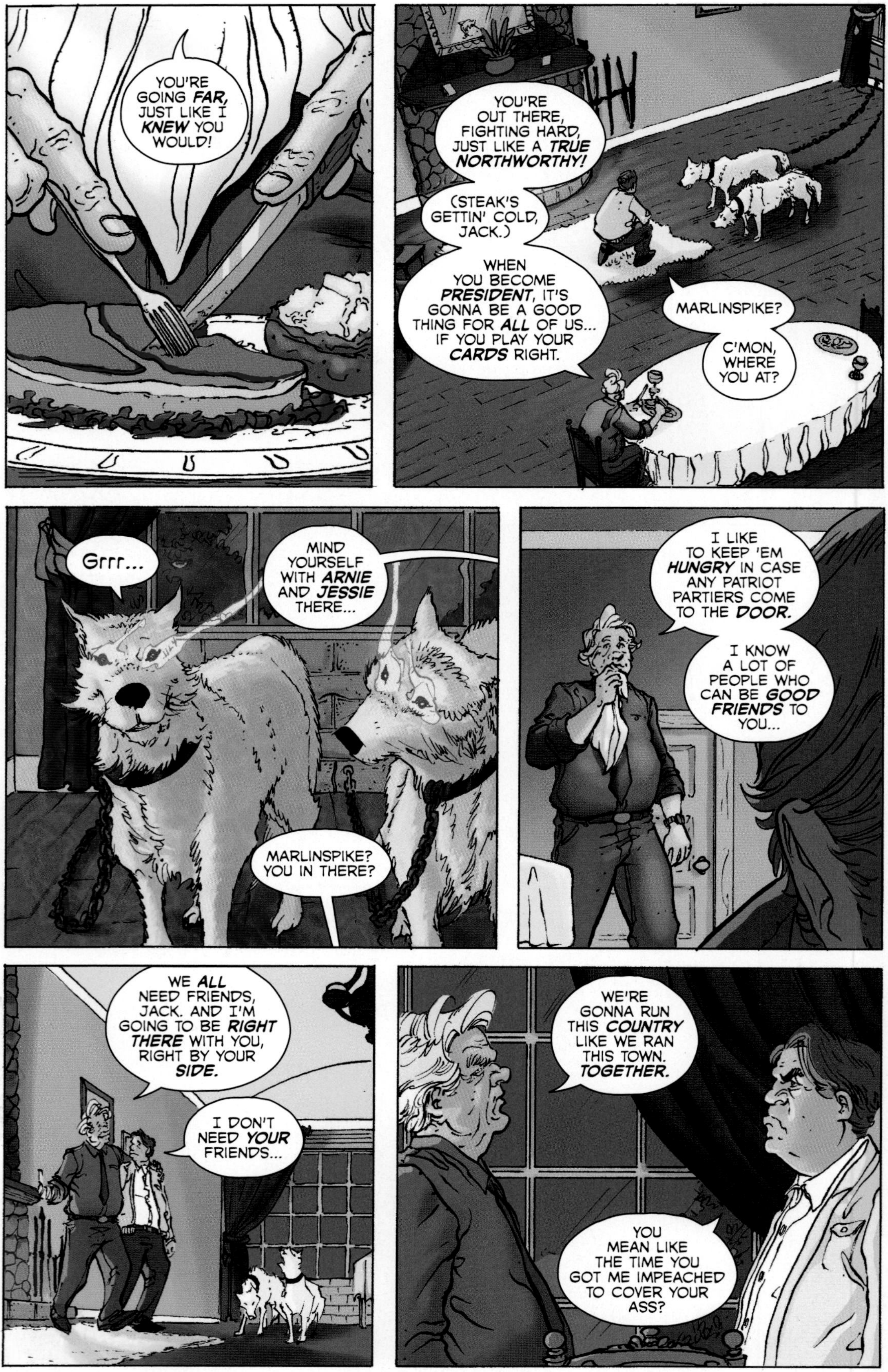

YOU'RE GOING FAR, JUST LIKE I KNEW YOU WOULD!
YOU'RE OUT THERE, FIGHTING HARD, JUST LIKE A TRUE NORTHWORTHY!
(STEAK'S GETTIN' COLD, JACK.)
WHEN YOU BECOME PRESIDENT, IT'S GONNA BE A GOOD THING FOR ALL OF US... IF YOU PLAY YOUR CARDS RIGHT.
MARLINSPIKE?
C'MON, WHERE YOU AT?
Grrr...
MIND YOURSELF WITH ARNIE AND JESSIE THERE...
MARLINSPIKE? YOU IN THERE?
I LIKE TO KEEP 'EM HUNGRY IN CASE ANY PATRIOT PARTIERS COME TO THE DOOR.
I KNOW A LOT OF PEOPLE WHO CAN BE GOOD FRIENDS TO YOU...
WE ALL NEED FRIENDS, JACK. AND I'M GOING TO BE RIGHT THERE WITH YOU, RIGHT BY YOUR SIDE.
I DON'T NEED YOUR FRIENDS...
WE'RE GONNA RUN THIS COUNTRY LIKE WE RAN THIS TOWN. TOGETHER.
YOU MEAN LIKE THE TIME YOU GOT ME IMPEACHED TO COVER YOUR ASS?

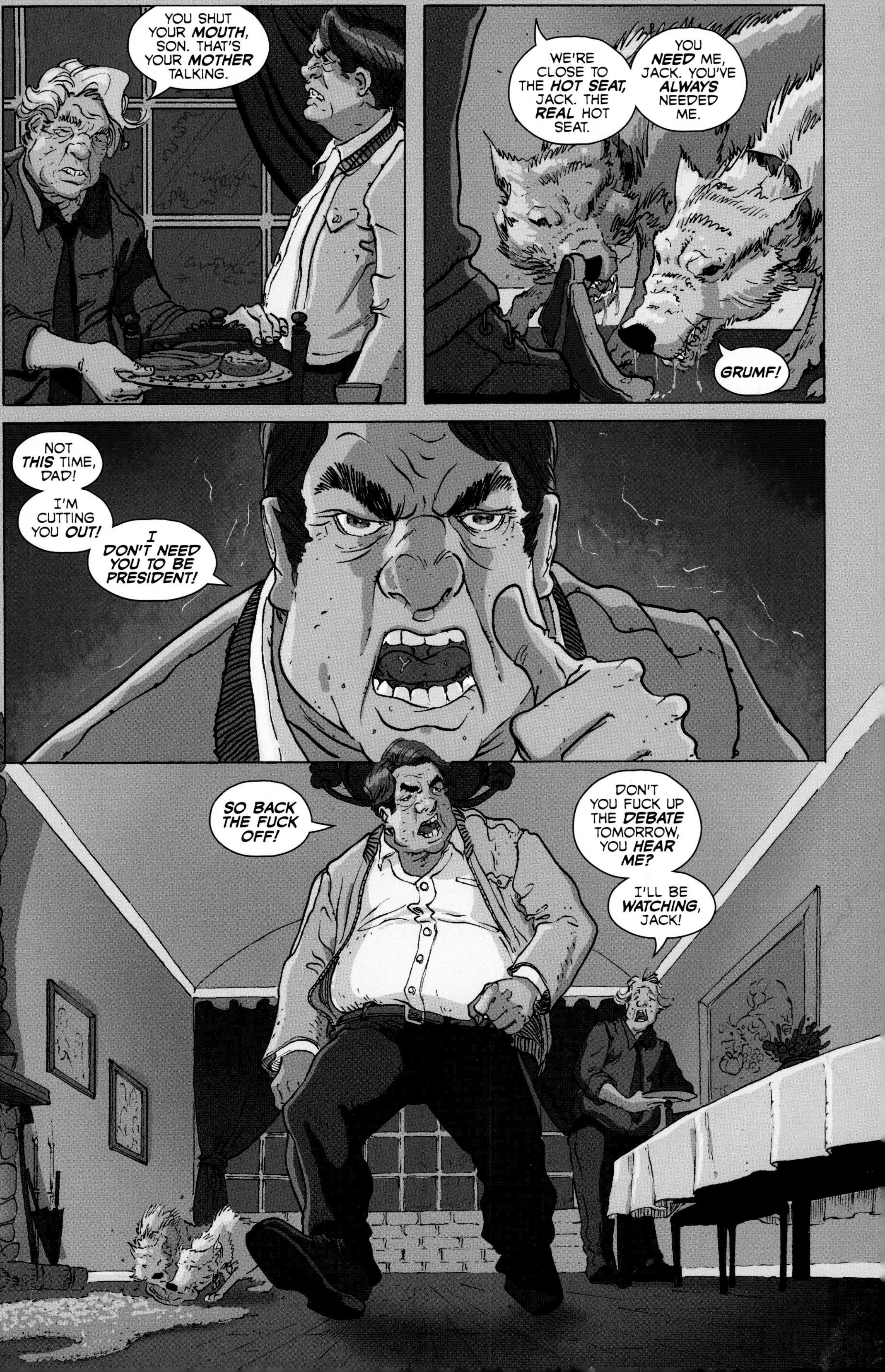
YOU SHUT YOUR MOUTH, SON. THAT'S YOUR MOTHER TALKING.
WE'RE CLOSE TO THE HOT SEAT, JACK. THE REAL HOT SEAT.
YOU NEED ME, JACK. YOU'VE ALWAYS NEEDED ME.
GRUMF!
NOT THIS TIME, DAD!
I'M CUTTING YOU OUT!
I DON'T NEED YOU TO BE PRESIDENT!
SO BACK THE FUCK OFF!
DON'T YOU FUCK UP THE DEBATE TOMORROW, YOU HEAR ME?
I'LL BE WATCHING, JACK!

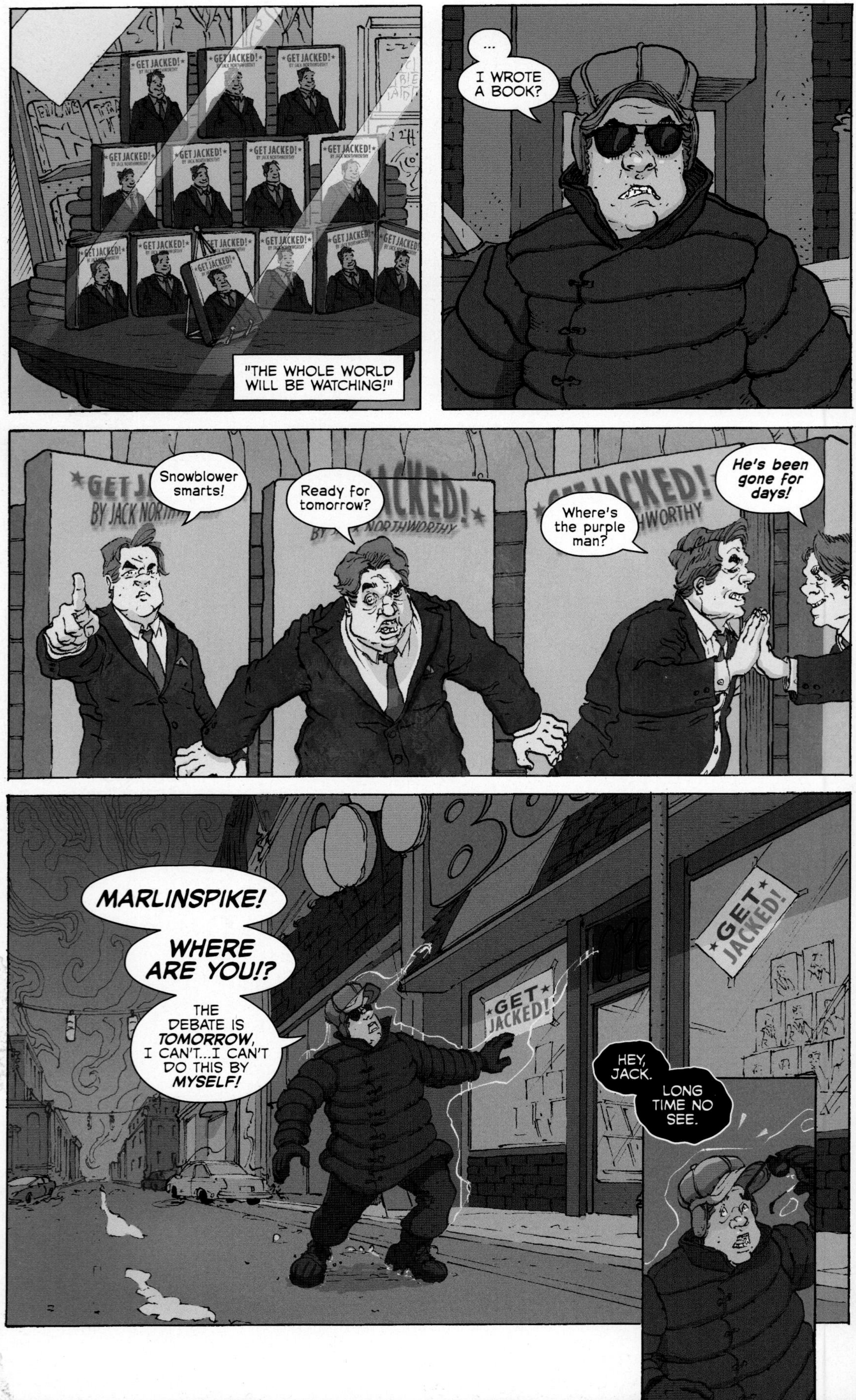
GET JACKED! BY JACK NORTHWORTHY
"THE WHOLE WORLD WILL BE WATCHING!"
...
I WROTE A BOOK?
GET JACKED! BY JACK NORTHWORTHY
Snowblower smarts!
Ready for tomorrow?
Where's the purple man?
He's been gone for days!
MARLINSPIKE!
WHERE ARE YOU!?
THE DEBATE IS TOMORROW, I CAN'T...I CAN'T DO THIS BY MYSELF!
GET JACKED!
GET JACKED!
HEY, JACK.
LONG TIME NO SEE.

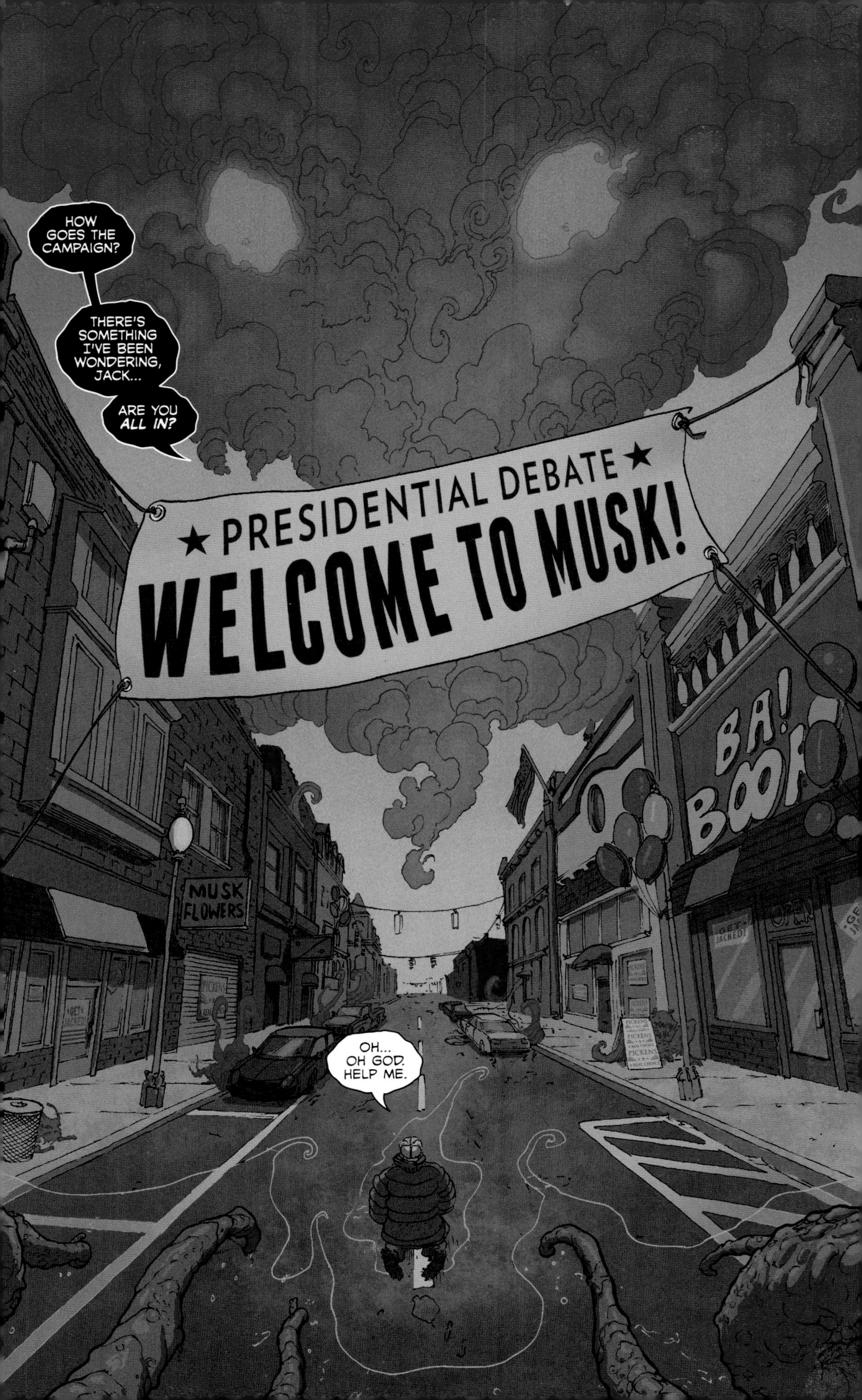
HOW GOES THE CAMPAIGN?
THERE'S SOMETHING I'VE BEEN WONDERING, JACK...
ARE YOU *ALL IN?*
★ PRESIDENTIAL DEBATE ★
WELCOME TO MUSK!
BA! BOO
MUSK FLOWERS
GET JACKED!
OPEN
PICKENS
OH... OH GOD. HELP ME.

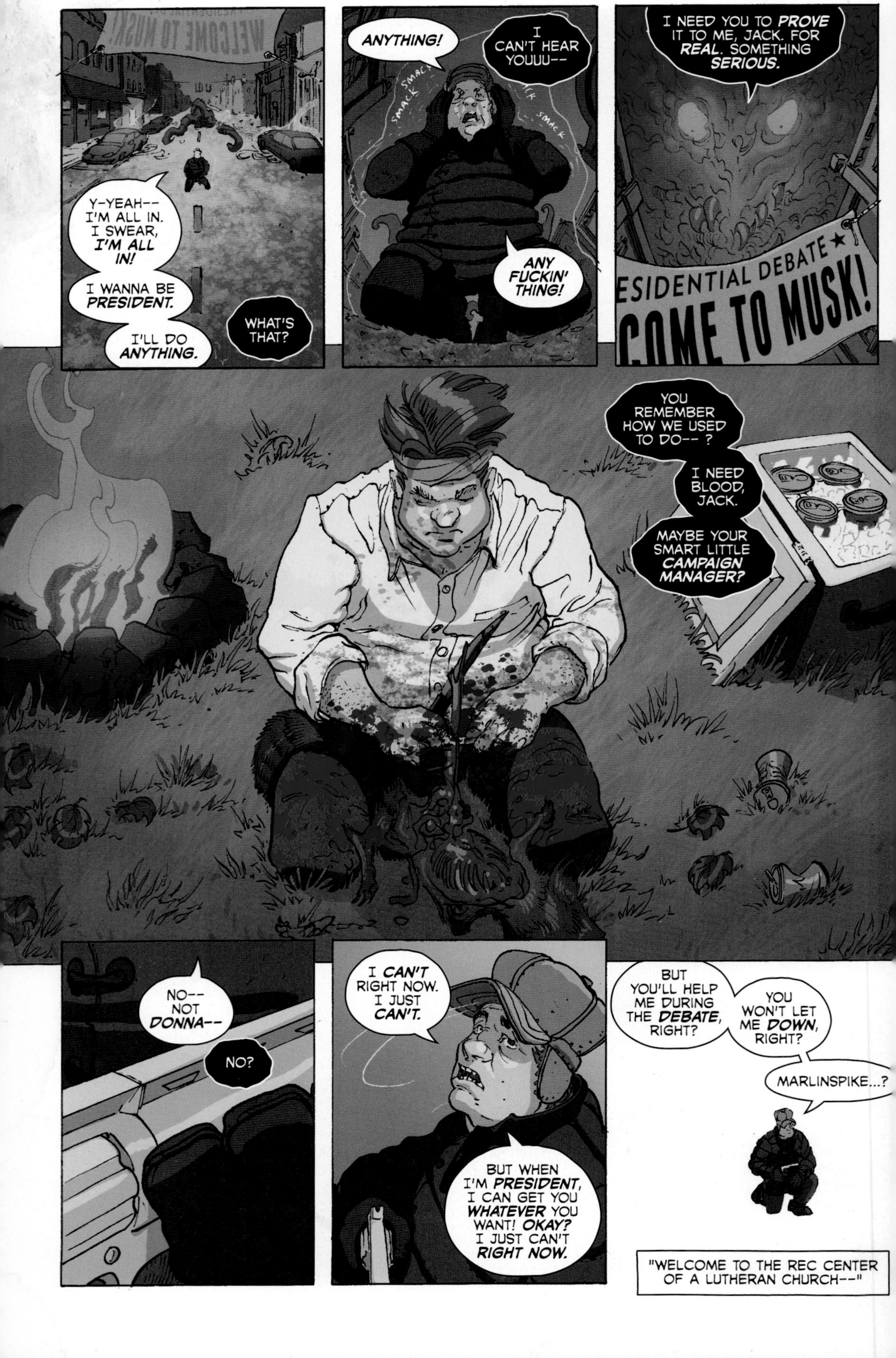

Y-YEAH--
I'M ALL IN.
I SWEAR,
I'M ALL IN!
I WANNA BE *PRESIDENT.*
I'LL DO *ANYTHING.*
WHAT'S THAT?
ANYTHING!
I CAN'T HEAR YOUUU--
SMACK
SMACK
ANY FUCKIN' THING!
I NEED YOU TO *PROVE* IT TO ME, JACK. FOR *REAL.* SOMETHING *SERIOUS.*
ESIDENTIAL DEBATE ★
COME TO MUSK!
YOU REMEMBER HOW WE USED TO DO-- ?
I NEED BLOOD, JACK.
MAYBE YOUR SMART LITTLE *CAMPAIGN MANAGER?*
NO-- NOT *DONNA--*
NO?
I *CAN'T* RIGHT NOW. I JUST *CAN'T.*
BUT WHEN I'M *PRESIDENT,* I CAN GET YOU *WHATEVER* YOU WANT! *OKAY?* I JUST CAN'T *RIGHT NOW.*
BUT YOU'LL HELP ME DURING THE *DEBATE,* RIGHT?
YOU WON'T LET ME *DOWN,* RIGHT?
MARLINSPIKE...?
"WELCOME TO THE REC CENTER OF A LUTHERAN CHURCH--"

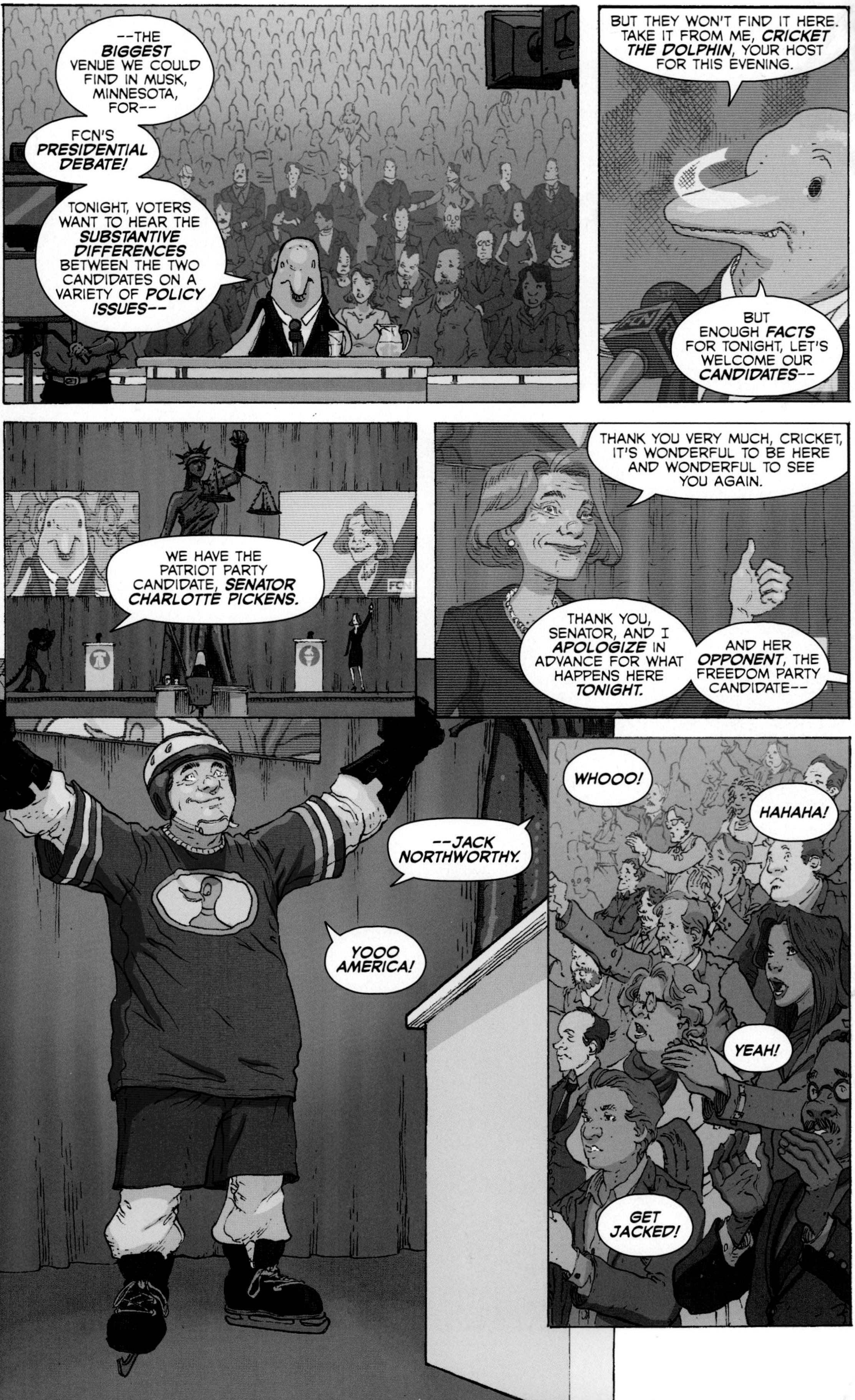
--THE BIGGEST VENUE WE COULD FIND IN MUSK, MINNESOTA, FOR--
FCN'S PRESIDENTIAL DEBATE!
TONIGHT, VOTERS WANT TO HEAR THE SUBSTANTIVE DIFFERENCES BETWEEN THE TWO CANDIDATES ON A VARIETY OF POLICY ISSUES--
BUT THEY WON'T FIND IT HERE. TAKE IT FROM ME, CRICKET THE DOLPHIN, YOUR HOST FOR THIS EVENING.
BUT ENOUGH FACTS FOR TONIGHT, LET'S WELCOME OUR CANDIDATES--
WE HAVE THE PATRIOT PARTY CANDIDATE, SENATOR CHARLOTTE PICKENS.
THANK YOU VERY MUCH, CRICKET, IT'S WONDERFUL TO BE HERE AND WONDERFUL TO SEE YOU AGAIN.
THANK YOU, SENATOR, AND I APOLOGIZE IN ADVANCE FOR WHAT HAPPENS HERE TONIGHT.
AND HER OPPONENT, THE FREEDOM PARTY CANDIDATE--
--JACK NORTHWORTHY.
YOOO AMERICA!
WHOOO!
HAHAHA!
YEAH!
GET JACKED!

QUIET FROM THE AUDIENCE...THIS ISN'T A *GAME SHOW!*

FIRST QUESTION FOR MAYOR NORTHWORTHY. SENATOR PICKENS HAS SAID YOU *LACK THE QUALIFICATIONS* TO BE PRESIDENT. DO YOU THINK YOU ARE *BEST CHOICE* FOR THE JOB?

FIRST OF ALL, YOU'RE LOOKING *GREAT,* CRICKET!

PICKENS IS A *POLITICIAN!* EVERYTHING SHE SAYS IS JARGON AND *DOUBLE-TALK!* BUT I'VE GOT SOMETHING SHE'LL NEVER HAVE--

SNOWBLOWER SMARTS!

CRICKET, MR. NORTHWORTHY'S CAMPAIGN GETS *FRUSTRATED* WHEN WE BRING THIS UP, AS WELL THEY *SHOULD.*

AMERICA NEEDS A *LEADER* IN THE WHITE HOUSE, NOT A SERIES OF OUTLANDISH *ONLINE VIDEOS.*

YOU'RE RIGHT, JACK. I'M A *POLITICIAN.* WITH SUBSTANCE, DEPTH, AND EXPERIENCE.

MR. NORTHWORTHY, YOU ARE A *PERFORMER* AND A *PHONY,* AS YOU YOURSELF HAVE PROVEN TONIGHT WITH YOUR *LITTLE COSTUME.*

YOU HAVE NO *PRINCIPLES,* YOU HAVE NO *VALUES--* ALL YOU HAVE IS *SCHTICK,* AND I DARE YOU--

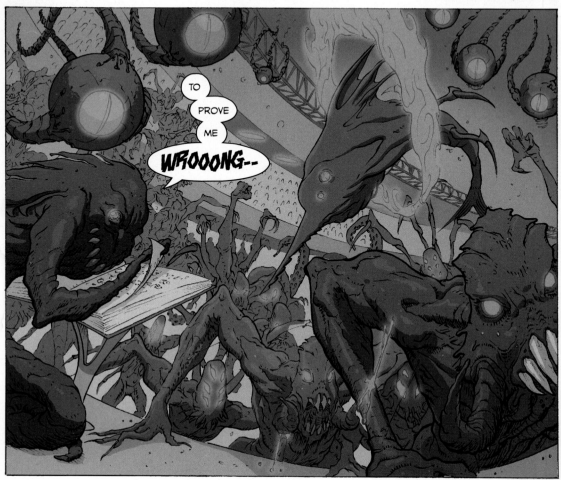

TO PROVE ME *WROOONG--*

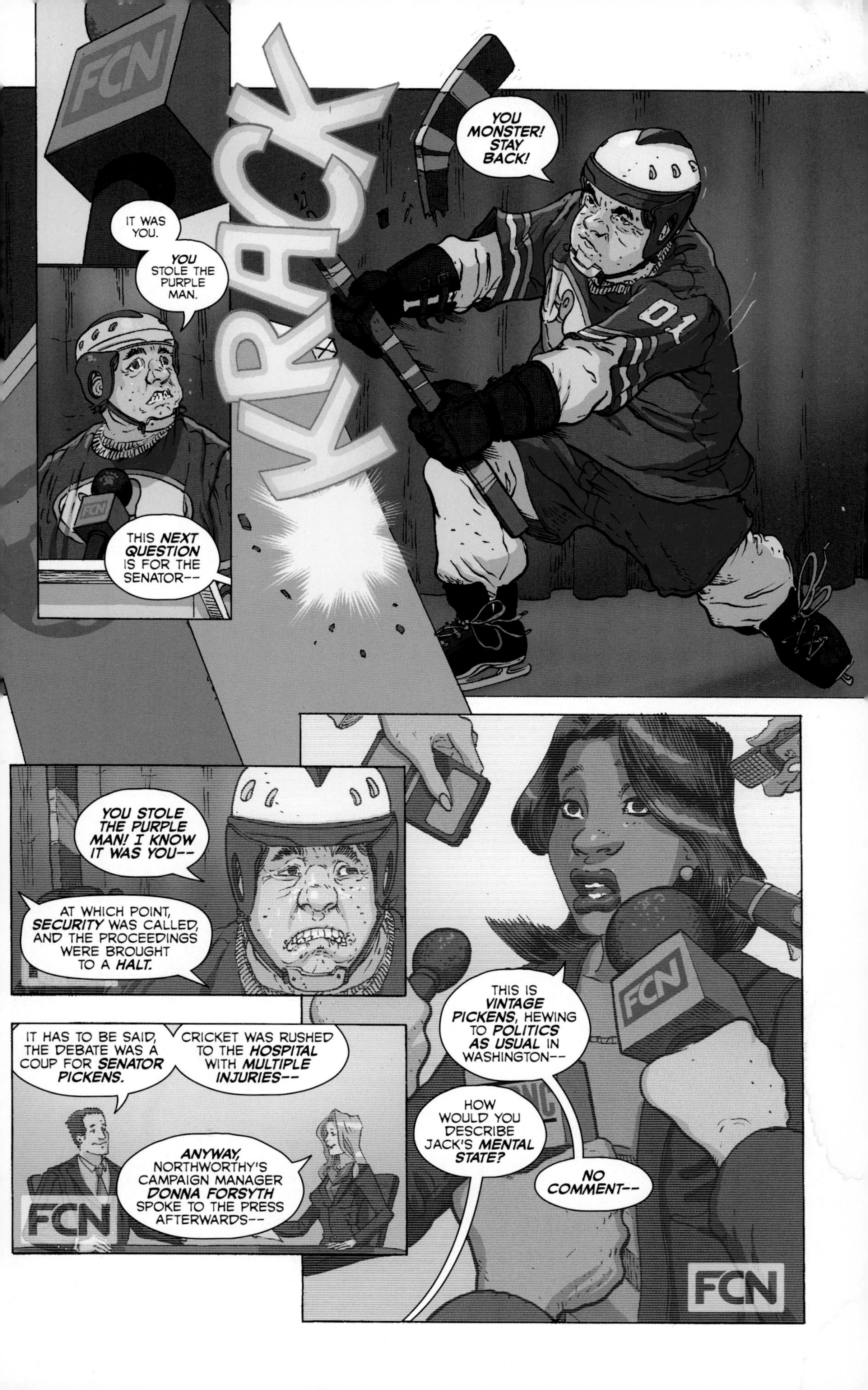

FCN
KRACK
YOU MONSTER! STAY BACK!
IT WAS YOU.
YOU STOLE THE PURPLE MAN.
FCN
THIS NEXT QUESTION IS FOR THE SENATOR--
YOU STOLE THE PURPLE MAN! I KNOW IT WAS YOU--
AT WHICH POINT, SECURITY WAS CALLED, AND THE PROCEEDINGS WERE BROUGHT TO A HALT.
IT HAS TO BE SAID, THE DEBATE WAS A COUP FOR SENATOR PICKENS.
CRICKET WAS RUSHED TO THE HOSPITAL WITH MULTIPLE INJURIES--
ANYWAY, NORTHWORTHY'S CAMPAIGN MANAGER DONNA FORSYTH SPOKE TO THE PRESS AFTERWARDS--
FCN
THIS IS VINTAGE PICKENS, HEWING TO POLITICS AS USUAL IN WASHINGTON--
FCN
HOW WOULD YOU DESCRIBE JACK'S MENTAL STATE?
NO COMMENT--
FCN

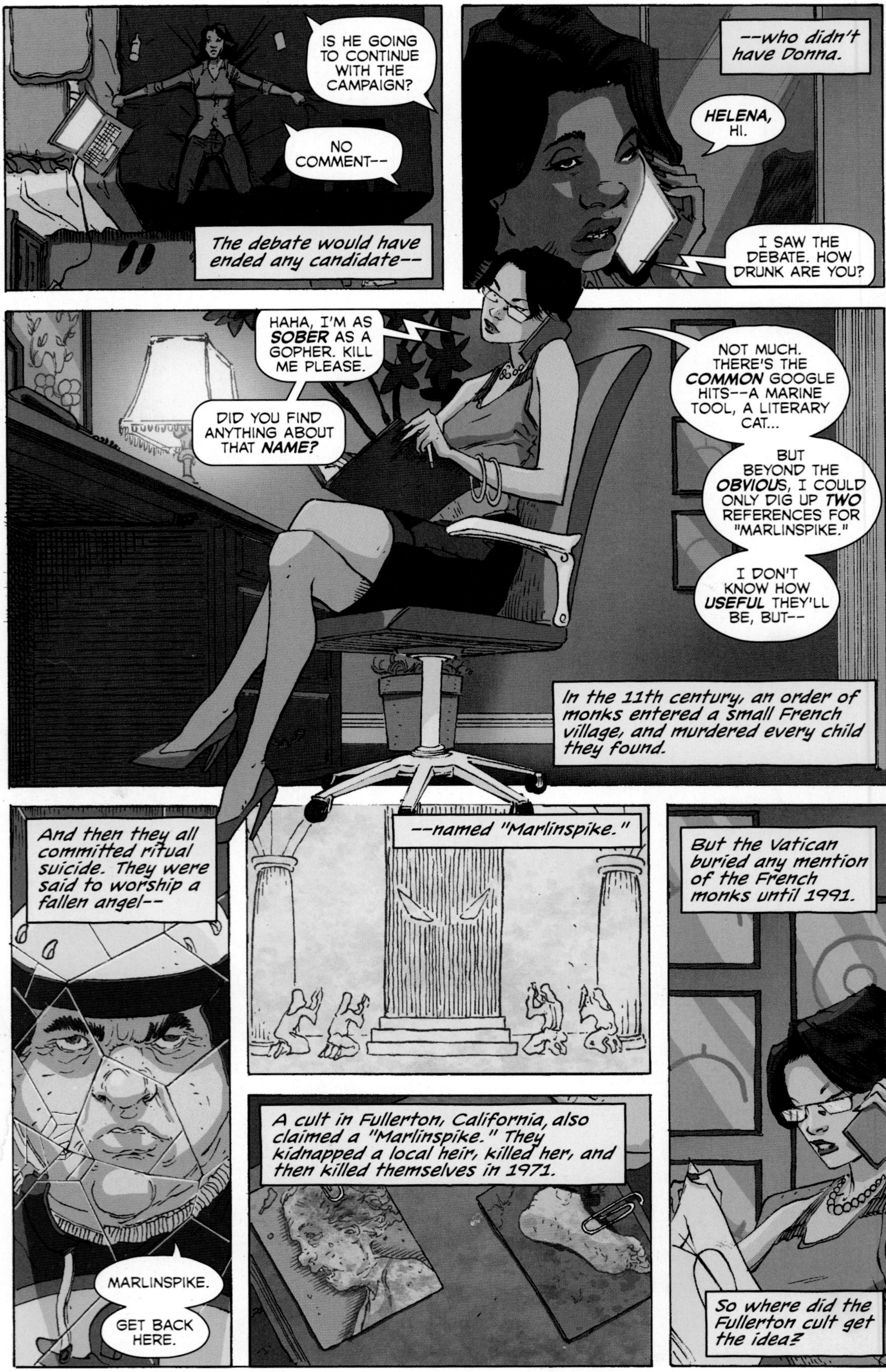
IS HE GOING TO CONTINUE WITH THE CAMPAIGN?
NO COMMENT--
The debate would have ended any candidate--
--who didn't have Donna.
HELENA, HI.
I SAW THE DEBATE. HOW DRUNK ARE YOU?
HAHA, I'M AS SOBER AS A GOPHER. KILL ME PLEASE.
DID YOU FIND ANYTHING ABOUT THAT NAME?
NOT MUCH. THERE'S THE COMMON GOOGLE HITS--A MARINE TOOL, A LITERARY CAT...
BUT BEYOND THE OBVIOUS, I COULD ONLY DIG UP TWO REFERENCES FOR "MARLINSPIKE."
I DON'T KNOW HOW USEFUL THEY'LL BE, BUT--
In the 11th century, an order of monks entered a small French village, and murdered every child they found.
And then they all committed ritual suicide. They were said to worship a fallen angel--
--named "Marlinspike."
But the Vatican buried any mention of the French monks until 1991.
MARLINSPIKE.
GET BACK HERE.
A cult in Fullerton, California, also claimed a "Marlinspike." They kidnapped a local heir, killed her, and then killed themselves in 1971.
So where did the Fullerton cult get the idea?

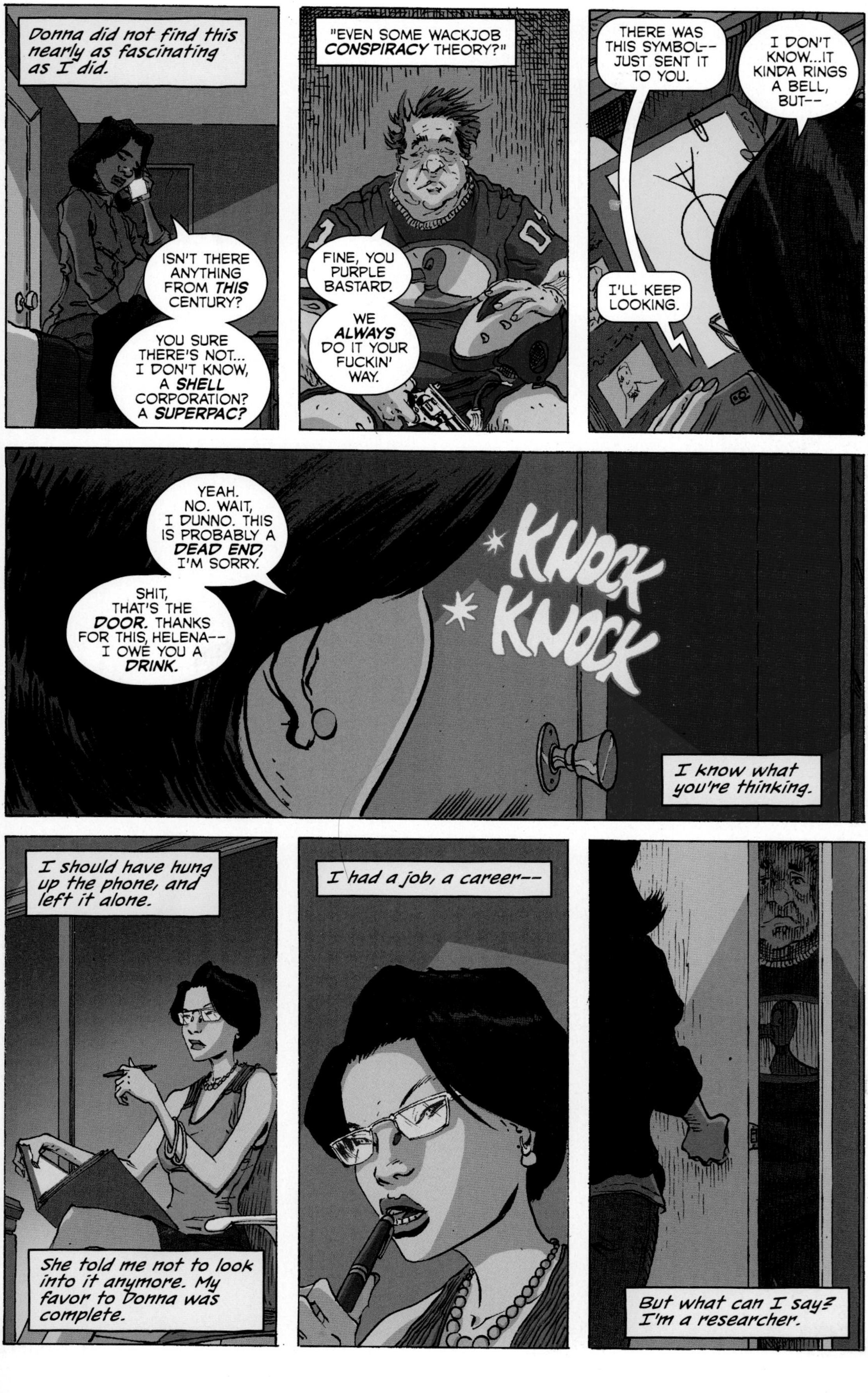
Donna did not find this nearly as fascinating as I did.
ISN'T THERE ANYTHING FROM THIS CENTURY?
YOU SURE THERE'S NOT... I DON'T KNOW, A SHELL CORPORATION? A SUPERPAC?
"EVEN SOME WACKJOB CONSPIRACY THEORY?"
FINE, YOU PURPLE BASTARD.
WE ALWAYS DO IT YOUR FUCKIN' WAY.
THERE WAS THIS SYMBOL-- JUST SENT IT TO YOU.
I DON'T KNOW...IT KINDA RINGS A BELL, BUT--
I'LL KEEP LOOKING.
YEAH. NO. WAIT, I DUNNO. THIS IS PROBABLY A DEAD END, I'M SORRY.
SHIT, THAT'S THE DOOR. THANKS FOR THIS, HELENA-- I OWE YOU A DRINK.
KNOCK KNOCK
I know what you're thinking.
I should have hung up the phone, and left it alone.
She told me not to look into it anymore. My favor to Donna was complete.
I had a job, a career--
But what can I say? I'm a researcher.

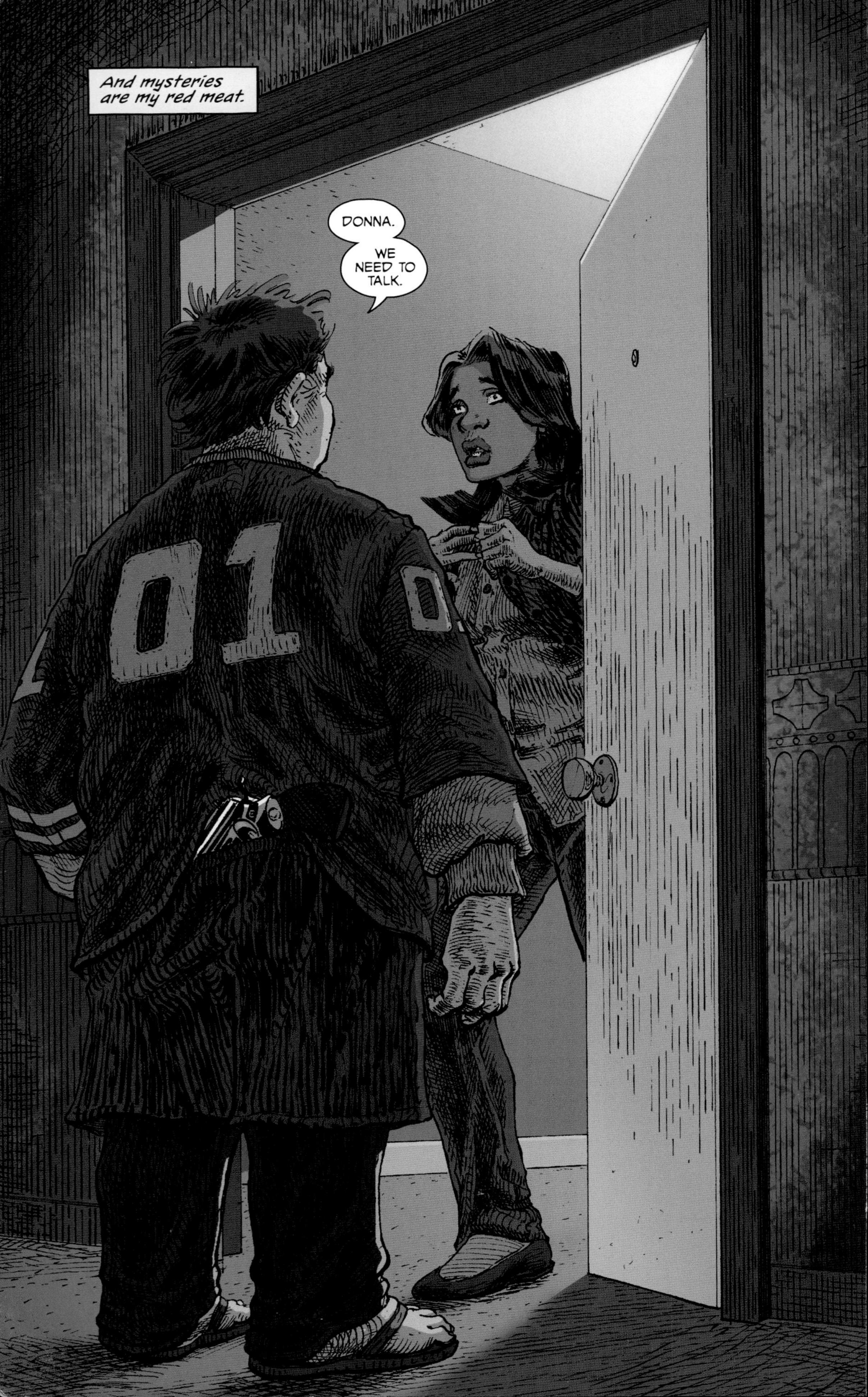
And mysteries are my red meat.
DONNA.
WE NEED TO TALK.
01

AND NOW *YOU'RE* GONNA QUIT ON ME TOO, RIGHT?

I'M *DEAD WEIGHT*. YOU'RE AFRAID I'M GONNA *DRAG* YOU DOWN WITH ME..

WHO WERE YOU ON THE PHONE WITH?

...

JOHN FROM PUBLICITY. FIRE FIGHT *CANCELLED* THE INTERVIEW.

SEEING AS HOW YOU *ATTACKED* THEIR HOST AND ALL...

JACK, TONIGHT WAS... A *DISASTER*. SURE.

BUT A CAMPAIGN IS MADE OF *MONTHS*, NOT *ONE NIGHT*.

WE'RE NOT DEAD *YET*, BUT--

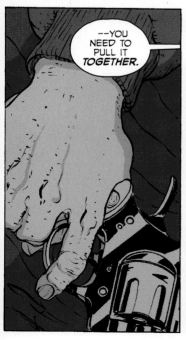

--YOU NEED TO PULL IT *TOGETHER*.

DONNA--

I CAN'T--

YES YOU *CAN*, JACK.

I'LL *HELP* YOU. WE'LL DO IT *TOGETHER*.

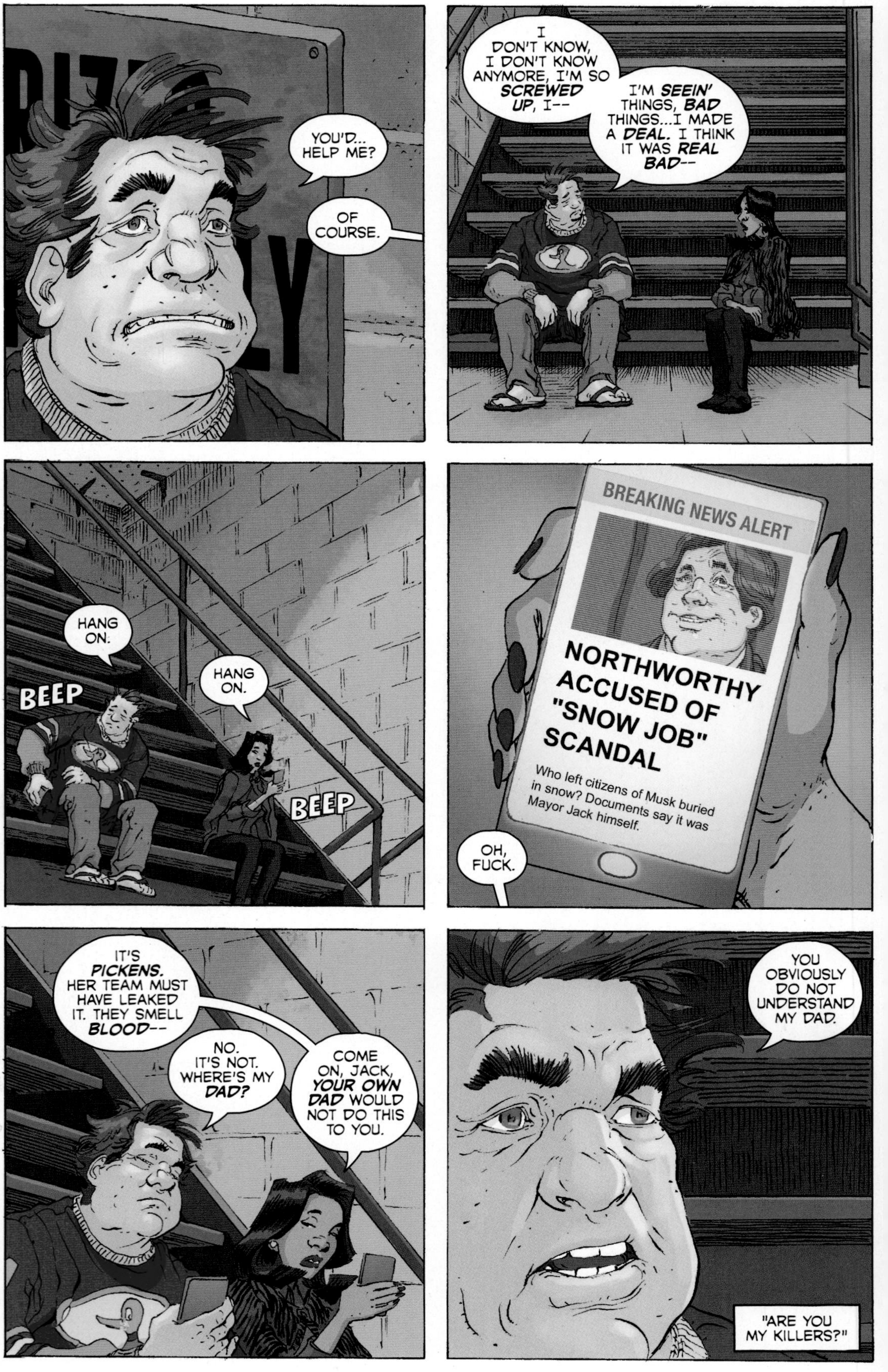

YOU'D.. HELP ME?
OF COURSE.
I DON'T KNOW, I DON'T KNOW ANYMORE, I'M SO *SCREWED UP*, I--
I'M *SEEIN'* THINGS, *BAD* THINGS...I MADE A *DEAL.* I THINK IT WAS *REAL BAD*--
HANG ON.
BEEP
HANG ON.
BEEP
BREAKING NEWS ALERT
NORTHWORTHY ACCUSED OF "SNOW JOB" SCANDAL
Who left citizens of Musk buried in snow? Documents say it was Mayor Jack himself.
OH, FUCK.
IT'S *PICKENS.* HER TEAM MUST HAVE LEAKED IT. THEY SMELL *BLOOD*--
NO. IT'S NOT. WHERE'S MY *DAD?*
COME ON, JACK, *YOUR OWN DAD* WOULD NOT DO THIS TO YOU.
YOU OBVIOUSLY DO NOT UNDERSTAND MY DAD.
"ARE YOU MY KILLERS?"

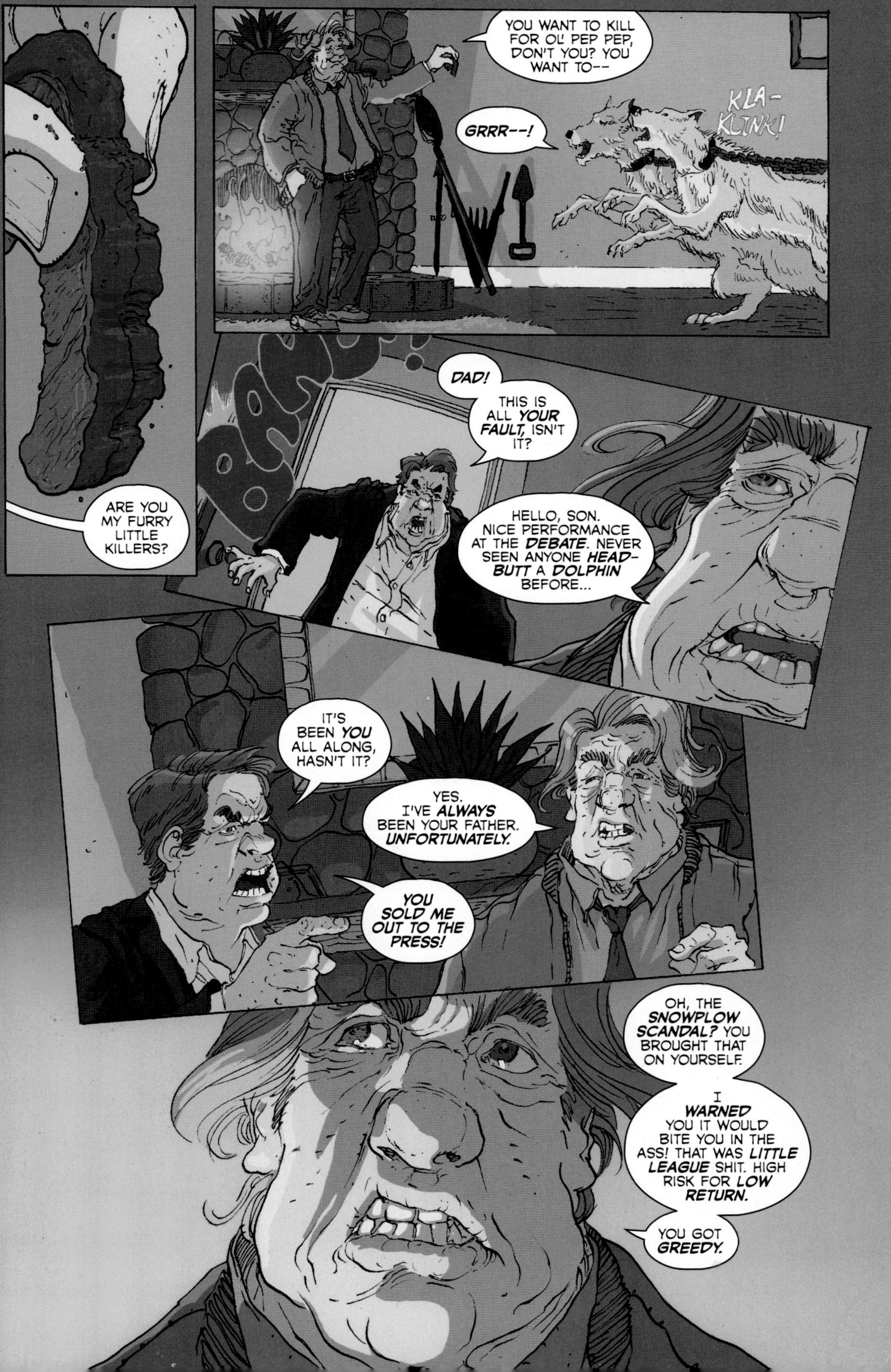
ARE YOU MY FURRY LITTLE KILLERS?
YOU WANT TO KILL FOR OL' PEP PEP, DON'T YOU? YOU WANT TO--
GRRR--!
KLA-KLINK!
DAD!
THIS IS ALL YOUR FAULT, ISN'T IT?
HELLO, SON. NICE PERFORMANCE AT THE DEBATE. NEVER SEEN ANYONE HEAD-BUTT A DOLPHIN BEFORE...
IT'S BEEN YOU ALL ALONG, HASN'T IT?
YES. I'VE ALWAYS BEEN YOUR FATHER. UNFORTUNATELY.
YOU SOLD ME OUT TO THE PRESS!
OH, THE SNOWPLOW SCANDAL? YOU BROUGHT THAT ON YOURSELF.
I WARNED YOU IT WOULD BITE YOU IN THE ASS! THAT WAS LITTLE LEAGUE SHIT. HIGH RISK FOR LOW RETURN.
YOU GOT GREEDY.

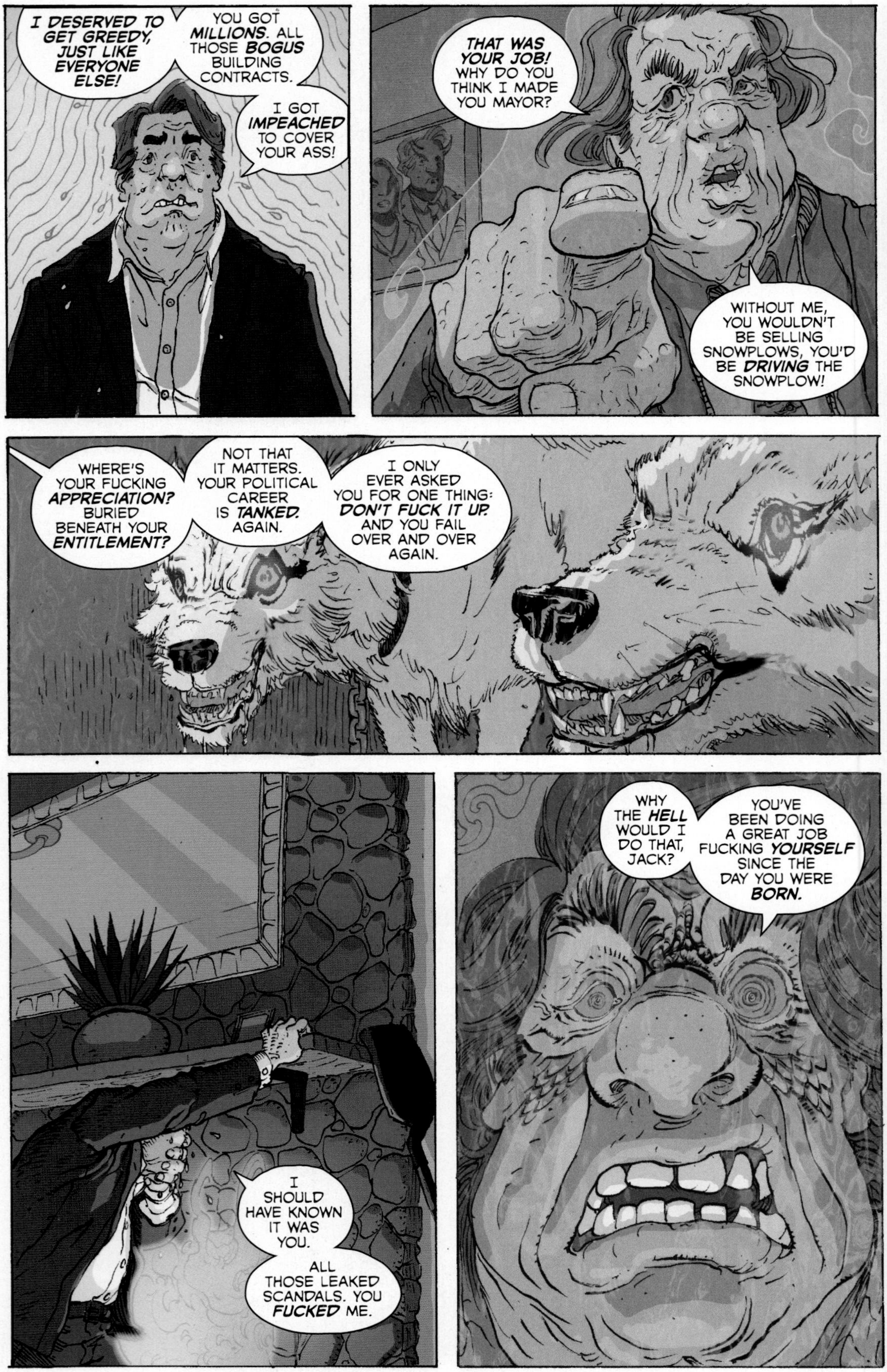
I DESERVED TO GET GREEDY, JUST LIKE EVERYONE ELSE!
YOU GOT MILLIONS. ALL THOSE BOGUS BUILDING CONTRACTS.
I GOT IMPEACHED TO COVER YOUR ASS!
THAT WAS YOUR JOB! WHY DO YOU THINK I MADE YOU MAYOR?
WITHOUT ME, YOU WOULDN'T BE SELLING SNOWPLOWS, YOU'D BE DRIVING THE SNOWPLOW!
WHERE'S YOUR FUCKING APPRECIATION? BURIED BENEATH YOUR ENTITLEMENT?
NOT THAT IT MATTERS. YOUR POLITICAL CAREER IS TANKED. AGAIN.
I ONLY EVER ASKED YOU FOR ONE THING: DON'T FUCK IT UP. AND YOU FAIL OVER AND OVER AGAIN.
I SHOULD HAVE KNOWN IT WAS YOU.
ALL THOSE LEAKED SCANDALS. YOU FUCKED ME.
WHY THE HELL WOULD I DO THAT, JACK?
YOU'VE BEEN DOING A GREAT JOB FUCKING YOURSELF SINCE THE DAY YOU WERE BORN.

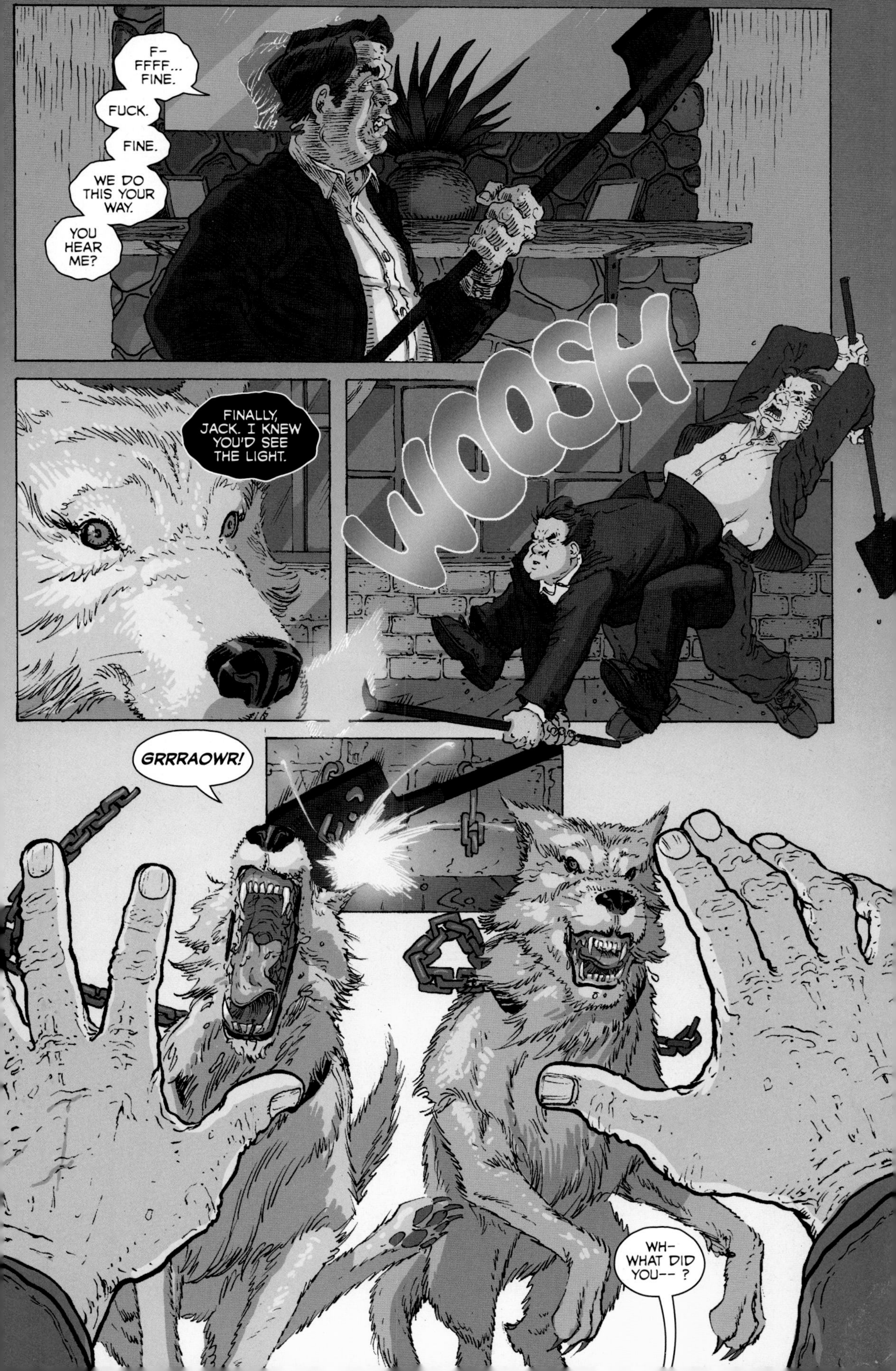
F-
FFFF... FINE.
FUCK.
FINE.
WE DO THIS YOUR WAY.
YOU HEAR ME?
FINALLY, JACK. I KNEW YOU'D SEE THE LIGHT.
WOOSH
GRRRAOWR!
WH- WHAT DID YOU-- ?

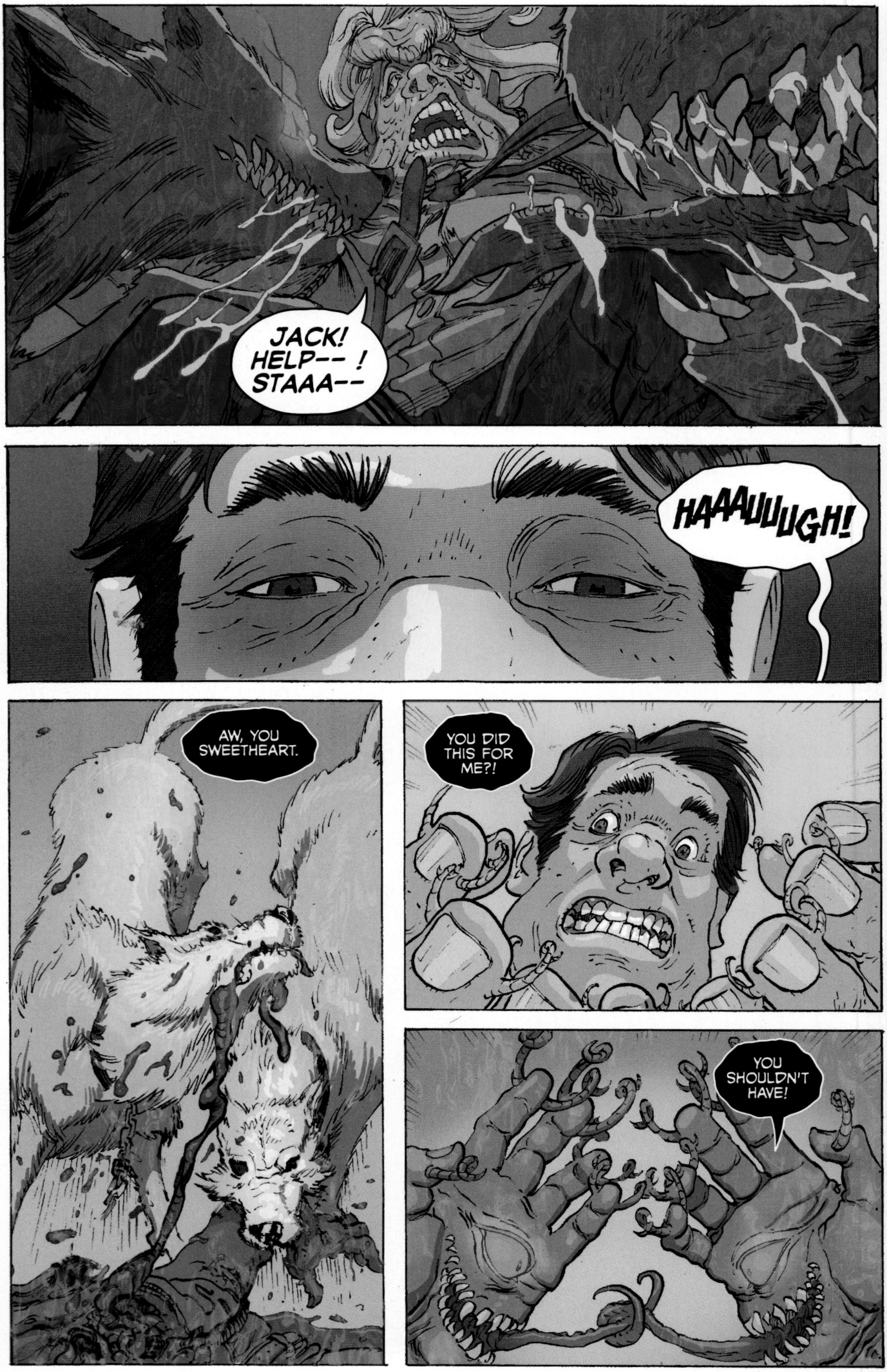
JACK! HELP-- ! STAAA--
HAAAUUUGH!
AW, YOU SWEETHEART.
YOU DID THIS FOR ME?!
YOU SHOULDN'T HAVE!

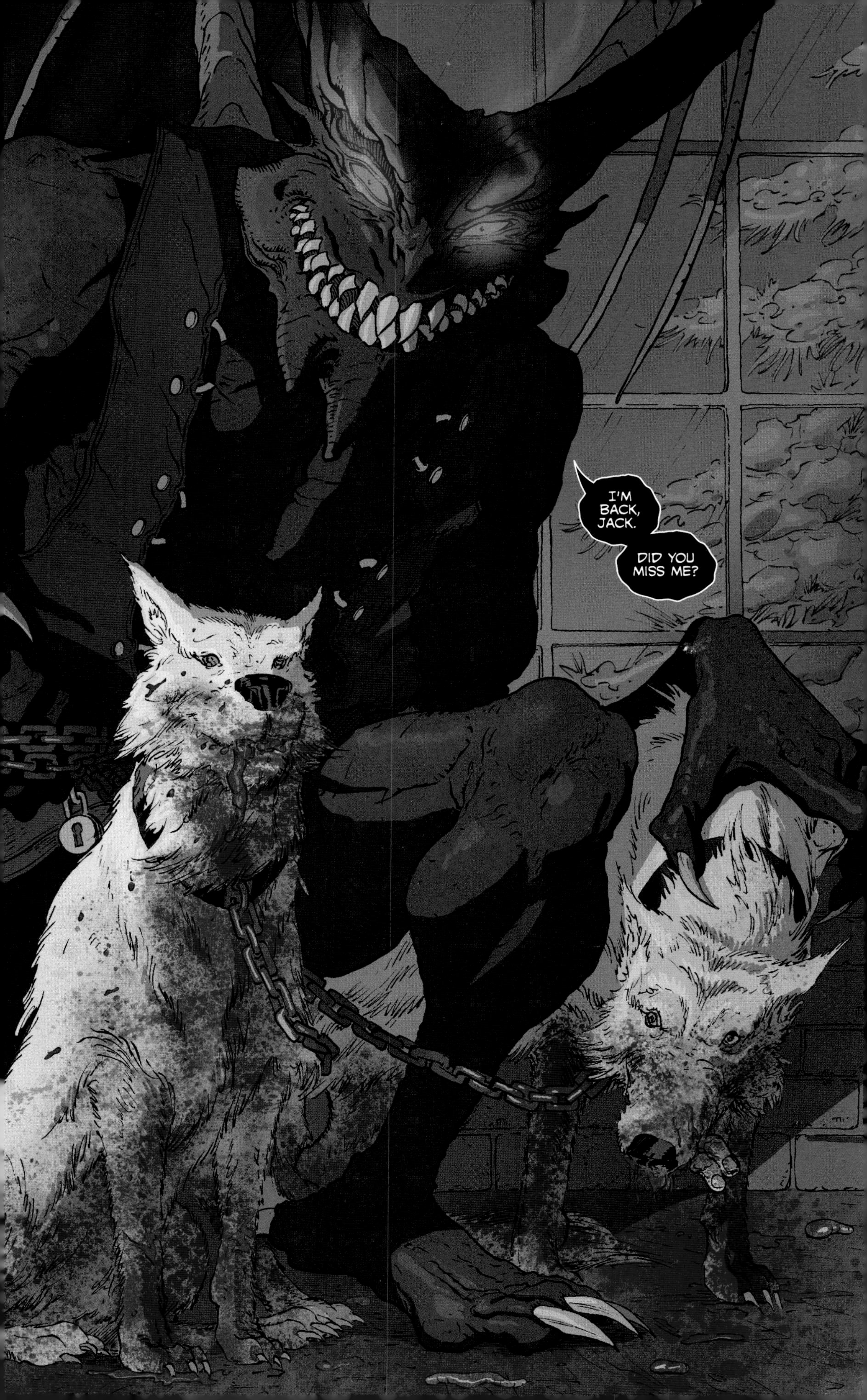
I'M BACK, JACK.
DID YOU MISS ME?

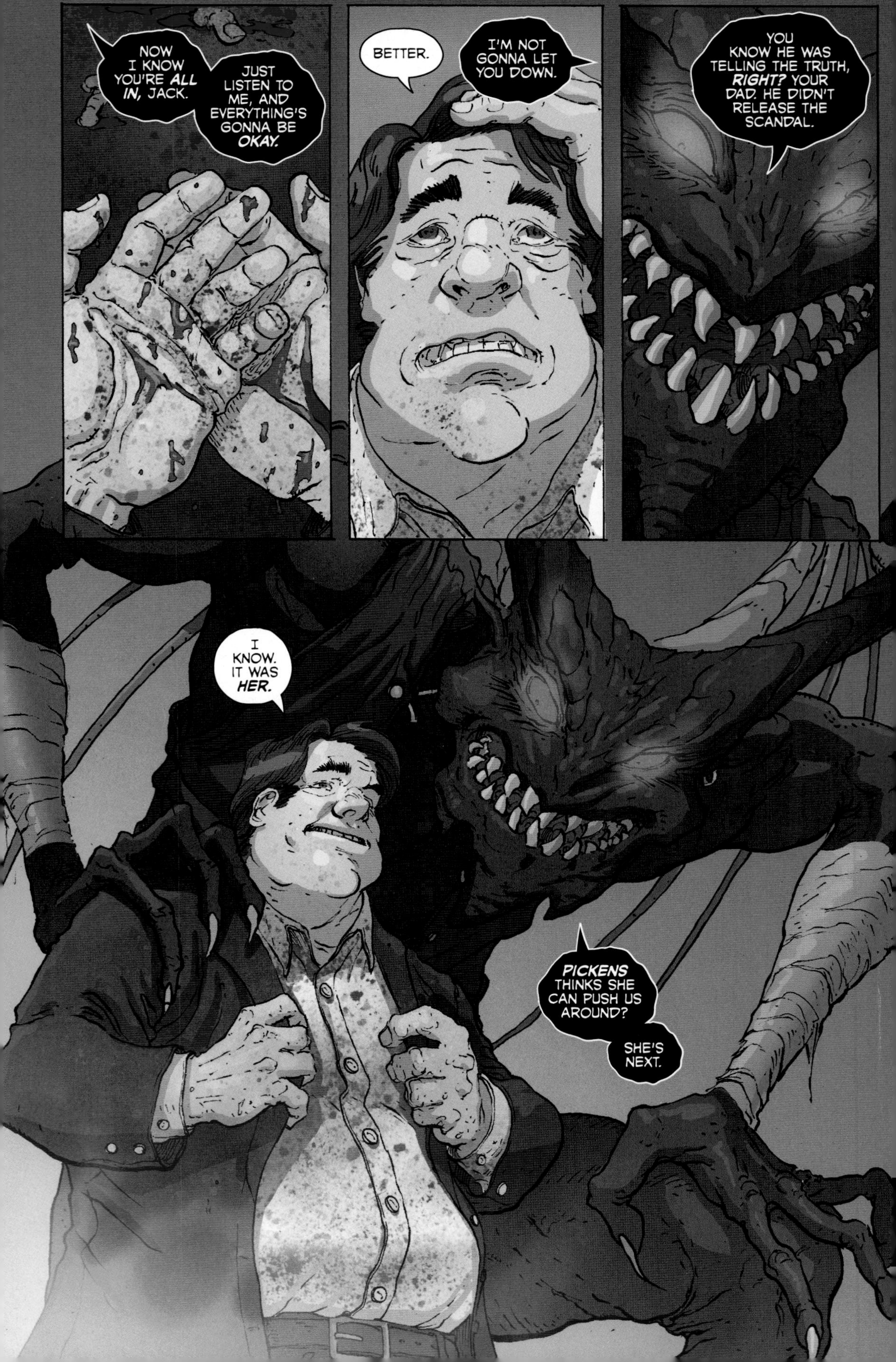
NOW I KNOW YOU'RE ALL IN, JACK.
JUST LISTEN TO ME, AND EVERYTHING'S GONNA BE OKAY.
BETTER.
I'M NOT GONNA LET YOU DOWN.
YOU KNOW HE WAS TELLING THE TRUTH, RIGHT? YOUR DAD. HE DIDN'T RELEASE THE SCANDAL.
I KNOW. IT WAS HER.
PICKENS THINKS SHE CAN PUSH US AROUND?
SHE'S NEXT.

CHAPTER 5
THE ABYSS

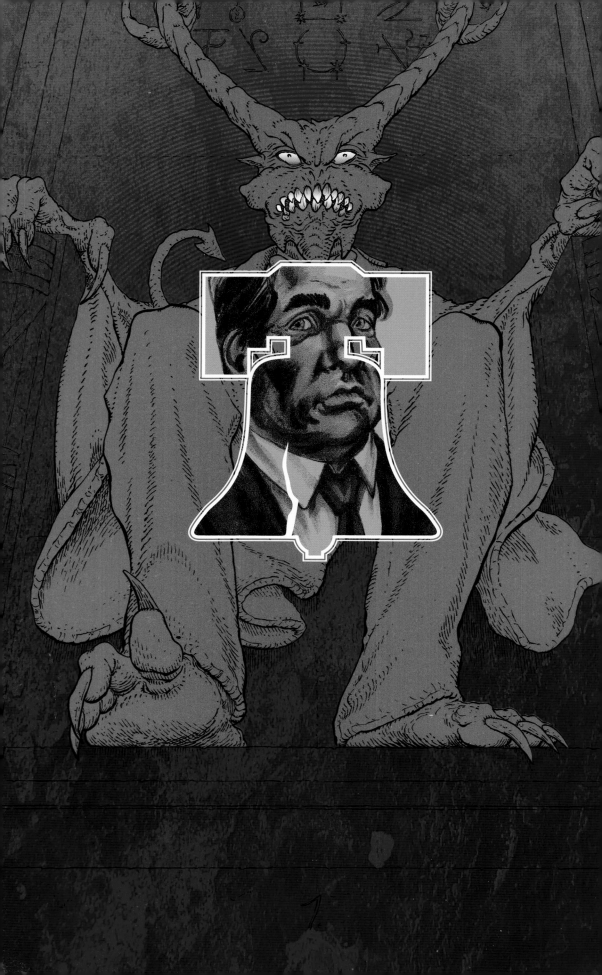

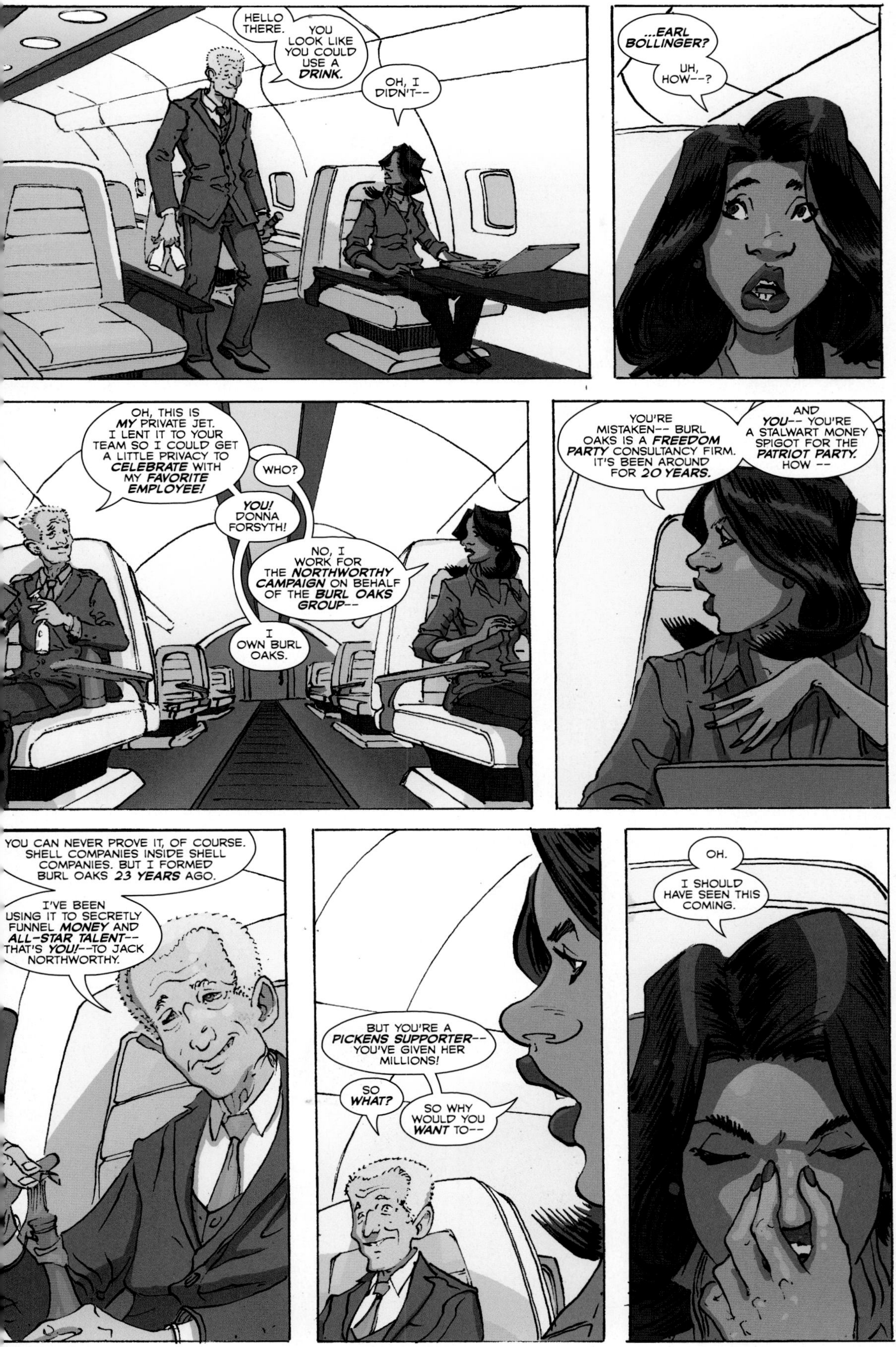
HELLO THERE.
YOU LOOK LIKE YOU COULD USE A DRINK.
OH, I DIDN'T--
...EARL BOLLINGER?
UH, HOW--?
OH, THIS IS MY PRIVATE JET. I LENT IT TO YOUR TEAM SO I COULD GET A LITTLE PRIVACY TO CELEBRATE WITH MY FAVORITE EMPLOYEE!
WHO?
YOU! DONNA FORSYTH!
NO, I WORK FOR THE NORTHWORTHY CAMPAIGN ON BEHALF OF THE BURL OAKS GROUP--
I OWN BURL OAKS.
YOU'RE MISTAKEN-- BURL OAKS IS A FREEDOM PARTY CONSULTANCY FIRM. IT'S BEEN AROUND FOR 20 YEARS.
AND YOU-- YOU'RE A STALWART MONEY SPIGOT FOR THE PATRIOT PARTY. HOW --
YOU CAN NEVER PROVE IT, OF COURSE. SHELL COMPANIES INSIDE SHELL COMPANIES. BUT I FORMED BURL OAKS 23 YEARS AGO.
I'VE BEEN USING IT TO SECRETLY FUNNEL MONEY AND ALL-STAR TALENT-- THAT'S YOU!--TO JACK NORTHWORTHY.
BUT YOU'RE A PICKENS SUPPORTER-- YOU'VE GIVEN HER MILLIONS!
SO WHAT?
SO WHY WOULD YOU WANT TO--
OH.
I SHOULD HAVE SEEN THIS COMING.

YOU WANT PICKENS IN THE *WHITE HOUSE.* YOU THOUGHT HER PRESUMED RIVAL *HONEYCUTT* WAS LOOKING *TOUGHER* THAN YOU'D LIKE.

YOU FINANCED *JACK* TO BEAT UP HONEYCUTT IN THE *PRIMARIES,* SO HONEYCUTT WOULD BE *WEAK* AGAINST *PICKENS* IN THE *GENERAL ELECTION,* AND--

CORRECTAMUNDO!

LOOKED LIKE A *SLAM DUNK* FOR PICKENS. EXCEEEEPT--

THOK

HONEYCUTT *DIED.*

R.I.P. GOOD MAN. CRYING SHAME. A WASTE OF A PERFECTLY *TENDERIZED STEAK.*

AND *NOW...*

NOW YOU HAVE TO FACE JACK.

JACK HAS GONE MUCH FURTHER THAN ANY OF US THOUGHT. THAT'S A *COMPLIMENT,* DONNA. FRANKLY, I THOUGHT HE WAS *UNELECTABLE.*

YOU'VE BEEN A *GOOD SOLDIER.* YOU'VE BEEN OUT IN THE *COLD* FOR TOO LONG. TIME TO COME BACK TO THE WARM EMBRACE OF YOUR HOME, THE *PATRIOT PARTY.*

YOU WANT ME TO QUIT JACK'S CAMPAIGN.

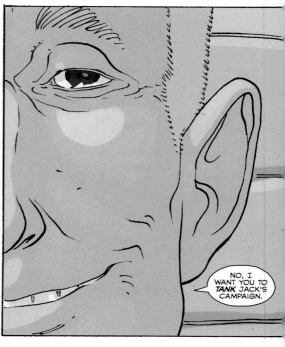

NO, I WANT YOU TO *TANK* JACK'S CAMPAIGN.

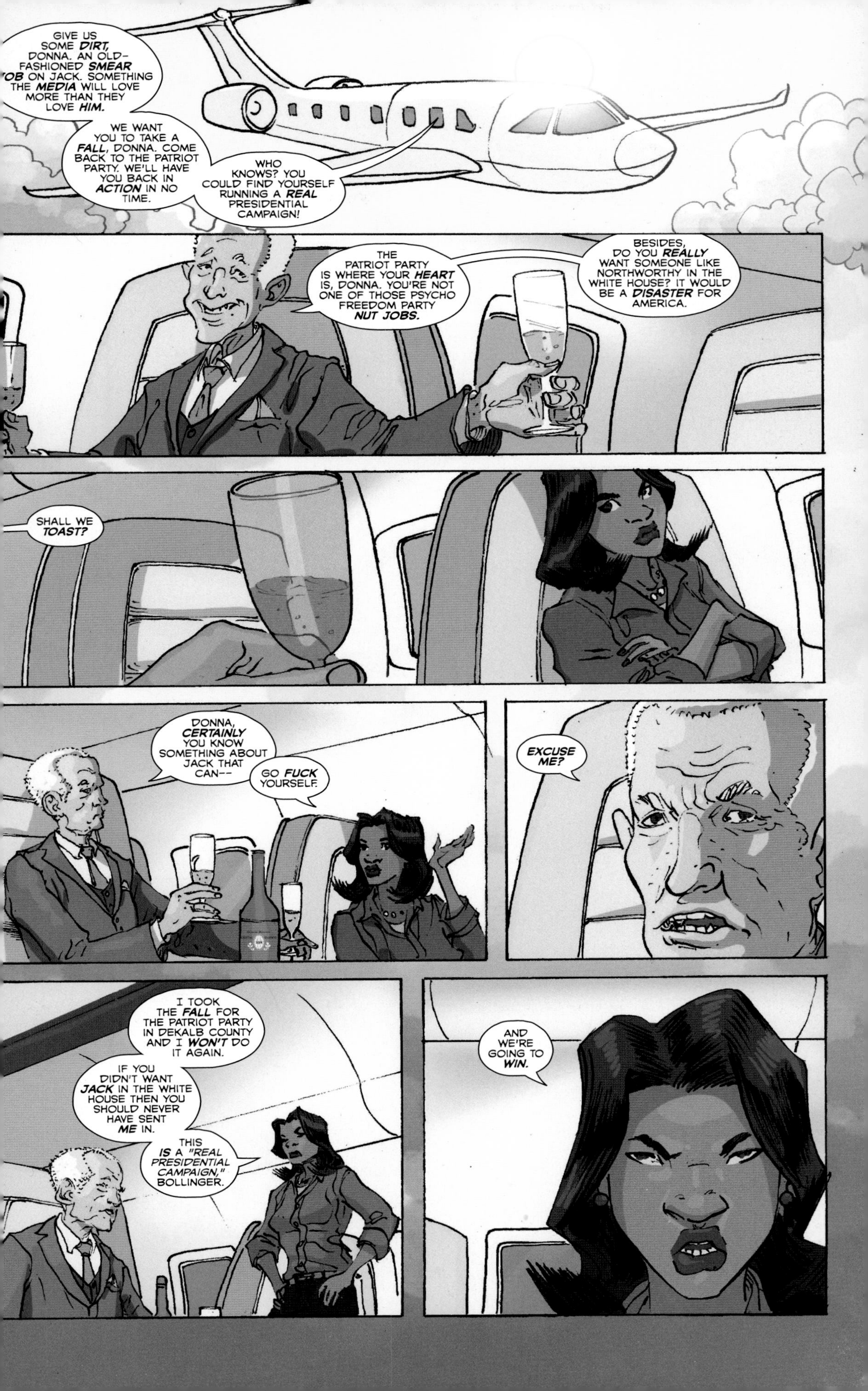
GIVE US SOME DIRT, DONNA. AN OLD-FASHIONED SMEAR JOB ON JACK. SOMETHING THE MEDIA WILL LOVE MORE THAN THEY LOVE HIM.
WE WANT YOU TO TAKE A FALL, DONNA. COME BACK TO THE PATRIOT PARTY. WE'LL HAVE YOU BACK IN ACTION IN NO TIME.
WHO KNOWS? YOU COULD FIND YOURSELF RUNNING A REAL PRESIDENTIAL CAMPAIGN!
THE PATRIOT PARTY IS WHERE YOUR HEART IS, DONNA. YOU'RE NOT ONE OF THOSE PSYCHO FREEDOM PARTY NUT JOBS.
BESIDES, DO YOU REALLY WANT SOMEONE LIKE NORTHWORTHY IN THE WHITE HOUSE? IT WOULD BE A DISASTER FOR AMERICA.
SHALL WE TOAST?
DONNA, CERTAINLY YOU KNOW SOMETHING ABOUT JACK THAT CAN--
GO FUCK YOURSELF.
EXCUSE ME?
I TOOK THE FALL FOR THE PATRIOT PARTY IN DEKALB COUNTY AND I WON'T DO IT AGAIN.
IF YOU DIDN'T WANT JACK IN THE WHITE HOUSE THEN YOU SHOULD NEVER HAVE SENT ME IN.
THIS IS A "REAL PRESIDENTIAL CAMPAIGN," BOLLINGER.
AND WE'RE GOING TO WIN.

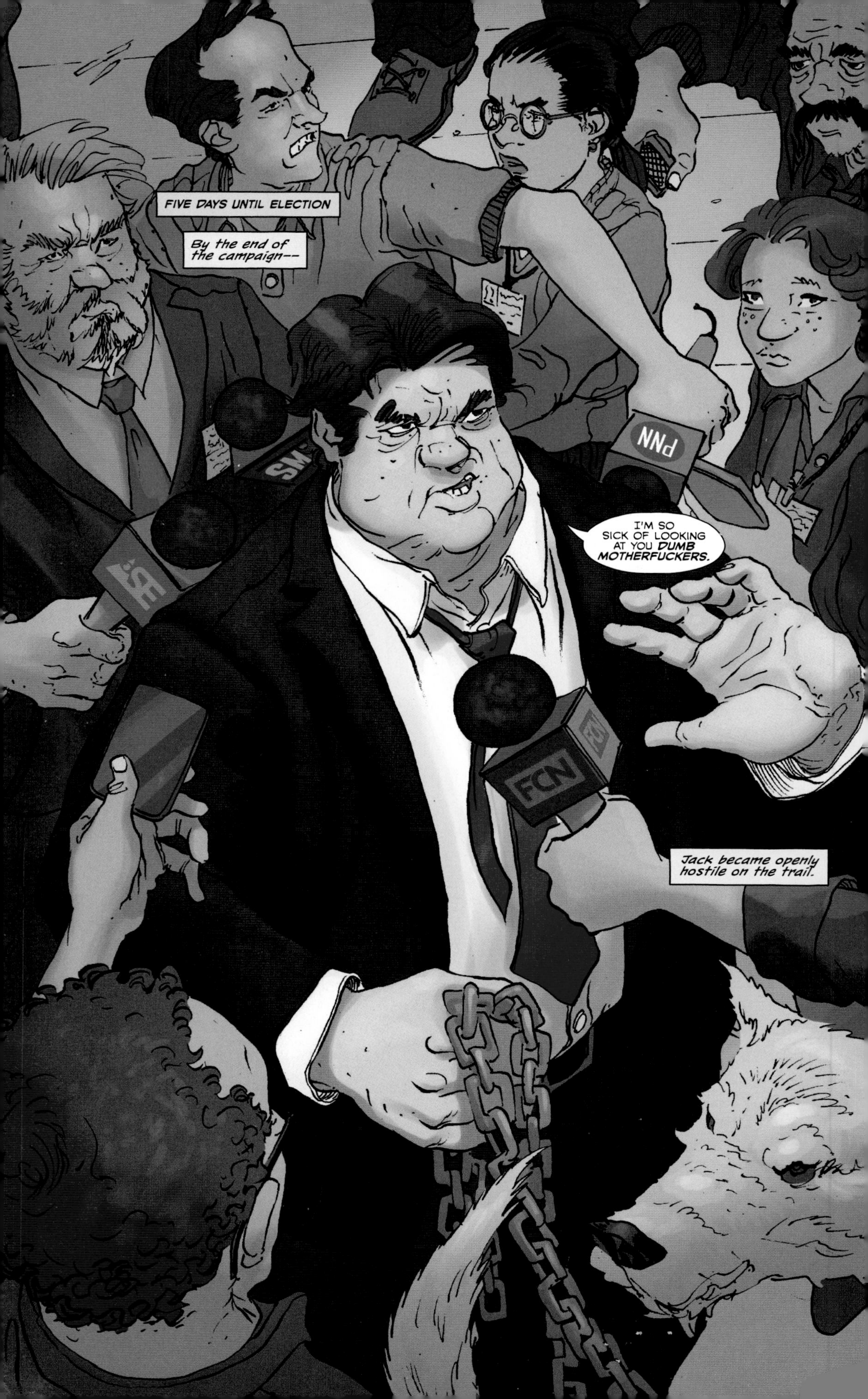
FIVE DAYS UNTIL ELECTION
By the end of the campaign--
I'M SO SICK OF LOOKING AT YOU DUMB MOTHERFUCKERS.
Jack became openly hostile on the trail.

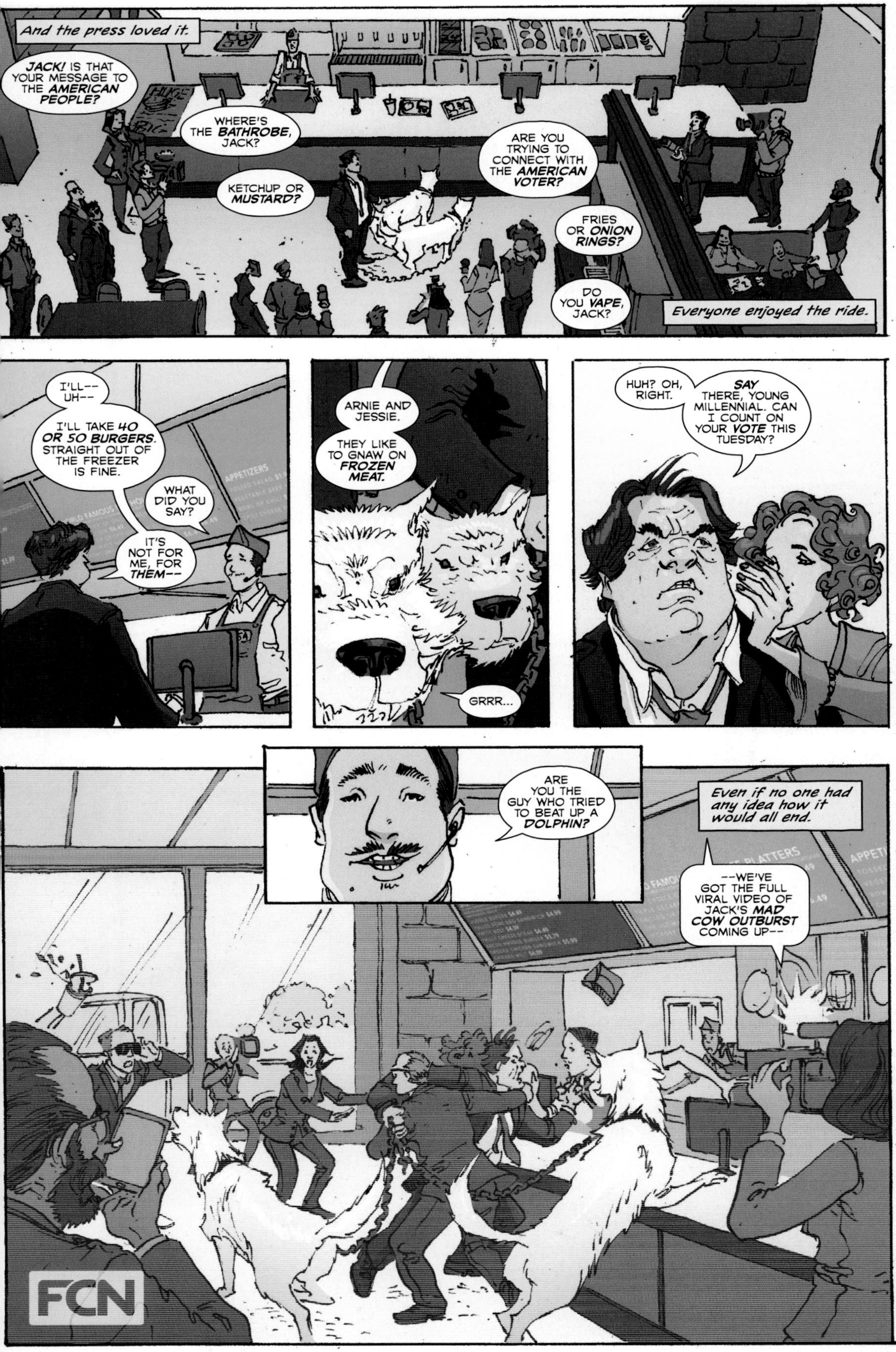
And the press loved it.
JACK! IS THAT YOUR MESSAGE TO THE AMERICAN PEOPLE?
WHERE'S THE BATHROBE, JACK?
KETCHUP OR MUSTARD?
ARE YOU TRYING TO CONNECT WITH THE AMERICAN VOTER?
FRIES OR ONION RINGS?
DO YOU VAPE, JACK?
Everyone enjoyed the ride.
I'LL-- UH--
I'LL TAKE 40 OR 50 BURGERS. STRAIGHT OUT OF THE FREEZER IS FINE.
WHAT DID YOU SAY?
IT'S NOT FOR ME, FOR THEM--
ARNIE AND JESSIE.
THEY LIKE TO GNAW ON FROZEN MEAT.
GRRR...
HUH? OH, RIGHT.
SAY THERE, YOUNG MILLENNIAL. CAN I COUNT ON YOUR VOTE THIS TUESDAY?
ARE YOU THE GUY WHO TRIED TO BEAT UP A DOLPHIN?
Even if no one had any idea how it would all end.
--WE'VE GOT THE FULL VIRAL VIDEO OF JACK'S MAD COW OUTBURST COMING UP--
FCN

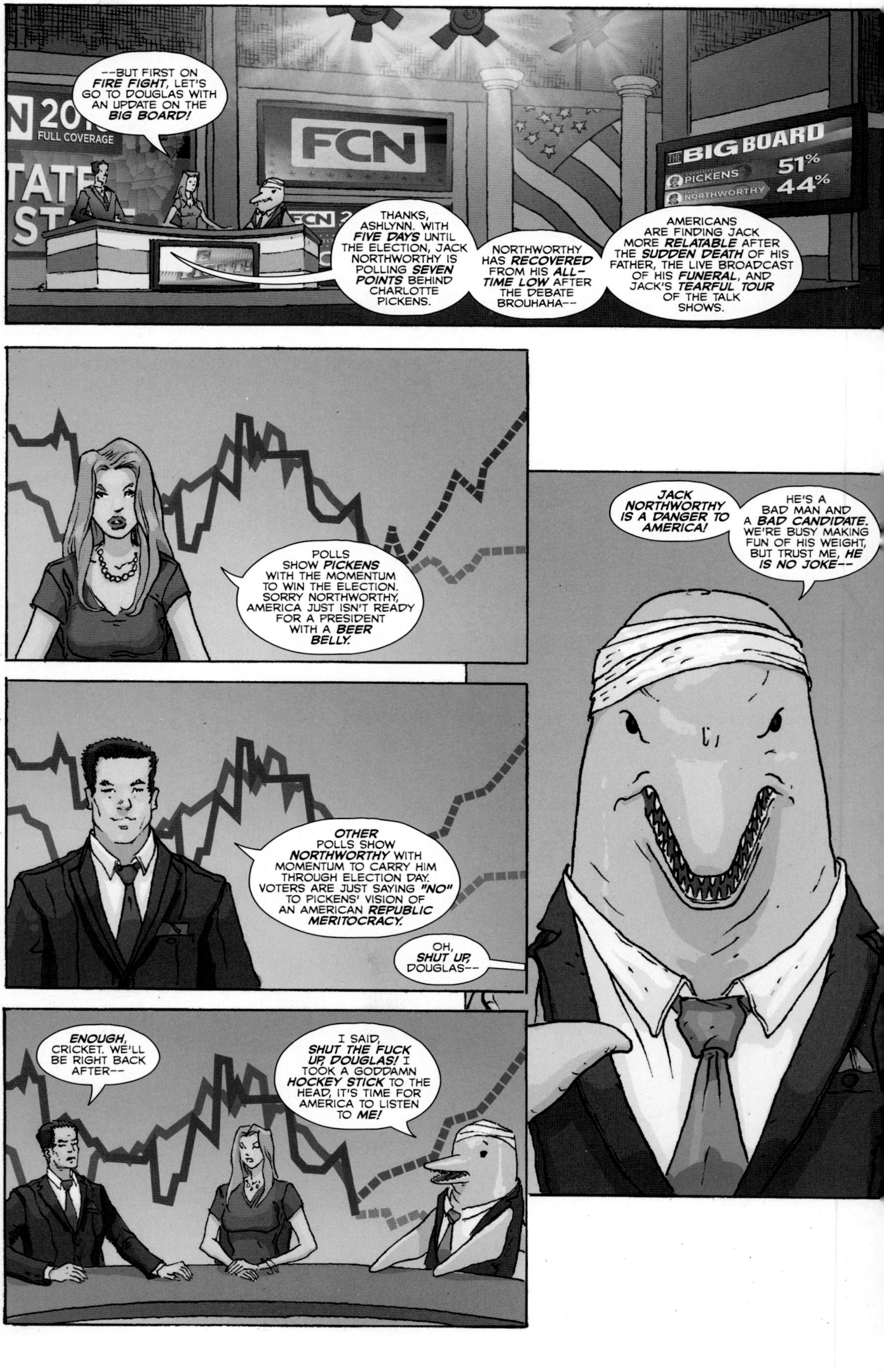

FULL COVERAGE
FCN
THE BIG BOARD
PICKENS 51%
NORTHWORTHY 44%
--BUT FIRST ON FIRE FIGHT, LET'S GO TO DOUGLAS WITH AN UPDATE ON THE BIG BOARD!
THANKS, ASHLYNN. WITH FIVE DAYS UNTIL THE ELECTION, JACK NORTHWORTHY IS POLLING SEVEN POINTS BEHIND CHARLOTTE PICKENS.
NORTHWORTHY HAS RECOVERED FROM HIS ALL-TIME LOW AFTER THE DEBATE BROUHAHA--
AMERICANS ARE FINDING JACK MORE RELATABLE AFTER THE SUDDEN DEATH OF HIS FATHER, THE LIVE BROADCAST OF HIS FUNERAL, AND JACK'S TEARFUL TOUR OF THE TALK SHOWS.
POLLS SHOW PICKENS WITH THE MOMENTUM TO WIN THE ELECTION. SORRY NORTHWORTHY, AMERICA JUST ISN'T READY FOR A PRESIDENT WITH A BEER BELLY.
JACK NORTHWORTHY IS A DANGER TO AMERICA!
HE'S A BAD MAN AND A BAD CANDIDATE. WE'RE BUSY MAKING FUN OF HIS WEIGHT, BUT TRUST ME, HE IS NO JOKE--
OTHER POLLS SHOW NORTHWORTHY WITH MOMENTUM TO CARRY HIM THROUGH ELECTION DAY. VOTERS ARE JUST SAYING "NO" TO PICKENS' VISION OF AN AMERICAN REPUBLIC MERITOCRACY.
OH, SHUT UP, DOUGLAS--
ENOUGH, CRICKET. WE'LL BE RIGHT BACK AFTER--
I SAID, SHUT THE FUCK UP, DOUGLAS! I TOOK A GODDAMN HOCKEY STICK TO THE HEAD, IT'S TIME FOR AMERICA TO LISTEN TO ME!

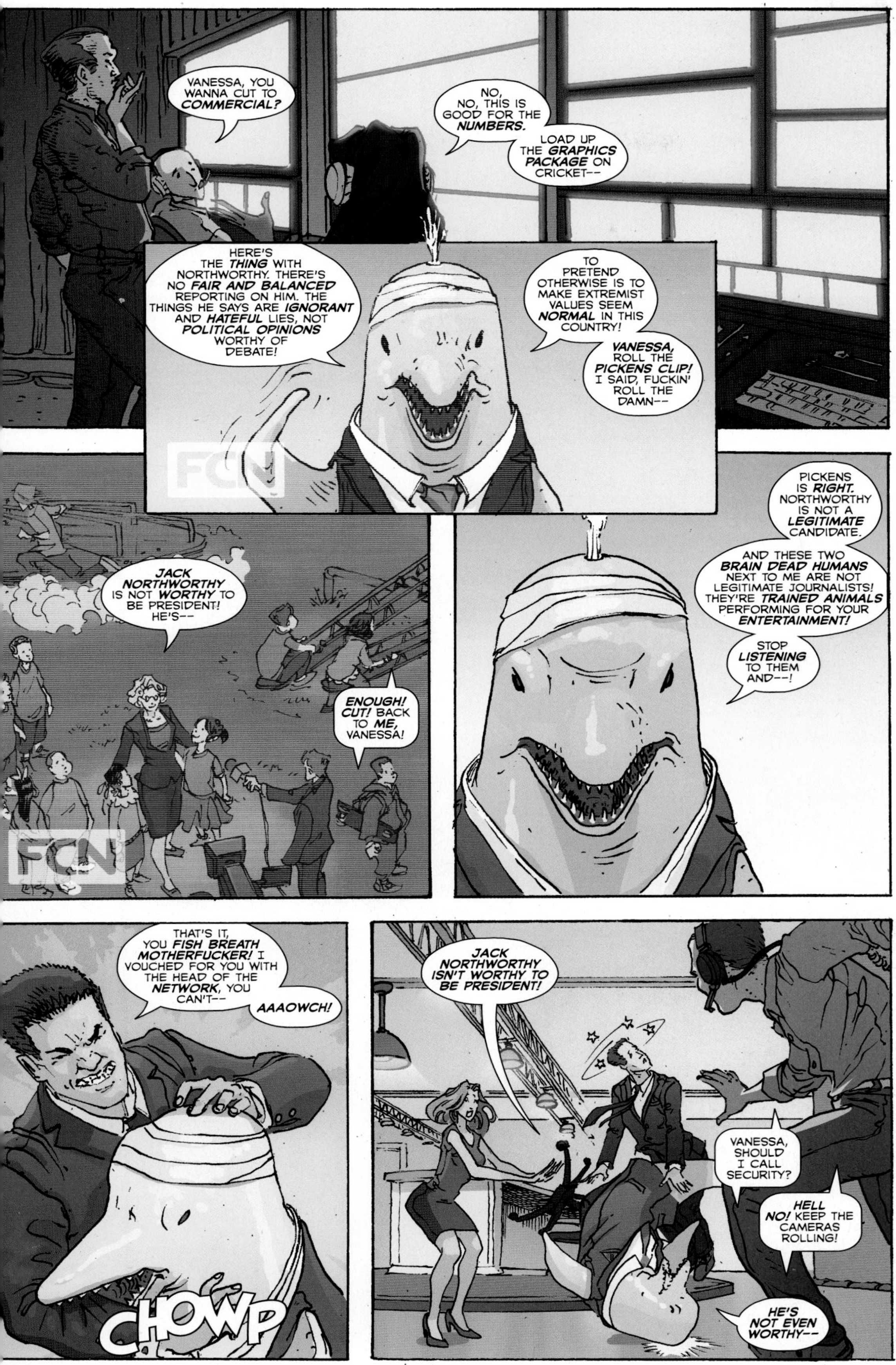
VANESSA, YOU WANNA CUT TO COMMERCIAL?
NO, NO, THIS IS GOOD FOR THE NUMBERS.
LOAD UP THE GRAPHICS PACKAGE ON CRICKET--
HERE'S THE THING WITH NORTHWORTHY. THERE'S NO FAIR AND BALANCED REPORTING ON HIM. THE THINGS HE SAYS ARE IGNORANT AND HATEFUL LIES, NOT POLITICAL OPINIONS WORTHY OF DEBATE!
TO PRETEND OTHERWISE IS TO MAKE EXTREMIST VALUES SEEM NORMAL IN THIS COUNTRY!
VANESSA, ROLL THE PICKENS CLIP! I SAID, FUCKIN' ROLL THE DAMN--
FCN
JACK NORTHWORTHY IS NOT WORTHY TO BE PRESIDENT! HE'S--
ENOUGH! CUT! BACK TO ME, VANESSA!
FCN
PICKENS IS RIGHT. NORTHWORTHY IS NOT A LEGITIMATE CANDIDATE.
AND THESE TWO BRAIN DEAD HUMANS NEXT TO ME ARE NOT LEGITIMATE JOURNALISTS! THEY'RE TRAINED ANIMALS PERFORMING FOR YOUR ENTERTAINMENT!
STOP LISTENING TO THEM AND--!
THAT'S IT, YOU FISH BREATH MOTHERFUCKER! I VOUCHED FOR YOU WITH THE HEAD OF THE NETWORK, YOU CAN'T--
AAAOWCH!
CHOWP
JACK NORTHWORTHY ISN'T WORTHY TO BE PRESIDENT!
VANESSA, SHOULD I CALL SECURITY?
HELL NO! KEEP THE CAMERAS ROLLING!
HE'S NOT EVEN WORTHY--

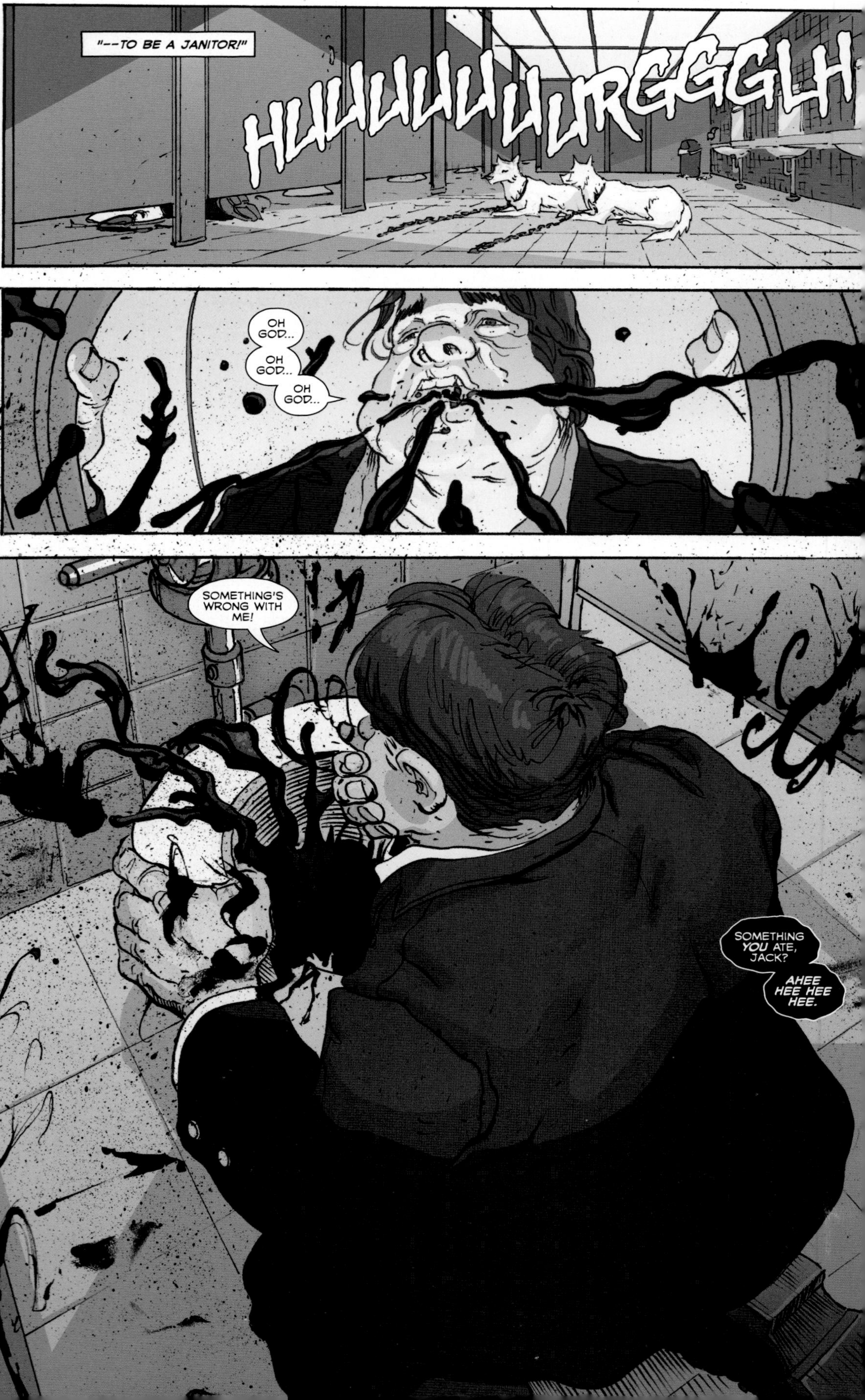
"--TO BE A JANITOR!"
HUUUUUUURGGGLH
OH GOD...
OH GOD...
OH GOD...
SOMETHING'S WRONG WITH ME!
SOMETHING *YOU* ATE, JACK?
AHEE HEE HEE HEE.

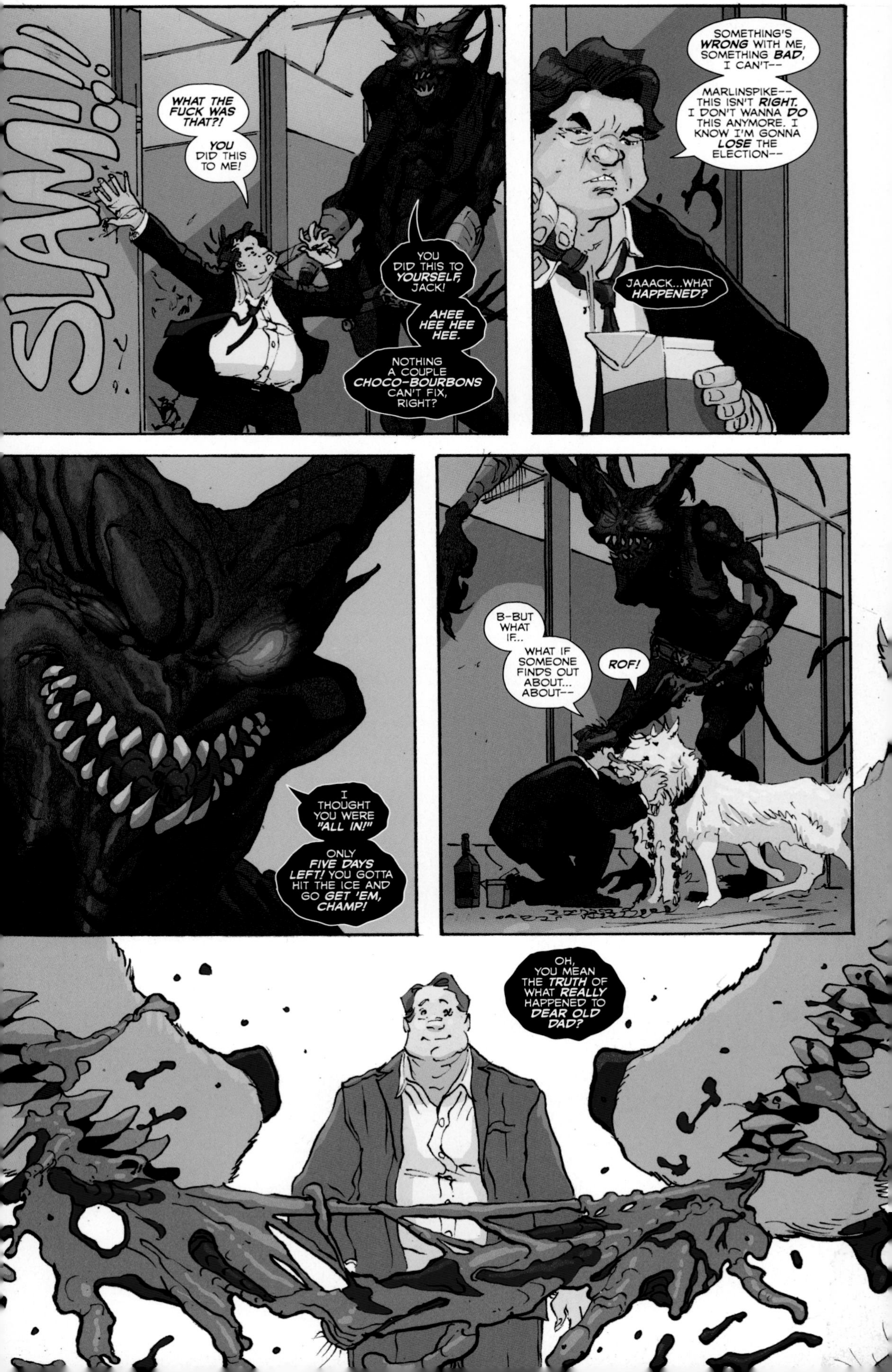

SLAM!!!
WHAT THE FUCK WAS THAT?!
YOU DID THIS TO ME!
YOU DID THIS TO YOURSELF, JACK!
AHEE HEE HEE HEE.
NOTHING A COUPLE CHOCO-BOURBONS CAN'T FIX, RIGHT?
SOMETHING'S WRONG WITH ME, SOMETHING BAD, I CAN'T--
MARLINSPIKE-- THIS ISN'T RIGHT. I DON'T WANNA DO THIS ANYMORE. I KNOW I'M GONNA LOSE THE ELECTION--
JAAACK...WHAT HAPPENED?
I THOUGHT YOU WERE "ALL IN!"
ONLY FIVE DAYS LEFT! YOU GOTTA HIT THE ICE AND GO GET 'EM, CHAMP!
B-BUT WHAT IF...
WHAT IF SOMEONE FINDS OUT ABOUT... ABOUT--
ROF!
OH, YOU MEAN THE TRUTH OF WHAT REALLY HAPPENED TO DEAR OLD DAD?

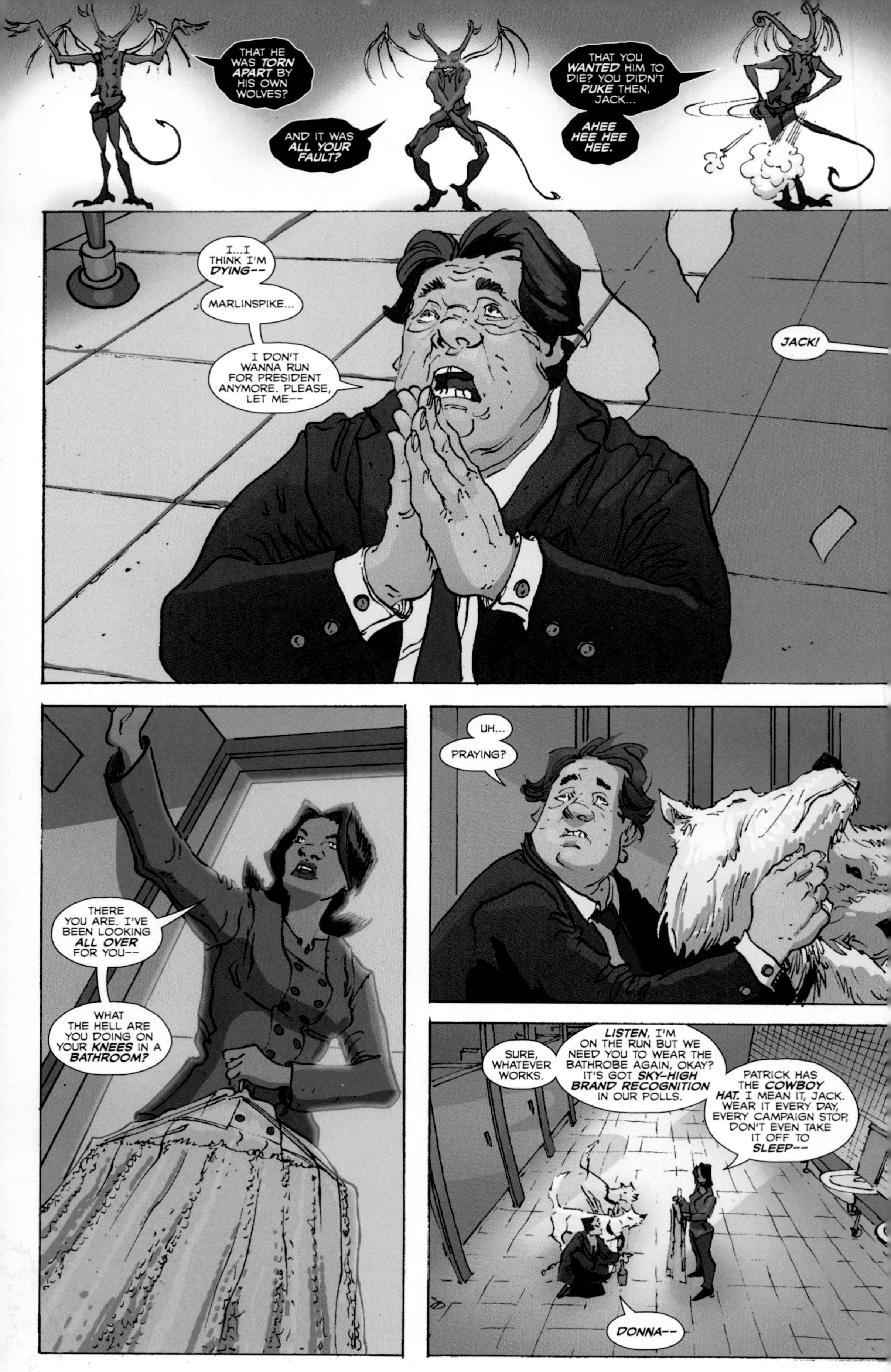
THAT HE WAS TORN APART BY HIS OWN WOLVES?
AND IT WAS ALL YOUR FAULT?
THAT YOU WANTED HIM TO DIE? YOU DIDN'T PUKE THEN, JACK...
AHEE HEE HEE HEE.
I...I THINK I'M DYING--
MARLINSPIKE...
I DON'T WANNA RUN FOR PRESIDENT ANYMORE. PLEASE, LET ME--
JACK!
THERE YOU ARE. I'VE BEEN LOOKING ALL OVER FOR YOU--
WHAT THE HELL ARE YOU DOING ON YOUR KNEES IN A BATHROOM?
UH...
PRAYING?
SURE, WHATEVER WORKS.
LISTEN, I'M ON THE RUN BUT WE NEED YOU TO WEAR THE BATHROBE AGAIN, OKAY? IT'S GOT SKY-HIGH BRAND RECOGNITION IN OUR POLLS.
PATRICK HAS THE COWBOY HAT. I MEAN IT, JACK. WEAR IT EVERY DAY, EVERY CAMPAIGN STOP, DON'T EVEN TAKE IT OFF TO SLEEP--
DONNA--

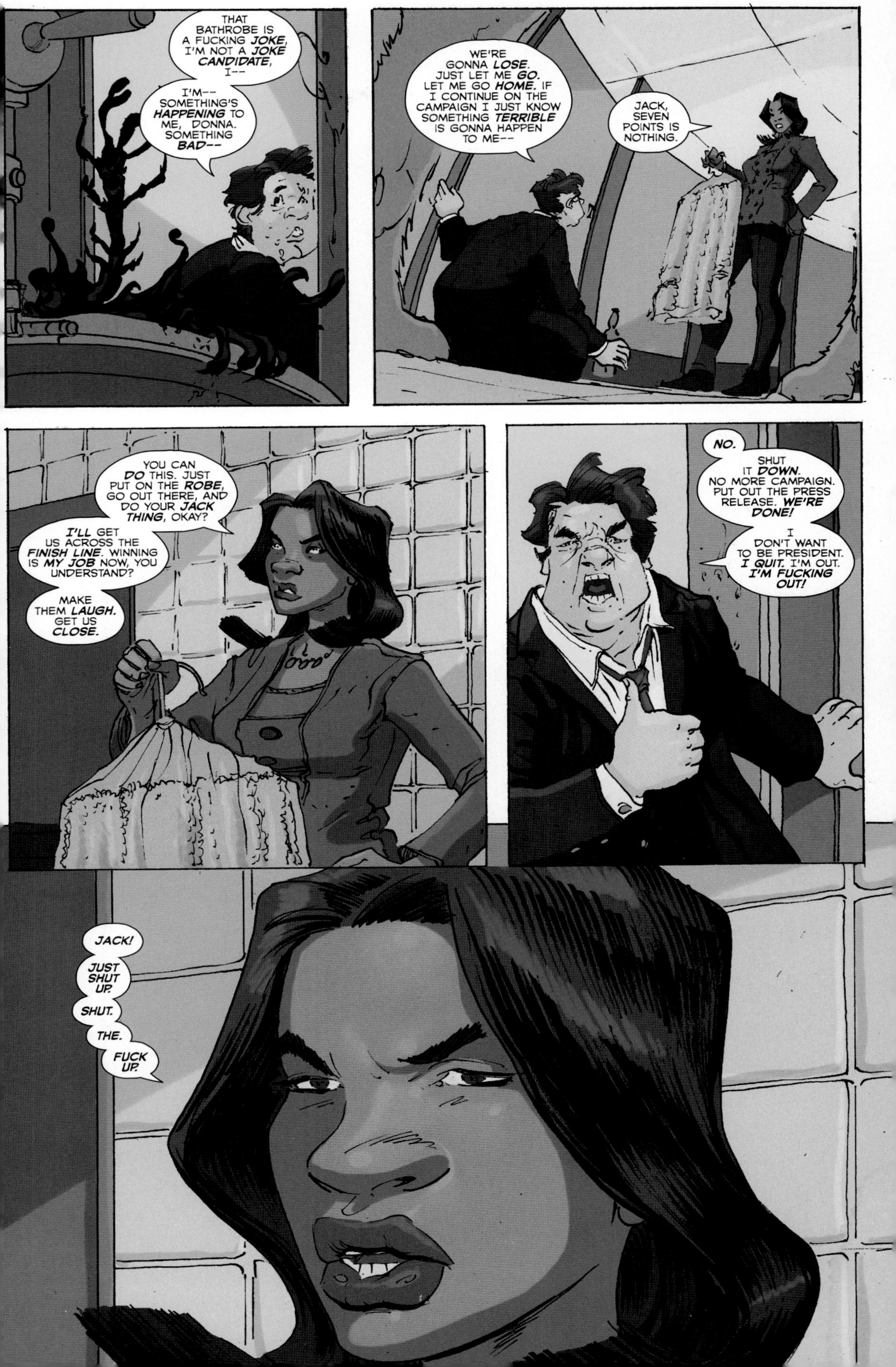
THAT BATHROBE IS A FUCKING JOKE, I'M NOT A JOKE CANDIDATE, I--
I'M-- SOMETHING'S HAPPENING TO ME, DONNA. SOMETHING BAD--
WE'RE GONNA LOSE. JUST LET ME GO. LET ME GO HOME. IF I CONTINUE ON THE CAMPAIGN I JUST KNOW SOMETHING TERRIBLE IS GONNA HAPPEN TO ME--
JACK, SEVEN POINTS IS NOTHING.
YOU CAN DO THIS. JUST PUT ON THE ROBE, GO OUT THERE, AND DO YOUR JACK THING, OKAY?
I'LL GET US ACROSS THE FINISH LINE. WINNING IS MY JOB NOW, YOU UNDERSTAND?
MAKE THEM LAUGH. GET US CLOSE.
NO.
SHUT IT DOWN. NO MORE CAMPAIGN. PUT OUT THE PRESS RELEASE. WE'RE DONE!
I DON'T WANT TO BE PRESIDENT. I QUIT. I'M OUT. I'M FUCKING OUT!
JACK!
JUST SHUT UP.
SHUT.
THE.
FUCK
UP.

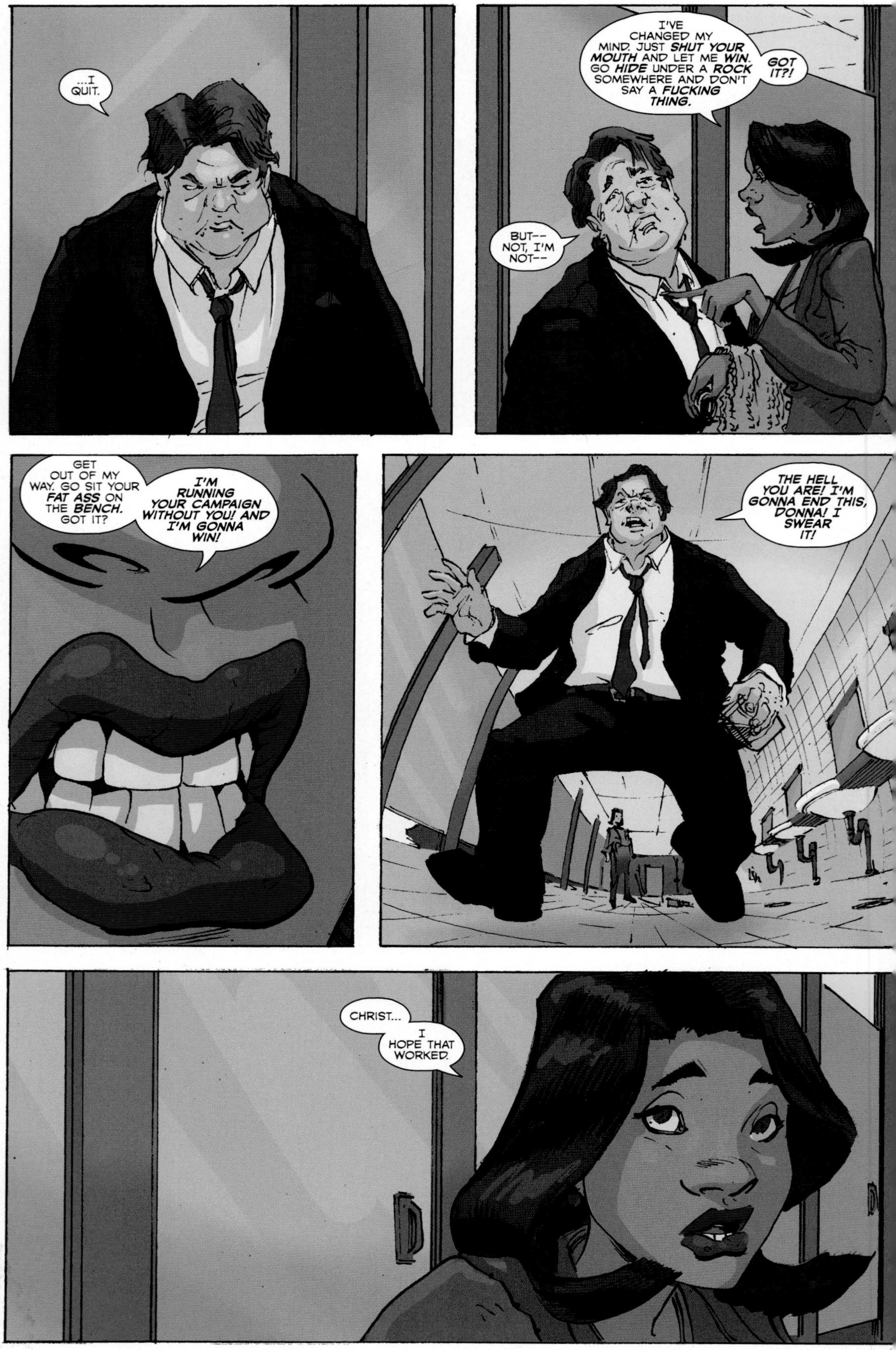

...I QUIT.
I'VE CHANGED MY MIND. JUST SHUT YOUR MOUTH AND LET ME WIN. GO HIDE UNDER A ROCK SOMEWHERE AND DON'T SAY A FUCKING THING.
GOT IT?!
BUT-- NOT, I'M NOT--
GET OUT OF MY WAY. GO SIT YOUR FAT ASS ON THE BENCH. GOT IT?
I'M RUNNING YOUR CAMPAIGN WITHOUT YOU! AND I'M GONNA WIN!
THE HELL YOU ARE! I'M GONNA END THIS, DONNA! I SWEAR IT!
CHRIST...
I HOPE THAT WORKED.

FOUR DAYS UNTIL ELECTION

WHEN I AM PRESIDENT, I WILL MAKE SURE THAT *CHILDREN* GET THE *HEALTH CARE* THEY NEED--

JACK, PICKENS WANTS TO FUND *CHILDRENS'* HOSPITALS, YOUR THOUGHTS?

UH...

YOU KNOW *WHAT?* *FUCK* KIDS. FUCK 'EM ALL.

GOD DAMN IT! IF I DROPPED THOSE *FUCKING KEYS* AGAIN, I CAN'T *REACH* THE GROUND--!

HELLO, CRICKET.

I *KNOW* YOU.

THEN YOU KNOW WHAT I *WANT.*

YOU WANT ME TO *BACK OFF* YOUR GUY.

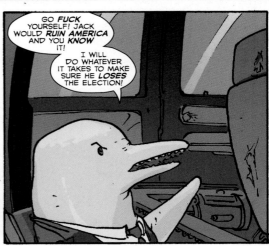

GO *FUCK* YOURSELF! JACK WOULD *RUIN AMERICA* AND YOU *KNOW* IT! I WILL DO WHATEVER IT TAKES TO MAKE SURE HE *LOSES* THE ELECTION!

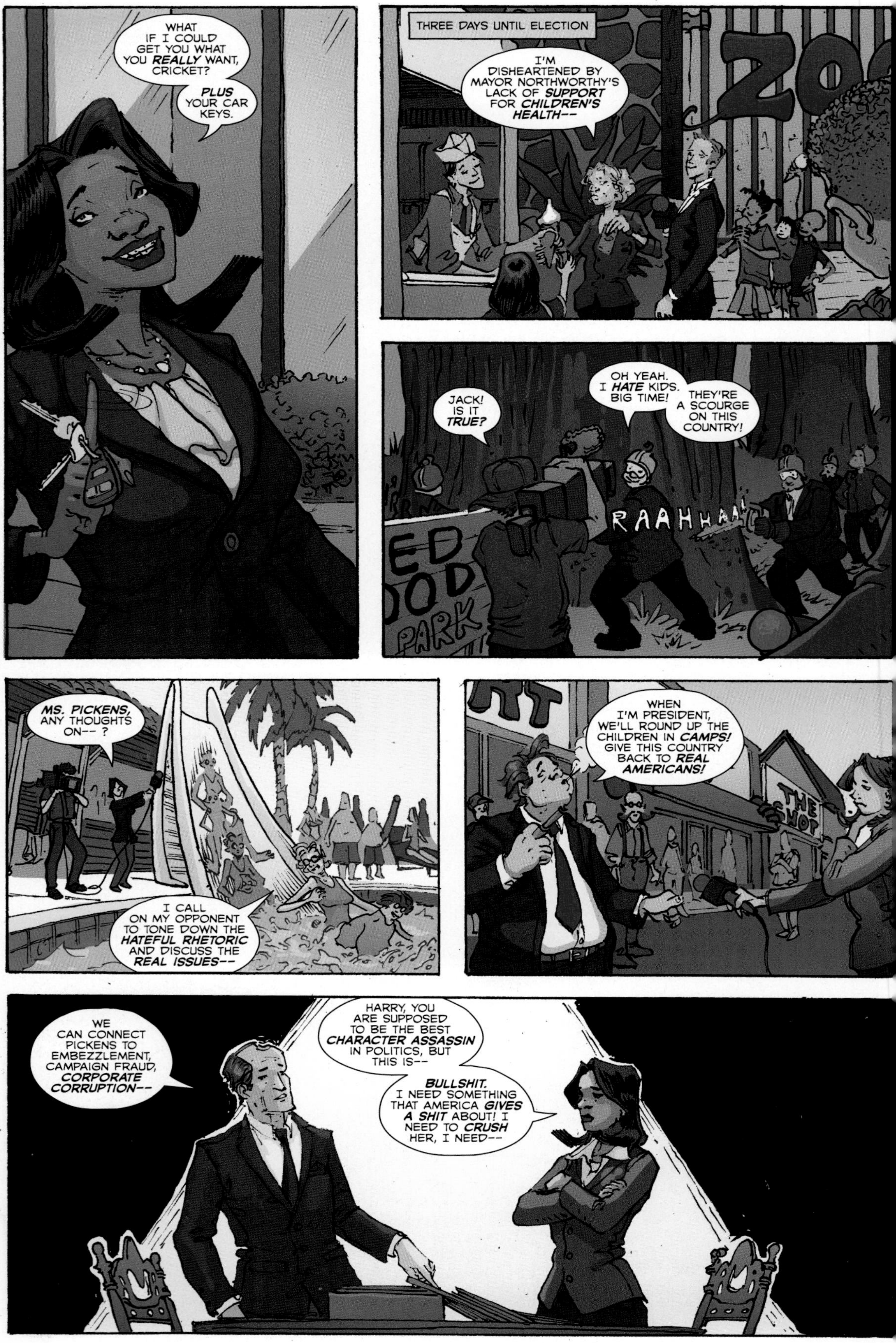
WHAT IF I COULD GET YOU WHAT YOU REALLY WANT, CRICKET?
PLUS YOUR CAR KEYS.
THREE DAYS UNTIL ELECTION
I'M DISHEARTENED BY MAYOR NORTHWORTHY'S LACK OF SUPPORT FOR CHILDREN'S HEALTH--
ZOO
JACK! IS IT TRUE?
OH YEAH. I HATE KIDS. BIG TIME!
THEY'RE A SCOURGE ON THIS COUNTRY!
RAAHHAA!
ED OOD PARK
MS. PICKENS, ANY THOUGHTS ON-- ?
I CALL ON MY OPPONENT TO TONE DOWN THE HATEFUL RHETORIC AND DISCUSS THE REAL ISSUES--
WHEN I'M PRESIDENT, WE'LL ROUND UP THE CHILDREN IN CAMPS! GIVE THIS COUNTRY BACK TO REAL AMERICANS!
WE CAN CONNECT PICKENS TO EMBEZZLEMENT, CAMPAIGN FRAUD, CORPORATE CORRUPTION--
HARRY, YOU ARE SUPPOSED TO BE THE BEST CHARACTER ASSASSIN IN POLITICS, BUT THIS IS--
BULLSHIT. I NEED SOMETHING THAT AMERICA GIVES A SHIT ABOUT! I NEED TO CRUSH HER, I NEED--

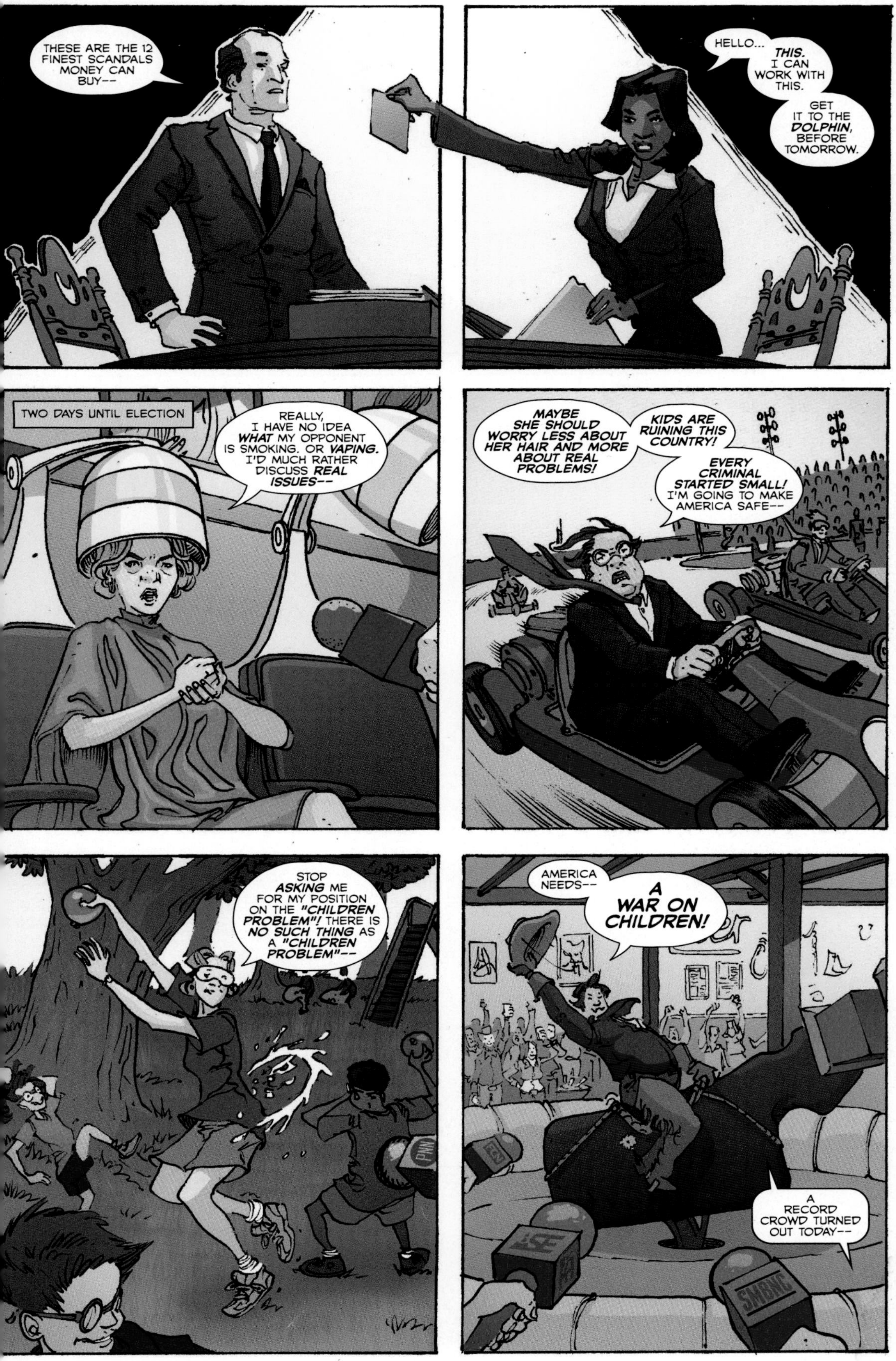
THESE ARE THE 12 FINEST SCANDALS MONEY CAN BUY--
HELLO... *THIS.* I CAN WORK WITH THIS.
GET IT TO THE *DOLPHIN,* BEFORE TOMORROW.
TWO DAYS UNTIL ELECTION
REALLY, I HAVE NO IDEA *WHAT* MY OPPONENT IS SMOKING. OR *VAPING.* I'D MUCH RATHER DISCUSS *REAL ISSUES*--
MAYBE SHE SHOULD WORRY LESS ABOUT HER HAIR AND MORE ABOUT REAL PROBLEMS!
KIDS ARE RUINING THIS COUNTRY!
EVERY CRIMINAL STARTED SMALL! I'M GOING TO MAKE AMERICA SAFE--
STOP *ASKING* ME FOR MY POSITION ON THE *"CHILDREN PROBLEM"!* THERE IS *NO SUCH THING* AS A *"CHILDREN PROBLEM"*--
AMERICA NEEDS--
A WAR ON CHILDREN!
A RECORD CROWD TURNED OUT TODAY--

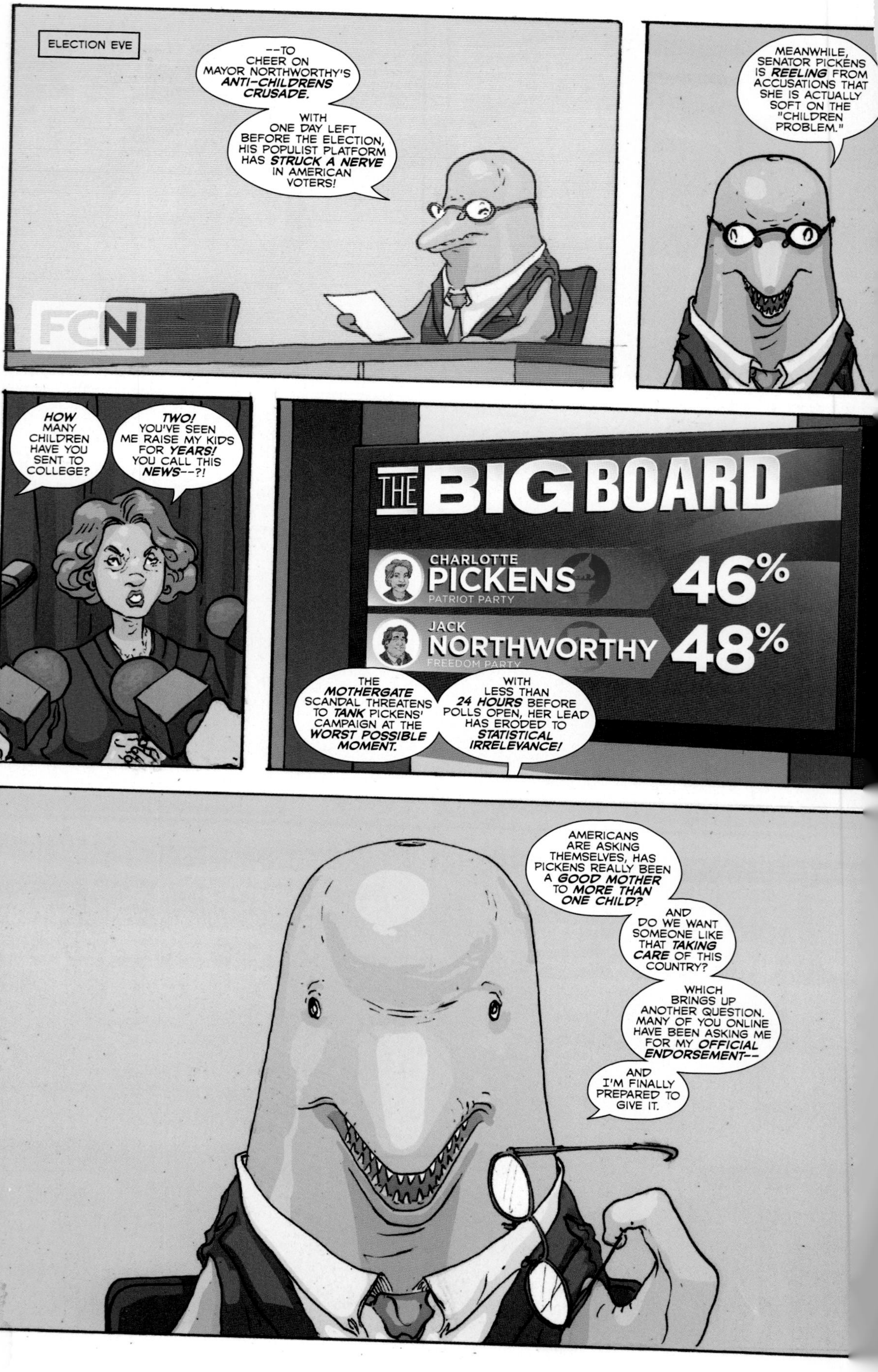
ELECTION EVE
--TO CHEER ON MAYOR NORTHWORTHY'S ANTI-CHILDRENS CRUSADE.
WITH ONE DAY LEFT BEFORE THE ELECTION, HIS POPULIST PLATFORM HAS STRUCK A NERVE IN AMERICAN VOTERS!
FCN
MEANWHILE, SENATOR PICKENS IS REELING FROM ACCUSATIONS THAT SHE IS ACTUALLY SOFT ON THE "CHILDREN PROBLEM."
HOW MANY CHILDREN HAVE YOU SENT TO COLLEGE?
TWO! YOU'VE SEEN ME RAISE MY KIDS FOR YEARS! YOU CALL THIS NEWS--?!
THE BIG BOARD
CHARLOTTE PICKENS
PATRIOT PARTY
46%
JACK NORTHWORTHY
FREEDOM PARTY
48%
THE MOTHERGATE SCANDAL THREATENS TO TANK PICKENS' CAMPAIGN AT THE WORST POSSIBLE MOMENT.
WITH LESS THAN 24 HOURS BEFORE POLLS OPEN, HER LEAD HAS ERODED TO STATISTICAL IRRELEVANCE!
AMERICANS ARE ASKING THEMSELVES, HAS PICKENS REALLY BEEN A GOOD MOTHER TO MORE THAN ONE CHILD?
AND DO WE WANT SOMEONE LIKE THAT TAKING CARE OF THIS COUNTRY?
WHICH BRINGS UP ANOTHER QUESTION. MANY OF YOU ONLINE HAVE BEEN ASKING ME FOR MY OFFICIAL ENDORSEMENT--
AND I'M FINALLY PREPARED TO GIVE IT.

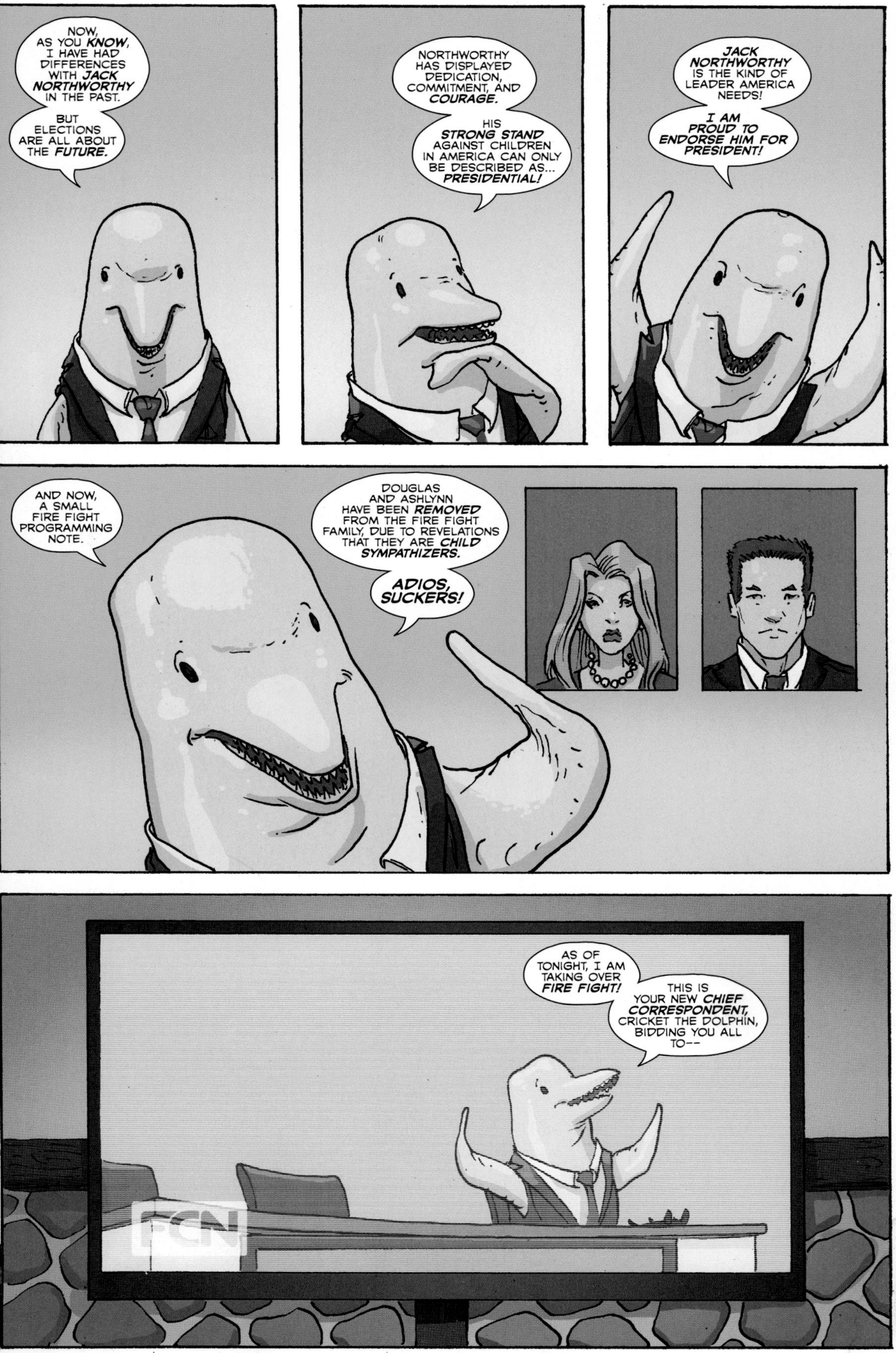
NOW, AS YOU KNOW, I HAVE HAD DIFFERENCES WITH JACK NORTHWORTHY IN THE PAST.
BUT ELECTIONS ARE ALL ABOUT THE FUTURE.
NORTHWORTHY HAS DISPLAYED DEDICATION, COMMITMENT, AND COURAGE.
HIS STRONG STAND AGAINST CHILDREN IN AMERICA CAN ONLY BE DESCRIBED AS... PRESIDENTIAL!
JACK NORTHWORTHY IS THE KIND OF LEADER AMERICA NEEDS!
I AM PROUD TO ENDORSE HIM FOR PRESIDENT!
AND NOW, A SMALL FIRE FIGHT PROGRAMMING NOTE.
DOUGLAS AND ASHLYNN HAVE BEEN REMOVED FROM THE FIRE FIGHT FAMILY, DUE TO REVELATIONS THAT THEY ARE CHILD SYMPATHIZERS.
ADIOS, SUCKERS!
AS OF TONIGHT, I AM TAKING OVER FIRE FIGHT!
THIS IS YOUR NEW CHIEF CORRESPONDENT, CRICKET THE DOLPHIN, BIDDING YOU ALL TO--
FCN

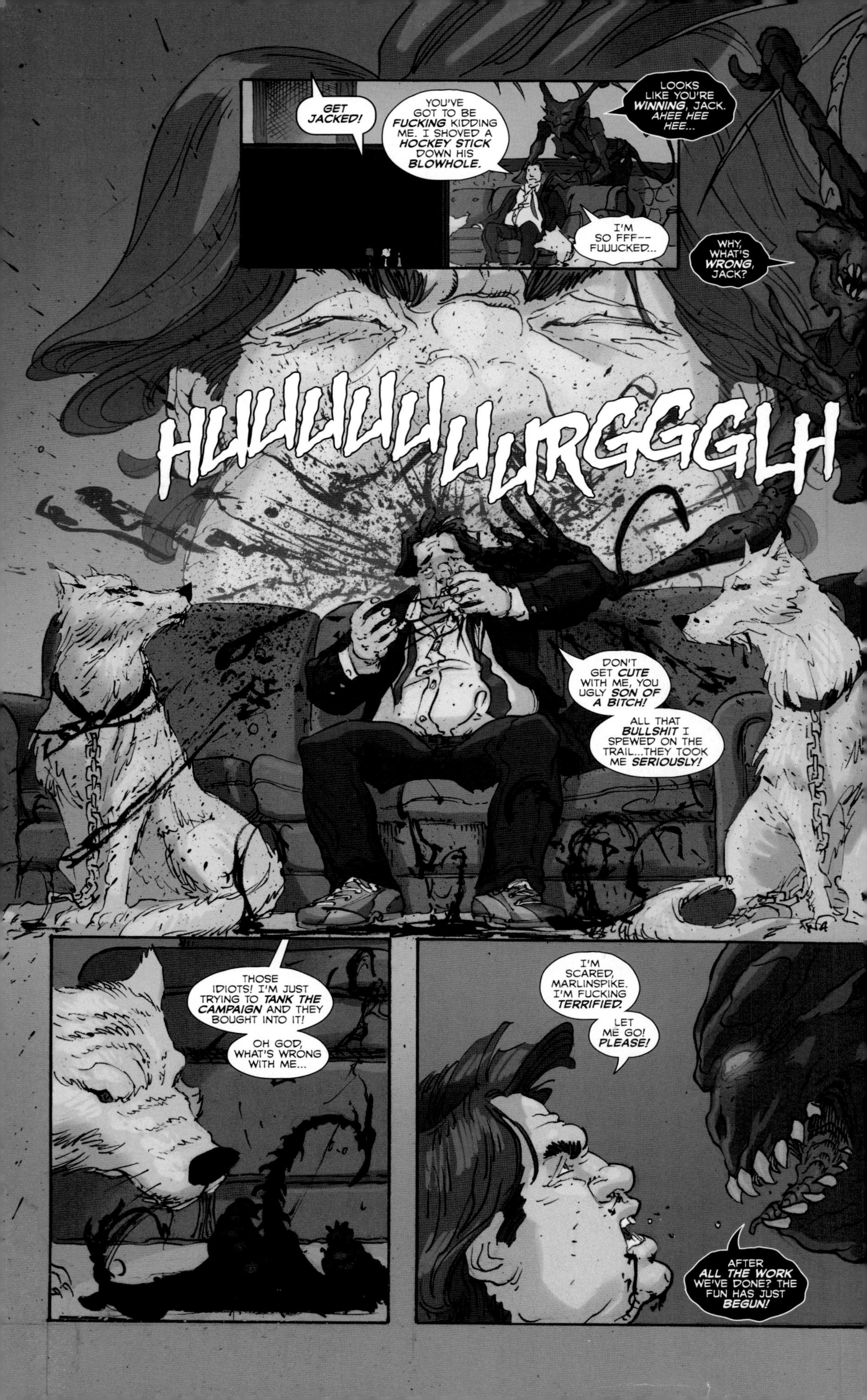
GET JACKED!
YOU'VE GOT TO BE FUCKING KIDDING ME. I SHOVED A HOCKEY STICK DOWN HIS BLOWHOLE.
LOOKS LIKE YOU'RE WINNING, JACK. AHEE HEE HEE...
I'M SO FFF-- FUUUCKED...
WHY, WHAT'S WRONG, JACK?
HUUUUUUURGGGLH
DON'T GET CUTE WITH ME, YOU UGLY SON OF A BITCH!
ALL THAT BULLSHIT I SPEWED ON THE TRAIL...THEY TOOK ME SERIOUSLY!
THOSE IDIOTS! I'M JUST TRYING TO TANK THE CAMPAIGN AND THEY BOUGHT INTO IT!
OH GOD, WHAT'S WRONG WITH ME...
I'M SCARED, MARLINSPIKE. I'M FUCKING TERRIFIED.
LET ME GO! PLEASE!
AFTER ALL THE WORK WE'VE DONE? THE FUN HAS JUST BEGUN!

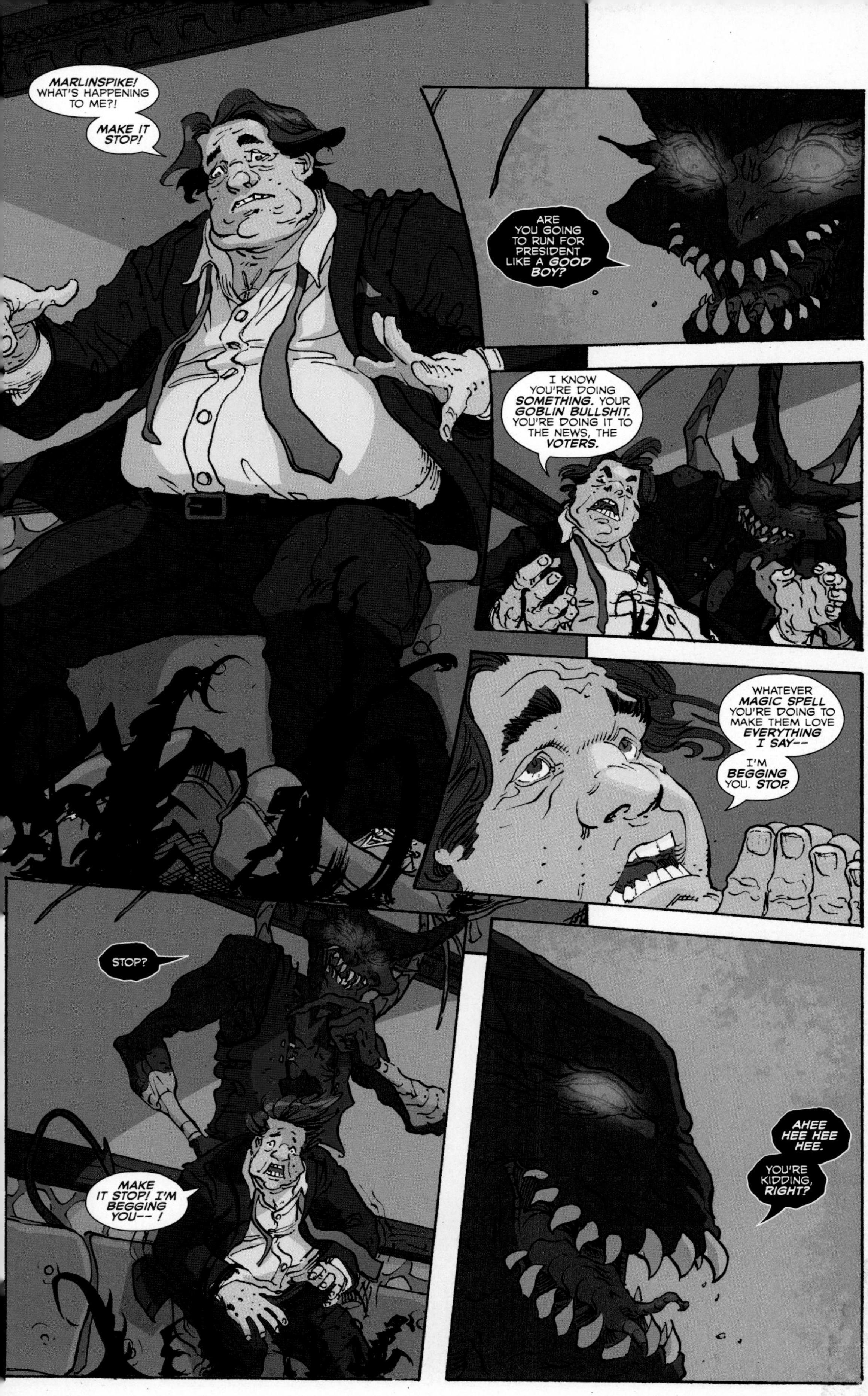
MARLINSPIKE! WHAT'S HAPPENING TO ME?!
MAKE IT STOP!
ARE YOU GOING TO RUN FOR PRESIDENT LIKE A GOOD BOY?
I KNOW YOU'RE DOING SOMETHING. YOUR GOBLIN BULLSHIT. YOU'RE DOING IT TO THE NEWS, THE VOTERS.
WHATEVER MAGIC SPELL YOU'RE DOING TO MAKE THEM LOVE EVERYTHING I SAY--
I'M BEGGING YOU. STOP.
STOP?
MAKE IT STOP! I'M BEGGING YOU-- !
AHEE HEE HEE HEE.
YOU'RE KIDDING, RIGHT?

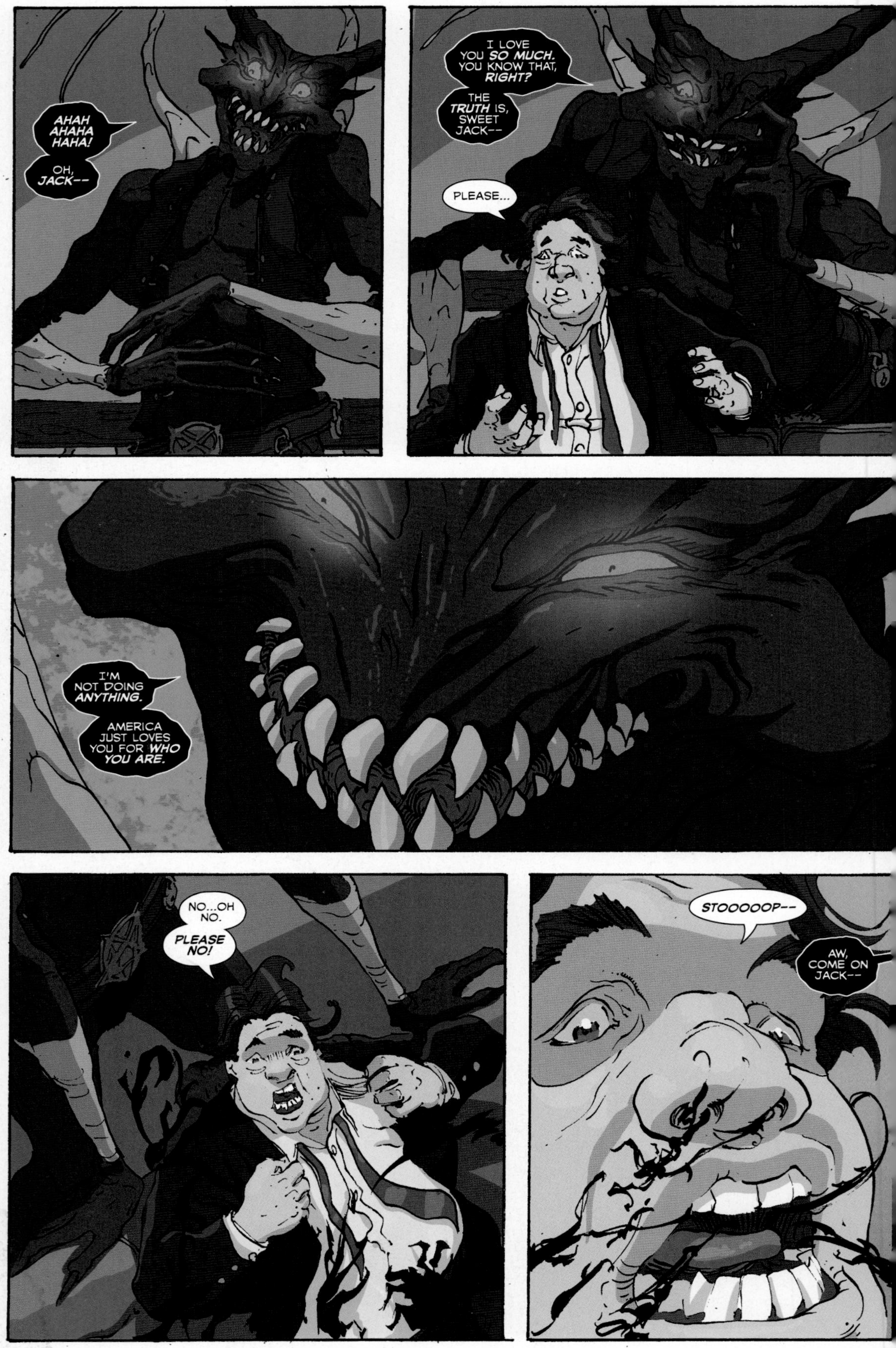
AHAH AHAHA HAHA!
OH, JACK--
I LOVE YOU SO MUCH. YOU KNOW THAT, RIGHT?
THE TRUTH IS, SWEET JACK--
PLEASE...
I'M NOT DOING ANYTHING.
AMERICA JUST LOVES YOU FOR WHO YOU ARE.
NO...OH NO. PLEASE NO!
STOOOOOP--
AW, COME ON JACK--

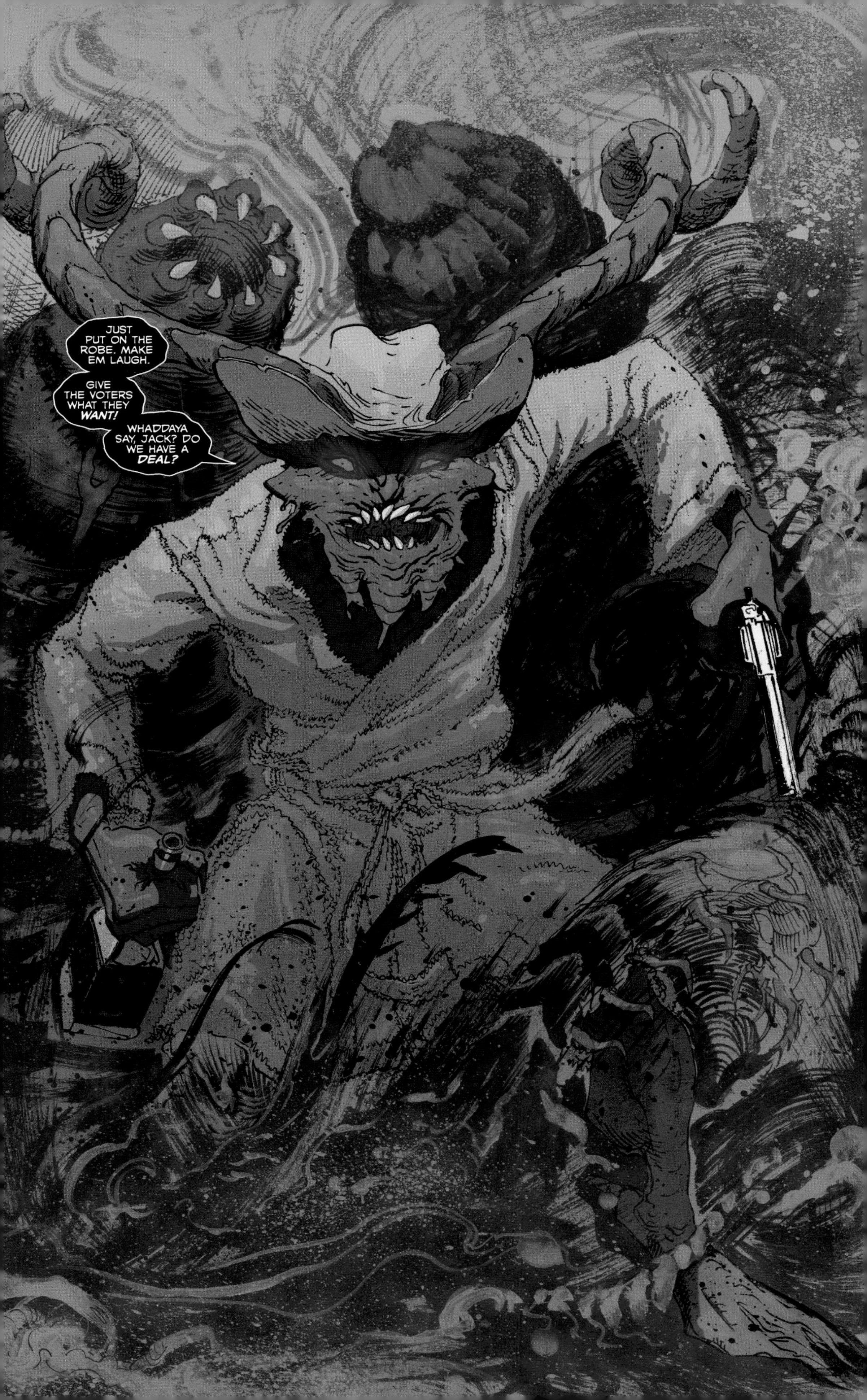
JUST PUT ON THE ROBE. MAKE EM LAUGH.
GIVE THE VOTERS WHAT THEY *WANT!*
WHADDAYA SAY, JACK? DO WE HAVE A *DEAL?*

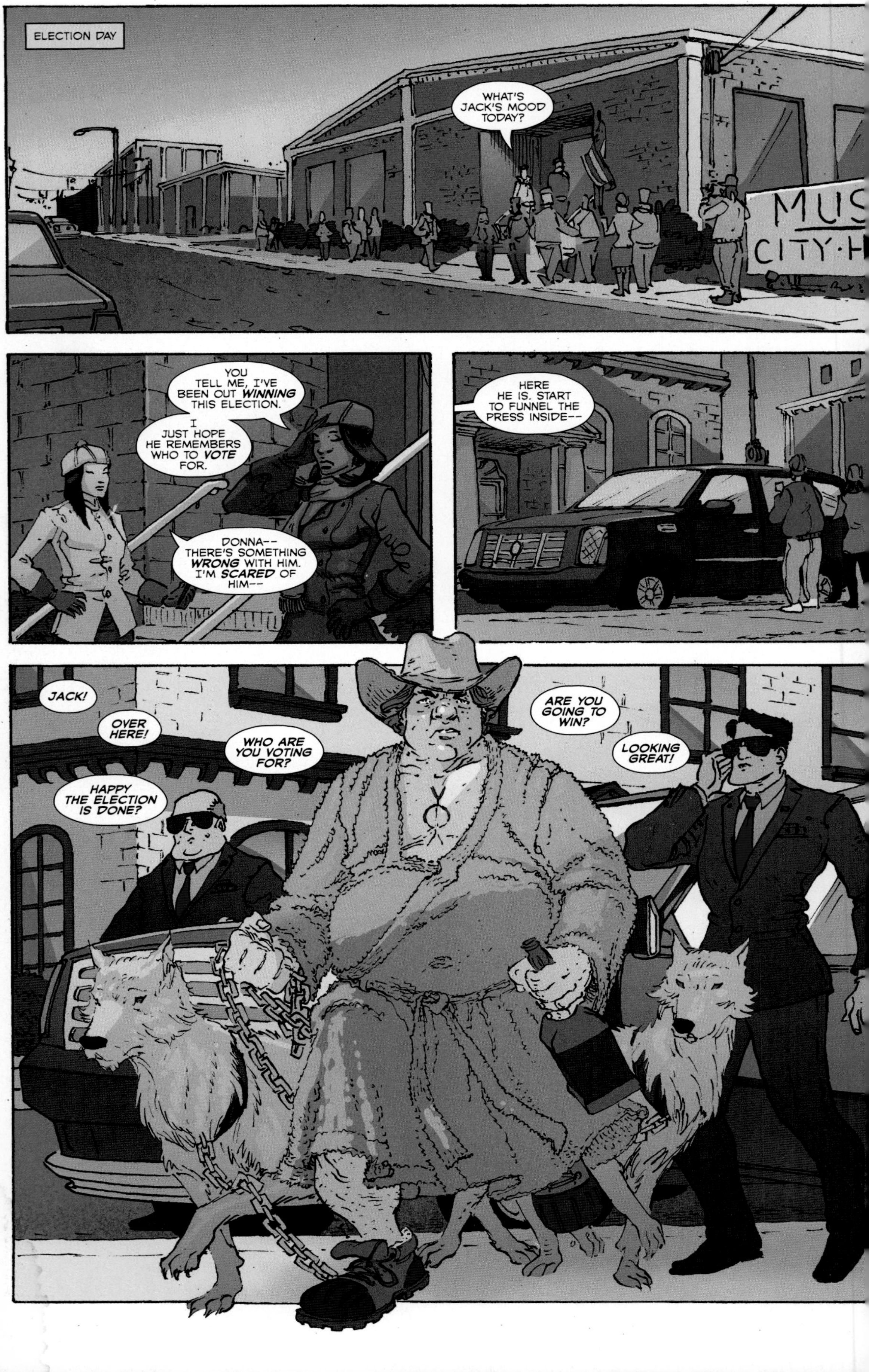
ELECTION DAY
WHAT'S JACK'S MOOD TODAY?
MUS
CITY·H
YOU TELL ME, I'VE BEEN OUT WINNING THIS ELECTION.
I JUST HOPE HE REMEMBERS WHO TO VOTE FOR.
DONNA-- THERE'S SOMETHING WRONG WITH HIM. I'M SCARED OF HIM--
HERE HE IS. START TO FUNNEL THE PRESS INSIDE--
JACK!
OVER HERE!
WHO ARE YOU VOTING FOR?
HAPPY THE ELECTION IS DONE?
ARE YOU GOING TO WIN?
LOOKING GREAT!

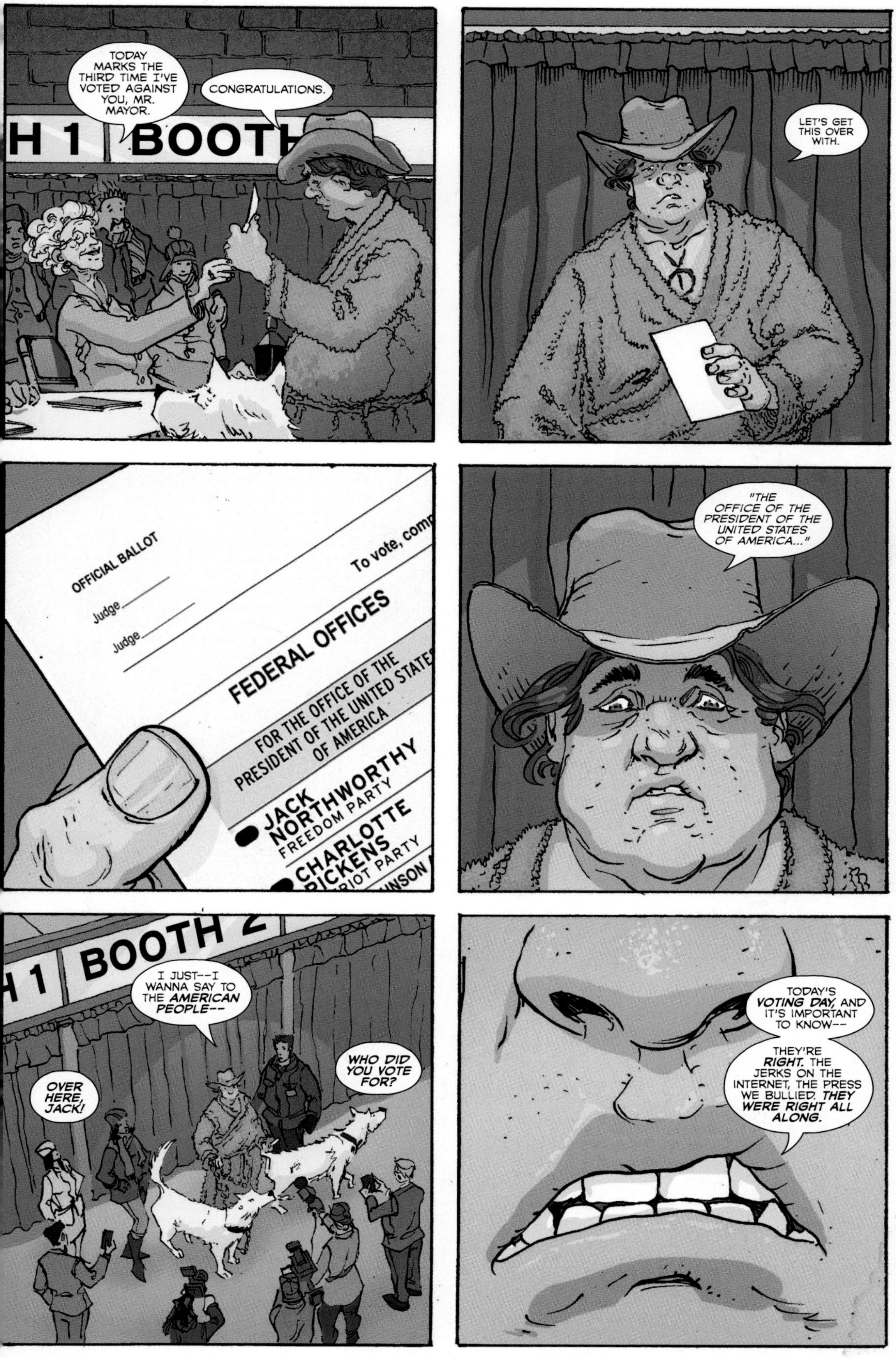
TODAY MARKS THE THIRD TIME I'VE VOTED AGAINST YOU, MR. MAYOR.
CONGRATULATIONS.
H 1 BOOTH
LET'S GET THIS OVER WITH.
OFFICIAL BALLOT
Judge
Judge
To vote, com
FEDERAL OFFICES
FOR THE OFFICE OF THE PRESIDENT OF THE UNITED STATES OF AMERICA
JACK NORTHWORTHY
FREEDOM PARTY
CHARLOTTE RICKENS
"THE OFFICE OF THE PRESIDENT OF THE UNITED STATES OF AMERICA..."
H 1 BOOTH 2
I JUST--I WANNA SAY TO THE AMERICAN PEOPLE--
OVER HERE, JACK!
WHO DID YOU VOTE FOR?
TODAY'S VOTING DAY, AND IT'S IMPORTANT TO KNOW--
THEY'RE RIGHT. THE JERKS ON THE INTERNET, THE PRESS WE BULLIED. THEY WERE RIGHT ALL ALONG.

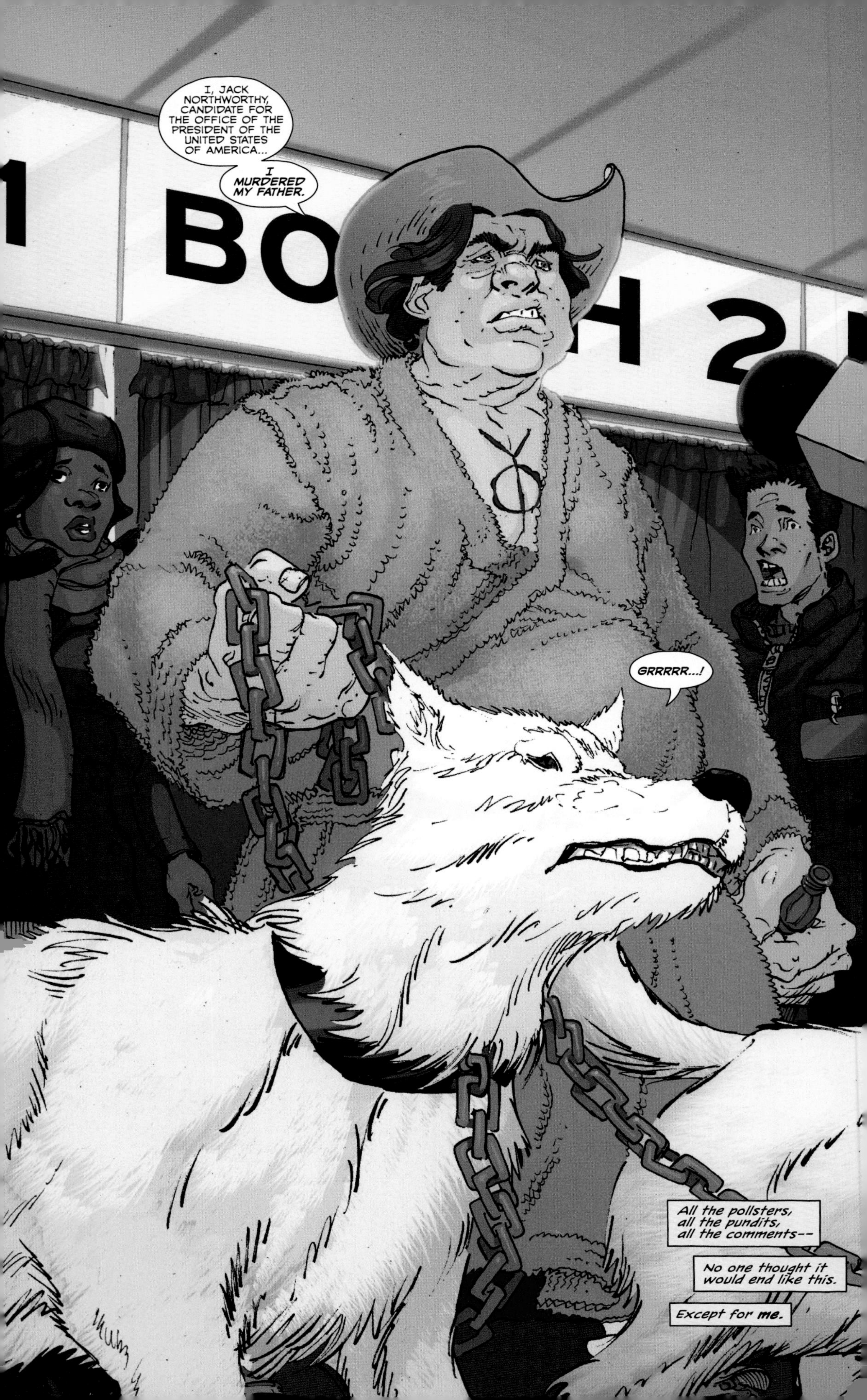
I, JACK NORTHWORTHY, CANDIDATE FOR THE OFFICE OF THE PRESIDENT OF THE UNITED STATES OF AMERICA...
I MURDERED MY FATHER.
BO H 2
GRRRRR...!
All the pollsters, all the pundits, all the comments--
No one thought it would end like this.
Except for **me.**

CHAPTER 6

THE END
OF THE ROAD

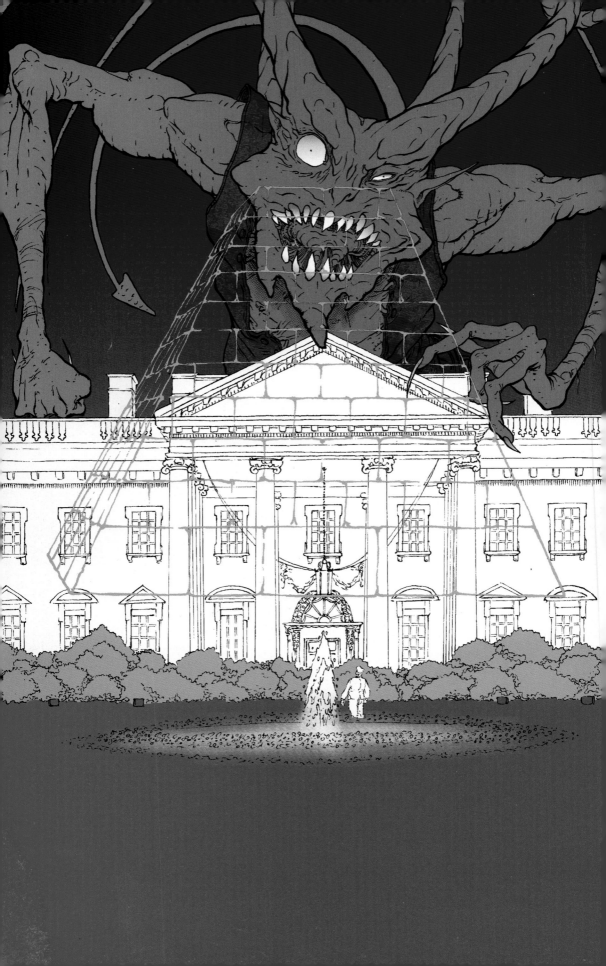

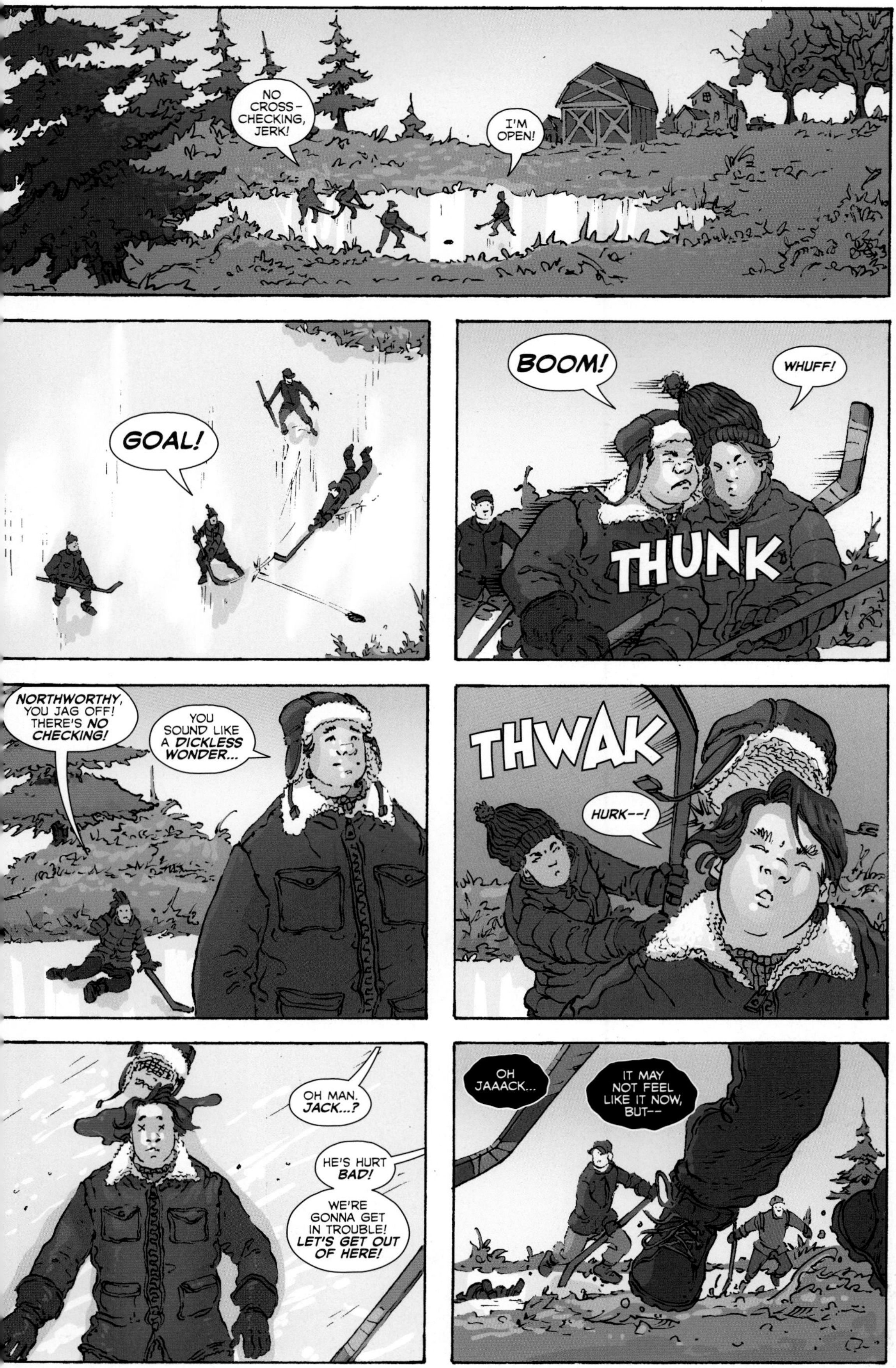
NO CROSS-CHECKING, JERK!
I'M OPEN!
GOAL!
BOOM!
WHUFF!
THUNK
NORTHWORTHY, YOU JAG OFF! THERE'S NO CHECKING!
YOU SOUND LIKE A DICKLESS WONDER...
THWAK
HURK--!
OH MAN. JACK...?
HE'S HURT BAD!
WE'RE GONNA GET IN TROUBLE! LET'S GET OUT OF HERE!
OH JAAACK...
IT MAY NOT FEEL LIKE IT NOW, BUT--

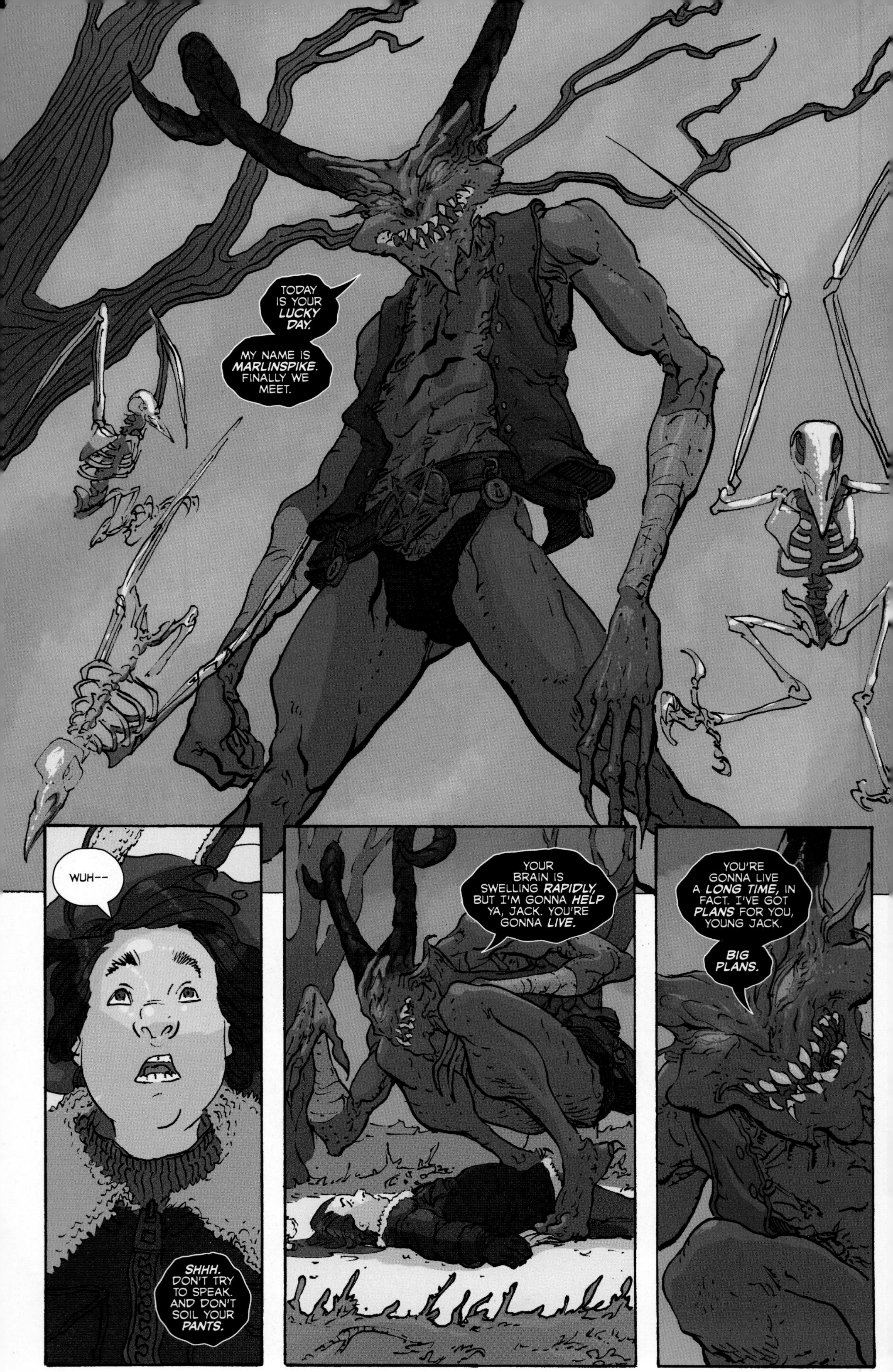
TODAY IS YOUR LUCKY DAY.
MY NAME IS MARLINSPIKE. FINALLY WE MEET.
WUH--
SHHH. DON'T TRY TO SPEAK. AND DON'T SOIL YOUR PANTS.
YOUR BRAIN IS SWELLING RAPIDLY, BUT I'M GONNA HELP YA, JACK. YOU'RE GONNA LIVE.
YOU'RE GONNA LIVE A LONG TIME, IN FACT. I'VE GOT PLANS FOR YOU, YOUNG JACK.
BIG PLANS.

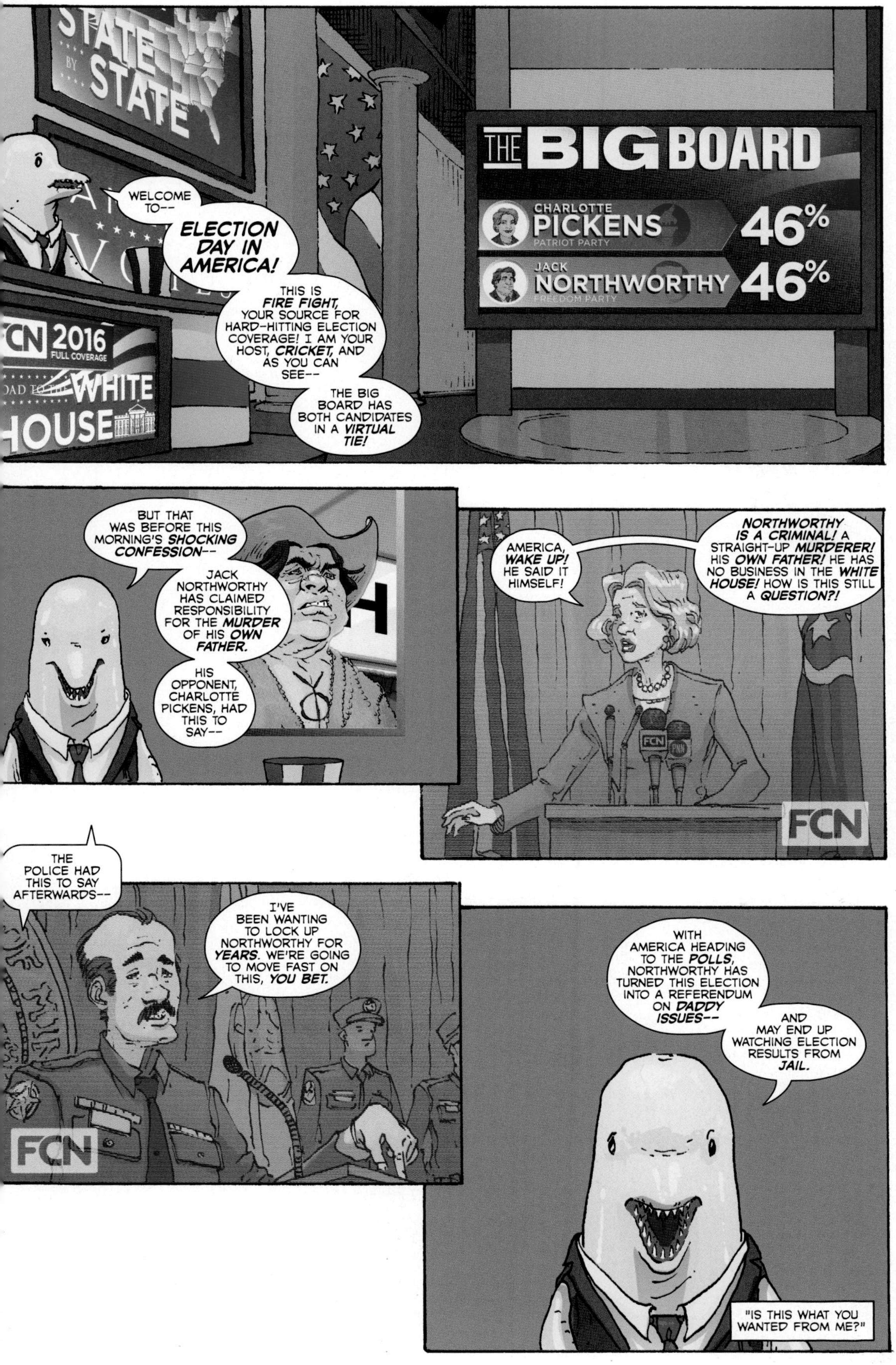
STATE BY STATE
THE BIG BOARD
CHARLOTTE PICKENS PATRIOT PARTY 46%
JACK NORTHWORTHY FREEDOM PARTY 46%
FCN 2016 FULL COVERAGE
WHITE HOUSE
WELCOME TO--
ELECTION DAY IN AMERICA!
THIS IS FIRE FIGHT, YOUR SOURCE FOR HARD-HITTING ELECTION COVERAGE! I AM YOUR HOST, CRICKET, AND AS YOU CAN SEE--
THE BIG BOARD HAS BOTH CANDIDATES IN A VIRTUAL TIE!
BUT THAT WAS BEFORE THIS MORNING'S SHOCKING CONFESSION--
JACK NORTHWORTHY HAS CLAIMED RESPONSIBILITY FOR THE MURDER OF HIS OWN FATHER.
HIS OPPONENT, CHARLOTTE PICKENS, HAD THIS TO SAY--
AMERICA, WAKE UP! HE SAID IT HIMSELF!
NORTHWORTHY IS A CRIMINAL! A STRAIGHT-UP MURDERER! HIS OWN FATHER! HE HAS NO BUSINESS IN THE WHITE HOUSE! HOW IS THIS STILL A QUESTION?!
FCN
THE POLICE HAD THIS TO SAY AFTERWARDS--
I'VE BEEN WANTING TO LOCK UP NORTHWORTHY FOR YEARS. WE'RE GOING TO MOVE FAST ON THIS, YOU BET.
FCN
WITH AMERICA HEADING TO THE POLLS, NORTHWORTHY HAS TURNED THIS ELECTION INTO A REFERENDUM ON DADDY ISSUES--
AND MAY END UP WATCHING ELECTION RESULTS FROM JAIL.
"IS THIS WHAT YOU WANTED FROM ME?"

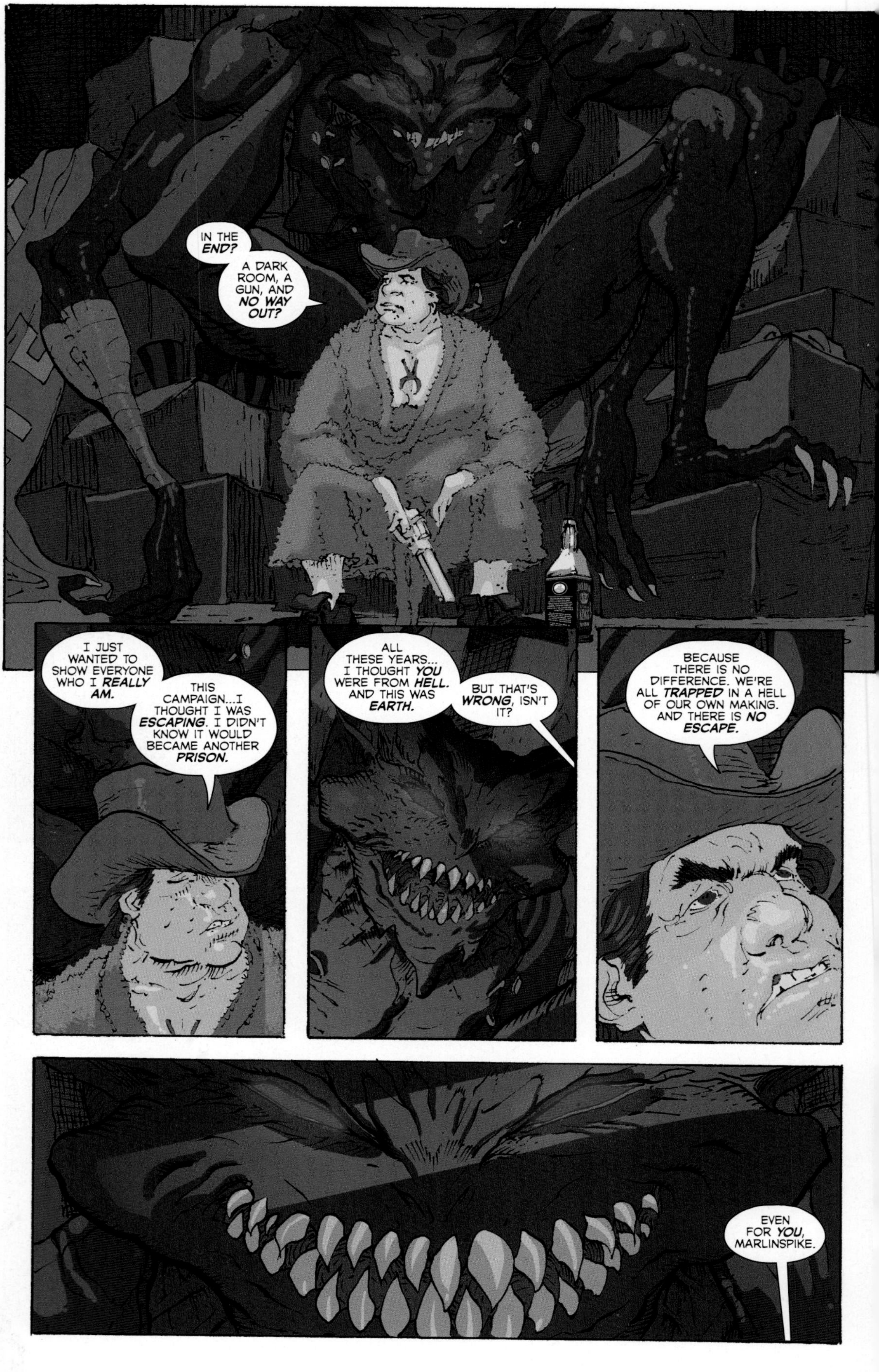
IN THE END?
A DARK ROOM, A GUN, AND NO WAY OUT?
I JUST WANTED TO SHOW EVERYONE WHO I REALLY AM.
THIS CAMPAIGN...I THOUGHT I WAS ESCAPING. I DIDN'T KNOW IT WOULD BECAME ANOTHER PRISON.
ALL THESE YEARS... I THOUGHT YOU WERE FROM HELL. AND THIS WAS EARTH.
BUT THAT'S WRONG, ISN'T IT?
BECAUSE THERE IS NO DIFFERENCE. WE'RE ALL TRAPPED IN A HELL OF OUR OWN MAKING. AND THERE IS NO ESCAPE.
EVEN FOR YOU, MARLINSPIKE.

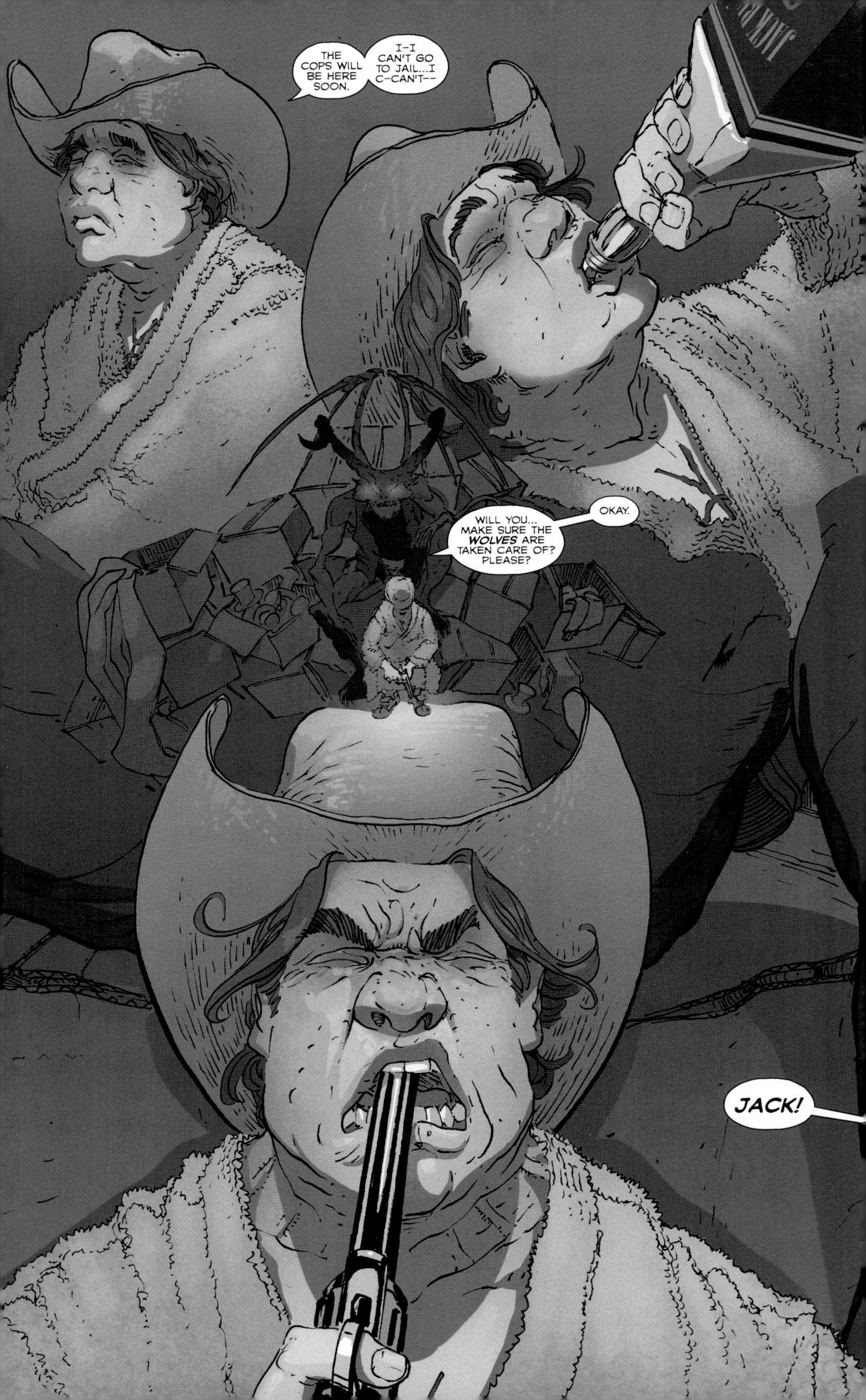
THE COPS WILL BE HERE SOON.
I-I CAN'T GO TO JAIL...I C-CAN'T--
WILL YOU... MAKE SURE THE *WOLVES* ARE TAKEN CARE OF? PLEASE?
OKAY.
JACK!

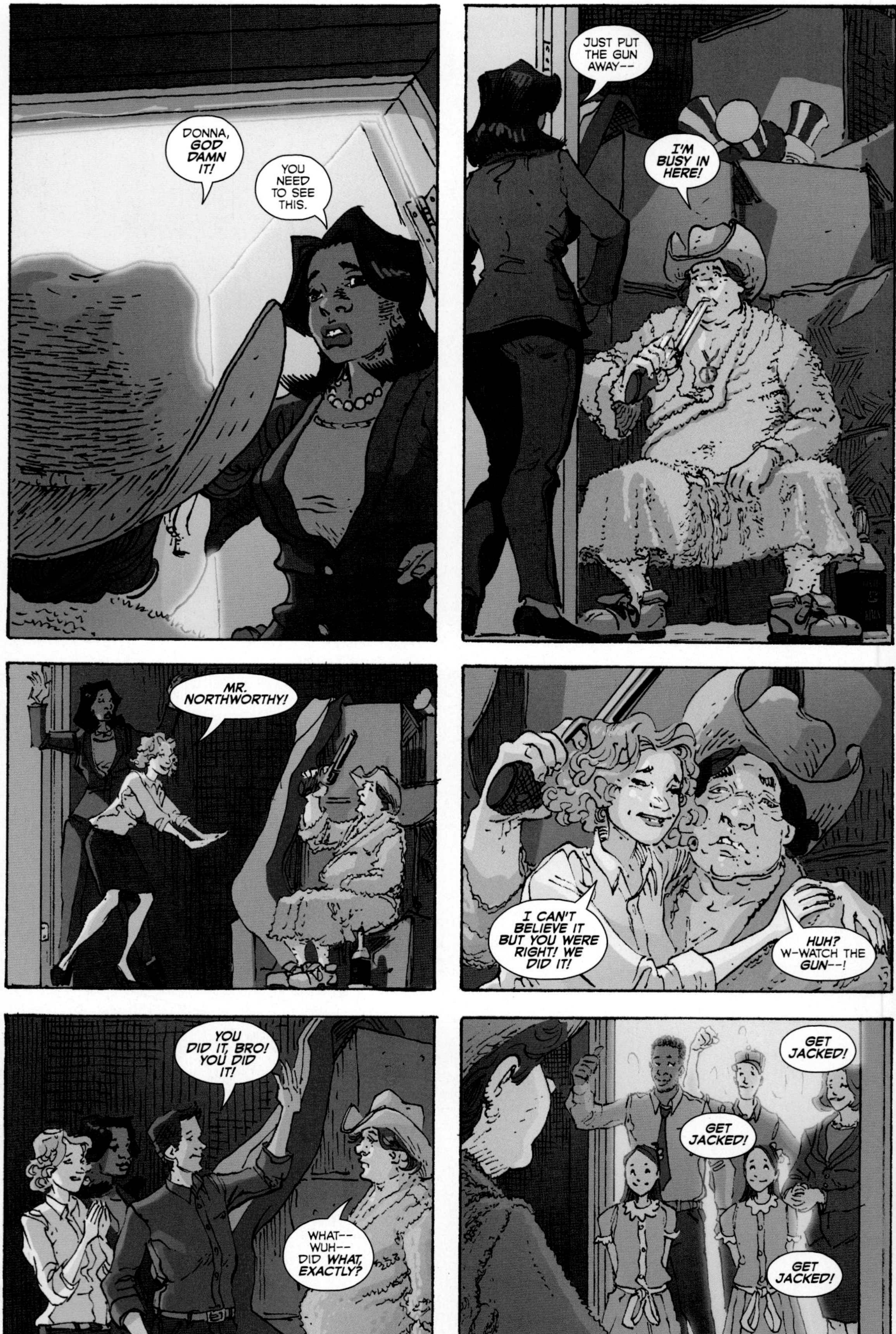
DONNA, GOD DAMN IT!
YOU NEED TO SEE THIS.
JUST PUT THE GUN AWAY--
I'M BUSY IN HERE!
MR. NORTHWORTHY!
I CAN'T BELIEVE IT BUT YOU WERE RIGHT! WE DID IT!
HUH? W-WATCH THE GUN--!
YOU DID IT, BRO! YOU DID IT!
WHAT-- WUH-- DID WHAT, EXACTLY?
GET JACKED!
GET JACKED!
GET JACKED!

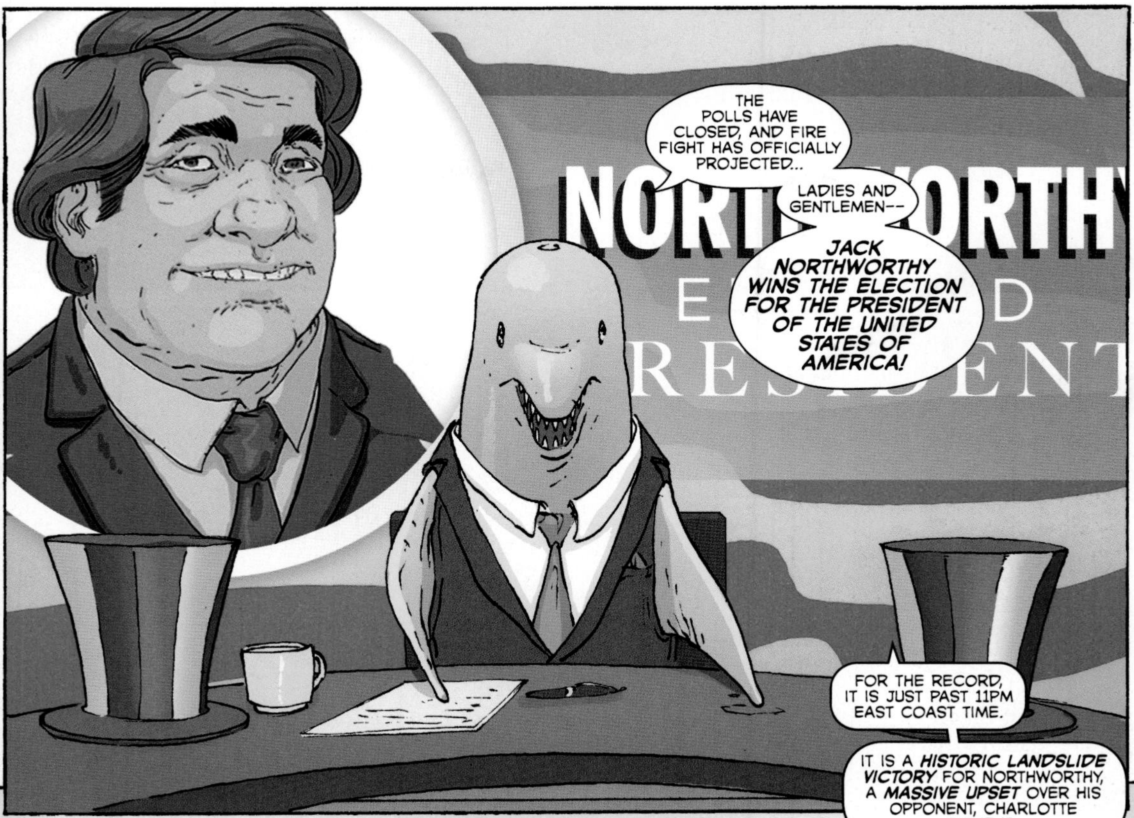
NORTHWORTHY
ELECTED
PRESIDENT
THE POLLS HAVE CLOSED, AND FIRE FIGHT HAS OFFICIALLY PROJECTED...
LADIES AND GENTLEMEN--
JACK NORTHWORTHY WINS THE ELECTION FOR THE PRESIDENT OF THE UNITED STATES OF AMERICA!
FOR THE RECORD, IT IS JUST PAST 11PM EAST COAST TIME.
IT IS A HISTORIC LANDSLIDE VICTORY FOR NORTHWORTHY, A MASSIVE UPSET OVER HIS OPPONENT, CHARLOTTE PICKENS.

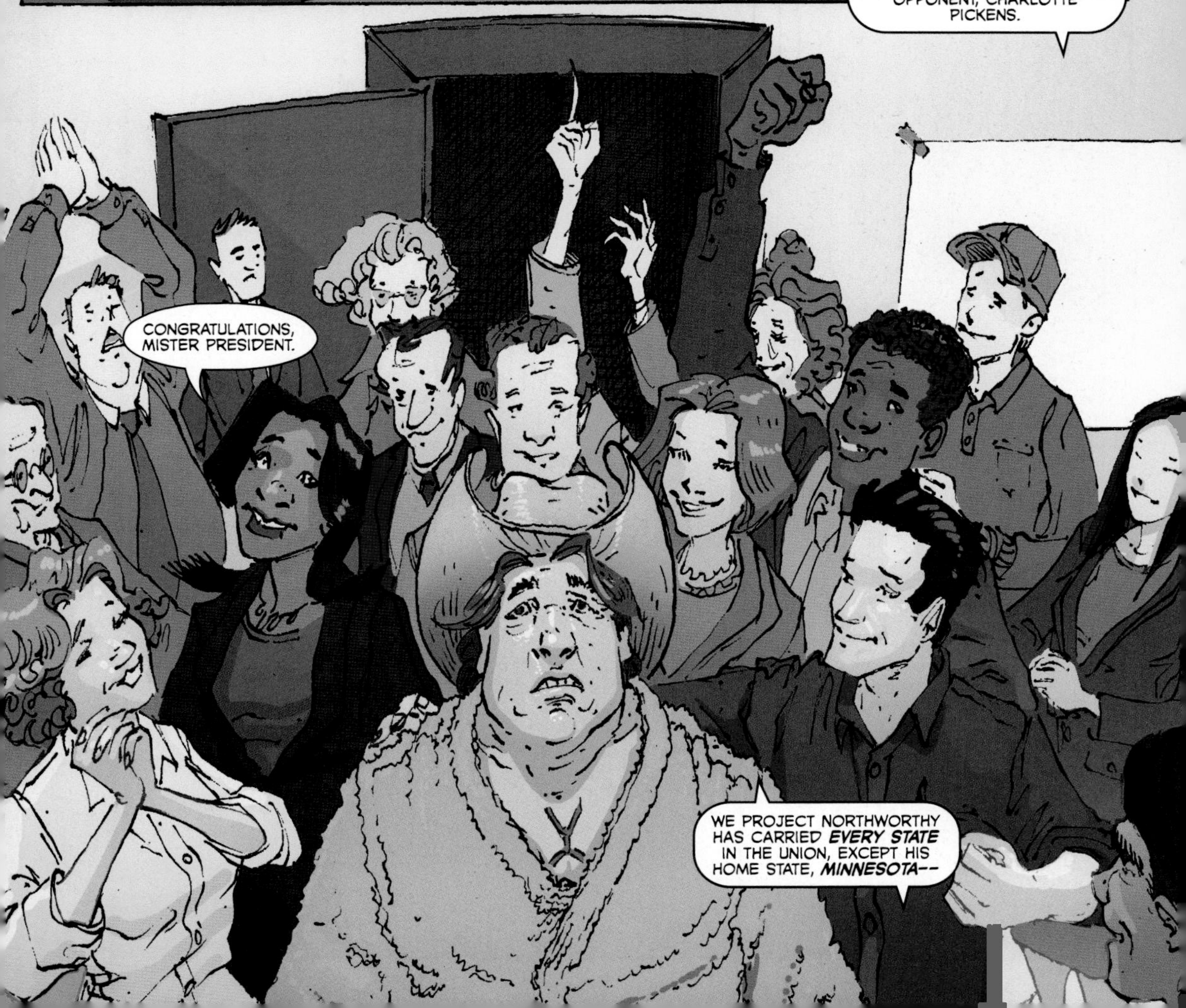
CONGRATULATIONS, MISTER PRESIDENT.
WE PROJECT NORTHWORTHY HAS CARRIED EVERY STATE IN THE UNION, EXCEPT HIS HOME STATE, MINNESOTA--

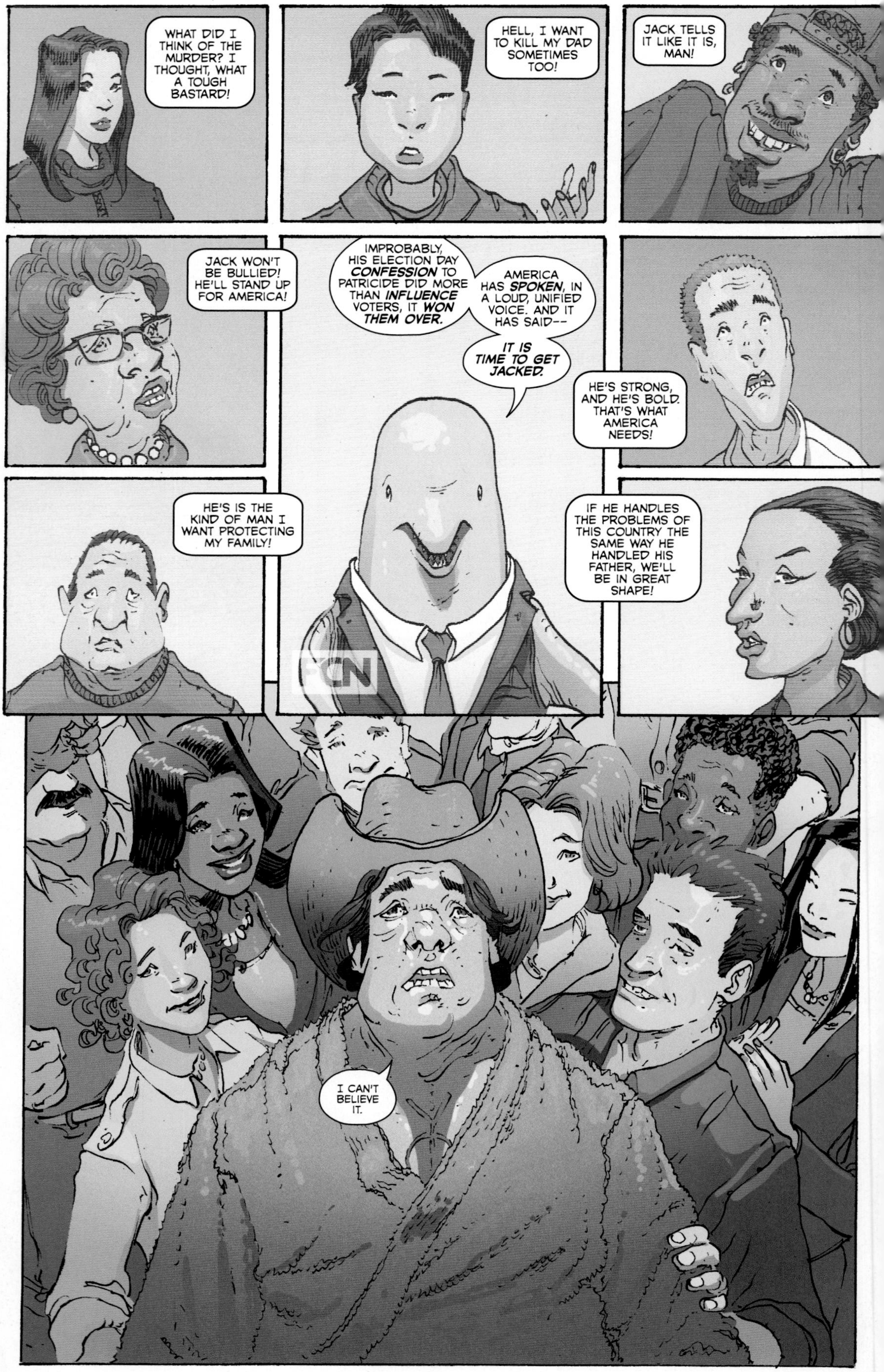
WHAT DID I THINK OF THE MURDER? I THOUGHT, WHAT A TOUGH BASTARD!
HELL, I WANT TO KILL MY DAD SOMETIMES TOO!
JACK TELLS IT LIKE IT IS, MAN!
JACK WON'T BE BULLIED! HE'LL STAND UP FOR AMERICA!
IMPROBABLY, HIS ELECTION DAY CONFESSION TO PATRICIDE DID MORE THAN INFLUENCE VOTERS, IT WON THEM OVER.
AMERICA HAS SPOKEN, IN A LOUD, UNIFIED VOICE. AND IT HAS SAID--
IT IS TIME TO GET JACKED.
HE'S STRONG, AND HE'S BOLD. THAT'S WHAT AMERICA NEEDS!
HE'S IS THE KIND OF MAN I WANT PROTECTING MY FAMILY!
IF HE HANDLES THE PROBLEMS OF THIS COUNTRY THE SAME WAY HE HANDLED HIS FATHER, WE'LL BE IN GREAT SHAPE!
FCN
I CAN'T BELIEVE IT.

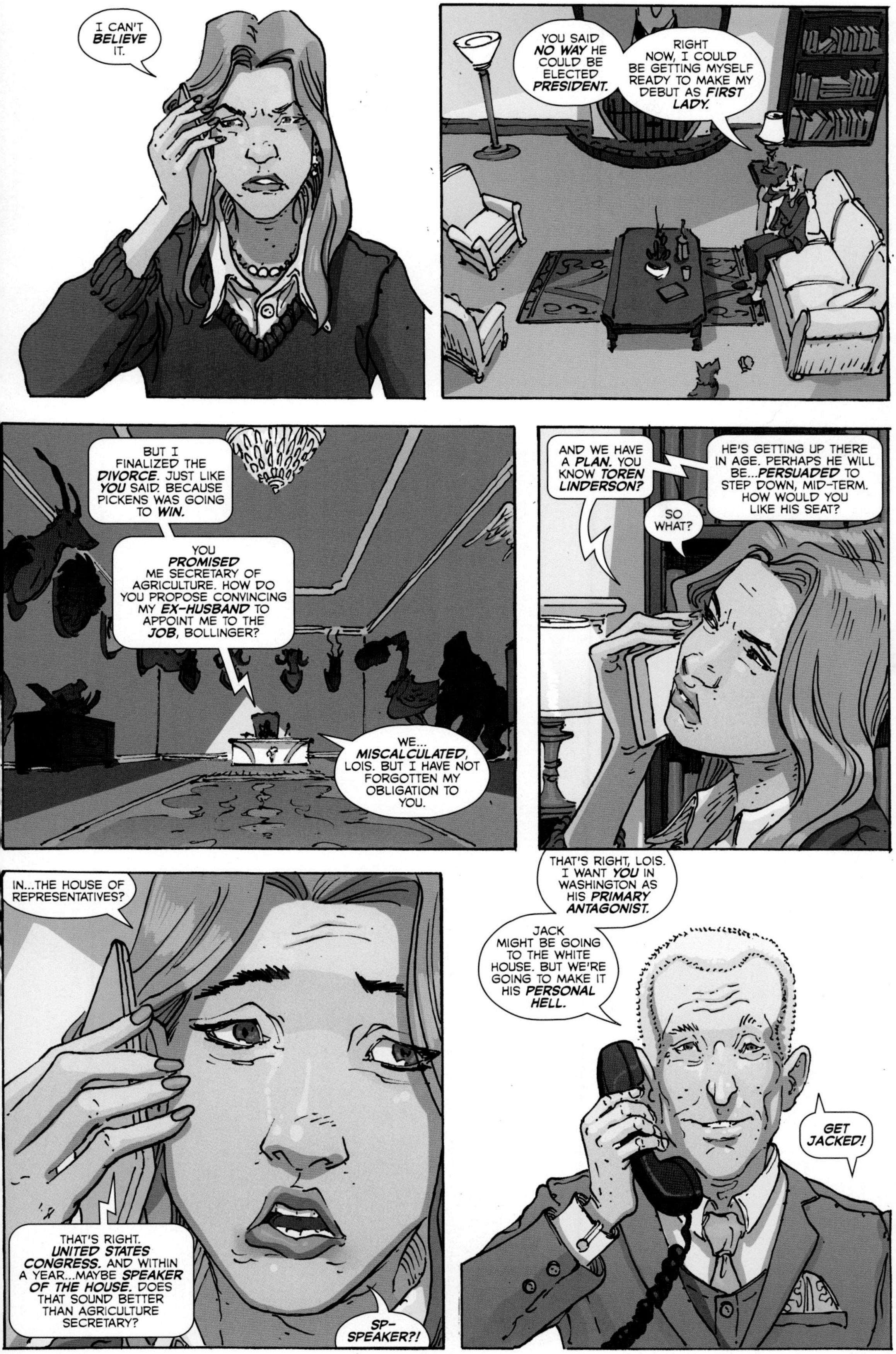
I CAN'T BELIEVE IT.
YOU SAID NO WAY HE COULD BE ELECTED PRESIDENT.
RIGHT NOW, I COULD BE GETTING MYSELF READY TO MAKE MY DEBUT AS FIRST LADY.
BUT I FINALIZED THE DIVORCE. JUST LIKE YOU SAID. BECAUSE PICKENS WAS GOING TO WIN.
YOU PROMISED ME SECRETARY OF AGRICULTURE. HOW DO YOU PROPOSE CONVINCING MY EX-HUSBAND TO APPOINT ME TO THE JOB, BOLLINGER?
WE... MISCALCULATED, LOIS. BUT I HAVE NOT FORGOTTEN MY OBLIGATION TO YOU.
AND WE HAVE A PLAN. YOU KNOW TOREN LINDERSON?
SO WHAT?
HE'S GETTING UP THERE IN AGE. PERHAPS HE WILL BE...PERSUADED TO STEP DOWN, MID-TERM. HOW WOULD YOU LIKE HIS SEAT?
IN...THE HOUSE OF REPRESENTATIVES?
THAT'S RIGHT. UNITED STATES CONGRESS. AND WITHIN A YEAR...MAYBE SPEAKER OF THE HOUSE. DOES THAT SOUND BETTER THAN AGRICULTURE SECRETARY?
SP-SPEAKER?!
THAT'S RIGHT, LOIS. I WANT YOU IN WASHINGTON AS HIS PRIMARY ANTAGONIST.
JACK MIGHT BE GOING TO THE WHITE HOUSE. BUT WE'RE GOING TO MAKE IT HIS PERSONAL HELL.
GET JACKED!

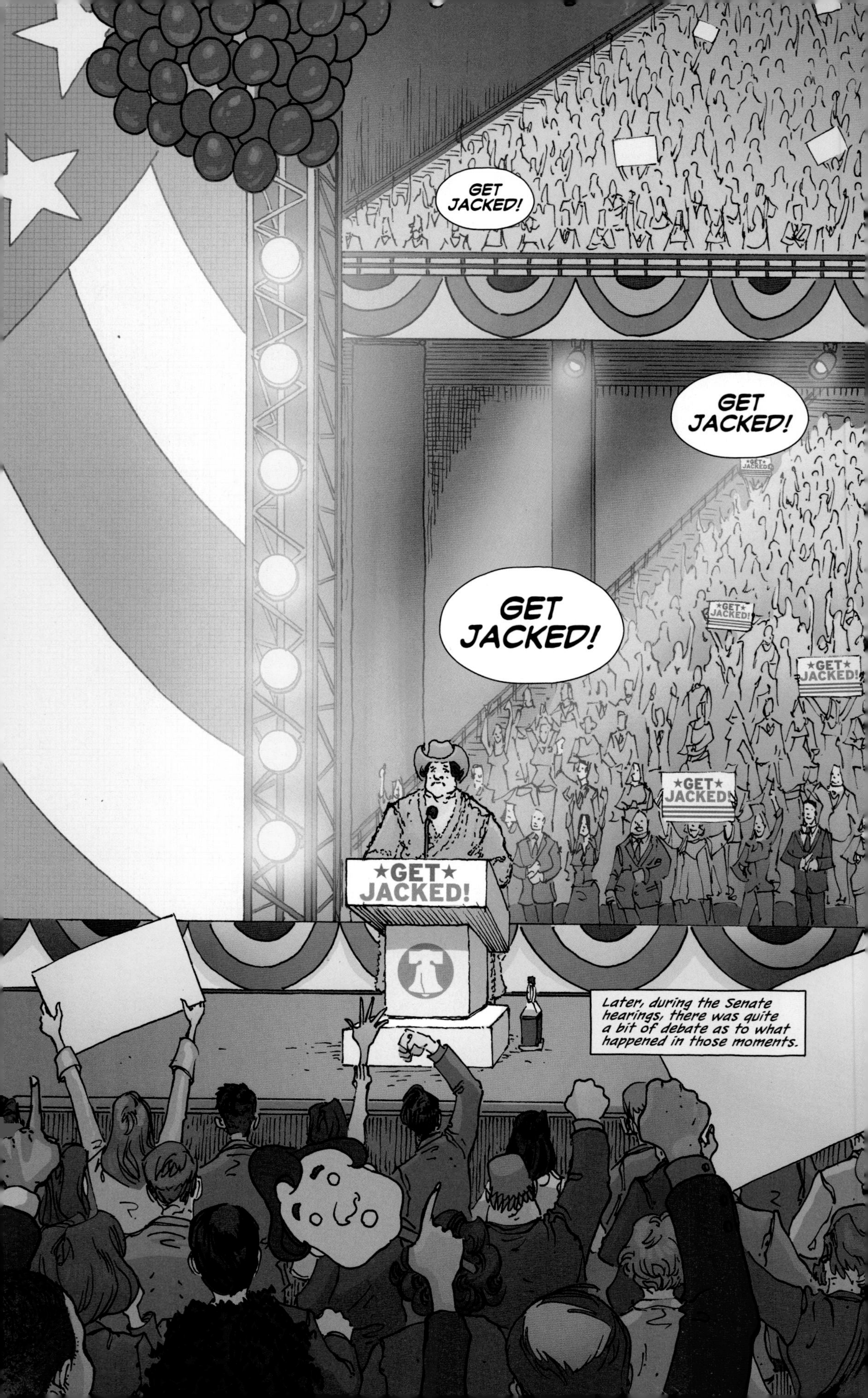
GET JACKED!
GET JACKED!
GET JACKED!
★GET★ JACKED!
★GET★ JACKED!
★GET★ JACKED!
★GET★ JACKED!
Later, during the Senate hearings, there was quite a bit of debate as to what happened in those moments.

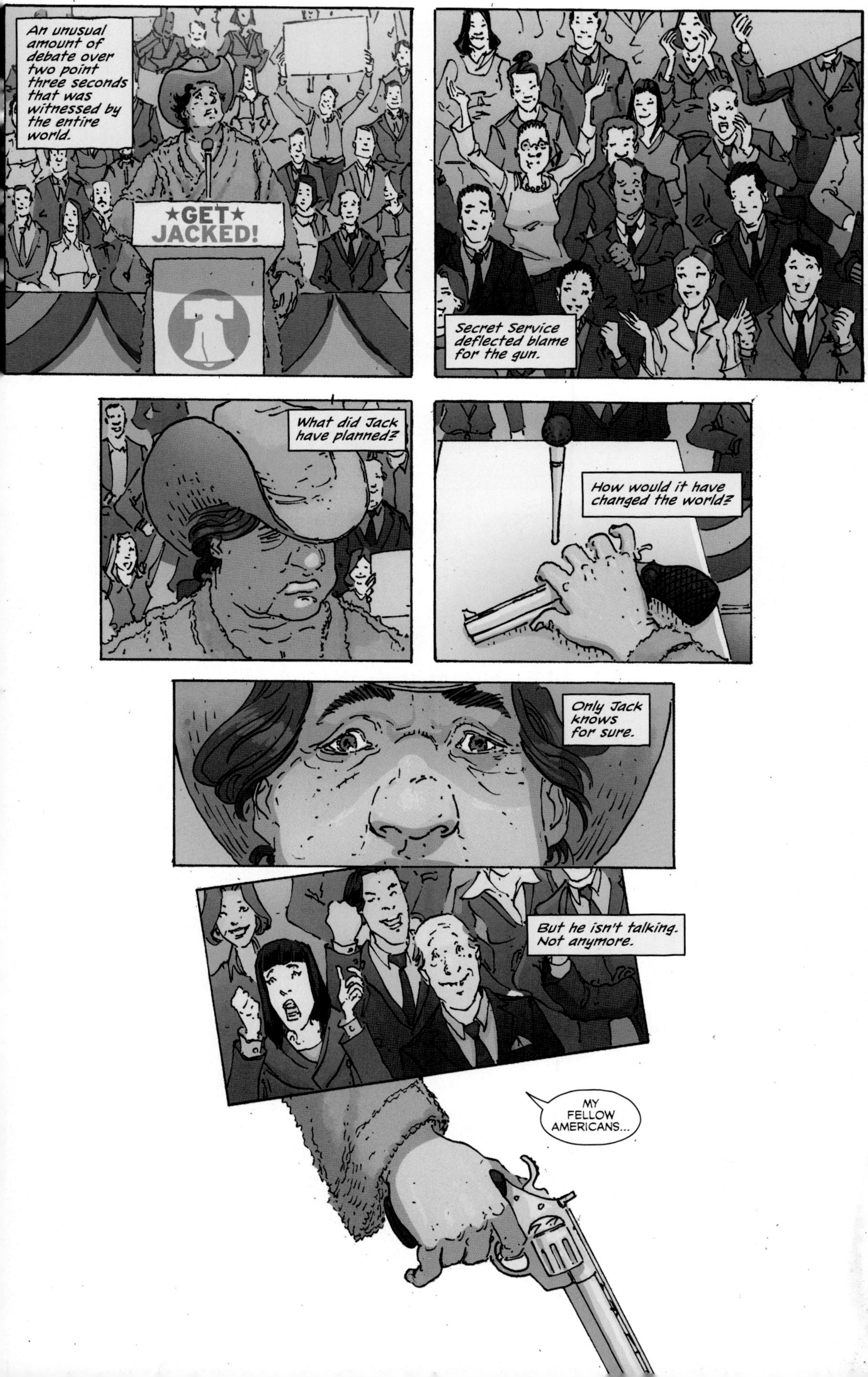
An unusual amount of debate over two point three seconds that was witnessed by the entire world.
★GET★ JACKED!
Secret Service deflected blame for the gun.
What did Jack have planned?
How would it have changed the world?
Only Jack knows for sure.
But he isn't talking. Not anymore.
MY FELLOW AMERICANS...

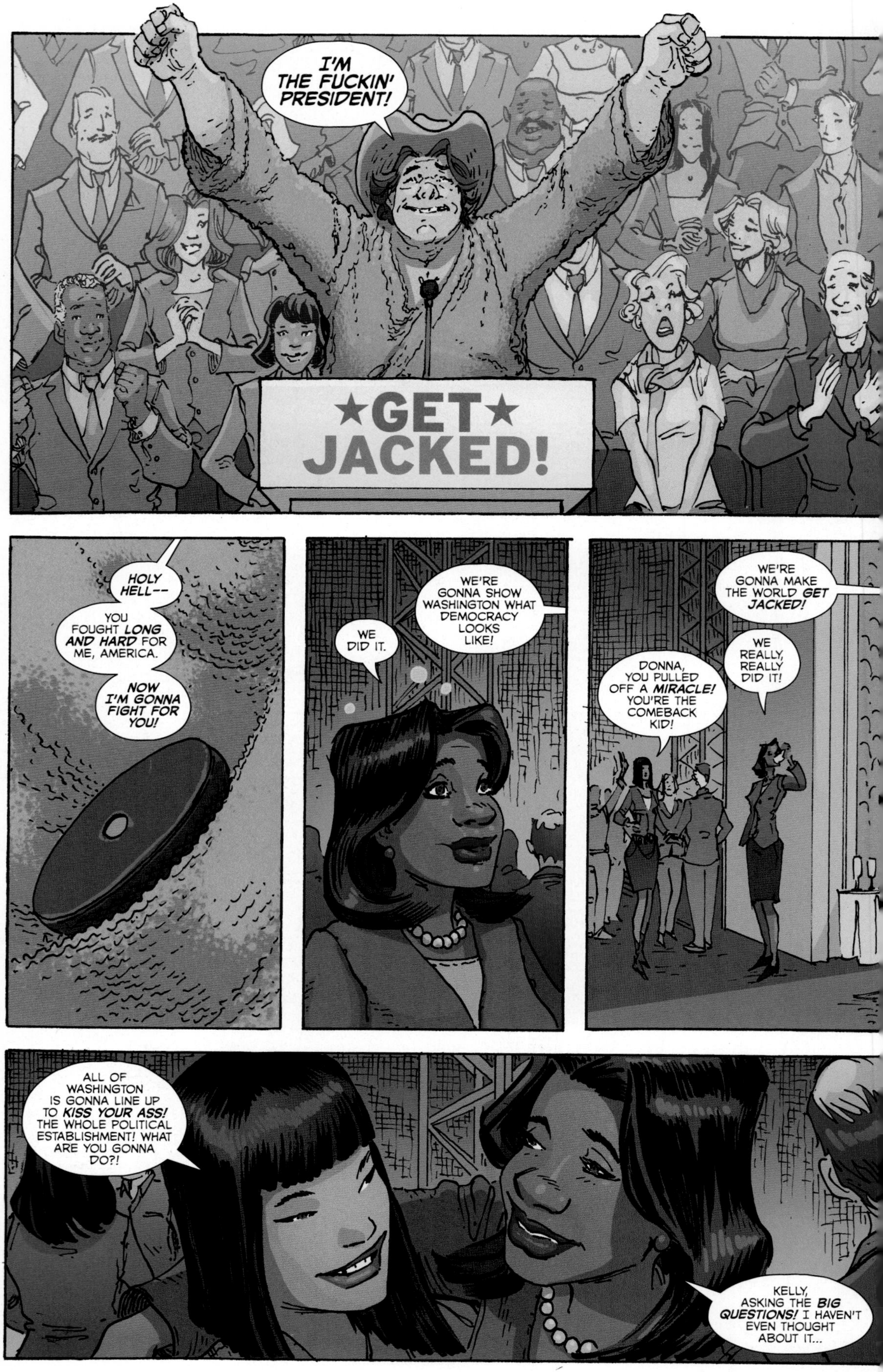
I'M THE FUCKIN' PRESIDENT!
★GET★ JACKED!
HOLY HELL--
YOU FOUGHT LONG AND HARD FOR ME, AMERICA.
NOW I'M GONNA FIGHT FOR YOU!
WE DID IT.
WE'RE GONNA SHOW WASHINGTON WHAT DEMOCRACY LOOKS LIKE!
WE'RE GONNA MAKE THE WORLD GET JACKED!
WE REALLY, REALLY DID IT!
DONNA, YOU PULLED OFF A MIRACLE! YOU'RE THE COMEBACK KID!
ALL OF WASHINGTON IS GONNA LINE UP TO KISS YOUR ASS! THE WHOLE POLITICAL ESTABLISHMENT! WHAT ARE YOU GONNA DO?!
KELLY, ASKING THE BIG QUESTIONS! I HAVEN'T EVEN THOUGHT ABOUT IT...

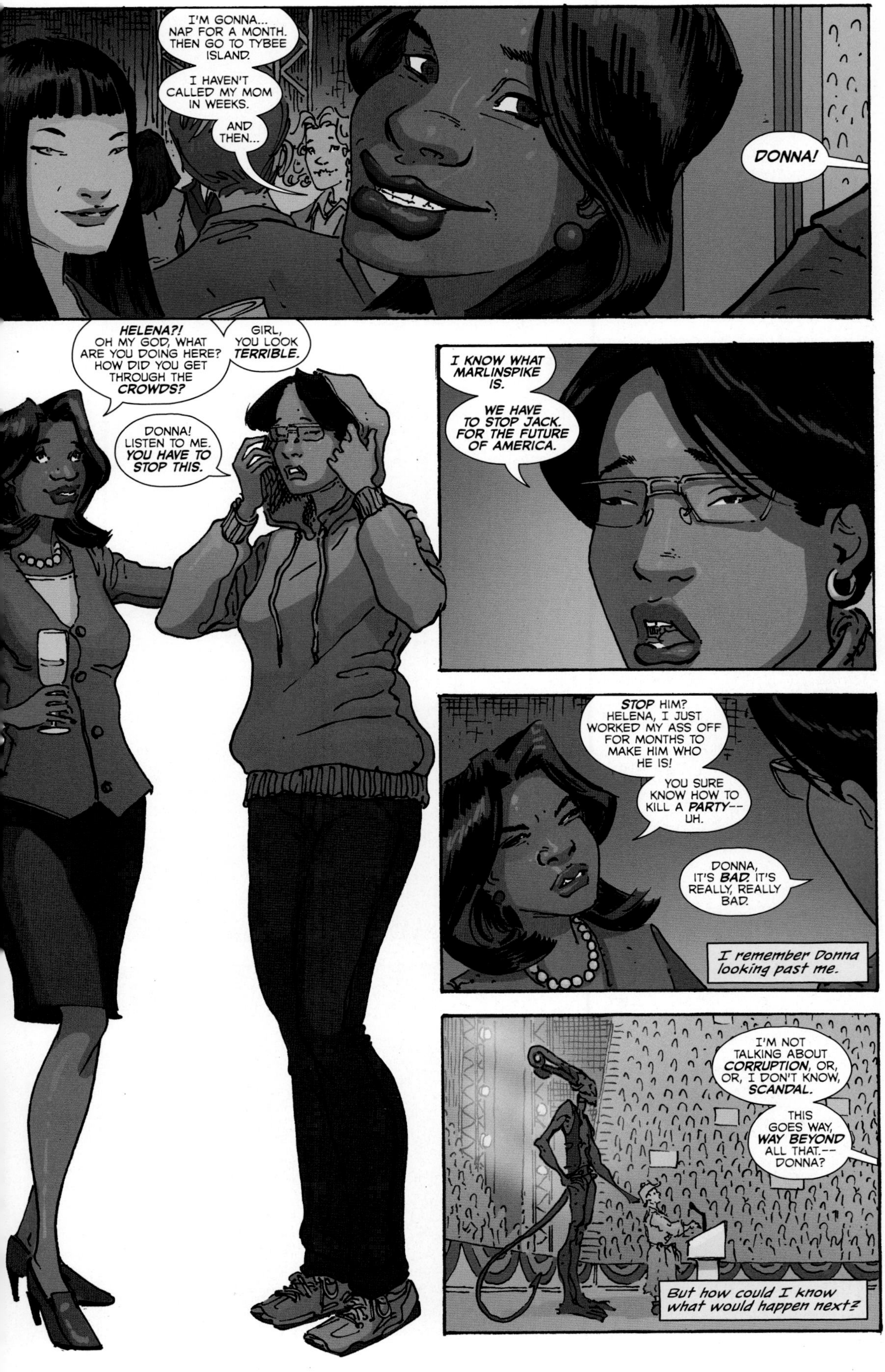
I'M GONNA... NAP FOR A MONTH. THEN GO TO TYBEE ISLAND.
I HAVEN'T CALLED MY MOM IN WEEKS.
AND THEN...
DONNA!
HELENA?! OH MY GOD, WHAT ARE YOU DOING HERE? HOW DID YOU GET THROUGH THE CROWDS?
GIRL, YOU LOOK TERRIBLE.
DONNA! LISTEN TO ME. YOU HAVE TO STOP THIS.
I KNOW WHAT MARLINSPIKE IS.
WE HAVE TO STOP JACK. FOR THE FUTURE OF AMERICA.
STOP HIM? HELENA, I JUST WORKED MY ASS OFF FOR MONTHS TO MAKE HIM WHO HE IS!
YOU SURE KNOW HOW TO KILL A PARTY-- UH.
DONNA, IT'S BAD. IT'S REALLY, REALLY BAD.
I remember Donna looking past me.
I'M NOT TALKING ABOUT CORRUPTION, OR, OR, I DON'T KNOW, SCANDAL.
THIS GOES WAY, WAY BEYOND ALL THAT.-- DONNA?
But how could I know what would happen next?

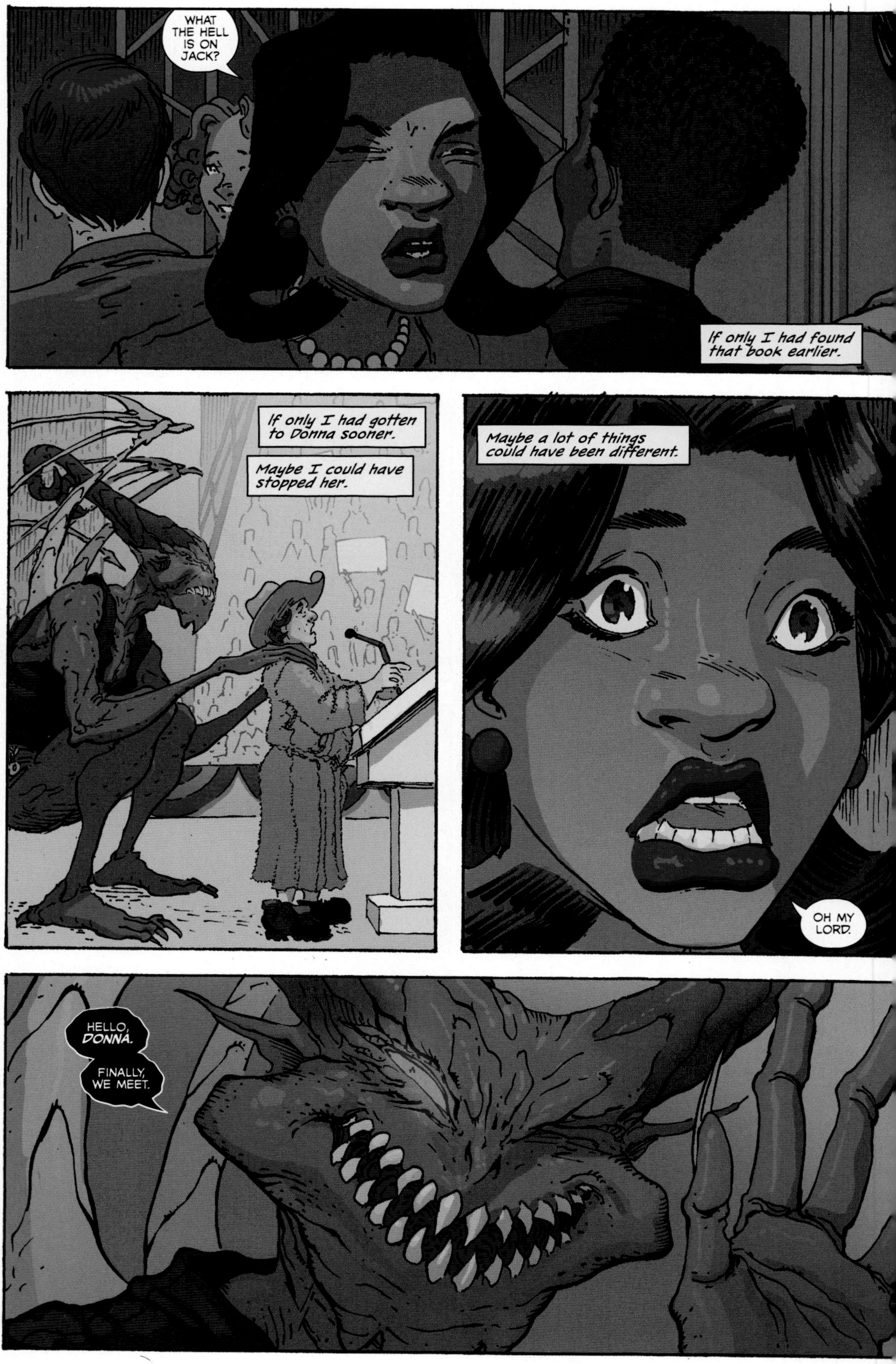
WHAT THE HELL IS ON JACK?
If only I had found that book earlier.
If only I had gotten to Donna sooner.
Maybe I could have stopped her.
Maybe a lot of things could have been different.
OH MY LORD.
HELLO, DONNA.
FINALLY, WE MEET.

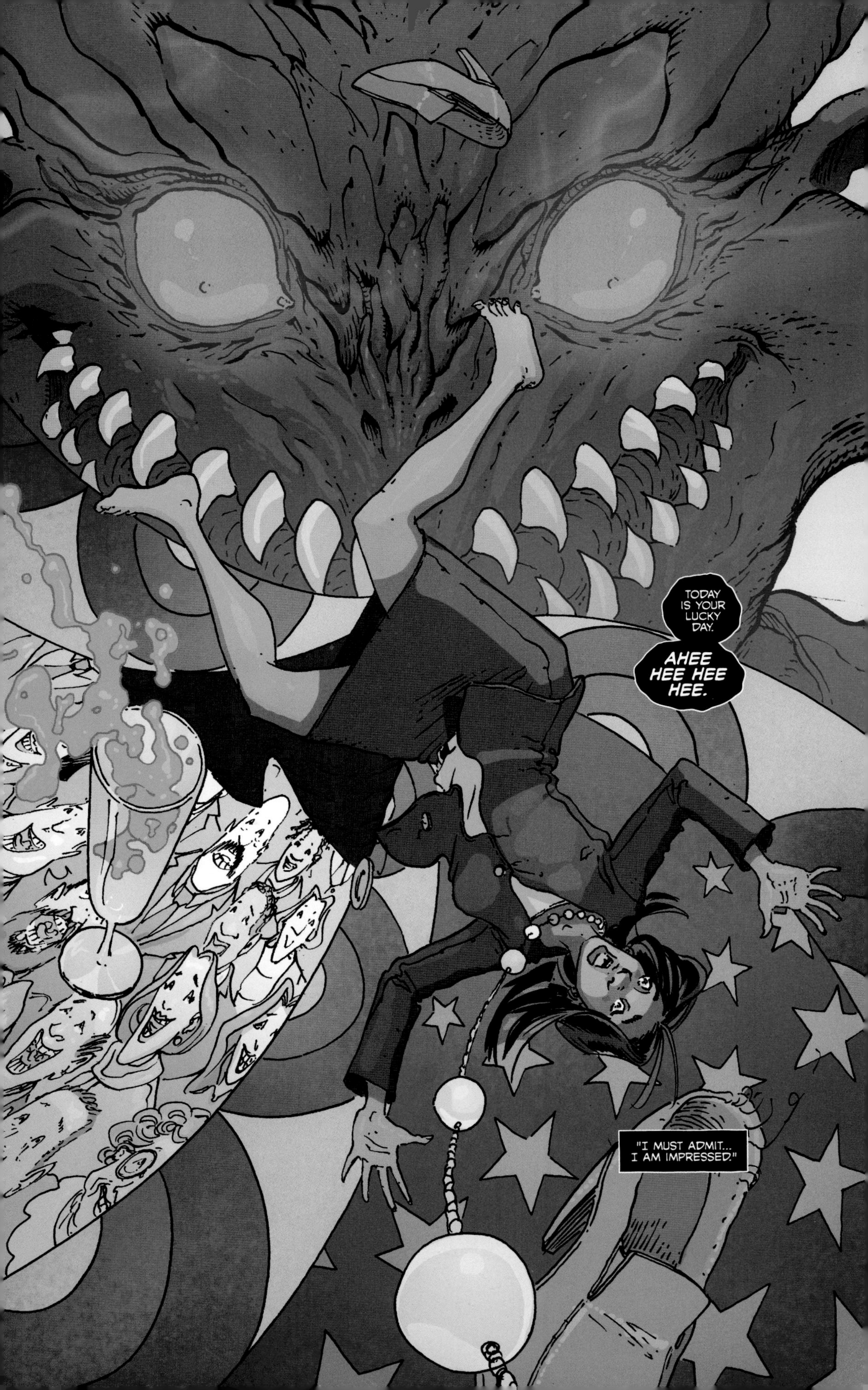
TODAY IS YOUR LUCKY DAY.
AHEE HEE HEE HEE.
"I MUST ADMIT... I AM IMPRESSED."

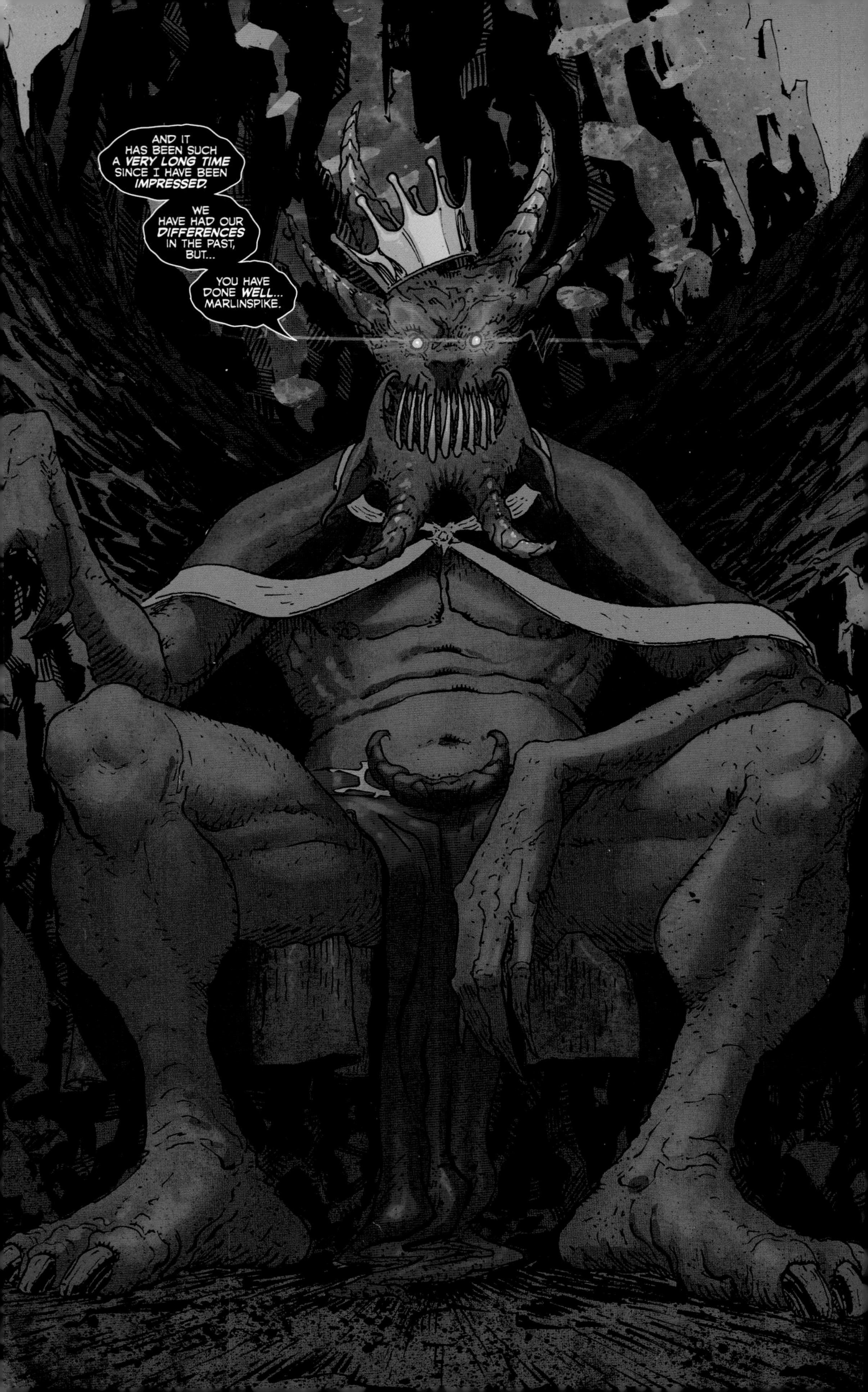

AND IT HAS BEEN SUCH A VERY LONG TIME SINCE I HAVE BEEN IMPRESSED.
WE HAVE HAD OUR DIFFERENCES IN THE PAST, BUT...
YOU HAVE DONE WELL... MARLINSPIKE.

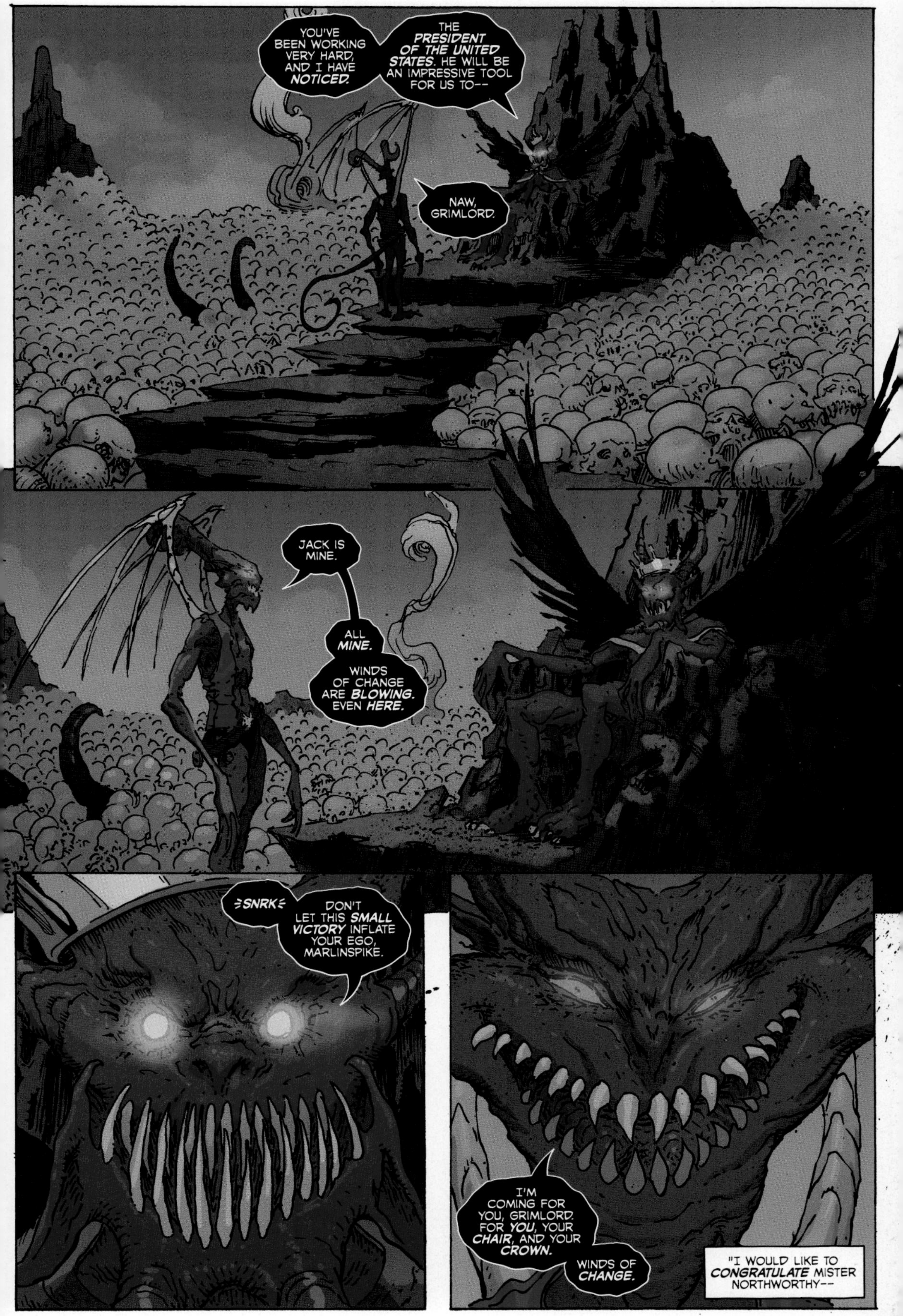

YOU'VE BEEN WORKING VERY HARD, AND I HAVE NOTICED.
THE PRESIDENT OF THE UNITED STATES. HE WILL BE AN IMPRESSIVE TOOL FOR US TO--
NAW, GRIMLORD.
JACK IS MINE.
ALL MINE.
WINDS OF CHANGE ARE BLOWING. EVEN HERE.
SNRK
DON'T LET THIS SMALL VICTORY INFLATE YOUR EGO, MARLINSPIKE.
I'M COMING FOR YOU, GRIMLORD. FOR YOU, YOUR CHAIR, AND YOUR CROWN.
WINDS OF CHANGE.
"I WOULD LIKE TO CONGRATULATE MISTER NORTHWORTHY--

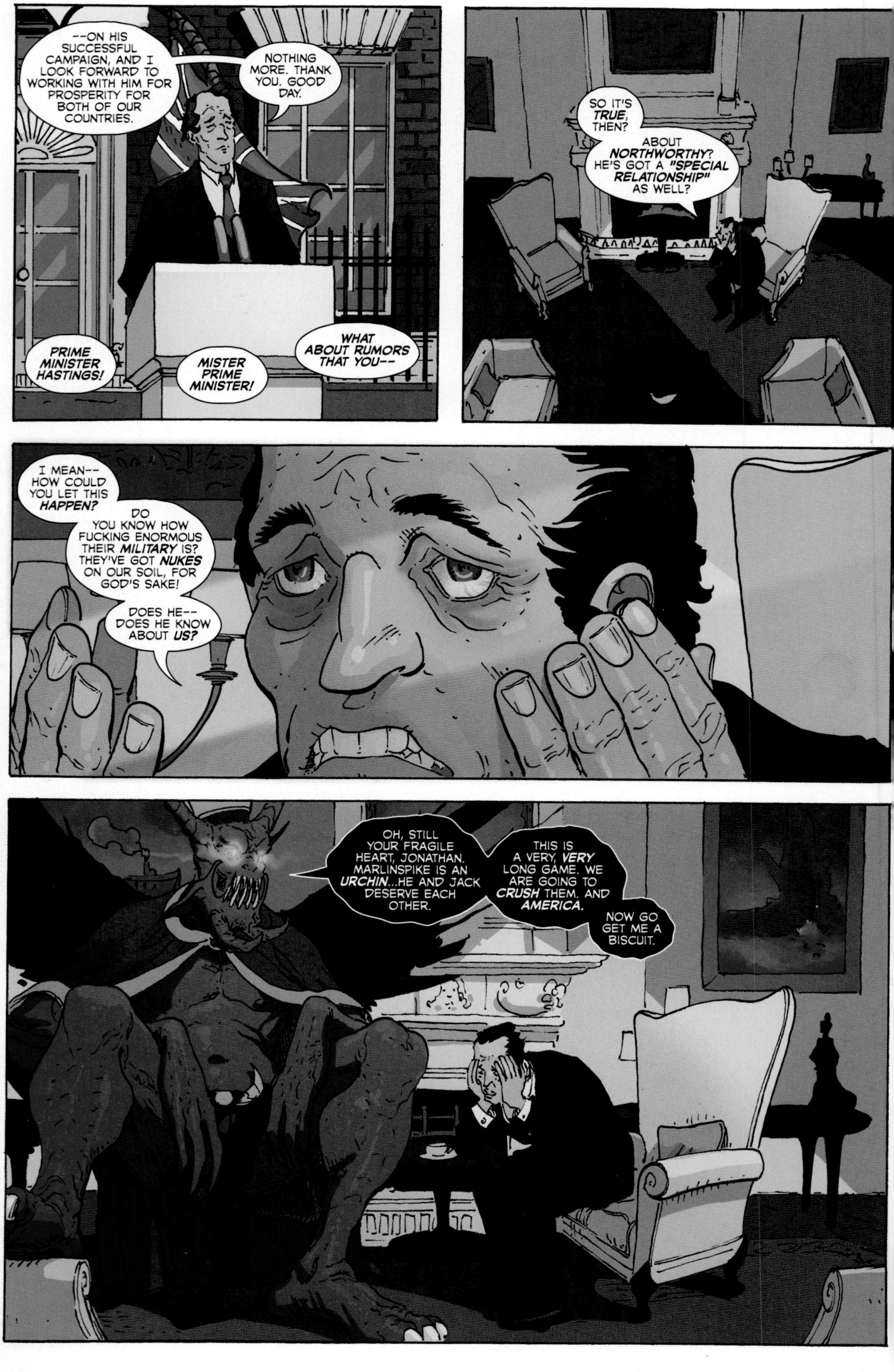
--ON HIS SUCCESSFUL CAMPAIGN, AND I LOOK FORWARD TO WORKING WITH HIM FOR PROSPERITY FOR BOTH OF OUR COUNTRIES.
NOTHING MORE. THANK YOU. GOOD DAY.
PRIME MINISTER HASTINGS!
MISTER PRIME MINISTER!
WHAT ABOUT RUMORS THAT YOU--
SO IT'S TRUE, THEN?
ABOUT NORTHWORTHY? HE'S GOT A "SPECIAL RELATIONSHIP" AS WELL?
I MEAN-- HOW COULD YOU LET THIS HAPPEN?
DO YOU KNOW HOW FUCKING ENORMOUS THEIR MILITARY IS? THEY'VE GOT NUKES ON OUR SOIL, FOR GOD'S SAKE!
DOES HE-- DOES HE KNOW ABOUT US?
OH, STILL YOUR FRAGILE HEART, JONATHAN. MARLINSPIKE IS AN URCHIN...HE AND JACK DESERVE EACH OTHER.
THIS IS A VERY, VERY LONG GAME. WE ARE GOING TO CRUSH THEM. AND AMERICA.
NOW GO GET ME A BISCUIT.

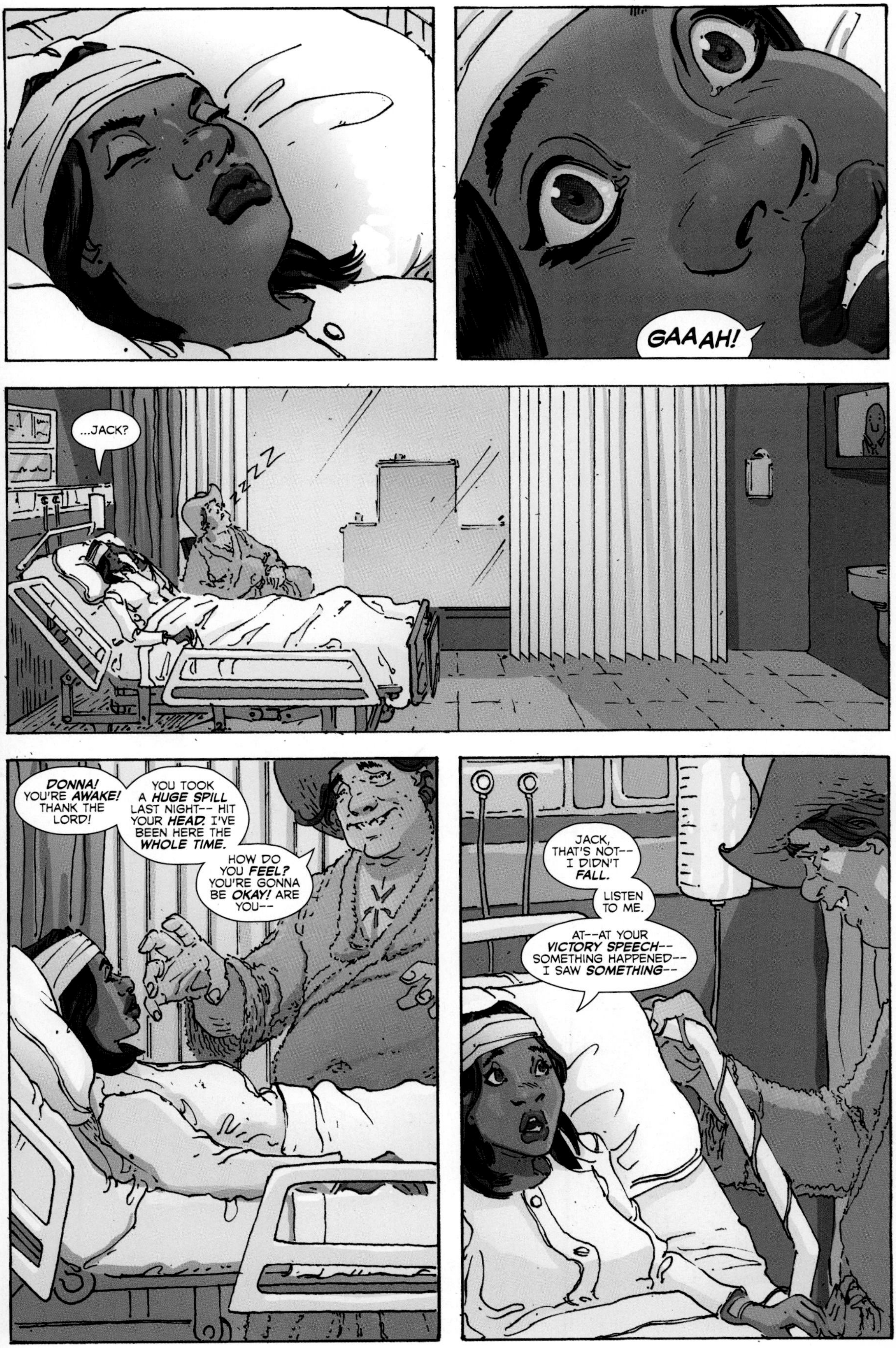
GAAAH!
...JACK?
ZZZZ
DONNA! YOU'RE AWAKE! THANK THE LORD!
YOU TOOK A HUGE SPILL LAST NIGHT-- HIT YOUR HEAD. I'VE BEEN HERE THE WHOLE TIME.
HOW DO YOU FEEL? YOU'RE GONNA BE OKAY! ARE YOU--
JACK, THAT'S NOT-- I DIDN'T FALL.
LISTEN TO ME.
AT--AT YOUR VICTORY SPEECH-- SOMETHING HAPPENED-- I SAW SOMETHING--

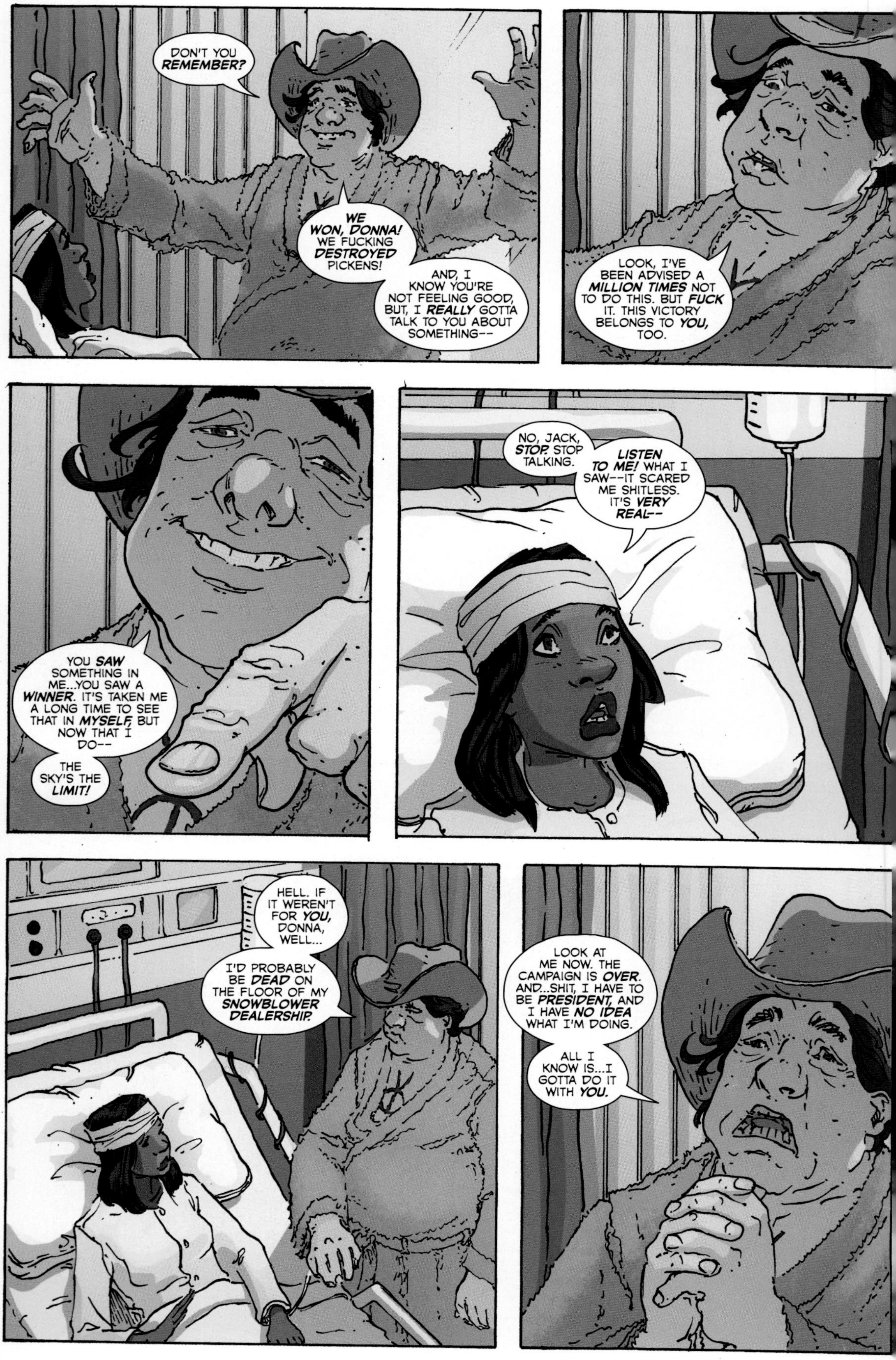
DON'T YOU REMEMBER?
WE WON, DONNA! WE FUCKING DESTROYED PICKENS!
AND, I KNOW YOU'RE NOT FEELING GOOD, BUT, I REALLY GOTTA TALK TO YOU ABOUT SOMETHING--
LOOK, I'VE BEEN ADVISED A MILLION TIMES NOT TO DO THIS. BUT FUCK IT. THIS VICTORY BELONGS TO YOU, TOO.
YOU SAW SOMETHING IN ME...YOU SAW A WINNER. IT'S TAKEN ME A LONG TIME TO SEE THAT IN MYSELF, BUT NOW THAT I DO--
THE SKY'S THE LIMIT!
NO, JACK, STOP. STOP TALKING.
LISTEN TO ME! WHAT I SAW--IT SCARED ME SHITLESS. IT'S VERY REAL--
HELL. IF IT WEREN'T FOR YOU, DONNA, WELL...
I'D PROBABLY BE DEAD ON THE FLOOR OF MY SNOWBLOWER DEALERSHIP.
LOOK AT ME NOW. THE CAMPAIGN IS OVER. AND...SHIT, I HAVE TO BE PRESIDENT, AND I HAVE NO IDEA WHAT I'M DOING.
ALL I KNOW IS...I GOTTA DO IT WITH YOU.

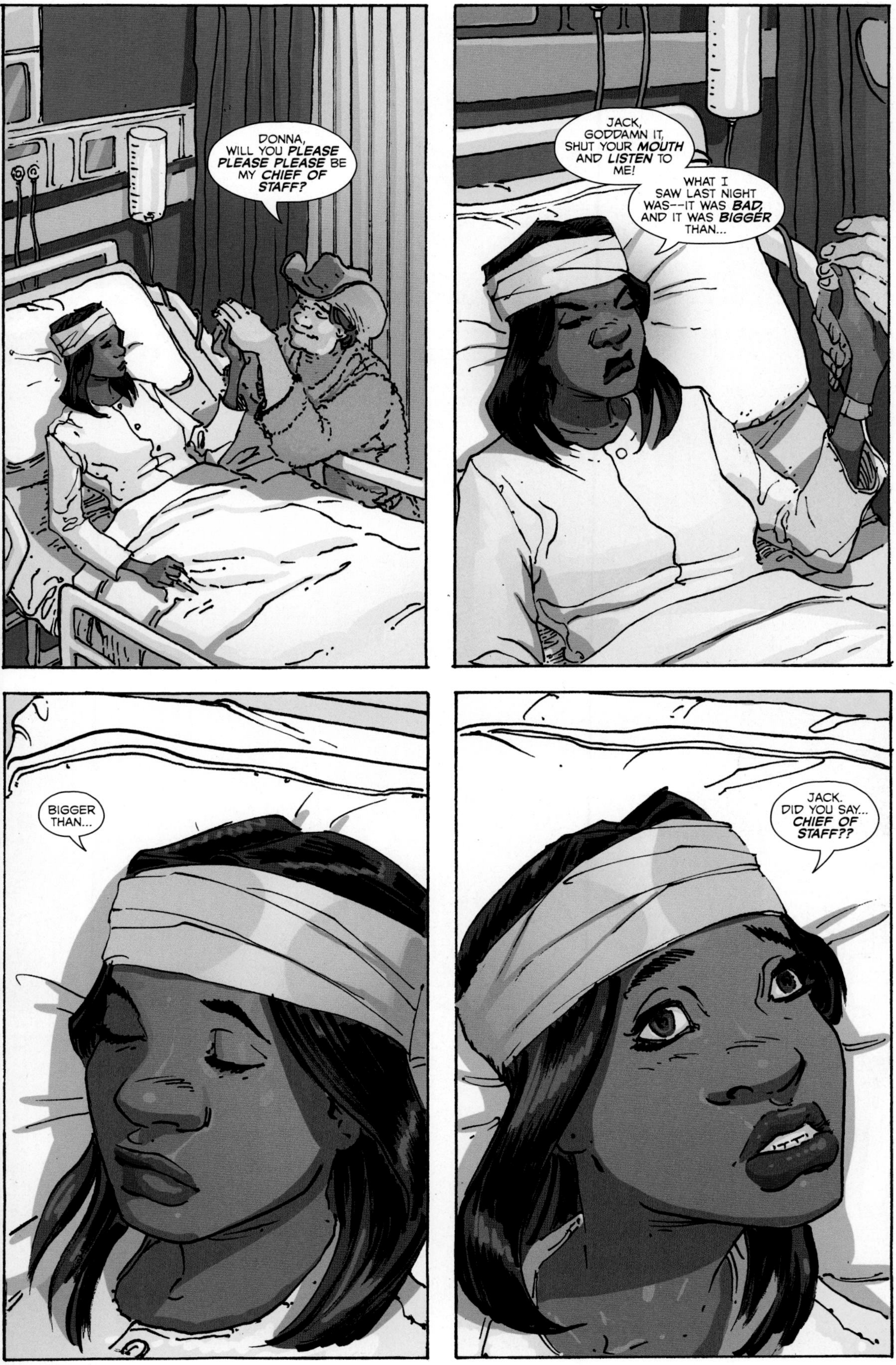
DONNA, WILL YOU PLEASE PLEASE PLEASE BE MY CHIEF OF STAFF?
JACK, GODDAMN IT, SHUT YOUR MOUTH AND LISTEN TO ME!
WHAT I SAW LAST NIGHT WAS--IT WAS BAD, AND IT WAS BIGGER THAN...
BIGGER THAN...
JACK. DID YOU SAY... CHIEF OF STAFF??

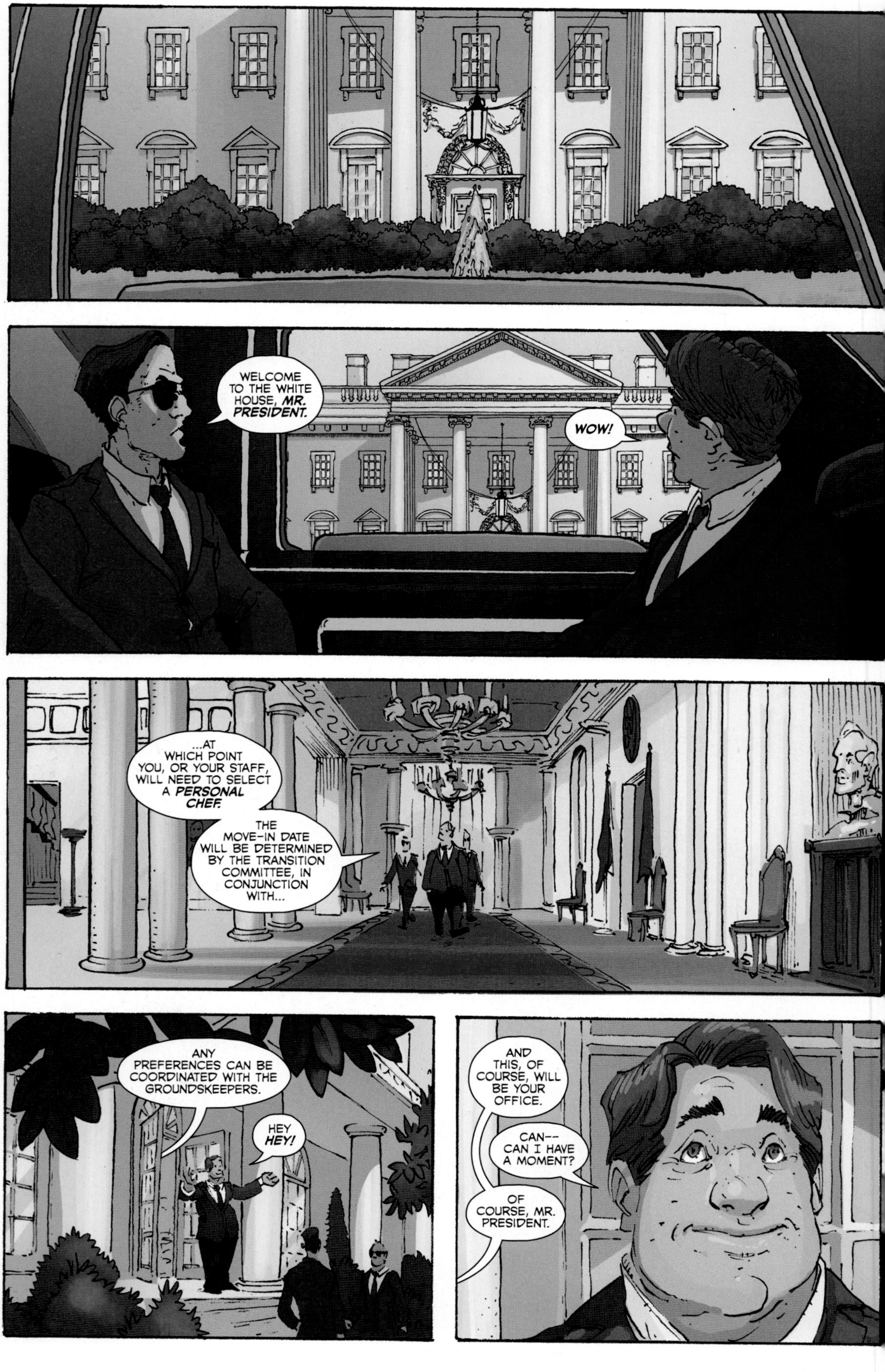
WELCOME TO THE WHITE HOUSE, MR. PRESIDENT.
WOW!
...AT WHICH POINT YOU, OR YOUR STAFF, WILL NEED TO SELECT A PERSONAL CHEF.
THE MOVE-IN DATE WILL BE DETERMINED BY THE TRANSITION COMMITTEE, IN CONJUNCTION WITH...
ANY PREFERENCES CAN BE COORDINATED WITH THE GROUNDSKEEPERS.
HEY HEY!
AND THIS, OF COURSE, WILL BE YOUR OFFICE.
CAN-- CAN I HAVE A MOMENT?
OF COURSE, MR. PRESIDENT.

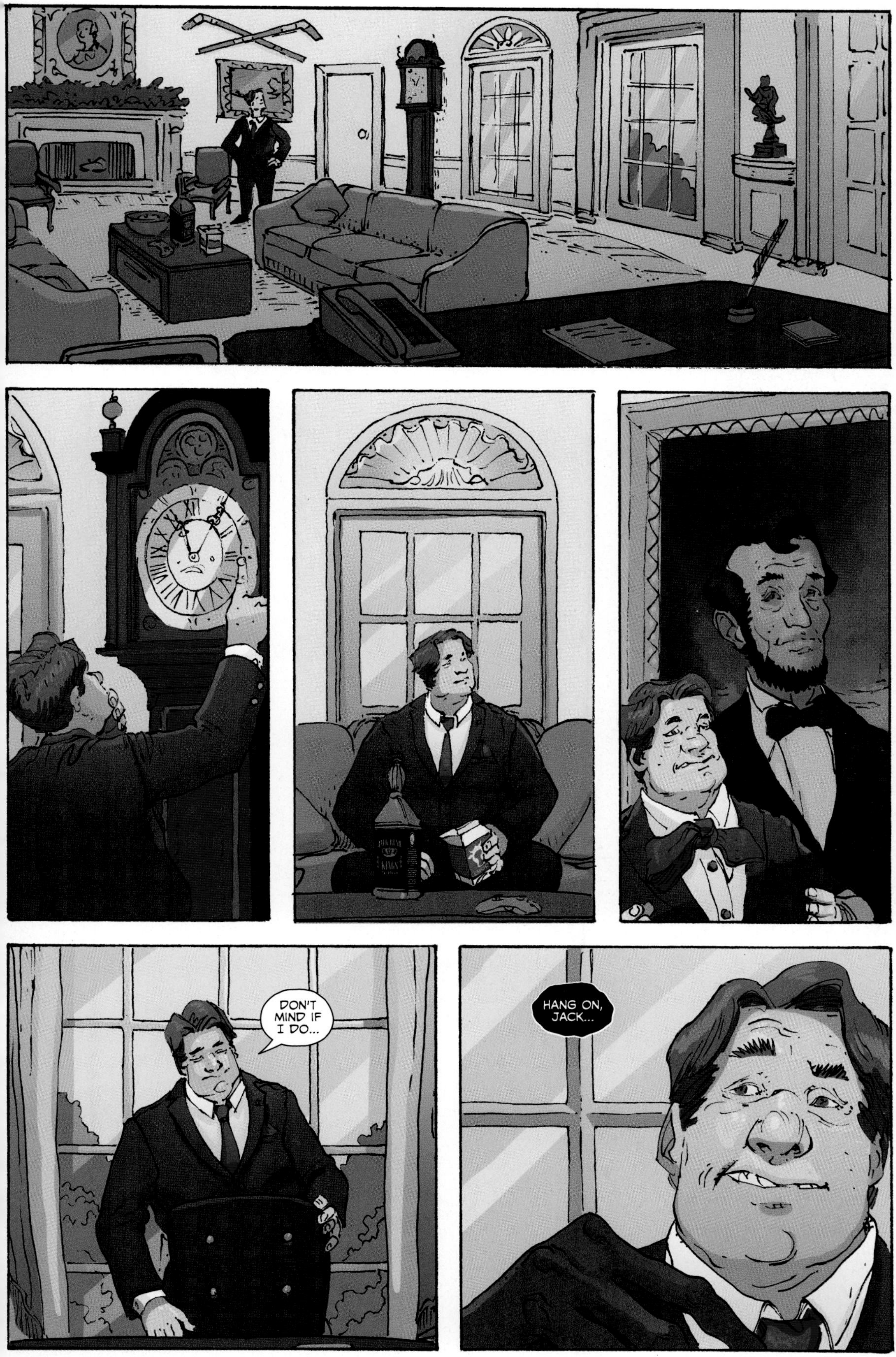
DON'T MIND IF I DO...
HANG ON, JACK...

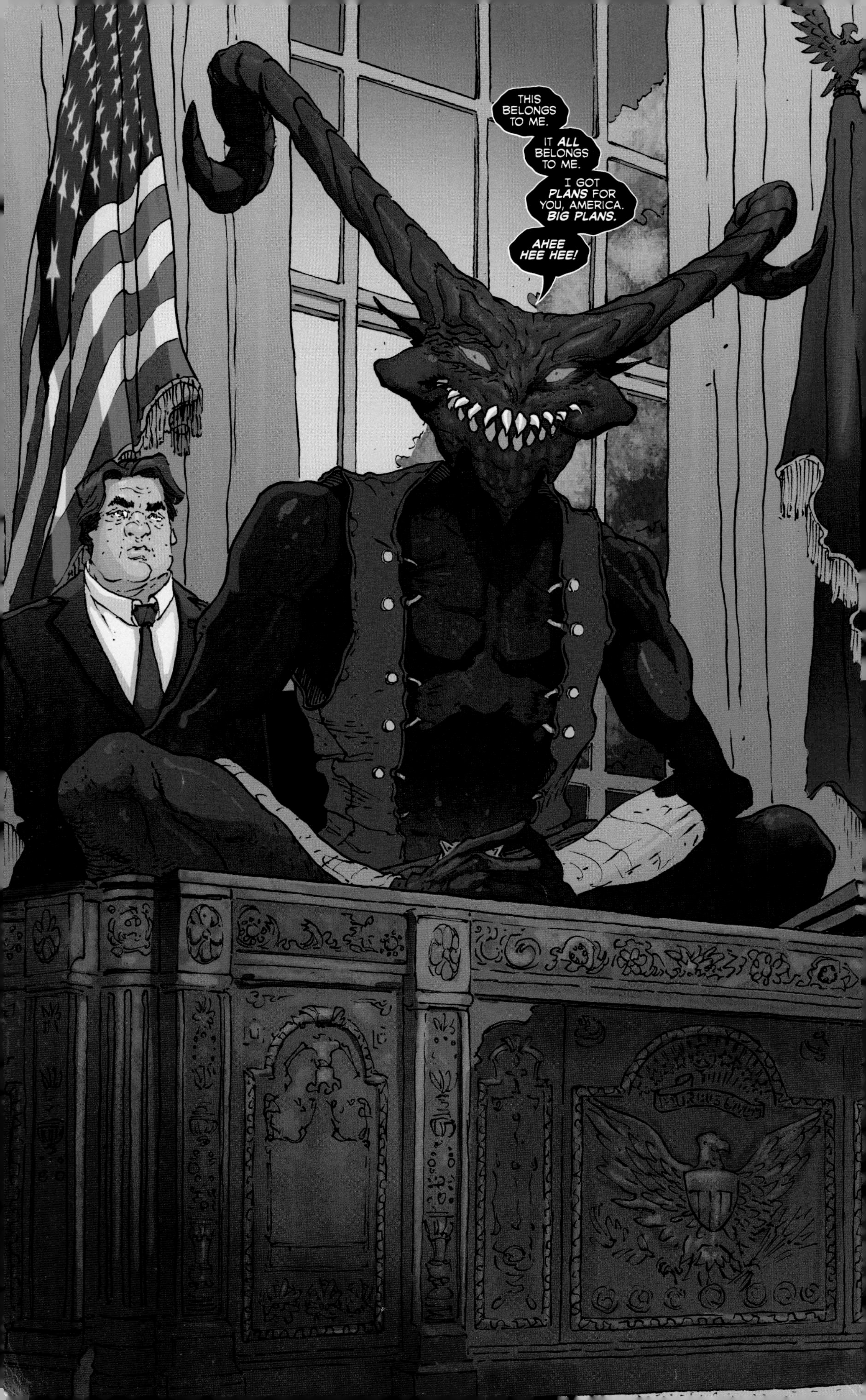
THIS BELONGS TO ME.
IT **ALL** BELONGS TO ME.
I GOT **PLANS** FOR YOU, AMERICA. **BIG PLANS.**
AHEE HEE HEE!

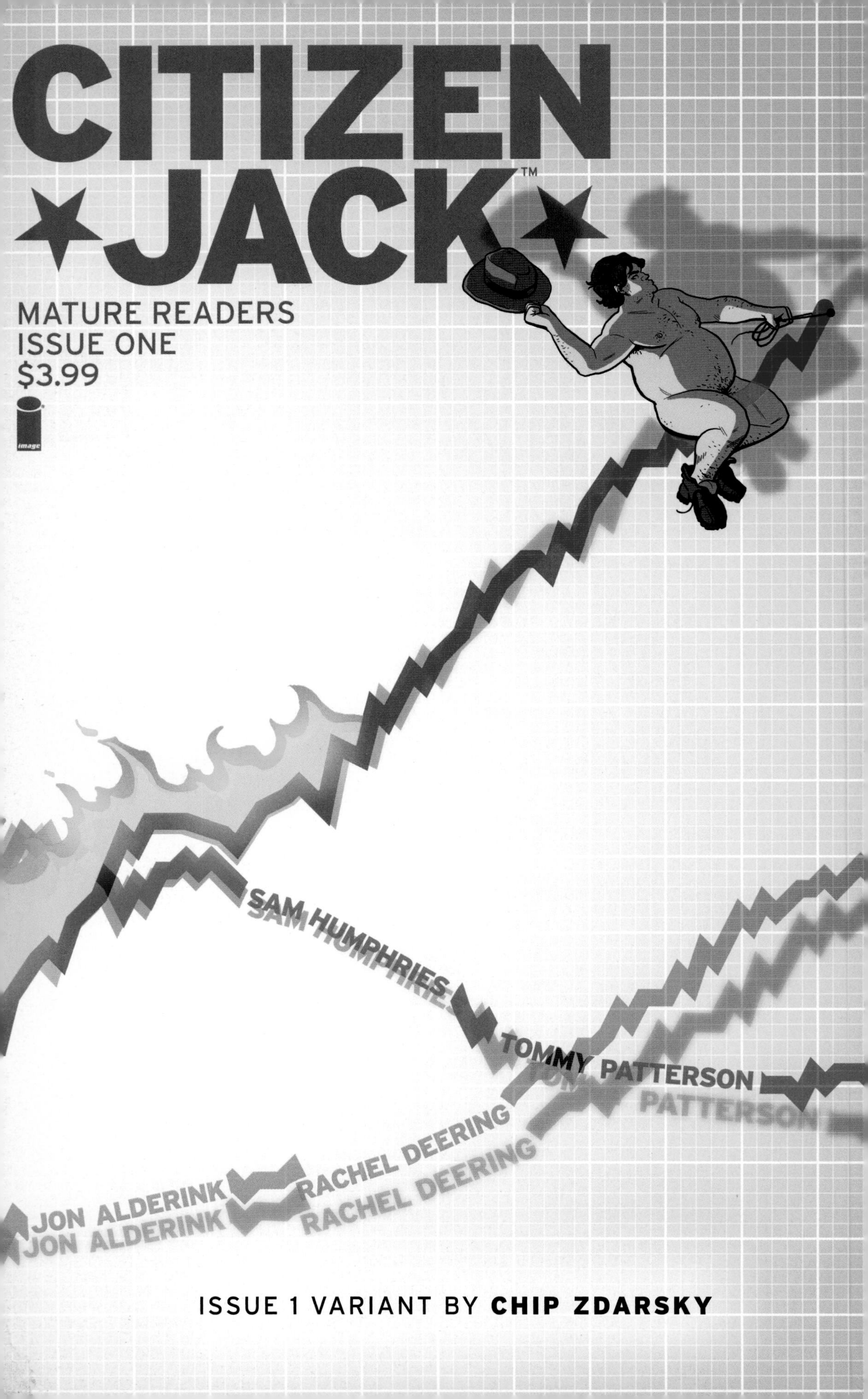
CITIZEN JACK™
MATURE READERS
ISSUE ONE
$3.99
image
SAM HUMPHRIES
TOMMY PATTERSON
RACHEL DEERING
JON ALDERINK

ISSUE 1 VARIANT BY **CHIP ZDARSKY**

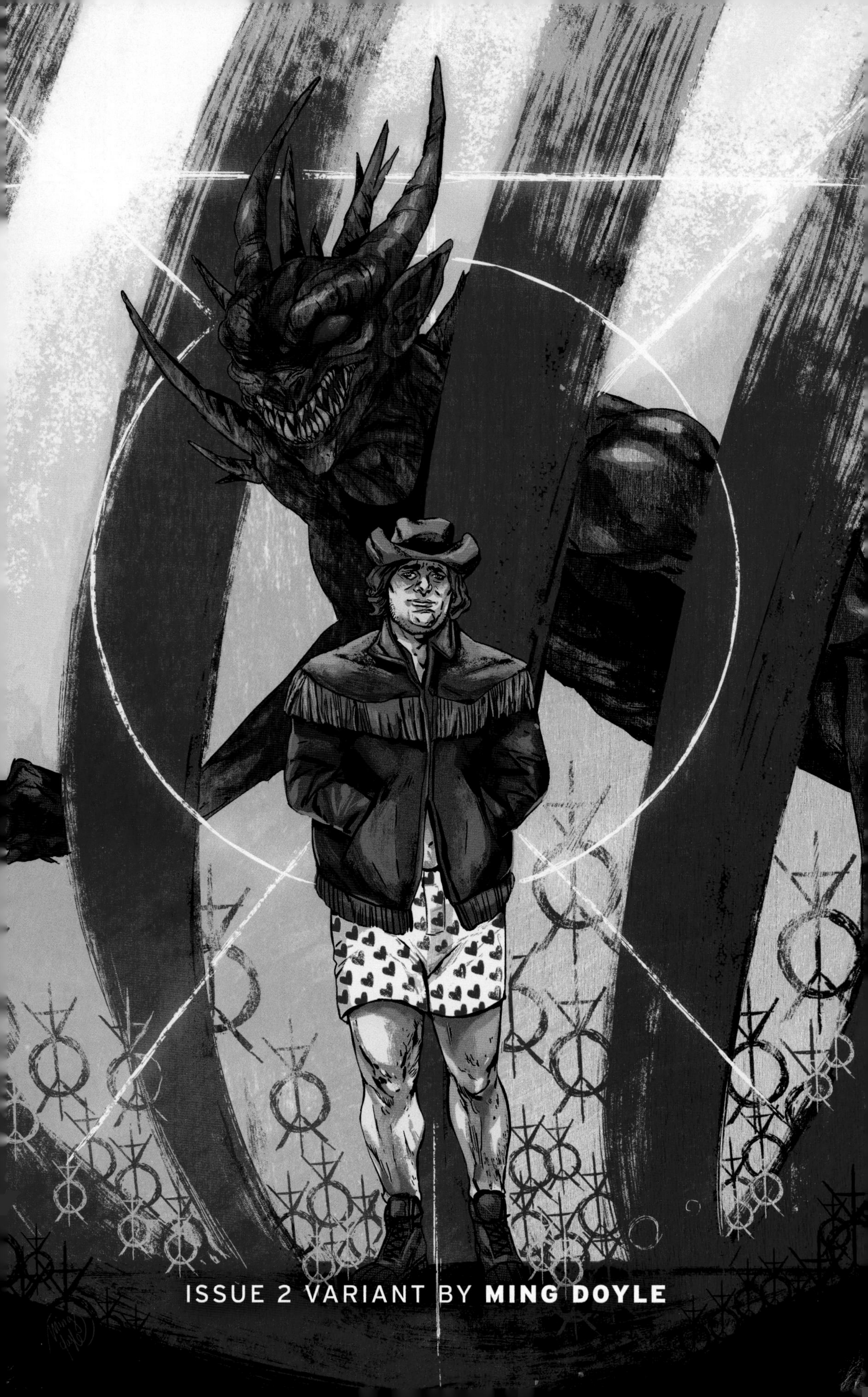
ISSUE 2 VARIANT BY **MING DOYLE**

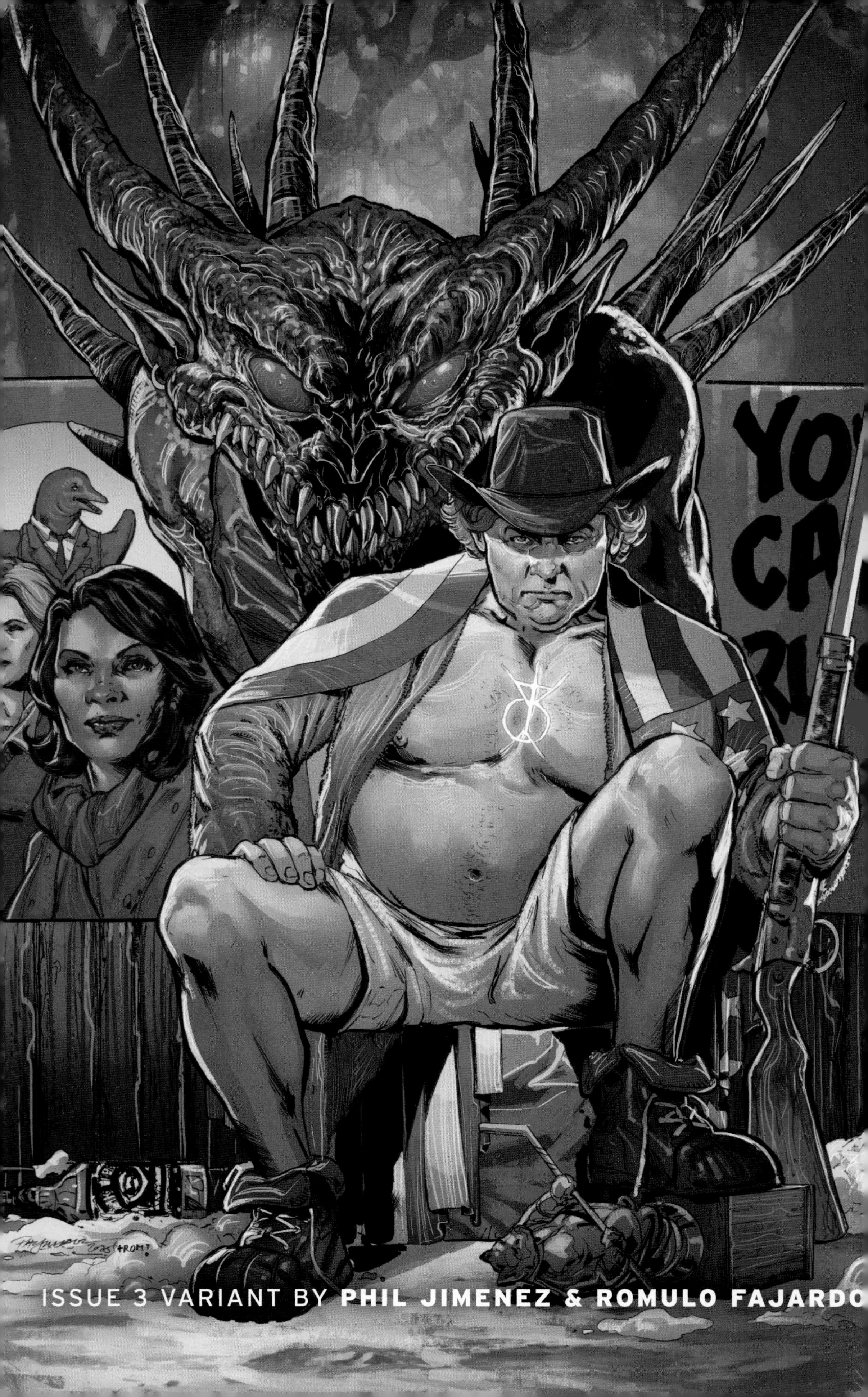

ISSUE 3 VARIANT BY **PHIL JIMENEZ & ROMULO FAJARDO**

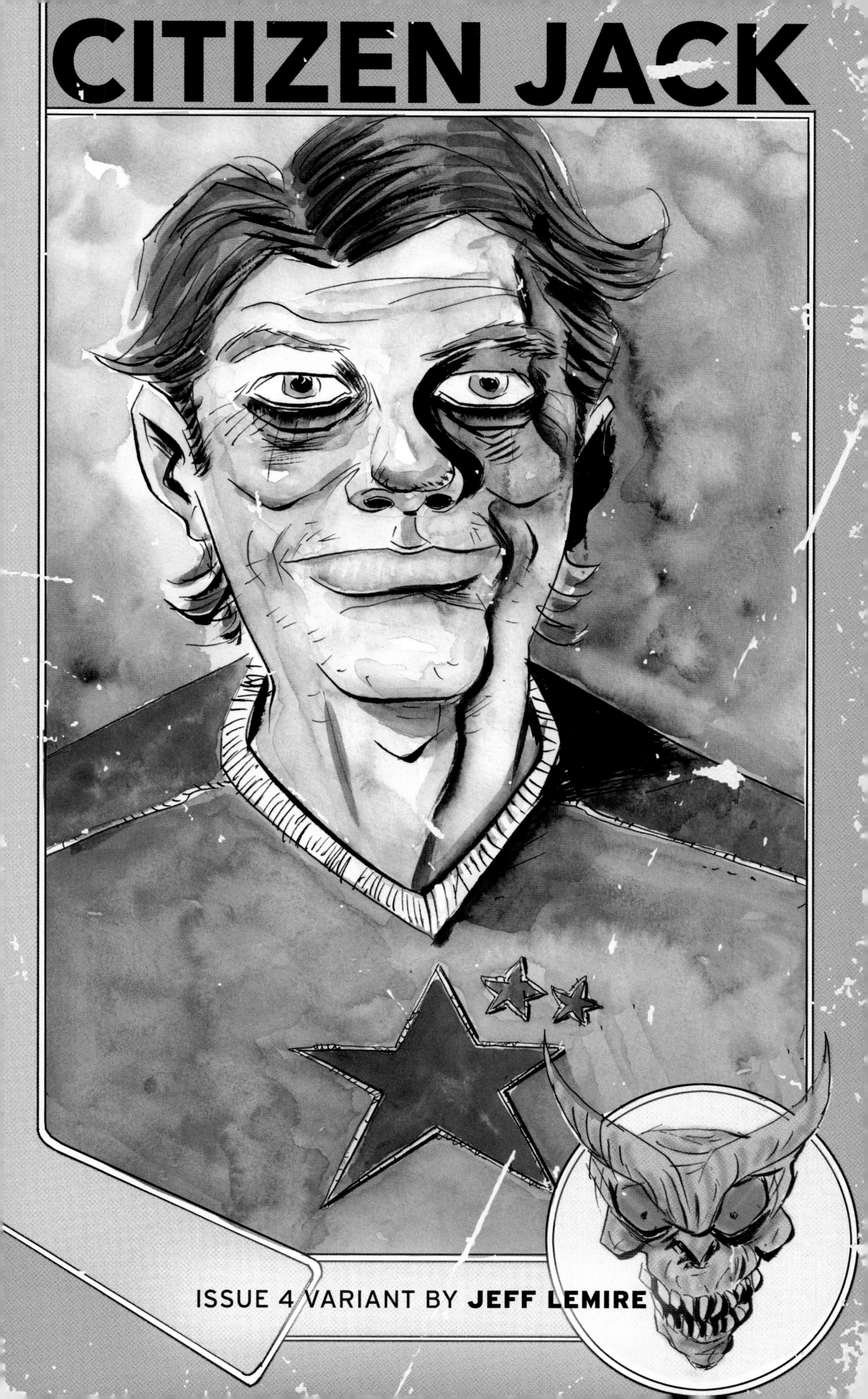
CITIZEN JACK
ISSUE 4 VARIANT BY **JEFF LEMIRE**

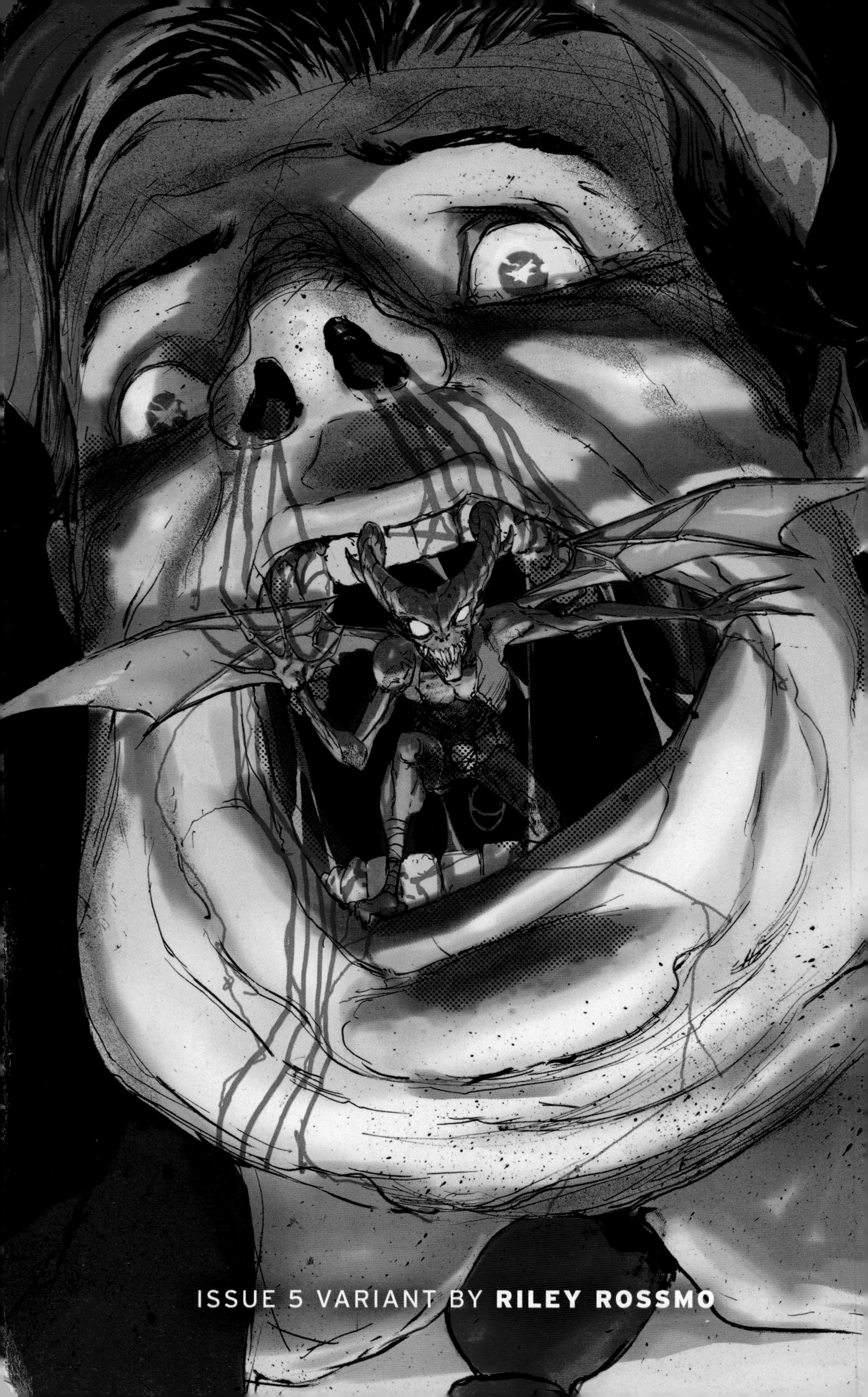

ISSUE 5 VARIANT BY **RILEY ROSSMO**

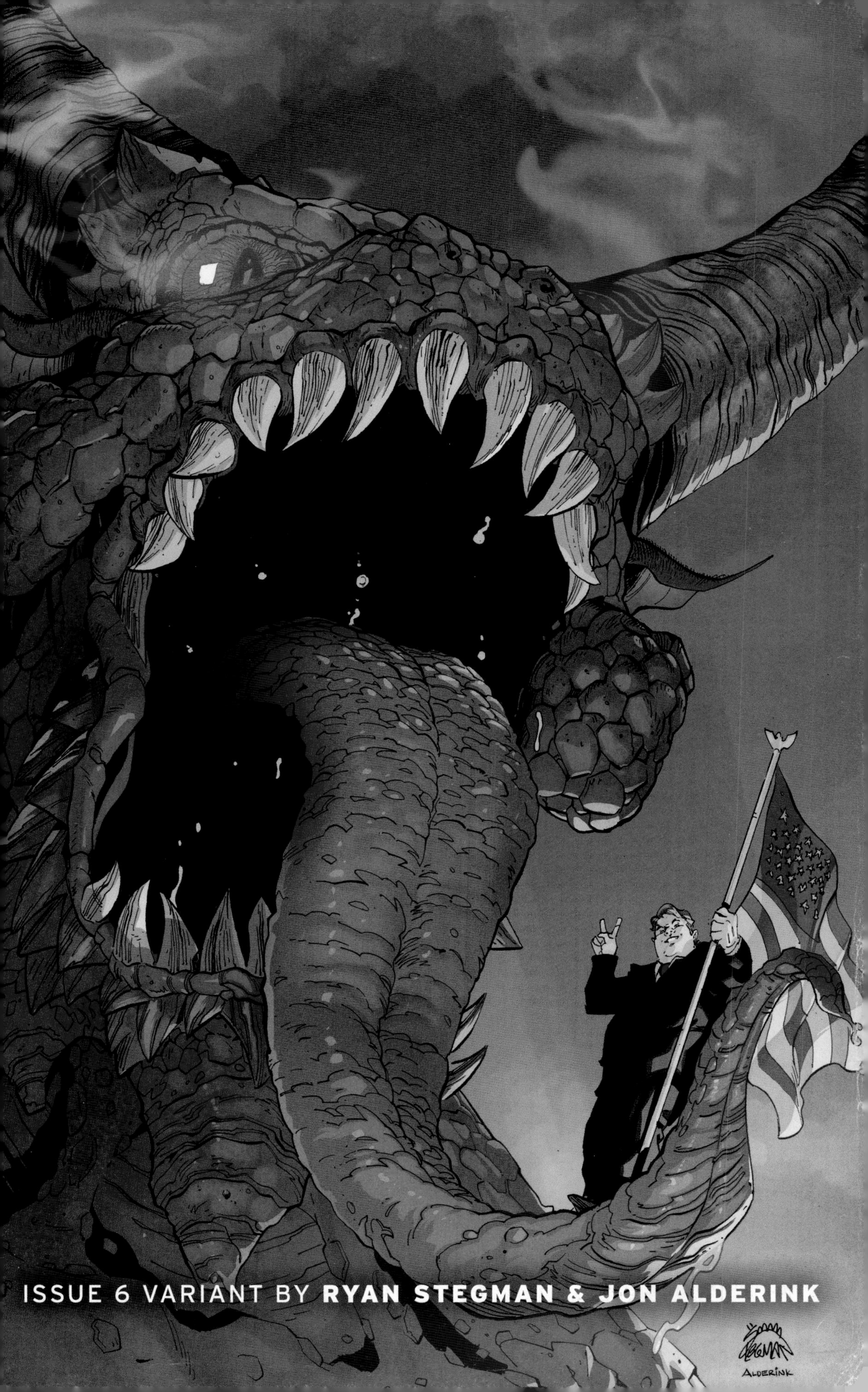
ALDERINK

ISSUE 6 VARIANT BY **RYAN STEGMAN & JON ALDERINK**

SAM HUMPHRIES is a comic book writer. He broke into comics with the runaway self-published hits OUR LOVE IS REAL and SACRIFICE. Since then, he has written high profile books such as LEGENDARY STAR-LORD for Marvel and GREEN LANTERNS for DC Entertainment. He lives in Los Angeles, but his home state... is Minnesota.

* *

TOMMY PATTERSON is a *New York Times* bestselling comic artist from Western Kentucky. He graduated with a degree in Studio Art from Murray State University and made his way into comics a few years later starting with FARSCAPE from BOOM! Comics. A four-year run on A GAME OF THRONES for Dynamite Entertainment raised his profile, and multiple bestselling trades later he got the itch for creator-owned comics. With the power of Marlinspike, he and Sam Humphries created the critically-acclaimed CITIZEN JACK!

* *

JON ALDERINK was trained at The Kubert School, and broke into comics after illustrating children's fairy tales. He fell in love with digital art and subsequently, color art for comics. He is currently earning his degree in Digital Media at Kendall College of Art and Design in Grand Rapids, MI, where he lives with his amazing wife and daughter. He likes spookin' and spaghettin', and thoroughly enjoyed working on the horror/comedy that is CITIZEN JACK.

* *

RACHEL DEERING is an Eisner and Harvey Award-nominated writer, editor, and letterer from Columbus Ohio. She is a twisted old crone who travels the backwoods of Appalachia with an antique gramophone and her theater of shadow puppets, performing for the local flora and fauna.

* *

JEANINE SCHAEFER has been editing comics for over ten years. Titles include Marvel Comics' X-MEN, SHE-HULK, and the Eisner-nominated YA MYSTIC, JONESY at BOOM!, and the upcoming MOTOR CRUSH, PRIMA and AD from Image Comics. She also founded GIRL COMICS, an anthology celebrating the history of women at Marvel. She lives in Los Angeles with her husband and daughter/adorable tornado, and sporadically runs a tumblr celebrating the special relationship between nerds and cats.

* *

DYLAN TODD is an art director, graphic designer, and writer. When he's not reading comics, making comics, writing about comics, or designing stuff for comics, he can probably be found thinking about comics. You can find his pop culture and comics design portfolio at bigredrobot.net.